The cry went up suddenly from the rear of the caravan, and the shaykh, recognizing the voice of his first wife, turned in that direction. Getting his mount firmly under control, he rode quickly to her side to learn what was wrong. The others followed closely behind him.

It didn't take long to find out what the matter was. The shaykh's thirteen-year-old daughter Murrah was missing. It must have been she that the Jinn took with him when he ascended into the sky, leaving the caravan to flounder in his wake.

"What would he want with your daughter?" Umar asked.

Nusair ibn Samman looked up and met the priest's gaze with eyes now reddened by tears as well as sand. His voice had a dead quality to it as he said, "He will eat her."

"That's barbaric," Prince Ahmad said. "We must do something."

"There's nothing that can be done," the shaykh said hollowly. "Estanash is immortal. So you see, the fight would be hopeless."

"You forget we now have a wizard of our own," Prince Ahmad said. "He will help us find a way to rid your people of this pestilence."

Jafar al-Sharif froze in cold fear. "Your Highness is very generous in his praise," he said, adding to himself, *and very quick to volunteer me in a cause.*

THE STORYTELLER AND THE JANN

STEPHEN GOLDIN

BANTAM BOOKS
TORONTO · NEW YORK · LONDON · SYDNEY · AUCKLAND

THE STORYTELLER AND THE JANN
A Bantam Spectra Book / October 1988

ISBN 0-553-27532-1

Published simultaneously in the United States and Canada

Bantam Books are published by Bantam Books, a division of Bantam Doubleday Dell Publishing Group, Inc. Its trademark, consisting of the words "Bantam Books" and the portrayal of a rooster, is Registered in U.S Patent and Trademark Office and in other countries. Marca Registrada. Bantam Books, 666 Fifth Avenue, New York, New York 10103.

PRINTED IN THE UNITED STATES OF AMERICA

O   0 9 8 7 6 5 4 3 2 1

CONTENTS

This book is dedicated to Melissa Ann Singer,
for all the time, effort, and love she put into it.

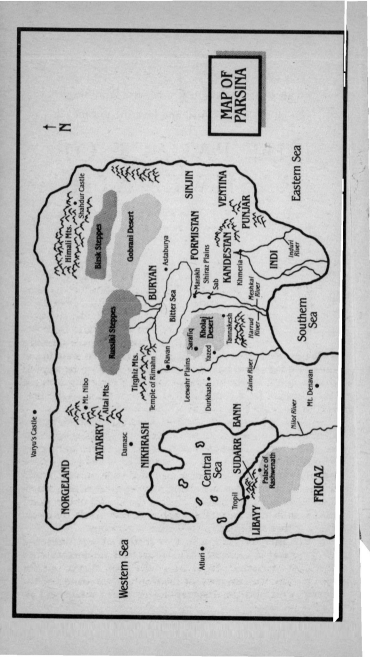

MAP OF
PARSINA

N

Eastern Sea

Varyu's Castle •

NORGELAND

Western Sea

TATARRY

Mt. Nibo •
Altai Mts.

Damasc •

NIKHRASH

Atluri •

Central
Sea

SUDARR

Tropil •

LIBAYY

BANN

Palace of
Rastwenath

FRICAZ

Tirghiz Mts.
Temple of Rimahn
Ravan •

Leewahr Plains
Durkhash •
Yazed •
Sarafiq •

Kholaj
Desert

Tannakesh •

Harrud River

Zaind River

Mt. Denavan •

Southern
Sea

Russiki Steppes

BURYAN

Bitter Sea

Astaburya •

Narakh •
Shiraz Plains
Sab •

Meshkal
River

KANDESTAN

Khmeria •

Induri
River

INDI

Bisk Steppes

Gobrani Desert

Himali Mts.
Shahdur Castle •

SINJIN

FORMISTAN

VENTINA

PUNJAR

1

THE PALACE OF RASHWENATH

T HE tale is told of a time when Hakem Rafi the accursed, the thief, the blackhearted, when this nefarious infidel violated the Temple of the Faith in the fabled city of Ravan and stole the golden jeweled urn of Aeshma from before the Bahram fire itself. The tale recounts how he escaped from the Holy City disguised as a soldier in Prince Ahmad's own wedding procession, only to be trapped in the ambush of the treacherous King Basir—and how, to save his own life, he smashed the urn and released Aeshma upon the unsuspecting world of Parsina once again.

Aeshma, the king of the daevas. Aeshma, satrap of the Pits of Torment. Aeshma, the personification of Rimahn upon the face of the earth. The power of pure evil had been bottled up for so many centuries within the Holy City—and now, in one earthshaking minute, this force exploded back into the world with devastating consequences for all who came near it, for all whose lives were touched by it. And the Cycles of the world ground on in their inevitable course, as one Cycle lay dying while another screamed in its birth contractions.

It was after receiving a hurried pledge of servitude, and with great fear in his heart, that Hakem Rafi the thief watched the release of Aeshma from his golden urn. Never one for bravery, only the certainty of his death at the hands of the brigands gave him the desperation that apes courage and al-

1

But Rashwenath had lived many millennia ago, in the Third Cycle of the world. As great as his power had been, it was now all for naught. Rashwenath was dead and dust, his name forgotten even by the storytellers, his history recounted only in the most obscure tomes. Hakem Rafi had never heard of the name, nor had anyone of his acquaintance. So when the thief asked Aeshma who Rashwenath was, it was pointless for the daeva to recount the magnificent history of this one-time emperor. Instead, Aeshma replied, "He was a great king many years ago. His palace stands empty now, and it is there I take you. Only that magnificent structure is grand enough to suit a man of your power and importance."

"If Rashwenath was such a great king, why does his palace stand empty?" Hakem Rafi asked suspiciously. He was not going to let Aeshma pull any tricks on him.

Aeshma could have told a story of political intrigues, of treachery, corruption, decay, and a rebellion that seethed across three continents—a rebellion in which he and his daevas played no small role—but he chose to keep the tale simple for the simple mind of a common thief. "Rashwenath died," he answered curtly. "His sons fought over the lands, and soon the empire was torn apart by civil wars. No one could afford to maintain such a magnificent palace, so it was abandoned and the empire soon disintegrated. No one has occupied the palace for thousands of years. But soon, if you so desire it, the palace will live again, a tribute to the power and majesty of my new master, Hakem Rafi."

Hakem Rafi had never been in even a small palace, let alone such a wonderful structure as the daeva was describing. He was intrigued by the possibilities. He reminded himself to start behaving like a man of wealth and property, for any riches he could imagine would soon be his for the asking. It was only right that he should occupy the grandest palace in the world and have an army of slaves to do his bidding. He felt he'd worked hard to steal Aeshma's urn and spirit it out of Ravan against all odds, he'd earned the right to live in lavish splendor.

They flew at great height and speed over the barren desert below, and Hakem Rafi's anticipation grew till he could barely wait to see this promised palace. On the horizon a chain of mountains came into view and began to grow as the two approached. The rukh descended now, making it apparent that their destination lay within those mountains.

Hakem Rafi's sharp eyes spotted something at the base of those hills, and as they drew closer he could see it looked like a vast city stretched out along the desert floor. Then, as they came closer still, the thief's eyes widened when he realized it was not a city he saw, but a single vast building stretching defiantly from the base of the mountains well into the desert. A single roof covered the grounds, with numerous small breaks for courtyards, gardens, and solaria; domes, towers, and minarets reached upward from its surface toward the sky. The stones of its walls were only slightly eroded after all this time, though the brightly colored facade and fabrics that had once graced its exterior had worn away. The structure was so huge that all of Yazed, Hakem Rafi's native town, could be hidden within the building's perimeter with yet room for a few minor country villages.

The rukh descended toward the roof of the palace. Setting Hakem Rafi down most gently, the rukh alit beside him and transformed itself once more. It became a cloud of oily black smoke, sulfurous and impenetrable, and shrank somewhat in size. As it shrank it condensed from a bird to a more vertical shape, until at last it took the features that could be called most natural for it—but for Hakem Rafi the new shape was far more frightening than the rukh.

Aeshma's form was an enormous obscene parody of a man. He stood well over five cubits tall and his skin was black as tar. His eyes glowed like red coals in his sockets and his teeth were a sharp set of fangs, upper and lower. Coarse, stringy black hair twined down to his powerfully muscled shoulders, and his arms and legs ended in twisted claws with razor-sharp nails. He was totally naked, and his grotesque penis was easily a cubit long with a barbed tip.

Hakem Rafi once again knew the fear that he might not be able to control this powerful being, yet even as he stood trembling the daeva made a proper salaam and said, "Welcome to your new home, O my master, if you will accept it as such."

"I—I'll have to look it over first."

"Certainly. There are stairs this way." So saying, Aeshma led the way to a staircase that descended from the roof into the center of the palace. The gigantic daeva had to stoop to avoid hitting his head on some of the entranceways, but in general the ceilings were high enough that he could walk upright with no problem. In Aeshma's hand appeared a large lamp with five wicks that lit the way for the thief. Behind Aeshma, Hakem Rafi followed cautiously, still fearing the power of his nominal slave.

At the bottom of the stairs they reached a central hall with arched ceilings high enough for three Aeshmas to have stood, one on another's shoulders. The open area of the floor was larger than the maidan in Ravan and corridors branched off from it in several directions. The smallest corridor could have accommodated five men walking abreast, while the largest was wider than most houses. Hakem Rafi looked down these diverging hallways and could see no end to any of them.

Through these hallways had once moved the commerce of three continents. Once the walls rang with the din of many different tongues crying in untold numbers of voices. Once ambassadors brought their legations here, and merchants their wares, and musicians their instruments. Once the air had been alive with the scent of spices and sweat, with the sound of bells and hawkers' cries, with the tang of oranges and wine, with the sight of camels and horses, and even elephants. Once these walls had known life and excitement, the intrigues of an empire, the lusts of a king alive with power.

Now the dust of the ages hung thickly in the air, making Hakem Rafi sneeze and cough. Insects buzzed unconcerned through the air, and the rats that fed on them chittered quietly in the corners. The air smelled musty and dry, and felt warm from the heat of the afternoon sun.

Hakem Rafi took a couple of steps as he looked around, and the sound of his boots on the tiled floor echoed through the chamber and down the corridors. His voice, when he spoke, echoed like a drum in the still air, frightening some of the rats back into their holes. "It's all so dead," he said. "I'm not sure I like that."

"With my help, O master, you will make it live again and restore the palace of Rashwenath to its former grandeur."

"It'd take an army of slaves a year to clean this up," the thief said, looking at the dust.

"It is but the work of a single night. When you awake in the morning, the palace shall gleam as it did on the day it was built. Just leave everything to me."

"Very well. First rid this room of its choking dust. But if I don't like the place when you're all done will you take me elsewhere and build me a new palace?"

"You are my master, and I am yours to command."

"Don't forget that," Hakem Rafi said.

"Of all the facts in all the world, that is one I never shall forget," the daeva replied, and added, "Is there anything you wish right now? Food and drink, perhaps?"

The mere mention of food reminded Hakem Rafi that he hadn't eaten since breakfast in the prince's camp early that morning. He'd become so used to going hungry during these last few weeks that he routinely ignored the insistent urges of his stomach—but there was no longer any reason to deprive himself of what he wanted.

"Yes," he said, "some food and drink sounds wonderful. Bring me some immediately."

"Do you have any preferences, O master?"

Hakem Rafi had so seldom been in a position where he had a choice that it was difficult to think. "Bring me a feast worthy of the wealthiest merchant in Ravan," he said with an arrogant wave of his hand.

"I hear and I obey," Aeshma acknowledged.

At Hakem Rafi's feet appeared a fine carpet of cerise, gold, black, and dark cedar green, so deep a man's fingers would sink into its pile up to the second knuckle, spread out invitingly with comfortable pillows around it. At the corners were several tall stands with silver inlaid brass lamps that illuminated the area around the rug, though the rest of the huge room was dim and the corners were lost in darkness. A leather sofreh covered the carpet's center and a white cloth sofreh was placed over that for æsthetic effect. On top of the cloth was a series of golden plates containing the largest feast Hakem Rafi had ever had served for himself alone. The scents exploded in his nostrils, filling them as the dust had done before. As the aromas of meat, fruit, and herbs wafted through the room, they seemed to drive the dust and rat droppings before them, till the faded dim hall at least was clean.

On the sofreh were a mixed herb plate served with feta cheese; an eggplant salad as well as a mixed green salad of romaine lettuce, cucumbers, tomatoes, radishes, and herbs; a dish of peach pickles; a plate of duck in walnut and pomegranate sauce served over chelo; a bowl of quince soup; a plate of nan-e lavash; a large pitcher of abdug; a bowl of apricots and plums; and an enormous platter heaped high with rahat lakhoum. Hakem Rafi had been fortunate enough to sample rahat lakhoum only twice before in his life, and never had he seen it piled in such generous quantities—and certainly never for one individual.

As a man with an eye toward the value of property—particularly other people's—Hakem Rafi was impressed at the quality of the materials Aeshma could produce; at the same time, as a man of ravenous appetite, he did not long ponder the supplementary details. He ate and drank heartily of this sumptuous repast, especially gorging on the rahat lakhoum, until even his monstrous appetite was sated and he sat on one velvet cushion feeling his stomach was about to burst.

The food had taken the edge off his fear, and the rahat lakhoum had made him bolder. He was no longer terrified of the daeva king who'd sworn to serve his wishes, and he was just beginning to realize exactly what all this could mean for him. Ever since stealing the urn and learning of its contents he'd dreamed of unlimited wealth—but dreams were one thing, and the fulfillment of them was something else entirely. The fact that he could become the richest, most powerful man in all Parsina, and that anything he wanted was his for the taking, was just starting to dawn in his simple mind. Hakem Rafi grinned and lay back on the carpeted floor, wallowing in the concept.

"Is there anything else my master wishes?" Aeshma asked smoothly.

With the hashish from the rahat lakhoum bubbling his thoughts, Hakem Rafi put his hands behind his head for a pillow and stared up at the high domed ceiling, lost in shadows overhead, considering the matter. "Yes," he said at last. "I'd like a woman to spend the night with me."

"Any particular woman?"

"A beautiful woman. The most beautiful woman in the world."

"I hear and—"

"No, wait," Hakem Rafi said, sitting up suddenly as an idea occured to him. A wicked smile broadened on his face as he turned the idea over in his mind. The incorruptible new wali of police in Yazed had been responsible for Hakem Rafi's abrupt departure from that city, and for his subsequent suffer-

ing in Ravan. A little revenge was called for here, and Hakem
Rafi's devious imagination conjured up a subtle form of retribution.

"Go to the home of the wali of police in Yazed. Bring me
his most beautiful wife or concubine and make sure no one
knows she's gone. Make her be passionately in love with me
and bring her here before me. Tonight I shall beget a son by
her. In the morning, return her with no memory of what has
happened here and let the wali think the boy is his and raise
him as his own. In this way will I cuckold the fool who drove
me from my home and avenge myself upon his line. But before you go, fashion me a golden bed studded with gems,
piled high with the softest silk pillows and filled with swan's
down, that I might welcome my guest properly. Oh yes, and
leave me some good silk ropes."

"I hear and I obey." The bed appeared in one corner of the
room exactly as Hakem Rafi had described it, and Aeshma
vanished, leaving the thief chuckling to himself.

The daeva returned shortly with the most attractive of the
wali's wives, and she was a beauty indeed. Her long black hair
flowed like silk down her back to the waist, and her dark
brown skin was soft and pure. Thick eyebrows topped her
almond-shaped eyes that burned with passion as she spied
Hakem Rafi. She walked boldly up to him, her slender hips
swaying sensuously with each stride. She knelt before him
and unfastened her milfa, then kissed the palms of his hands
and touched them to her body. Her lips were trembling with
her naked desire as she fell to her knees caressing him.

"Does my master require anything else?" Aeshma asked
discreetly.

Hakem Rafi could hardly take his eyes from the woman
kneeling before him. No woman had ever looked at him with
desire that way. "Uh, no, this will suffice. Go clean the palace
as you promised. Leave me in privacy until the morning."

"I hear and I obey," Aeshma said, and disappeared to another part of the palace. So besotted with hashish and desire
was Hakem Rafi that he didn't even hear the daeva laughing.

The light of morning shone into the palace of Rashwenath
through cleverly disguised skylights in the ceiling. Hakem
Rafi woke slowly as his mind cleared of the hashish and love-
making of the previous night. Beside him, the wali's wife still

lay naked and asleep, her body spent from the energy of their union. Hakem Rafi sat up slowly, then stared about him at the wonder that had occurred.

True to his word, the king of the daevas had restored the palace to its former glory. The cobwebs were cleared from the corners, and not a speck of dust lay anywhere about. The rats had vanished, their holes were plugged and plastered over, the insects were gone, and the air smelled lightly of lemon blossoms.

The hall he was in contained three fountains, each over five cubits in diameter, whose water was scented with citrus blossoms. Above each was a dome of paper-thin alabaster, allowing the softest filtered light of peach hue to color the creamy marble floor below. The marble was patterned in cream and gray in an intricate basket weave. At certain points on either side it became denser, outlining shallow pits filled with soft rugs and huge pillows.

The tapestries that were faded and dust filled the night before, now were bright depictions of erotic events. The largest and finest of these showed Hakem Rafi in the embrace of the wali's wife, as she was obviously straining to pull him to her. The portraiture was very flattering, and Hakem Rafi resolved to have the daeva make him similarly endowed as soon as possible.

The delicious bubbling sound of the fountains mingled with the songs of many birds in golden cages suspended from the carved onyx ceiling panels. They swayed gently in the breeze cooled by the fountains, and made the palace seem full of life. On the walls and stands were inlaid lamps that, come the night, would give the soft, sensual light shed by burning the finest oils.

Hakem Rafi stood up, gawking at the beauty of the building around him, until he realized suddenly that he was naked. He quickly donned the uniform he'd been wearing when Aeshma snatched him from the forest, and walked about the hallway to admire his new home. Everywhere he looked was beauty compounded on beauty—pictures, carpets, tiles, furniture, fixtures. And every bit of it was his. It was true. He was the richest, most powerful man in Parsina.

A sudden thought brought him up short. One man had possessed all this wealth before, and where was he now? Dead and dust, and his memory totally forgotten. Great though he was, Rashwenath was mortal and his name had died centuries ago. All he'd strived for was gone, all he'd built evaporated. Hakem Rafi was mortal, too; he'd never given the matter much thought before, but now it seemed suddenly of vital concern.

"Aeshma!" he called, and his voice echoed down the empty hallways, muffled only slightly by the restored tapestries.

The daeva's huge form materialized out of smoke before him. "Ever at my master's call," Aeshma said with surprising softness.

"I want you to make me immortal," the thief said brusquely.

For the first time, the daeva hesitated. "That I cannot do, O my master."

"You swore to obey all my commands," Hakem Rafi said in a petulant whine.

"And so I shall, in everything within my ability. My powers are unequaled upon the face of the earth, but power over death is not mine. Death was created by my lord Rimahn to inflict upon the creatures of Oromasd. I have not the ability to undo what my own lord and creator has done. I shall obey you in all things, save that I am powerless to forestall your eventual and inevitable death. As I promised you, I will not cause it—but neither can I stop it from happening some day."

Hakem Rafi the thief turned away from Aeshma to hide the bitterness in his soul. He had seldom thought about death before, merely tried to avoid it; he'd always thought himself too clever to be caught and executed, too skilled to lose any fight he didn't dodge. But now that he had everything, now that the world could be his if he chose, the irony that he could lose it all was a painful one. In a thousand years, would he be as forgotten as the great Rashwenath, a name never spoken, a presence never felt? What, then, would be the point of living at all, if everything was to vanish from him?

He must have voiced the question aloud without realizing it, for Aeshma answered in soft, seductive tones, "The answer, O my master, is to live as fully and as best you can. If it is all destined to vanish tomorrow, then enjoy it to the utmost today. At your command I can shower you with a thousand, thousand pleasures, with wealth beyond imagining, so when death does come it will find you with not a moment wasted, not a second left unenjoyed. Your days will be filled with delight and your nights will be rich with satisfactions most men dare not even dream of. Rashwenath is dead, and his glory with him, but it is said he never regretted a single moment of the life he lived. So let it be with you."

Hakem Rafi listened to the daeva's arguments, and they struck a chord in the thief's greedy soul. It was true that no man was granted immortality—but he, Hakem Rafi, had been granted more than any man could wish. Yes, he would bury himself in sensual pleasure and live as Aeshma suggested. He would have food, wine, women, power, and revenge on all those who'd belittled or insulted him, and he would not think of death again. It would come—but the object of life, as Aeshma had explained, was to have no regrets, no sorrows. When death did come, it would find Hakem Rafi happy and contented. No man could ask for more than that.

"Yes," he said aloud. "You're right, my wise slave. I'll wear you down in your efforts to please me."

"Whatever you command shall be yours," Aeshma replied.

"First prepare a feast of a breakfast, then take the woman back to the wali before she is missed," Hakem Rafi said. "Perhaps I'll enjoy her again sometime to beget more sons. When you return, we'll talk in more detail about the pleasures you can provide me."

"I hear and I obey."

The daeva escorted Hakem Rafi into an ornate dining hall where a breakfast meal as sumptuous as last night's dinner was spread before him. Then Aeshma vanished and scooped up the still-sleeping woman to fly her safely back to her home. He could not help a deep-throated chuckle as he went, thinking of how completely this foolish mortal was falling under his control.

Aeshma was a prideful being, and it chafed him sorely to be bound by oath to anyone but his lord Rimahn, let alone a petty mortal like Hakem Rafi. But bad though that was, being trapped and impotent in a golden urn before the fires of Oromasd for thousands of years had been even worse, a constant, searing torment that he was now relieved of.

Hakem Rafi was a mortal. Even without Aeshma's killing him, he would die. At most, he could be expected to live another forty years. If, at Aeshma's gentle insistence, he over-

dulged in food, wine, drugs, and sex, his life span might be
iminished that much further. What were a few more decades
o a creature who'd waited millennia for his freedom?

When Hakem Rafi died, Aeshma would be totally free—
ree to regain all his lost power, free to war against mankind,
ree to avenge himself on the enemy in the name of his lord
Rimahn. There would be no others to stand in his way; when
Aeshma was totally free, the world would quake and
Dromasd's ally, mankind, would vanish from the face of the
earth.

2

THE PRINCESS

ING Basir of Marakh, who called himself "the Blessed," was a man who worried. He was a short, plump man. Years of ruling Marakh had turned his hair prematurely gray and furrowed his wide forehead. His balding head could be hidden beneath his turban, but his gray beard, which grew in uneven patches on his face, was visible for all the world to see. The doctors told him its irregular growth was due to his constant worrying—but rather than setting his mind at ease, that only made him worry more that his appearance was less than regal and his subjects would not respect him.

King Basir wanted to be a great monarch. He wanted his people to love and respect him. He wanted his enemies to fear and respect him. He wanted his allies merely to respect him. But inspiring those emotions in others was never easy. There were so many decisions to be made all the time, and he was never sure what the right answers were. If he ruled harshly he was called a tyrant; if he showed mercy he was labeled weak. Worst of all, if he tried to take some middle position he was accused of being indecisive and everyone ended up despising him.

He knew what a good king, a strong king, should be. He grew up with a living example. His father, King Alnath, was universally regarded as a powerful monarch. It was King Alnath who expanded Marakh's hegemony south and west across the Shiraz Plains, and east well into neighboring For-

istan. King Alnath was a feared warrior and a stern ruler
ho'd commanded respect from friend and foe alike. Even
ow, with King Alnath dead these past twenty-seven years,
he neighboring lands still respected the power of Marakh
ven though King Basir had added nothing to the kingdom
nce taking the throne. Thus does a good reputation stand its
olders in good stead long after its basis has vanished.

King Alnath tried to instill in his son the lessons of power.
He would hold mock councils in which young Prince Basir
had to make decisions of state. Every time the prince made the
wrong decision, King Alnath would publicly mock him before his wazirs. Often the prince was beaten as well. In this
way did King Alnath seek to ensure that his successor would
be a man who thought carefully and made no bad decisions.
His son, he vowed, would be an even better king than he was,
because he would have learned from his father's mistakes.

It was with these high expectations of him that King Basir
ascended to the throne of Marakh. But with his father always
held up to him as an example of what a king should be, Basir
knew he could never be strong enough, never be wise enough,
never be brave enough to meet those demanding standards.
He also knew he never dared admit those self-doubts publicly.
Each decision, however small, was an agony to him, until he
worked himself into such a state that his stomach was in constant pain and he could eat only the blandest of foods.

As a futher disappointment in his life he produced four
daughters, but no sons. He was certain, somehow, that the
fault lay with him, that he was not strong enough to sire sons,
and out of guilt he lavished attention on the princesses—and
particularly on Oma, his oldest daughter.

From an early age she had the finest tutors and was given
the best education any woman could expect. She could read
and write, and she debated well with the best scholars in the
land. She played backgammon and chess, danced with a grace
to make gazelles jealous, and composed poetry of beauty and
perception. She sang with a voice to rival the nightingale, and
played excellently upon the lute, flute, and drum. To top it all
off, she was a pearl of matchless beauty, a girl of such exquisite
features and pale white skin, of long black hair and large black
eyes, of delicate figure and pleasing speech, that all who saw
or heard her fell instantly in love.

Little wonder she became the prize of King Basir's other wise harried life. He could deny her nothing. If he even tried to say no to her, she would pout and call him a failure as a father, and that would remind him of his many failures as a king. He would feel guilty for being so unreasonable, and always he would relent and give Princess Oma exactly what she wanted, no matter how exorbitant the price.

On one point alone did King Basir remain resolved against his daughter. Knowing that he might never have a male heir and wanting to secure the best marriage for her and his kingdom, he made a contract when she was just a girl to wed her to the equally young Prince Ahmad of Ravan. Princess Oma cried and screamed and pouted that she was being treated like a slave, and that she would never marry a man she'd never met and didn't love, but on this matter the king remained adamant. The future of the kingdom must be assured to prevent chaos after King Basir's death, and an alliance with Ravan would solidify Marakh's stature among the world's nations.

Yet even on this important matter King Basir could not remain constant. After the death of King Shunnar of Ravan, Shunnar's widow, Shammara, sent King Basir the gift of a lovely and enticing concubine named Rabah, who worked unstintingly to convince the king that Shammara's son, Prince Haroun—rather that Prince Ahmad, son of a concubine— would be the better marriage choice. Rabah became intimate friends with the young Princess Oma and tried to convince her of Haroun's desirability as well. At the same time one of the king's most trusted advisers, Tabib abu Saar, was also subverted to Shammara's cause and began counseling King Basir to betray his solemn contract regarding Prince Ahmad. Against pressure from all these sides, King Basir's resolve, never strong to begin with, could not stand up, and he agreed to betray the prince and wed his precious Oma to Prince Haroun instead.

Thus, with Shammara's aid, was the plan devised to lure Prince Ahmad out of Ravan by insisting he travel to Marakh to wed his bride. In a forest along the road, King Basir stationed two hundred of his best soldiers, outnumbering the wedding party by four to one. Once Ahmad was dead, Princess Oma could marry Prince Haroun and the two lands would be united as had always been the plan, with just a slight change of names in the leading roles.

But it was now several days after the ambush was sup-posed to occur, and King Basir had received no word from his men. His captain in the field had been given strict instructions to send a messenger back to Marakh on their fastest horse to bring the news of the mission's success. Even a failure should have merited some word, though that was unlikely consider-ing the relative size of the two forces involved. But days passed and no word came. King Basir worried and the fire in his stomach flamed like a blacksmith's furnace.

All sorts of horrible contingencies raced through his mind. Prince Ahmad could have defeated the ambush, returned to Ravan, killed Shammara, and even now be assembling an army to march in revenge against Marakh. Or Shammara could have double-crossed both sides to play out a subtle game of her own design. Scores of alternatives, each of them disastrous, danced through King Basir's mind, haunting his sleep and ruining his digestion. He considered sending out spies, but was too afraid of what they might find.

After a week and a half, the two retainers who'd gone to Ravan with Tabib abu Saar as King Basir's legation returned to Marakh via a most circuitous route. They were taken imme-diately before the king, where it was obvious they were frightened out of their wits—not by being in the king's pres-ence, but by what had happened to them upon the road. Un-der stern questioning by the king and his wazirs, they told their eerie tale.

At first, they said, all had gone as planned. The prince's party had walked into the ambush unprepared for battle. Tabib abu Saar and his retainers retreated from the scene the instant the fighting started and watched the skirmish from a safe distance down the road. The Marakhi soldiers far out-numbered Prince Ahmad's troops, and the battle was going well when suddenly a supernatural manifestation appeared.

An enormous black whirlwind arose from nowhere, tow-ering above the treetops, and from it streaked bolts of light-ning that struck the Marakhi warriors and burned them instantly like so many lumps of coal. The whirlwind did not harm the prince's men, and abu Saar's retainers speculated the prince must have had strong magic on his side to defeat the opposing force.

So fearsome was the whirlwind that abu Saar's horse reared in terror, spilling the Marakhi ambassador on the hard

ground and breaking both his legs. The servants' asses wer
braver, but still would not approach the whirlwind, and th
servants were afraid to dismount and help their master, les
the asses run off and leave them stranded in the forest.

Then the whirlwind transformed itself into a giant rukh
grabbed one of the prince's soldiers, and flew off into the sky
The retainers didn't know what to make of that, but though
perhaps the soldier might have been a sacrifice by the prince tc
the evil powers he'd summoned to defeat the ambushers.

Abu Saar had lain on the ground in pain, pleading with his
servants to help him, but they were afraid and didn't know
how. When some of the prince's men came looking for them,
they turned and fled, taking a long and devious route back to
their native city to avoid being followed and captured. They
knew nothing more of what had happened to Tabib abu Saar
and Prince Ahmad's party.

This news sent the king into profound fits of anxiety, and
he pulled out even more of his sparse beard. Shammara would
be awaiting word from him about the success of his raid.
Though he had never met the woman, her reputation was that
she was not a person to cross casually. Even though the ambush's failure was due to supernatural intervention and was no
fault of King Basir's, Shammara might well take strong action
that was bound to be unpleasant. She was even rumored to
have connections with the rimahniya, the secret religious cult
of fanatical assassins. King Basir did not wish to die from one
of their poisoned daggers stuck between his ribs.

With his stomach aflame he dismissed the gibbering servants and discussed the matter with his wazirs. He thoroughly
regretted letting himself be talked into betraying his contract
with Prince Ahmad, but nothing could rectify that now. He
had to evaluate the situation given but the flimsiest of evidence and make new plans on events as he understood them.

They had to assume Tabib abu Saar was captured and
questioned by Prince Ahmad. With both legs broken he
would not put up much resistance under interrogation, and
thus would tell Prince Ahmad all about the secret alliance between Shammara and King Basir. The prince was known as a
well-trained, but inexperienced, fighter, and it was con-
ceivable that his anger at the betrayal would lead him to take
some action against Marakh.

"Is it too late to apologize to him and offer him help against Shammara?" King Basir asked.

"Do you think he'd believe it after what happened?" his first wazir countered.

"No, no, I guess not," the king said weakly.

"Besides, Your Majesty, Prince Ahmad has but a handful of men. Marakh has one of the strongest armies in all Parsina. Any fight against us would mean his certain death."

"But he obviously has some powerful sorcerer working for him. That whirlwind—the rukh—"

"All the more reason to maintain your strong alliance with Shammara. We'll need help from the Holy City if we face a threat from magic."

"Shammara!" King Basir went suddenly cold at the thought of his powerful ally. "What will I do about her? What will I tell her? How can I explain . . . ?"

"You will explain nothing," the wazir said. "Are you not king of Marakh, ruler of the two rivers? A king need explain to no one. You will send her a message saying that, as agreed upon, your army attacked the prince's party on the road and prevented them from reaching Marakh. You will prepare Princess Oma's bridal party as quickly as possible and send her off to Ravan to marry Prince Haroun and further cement the alliance between Marakh and Ravan. When all is completed, how can Shammara complain?"

But King Basir did not likewise underestimate Shammara's critical abilities. "What if Prince Ahmad returns and claims his rights?" he asked.

"Then you denounce him as an impostor and deal with him accordingly. That's why you must send your daughter to Ravan and have the marriage take place as quickly as possible. Once the union's been consummated it will be in Shammara's best interest to have Ahmad declared a fraud. With the combined armies of Marakh and Ravan aligned against him, Prince Ahmad would have no chance of victory—and I'm sure he's wise enough to know that and not even try."

King Basir mused on his wazir's words. It was often true, he knew, that a good bluster could get a monarch through the most embarrassing of circumstances. He'd lived up to his part of the bargain with Shammara; it wasn't his fault the prince escaped. With any luck at all, Prince Ahmad would flee to distant parts of Parsina and never be heard from again, and King Basir's word on the story would never be challenged. And if Ahmad did show up trying to reclaim his bride and his throne, what choice did Shammara have but to back Basir's story that the young man was just a clever imposter and the real prince died at the hands of brigands on the road to Marakh?

"Very well," he commanded, trying to make his voice sound authoritative. "Have my scribe prepare a message that the prince was killed in the woods by brigands and Princess Oma, grief-stricken though she is by the death of her fiancé, will travel to Ravan to fulfill the marriage contract by marrying Prince Haroun. We'll send the note to Ravan by the fastest messenger, and Princess Oma's party shall follow within a few weeks."

He paused. "We'll give Oma a full military escort, of course. Travel along the roads these days is full of hazards, as the poor departed Prince Ahmad found out, and nothing untoward is going to happen to my daughter on the way to her wedding."

One of the servants who had brought stomach-soothing pilau to the king during the council session was in the direct employ of Princess Oma. As soon as he was dismissed from his duties he reported directly to her all that had occured and the decisions that had been made. The princess thanked him, paid him a generous bonus, and sent him off to find what else he could learn about the plans for her future. Then she sat down to ponder what she herself must do about the situation.

Princess Oma was one of those unfortunate women cursed with an abundance of blessings, and therefore never realized she was cursed. Though not quite seventeen her beauty was already fabled throughout the land—and in truth her long, silken black hair, her large, clear eyes, her smooth white skin and her supple figure fully justified any praise she could receive. She was smarter than anyone in the palace except a few of her teachers, and the training she'd received from them only sharpened her mental skills. She had a melodious voice coupled with grace and a smile that could have charmed Rimahn himself, so it was said. She was possessed of a driving energy and a passion for living that burned deep within her soul.

Few indeed were the people who could say no to her. This was the single great tragedy of Princess Oma.

She sat alone in her private bedroom, thinking what to do. The room was not large, but well appointed. Richly woven peacock green and white tapestries hung upon the walls, and the floor was heaped with sheepskin rugs. The large, carved oak bed was overhung by a canopy, from which draped a pale silver gauze that floated sensuously to the floor or wafted in the occasional breeze. From the garden below, hidden by an extra screen, women musicians played Oma's favorite music so that her days were filled with songs. An ebony closet with ivory inlay stood in one corner, and a full-length mirror, framed with electrum and set with diamonds, stood in another. Huge bowls of flowers, cut each morning in her own garden, filled the air with the sweet scent of jasmine.

Princess Oma watched her reflection carefully in the glass as she practiced her pout. She wondered whether it would be worth starting a tantrum to make her father cancel his plans to send her to Ravan, but realized that move would fail now as it had before because her father was more desperate now than ever. She would only end up looking silly, and she hated looking silly.

She walked to the door and told her slave, "Find Rabah and tell her I want to see her immediately." Rabah was her friend; Rabah always knew what to do. Rabah would give her the advice she needed.

When Rabah arrived a short time later, she found Princess Oma lying prone and naked on her bed. The slave was dismissed, leaving the two women alone, and Princess Oma said, "Oh Rabah, my angel, could you rub my back for me? The skin feels so dry and coarse."

"As you wish, O my princess," Rabah said with a slight smile. Rabah was a tall, willowy woman in her early thirties, with short brown hair and strangely intense eyes, one blue and one green. Her facial expressions were always controlled so it was impossible to tell her thoughts, and she moved with the springy gracefulness of a tigress on a casual prowl. Now she lightly crossed the room to the closet, where a vial of massage oil was kept in a bottom drawer. She warmed the oil on her palms and then began rubbing it into the princess's back. Rabah's touch was gentle, but there was a reserved strength in her hands that could have made her dangerous had she chosen to be. This gave a touch of spice to the experience that the princess savored.

As Rabah's fingers sensuously explored the silken skin of Oma's back, the princess confided to her all that had transpired in her father's council chamber. "I will not be passed from hand to hand, a jewel going to the highest bidder," she said stubbornly.

"That is ever the lot of women," Rabah said.

"Well, it won't be that way for me. I shall control my own destiny. I'll love whom I please and take my pleasure where I like. No man will control me."

"Brave words, Your Highness."

"But you disapprove, is that it?" Princess Oma said, reading the older woman's tone.

"I would counsel wisdom to back up the bravery," Rabah said as her hands soothed the tension of anger from Oma's lithe body. "It's the way of the world that men believe they have control. To defy that would be to stand against the current of a powerful river; if one but swims the river instead, it's easier to reach one's destination."

"I don't want to marry Haroun. I hear he's perfectly awful, and he does cruel things to slave girls."

"Yet you helped me convince your father to betray his agreement with Ahmad."

"I didn't want to marry Ahmad, either," Princess Oma said with a pout. "I don't want to marry anyone. Why should I be shackled to only one lover all my life when my husband can have many wives and concubines? I want the freedom to love whom I choose, when I choose, how I choose. Is that so terrible?"

"Not at all," Rabah said. "But in the world as it is, we women must practice a little caution." She hesitated a moment. "Could it be that Your Highness is afraid of a man's love?" Rabah knew that Oma had been raised among women; the only men she saw were eunuchs, some of her tutors, and her father. Some trepidation on her part would be perfectly natural.

"I've never tried any men, of course," Oma said. "A princess's maidenhead is a valuable commodity, and I'm not going to throw it away on a whim."

"If you'll accept my word for now, the love of a man can be just as exciting as the love of a woman," Rabah told her.

"Thank you. I'll look forward to it. But may Oromasd grant that my first experience not be with Prince Haroun."

Rabah's strong hands manipulated the muscles of Oma's back, relaxing the last of the tension beneath the taut young flesh. For several moments the two drifted in silence. Then Oma spoke again.

"They say Ahmad used powerful sorcery to escape my father's trap. Do you believe that?"

"Many things are possible."

"Ahmad, a sorcerer. Why, he could swoop into the room his very minute and cast a spell on us so neither of us could move. We'd be helpless before him and he could ravish us both on the spot if he chose, don't you think?"

"If that frightens you, all the more reason to go to Ravan. No magic can touch you in the Holy City."

"Frighten? Rabah, that would be the most exciting thing that ever happened to me." She sighed. "But it won't. They all say Ahmad's much too noble to do anything like that. Do you really *want* me to go to Ravan?"

"I think you *should* go," Rabah said carefully. "Marriage to Haroun is a price to pay, but in a few months he'll attain his majority and be crowned king of Ravan. That will make you queen. Haroun is a cipher, easily ignored. As long as you don't interfere with his mother's political rule, you'll be able to do as you wish. You'll have the freedom you say you want so badly. The price is your maidenhead."

"Haroun may get that from me, but he certainly won't get much else."

Princess Oma lay silent again for a while as Rabah's fingers kneaded her flesh. Then she said, "Rabah, *if* I go to Ravan, will you come with me?"

"I can't, O my princess, you know that. I'm your father's concubine; I belong here with him."

"I could make him give you to me as a servant. You know he'd do it if I asked him the right way."

"No." For just the faintest instant Rabah's fingers tightened on the muscles in the princess's neck. The pressure was gone again almost before Oma realized it was there. "I belong here with your father," Rabah continued emphatically.

"But I'll be alone and friendless in a strange city," Oma protested.

"You'll make new friends quickly enough, of that I have no doubt," Rabah smiled knowingly. "Once you're queen you can have friends of *both* sexes."

"But I want a familiar face to remind me of home."

"Why not take your handmaiden Hinda? You like her, and she'll remind you of home."

"Hinda has buck teeth and a hairy lip."

"But she also has very talented fingers." Rabah tickled the princess in a particularly sensitive place, and was rewarded with a delightful squeal.

Princess Oma turned over onto her back and looked up at the older woman. "I'll miss you, Rabah," she said, peering straight into the other's eyes.

"And I'll miss you, O my princess," Rabah said, returning the gaze. "Perhaps kismet will decree a short separation and we can be reunited again after all."

The princess reached up and wrapped her arms around her friend's neck. "Kiss me, Rabah," she whispered. "Give me something to remember if the nights in Ravan prove too long and lonely."

She pulled Rabah down on top of her and Rabah did indeed give her something to remember for many weeks to come.

Later, in the middle of the night when the young princess lay snoring gently from exhaustion, Rabah stole quietly from the room and returned to her own chambers. There she spent an hour composing two long, detailed letters on the thinnest rice paper from Sinjin. When they were done she sealed them and, donning her long black burqa and thawb, she slipped silently down the deserted halls and through the secret door out of the palace.

Under the darkness of night she moved like a cat's shadow through the streets of Marakh to the home of a certain rug merchant. He answered the door after a few minutes of her soft but insistent knocking, and she gave him the letters along with her instructions. The merchant nodded and Rabah returned to the palace without ever having been seen by unintended eyes.

Taking the letters, the merchant climbed the stairs to his roof where, in a secret compartment, he kept some specially trained pigeons. Folding the missives compactly, he tied each inside a special pouch attached to a different bird's leg. In the first light of morning he lifted the birds into the air and let them go. The birds flew high above the roof, circled a few times to get their bearings, and then flew off for their true homes more than a hundred parasangs away—one to a cave in the Tirghiz Mountains and the other to a coop atop the north tower of the palace of Ravan.

3

THE WIZARD'S
WRATH

T the northeast rim of the world stretch the
Himali Mountains, considered by knowl-
edgeable geographers to be the most forbidding peaks in all Parsina. Unscalable cliffs
tower over the clouds that float between
them, and few are the human eyes that have
seen more than a fraction of this inhospitable range. This is
one of the places where Rimahn's handiwork is most apparent, ripping apart the peaceful fabric of Oromasd's perfect creation and replacing it with jagged, naked rocks. It is not
uncommon for the highest summits to have snow on them for
ten or eleven months out of the year, and no animals, not even
birds, live naturally in the harsh climate except in the summer
when the warmth of the sun softens even this monument to
the chaos of Rimahn.

Perched atop the highest peak of the world's foremost
mountain chain like a lone sentinel against the infinite was
Shahdur Castle, home of the sightless wizard Akar. Carved
from the living stone, the castle was an integral part of the
very mountain that held it up to the sky. Towers rose at
strange angles, defying both gravity and common sense, and
the very walls of the castle reeked of magic. Such an aura was
inevitable, for the castle had been carved by supernatural
means. Working one of his strongest spells, the wizard Akar
had summoned an army of Marids from their shadowy realm,

bound them to his indomitable will, and forced them to labor for a year, a month, a week, and a day to carve the castle from the mountain's stone. Only when he was satisfied that the work had been done perfectly to his specifications did he release them from his spell and send them fleeing back to their homes in terror and anger at his power over them.

Though Shahdur Castle was the highest point in the world, it could not be said to overlook its surroundings because, like its master, the castle had no eyes. No windows were cut in its rocky walls, because its sole human inhabitant had no need to look out upon the landscape. Akar the wizard had traded his eyes many years ago for the power to read the hidden names of people and things, and the world was all equally dark to him. For all that, however, he saw into the arcane mysteries of Parsina better than most sighted people ever could.

On this particular day, the day when Aeshma was released from his golden urn to work his wickedness upon the world, Akar stood upon the roof of his castle raging into the gathering darkness of night. For all his wisdom, for all his knowledge, he had been cheated by a pair of ordinary people—Jafar al-Sharif and his daughter Selima. These clever rogues had claimed to be mighty wizards in possession of the urn of Aeshma, and Akar had rescued them from their predicament in Ravan expressly so they could share the urn with him. In return for his favors and hospitality, this pair of swindlers had stolen his priceless flying carpet and the ring that controlled the minor Jann named Cari.

As a powerful wizard, Akar was normally in total control of his emotions, but he still had one failing he could not alleviate: his fiery temper. When provoked he would fly into sudden rages surpassing all reason, and at such times all the force of his mighty power would be directed at the object of his fury. Not until his wrath was released would the calm of sanity return and he would be his dignified self once more.

Such a rage came upon him when he learned that his two guests were imposters, and that they were escaping with some of his possessions. Climbing the stairs of his castle, he came out onto the flat roof just as the thieves were making off with his treasures. Using the raised markings on the ground to guide him he walked with crisp, efficient steps to the very edge of his roof and looked out into the sky. Even without eyes, his sense for detecting magical power told him where the carpet was, and how far away. Had he been thinking in a rational manner he might have been surprised at the fact that the impostors could even get the carpet in motion. But Akar was beyond such considerations. He was interested solely in revenge.

Akar began speaking the words of power as he reached deep inside his soul to concentrate the energy he would use. This was his prime death spell, a curse that would wither any enemy within his considerable range. The words came fluently, the power flowed, and as the carpet flew to the limits of his detection Akar let forth the energy he'd been conjuring. Balls of pale green flame shot from his fingertips toward the escaping pair, carrying with them all the venom and hatred Akar could muster.

With the release of those fireballs, the anger drained instantly out of Akar—and with it went the power he'd focused for the spell. He could no longer sense the carpet, and had no idea how successful his spell had been, for he knew the fugitives had been at the very limits of his range when he shot the fireballs. It did not matter; he'd done what he could do for now.

There were more important matters demanding his attention. The urn of Aeshma had been opened; he knew that from the massive disturbance on the magical web that underlay the world. He had missed his best chance to control the king of the daevas, to harness that incredible power for his own ends. Aeshma would have been weakened after so many centuries confined within the golden urn, but with each passing second his strength would increase and his power would return. Akar knew he must devote his energies to capturing the daeva before he grew too powerful for any man to control.

If Jafar al-Sharif and Selima had escaped his death curse, it was of little consequence at the moment. At some later time, after he'd gained control of Aeshma, he could track them down wherever in the world they were and exact a fitting retribution upon them. For now they could be allowed to think they'd escaped his vengeance.

Turning, he started back toward the stairs when one of his servants, a tall hairy Jinn with skin as black as soot, approached him, "O master, forgive this bearer of bad tidings, but there is chaos loose in the castle. In the course of their escape the impostors left the door open at the bottom of the stairs and the winged tigers have come through. Your loyal servants have been fighting them, but the beasts are fierce and we have suffered many injuries."

Akar frowned. This was one more crime for which Jafar al-Sharif would pay heavily. "Go into my upper storeroom and bring me the ebony wand with the emerald insets. It will be on the eastern shelves, third shelf down from the top, seventh item from the left."

"Hearing and obeying," said the Jinn, and vanished quickly upon his errand. He returned but a few moments later, quaking in fear at the reaction he knew his news would provoke from his master.

"O my gracious lord, I cannot perform the task you set. The storeroom has been ransacked, the shelves have been overturned, and their contents are scattered all over the floor. It's impossible to find anything in there right now."

At this news Akar, who had thought his anger entirely vented by the spell he'd cast against the thieves, flared into rage anew at the indignity he'd suffered. His previous temper was as but a summer squall compared now to the full tempest of his wrath. He did not have the proper equipment to do the job of ridding his castle of tigers, but that scarcely mattered. He was Akar, the world's mightiest wizard, and his power alone would suffice.

Step by angry step he marched across the roof and down the spiral stone stairway into the depths of his mountaintop castle. Up from below came the sounds of chaos, as his magical servants battled the ferocious flying tigers with the flaming claws who lived in the mountain's hollow interior. Snarls and groans and yells of pain reached the wizard's ears, but he cared naught for any of them. He was coming to redeem his castle, to rid it of the last trace of interlopers and restore its integrity once more. What was his would be his again and forever. No one would deny him that.

He stepped out into the long corridor of rock and confronted his foes. He could not see the tigers, but he could smell their feline musk, hear their angry growls, feel the heat of their bodies and their fiery claws. There were at least ten of them, perhaps a score, but Akar knew no fear. He knew with utter precision the length, width, and depth of his power, and he knew with equal precision how to use it.

His servants who'd been fighting the tigers in the corridor disengaged from the battle at the sight of their master. They backed against the wall, or through doorways, or vanished altogether. They knew better than to stand between the mighty wizard and any target he set his attention to.

And the wizard Akar uplifted his hands and a hurricane swept down the corridor, a wild wind whistling its vengeance against Shahdur's defilers. Akar's body began to glow with a blazing radiance of rage at the beasts who'd invaded his stronghold. Slowly the fires of his fury increased until he stood in the hallway shining like the light of a dozen suns.

And Akar spoke but a single word. "Begone!" and it echoed like thunder down the smooth stone corridor.

The winged tigers roared their defiance. They spat and hissed and snarled, swiping their fiery claws in the air to menace a man who could not be swayed by such theatrical gestures. And as Akar stepped toward them they backed away reluctantly, afraid to challenge the brightly glowing figure before them.

Step by deliberate step, Akar herded the fierce creatures back into the stairway from which they'd come, back down the stairs and through the sturdy wooden door that separated the castle proper from the mountain's interior. And when all the tigers were back in their proper place, Akar slammed shut the heavy door and slid the bar closed, sealing off the threat. Shahdur Castle once more belonged to him.

As the menace disappeared, Akar could feel fatigue washing over him. Two angry surges of power so close together had proved a severe strain on his energies, and his strength was fading quickly. Akar climbed the stairs to his bedroom level, and each step seemed twice as high as the one preceding it. Akar struggled to his bedroom, panting when he reached it, and fell exhausted across the bed, where he slept for two solid days without waking.

When the sleep had eased his spirit and a good meal had renewed his strength, Akar faced the difficult task of putting his equipment back in order. For one of the very few times in his life he regretted the loss of his eyes, for the collection and inventory process would be infinitely more difficult without sight. Nor could he trust his servants to perform the task. Some of his implements were so sensitive they'd be destroyed if touched by inexperienced hands; others were so powerful they could kill the person touching them unless handled just so. As tedious as it was, Akar knew this was a chore he'd have to perform himself.

He entered the first storeroom crawling on hands and knees, for some of the scattered objects were so small and fragile he dared not risk crushing them underfoot. His hands scouted the ground before him, and each time he encountered something his sensitive fingers would surround it, noting its shape and size and texture and inscriptions, and Akar's magical senses would probe the object's very nature until he knew precisely what it was. Only then would he hand the object to one of his sighted servants to be catalogued and stored away properly.

Thus did Akar spend the waking hours of the following two weeks on his knees in his two upper storerooms, searching the floors with sensitive fingers until every piece of equipment, every jar of powder, every phial of precious liquid, every amulet, and every talisman, all were accounted for. New lists were made and compared to old lists, until finally Akar knew everything he still had and where it was.

Much to his relief he learned that only two items had been stolen: the flying carpet, a major loss, and the ring of Cari, an insignificant one. Even so, he had other methods of traveling at his disposal; and the world was filled with Jann he could enslave if he chose. What angered him most about the loss was not the value of the items stolen, but the fact that such a brazen upstart as Jafar al-Sharif would have the nerve to take anything at all from a man so obviously his superior. He was somewhat perplexed that a man such as Jafar could even operate the carpet, and he resolved to look over that spell again when he had time, to see whether it was too accessible, even to charlatans.

With his castle finally back in order, Akar once again set his mind on the true problem: finding the whereabouts of Aeshma and determining the status of the daeva king's situation. To do this, Akar descended to his meditation chamber, the room with its floor marked in arcane symbols and mystic designs. Here he would empty his mind of its mundane concerns and send it exploring out into the magical web, tracing the paths and patterns within that network, looking for evidence of Aeshma's existence.

There was no question that Aeshma was out there somewhere, but the daeva king was using his magical powers at
such a reduced level that they barely stood out among the
other practitioners of the mystic arts. Time after time Akar
followed a delicate trace of magic, only to locate another wizard at the other end. It took all his powers of observation, and
not a little intuitive deduction, to track down Aeshma's location.

He narrowed the area to a remote desert region south of
Sudarr, but the trace was so weak and so far away he could not
pinpoint it further by such indirect means. More detailed information would have to come from other sources.

Standing in the center of his conjuration room, surrounded by charms and talismans to protect him against the
might and power of the forces he evoked, Akar summoned to
him five Marids, second most powerful of all the levels of the
djinni. These Marids were all brothers, and all so tall they had
to stoop to fit in the room. They had green, scaly skin, folded
leathery wings like bats, and yellow eyes shining with malev-
olence. Their lower tusks curled around the sides of their
cheeks like a boar's and their long, thin tails, with edges like
swords, slashed the air angrily. They raged against being summoned by this mere mortal, but the force of Akar's will
bound them to his orders and they could not refuse him.

In his sternest voice Akar commanded the Marids to fly to
the desert south of Sudarr and find where Aeshma was. They
were to observe what was going on and report back to him
everything they learned. He also told them to keep a discreet
distance from Aeshma and try as best they could to remain
hidden from him. Akar knew the Marids were creatures normally bound to Aeshma by kinship and temperament. He had
placed them strongly under his control, but he didn't want to
take the chance of Aeshma wresting them away and learning
prematurely of Akar's interest in him.

The five Marids flew off and Akar waited another week
with the patience of a spider in the corner of her web. Four
Marids returned with their tale that they had found Aeshma
and spied on him until he spotted them. He tried to pull them
under his control, but Akar's power over them was too
strong. In a rage, Aeshma had killed one of the Marid brothers, but the others returned to tell what they'd learned.

Aeshma had taken up residence in the palace of Rash-wenath, along with a human whom he was apparently serving. The palace had been restored to its original splendor all for the benefit of this one man—but other than maintaining this fabulous palace, Aeshma was making no ventures into the wider world.

Akar digested that news slowly. The man who'd freed Aeshma had been clever enough to slip a noose around the daeva's abilities, and Aeshma was content for the moment not to fight for control. Knowing what he did about daevas, Akar suspected that state of affairs would not continue for very long, and then Aeshma would be on the loose once more. Further, Aeshma now knew there was someone in the world who knew where he was and was interested in him—someone powerful enough to control Marids and keep them from Aeshma's clutches. That forewarning made Aeshma extra dangerous to deal with. Special steps would have to be taken.

Akar dismissed the Marids and, after due consideration, began his elaborate series of preparations. He purged his body with laxatives and emetics for three days to cleanse the system of any impurities. He then spent two weeks on a strict vegetarian diet, with the meals rigorously prepared in certain steps at certain times of the day according to special arcane formulas. Akar spent most of his time in his vast library, refreshing his memory on a wide variety of spells and secrets by having his servants read selected passages from ancient manuscripts. He had one of his Jinn fly to the nearest village and steal a goat, which Akar promptly sacrificed on his private altar; he drank some of the goat's blood while it was still warm, and the rest he smeared over his naked body.

Most of his resting time was spent, not in sleep, but in deep meditative trances that cleansed his mind of impurities the way the purges had cleansed his body. His breathing slowed, his pulse rate dropped, and his soul stored up energy for the big struggle he knew lay ahead of him.

After these weeks of preparation, when he was at last ready for the ordeal he must endure, the wizard Akar walked into his newly reordered storerooms and picked carefully from among the tools, powders, and amulets in his possession, until he had precisely those that could benefit him the most in a wide variety of emergency situations. He bundled his implements neatly into a tiny pouch around his neck, then left the storeroom and walked up the spiral stairway to the flat roof of Shahdur Castle.

Standing alone on the rooftop, the blind wizard lifted his arms to the open sky and recited a spell of great power. He spoke slowly and in a deep voice, enunciating each syllable with delicate precision and putting the force of his will into every word he uttered. His voice rolled across the open valleys and echoed from the other mountains in a naked display of power.

When he finished the spell he stood patiently and waited. Soon he could hear the flapping of wings, and an enormous eagle, with a wingspan greater than the height of four tall men, flew down and landed beside him. Akar felt his way, awkwardly at first, to the bird's side and climbed onto its back, while the majestic creature raised not a cry of protest. When the wizard was securely in place he gave the eagle his command. The huge wings spread out and the bird soared off the castle roof high up into the chilly mountain air currents. The eagle made three long, slow circles of the area to orient itself, then turned in a southwesterly direction and began its long, silent flight to the palace of Rashwenath.

4

THE PURGE

I N Ravan the Holy City, Ravan the Blessed of Oromasd, Ravan the center of the world, a particular blight was spreading through its wide streets and beautiful buildings, its shaded bazaars and gilded domes. Ever since the death of the late beloved King Shunnar, his widow Shammara had been working her wiles to negate his last request and bring the city under her total control.

King Shunnar had willed that the crown should go to his elder son, Prince Ahmad, upon attaining his eighteenth birthday—even thought Ahmad was only his son by a concubine instead of an official wife. Shammara's son Haroun, just a few weeks younger, would only inherit if anything happened to Ahmad. King Shunnar's most trusted wazir, Kateb bin Salih, had been appointed regent until the new ruler was crowned—but Kateb bin Salih was now old and infirm, and incapable of thwarting Shammara's plans.

Several times Shammara had hired rimahniya assassins to enter the Temple of the Faith where Ahmad was being raised, but each time they were doomed to failure by the alertness of the priests of Oromasd. But not all her plans were so unsuccessful. Forging an alliance with the wali of police, she slowly tightened her grip on the city. Little was done without her permission, and she built slowly toward the day she could make her rule over Ravan more overt.

Shammara sent emissaries to all the neighboring kingdoms, bribing their way into favor and making allies for her on all sides. In particular she made a secret alliance with the weak King Basir of Marakh, finally convincing him to betray Prince Ahmad and marry his daughter Oma to Prince Haroun instead.

And even months before Prince Ahmad left the Holy City, Shammara had been spinning her plans for the takeover of Ravan. Shammara was a systematic person who compiled list upon list of things that must be done and people who must be replaced, so that she would be ready when her day of triumph came.

Her first list was of those people steadfastly loyal to Prince Ahmad who could not be subverted to Shammara's cause. This list was subdivided into three groups; those of Prince Ahmad's supporters who would have to be assassinated; those who could be neutralized by removing them from positions of power; and those who, while loyal, were no serious threat to Shammara's new regime.

Shammara's second list was of those people already committed to her side, and it was subdivided into two parts; those who already held positions of power, and those who could be called upon to fill other positions once Prince Ahmad's supporters were out of the way.

Her third list was of those people who were neutral in the silent struggle between Shammara and Prince Ahmad, and it was similarly divided into two groups; those neutrals who, either with threats or with promises, could likely be swayed into Shammara's camp once she held full power, and those who were not worth the bother to try.

The wali of police helped Shammara draw up her lists; he had spies everywhere in Ravan and was constantly gauging the direction and strength of the emotional winds. The wali was already firmly committed to Shammara, and had been promised the rank of wazir once her administration was in place. He would remain on top of this power swing, as he had all the others. He was known for his ability to select winners.

On the other side, Prince Ahmad continued his studies in the Royal Temple under the tutelage of his friend and instructor, high priest Umar bin Ibrahim. Although Umar was aware of Shammara's growing power he was uncertain how to combat it—and neither he nor the prince knew the extensive details of what Shammara was plotting. They continued to place their trust in Oromasd to preserve the proper order in the Holy City, and took no counteractions of their own.

Unwittingly, Umar bin Ibrahim even made Shammara's task much easier for her. Suspecting some act of treachery along the road to Marakh, he made certain that the prince's entourage consisted of those members of the Royal Guard and those palace servants who were the most loyal and dedicated to Prince Ahmad, and he added himself to the party as well. This considerably thinned out the ranks of the people on Shammara's first list of those loyal to Ahmad who would be left inside the city when the prince departed. Those who went with Prince Ahmad would be killed by King Basir's "brigands," or at the very least would be outside the city walls and powerless to prevent Shammara's takeover.

Prince Ahmad's wedding procession departed through Palace Gate at the northern end of the city with great ceremony and the cheers of the populace. Shammara watched the departure from an upper window of the palace with a growing feeling of destiny fulfilled.

Shammara was a tall, slender woman with piercing eyes, a small mouth, and prominent cheekbones. Not a trace of gray marred her long black hair, not a line or wrinkle disturbed the gaunt smoothness of her face. She'd been a beautiful woman in her youth; she'd lost none of the beauty, but age had put sharper lines on her features, emphasizing them even more strongly. Shammara was a woman of few compromises, either physically or politically.

She smiled to watch the prince's procession, knowing that the last significant opposition to her rule in the Holy City was now gone. Those people who would inevitably try to defy her would have no spokesman to rally behind, no symbol to unify them. Soon enough word would come of Prince Ahmad's tragic death upon the road to Marakh, and all opposition would collapse as people realized there was no other possible ruler for Ravan but Shammara's son, Prince Haroun.

The plans, long since made, proceeded automatically. Two hours after Prince Ahmad left the city, the wali of police dispatched his most trustworthy officers on missions of murder. Noble homes were broken into, their owners butchered unceremoniously until the grounds ran red with their blood. Powerful merchants who worked in the bazaar were accosted by hooded strangers and had long knives shoved into their bellies before they could react to possible danger. The assassins tried to keep the bloodshed to a minimum, killing only their assigned targets and sparing wives and minor children— but on those few occasions where their crimes were witnessed by servants or family members, the witnesses were slain as well to keep the acts as anonymous as possible.

A score of influential citizens died mysteriously that afternoon, leaving a tremendous power vacuum within Ravan. Shammara had deliberately kept the number small. A purge that was carried out with surgical precision would scarcely bother the general population; they didn't care who ruled them as long as their taxes were not too bothersome. A bloodbath, though, would stir fears in many people that they, too, might be slated for elimination, and could lead to a panic that would be counterproductive.

Shammara's biggest concern was of vendetta from family and friends of the victims. She hoped fear would silence most of them and keep them from protesting; if not, one or two more deaths as an example should silence all.

When news of these murders became known throughout Ravan, the wali of police expressed his shock that such violence could happen within Oromasd's Holy City and pledged that those responsible for the crimes would be quickly punished. Indeed, within a few more hours he had rounded up some of the city's worst criminals, all of whom confessed under torture that they had committed the crimes in question. They were all summarily executed, thus sparing the populace the agony of prolonged and confusing trials. The wali was a firm believer in the adage that justice delayed was justice denied, and he would never be accused of obstructing justice for those he felt deserved none to begin with.

Kateb bin Salih was summoned to confer with Shammara about how to deal with the crisis. The regent, once one of King Shunnar's wisest and most trusted wazirs, was now weak and senile. Though he tried to govern Ravan wisely in the name of Prince Ahmad, he was no longer any match for the wiles of Shammara.

Shammara arranged for the interview to occur in an audience room in the women's section of the vast palace. Here in a room of green and white carpeting, of emeralds set in alabaster pillars and a domed ceiling, she sat cross-legged on the carpeted leewan wearing her most demure milfa and an air of righteous indignation. The regent hobbled in aided by his servants, sat upon the carpet a discreet distance from Shammara, and squinted across at her with his aged eyes.

Shammara was the picture of concern, her voice calm but horrified at the indignities and tragedies the city had suffered. Her voice was heavy with emotion as she listed the names of the dead, honored names all, and spoke of the gaping vacancies left in official positions as a result.

After assuring the regent that she was as horrified by these events as he was, she gave him a list she'd thoughtfully prepared, suggesting people she thought would do a good job replacing those who'd been so tragically lost. The regent, once an old hand at internal politics, no longer kept abreast of affiliations and saw nothing wrong with the people Shammara suggested. He recognized most of the names on the list as being men of high standing and good family; he had no way of knowing they were all personally loyal to Shammara and would support her in all decisions against Ahmad.

Kateb bin Salih approved Shammara's list of people to replace those who had been murdered, with only a few changes—changes Shammara demurely accepted, praising his wise choices. Only two were troubling, and those were minor ones who could be dealt with later. The continuing good will of the old man was worth it, for a while. Thus, within twenty-four hours of Prince Ahmad's departure, Shammara's supporters were confirmed in their positions and held most offices of power within the Holy City.

With that much accomplished so easily, Shammara decided to wait and consolidate her gains rather than push for the rest of her program too quickly. Oromasd cautioned in favor of moderation and to avoid excess in everything, and Shammara was a firm believer in using minimal effort to achieve maximum effect. She was now in a position where few people in the city could seriously threaten her; she could afford to wait and let events develop at their own pace.

For most of the citizens, life went on as before. They had little contact with the people who ruled over them, and a change of wazirs and emirs had little effect on the price of food in the bazaars. This sort of thing happened all the time, and aside from some gossip there was little reaction to the purge.

Those people who traveled in court circles, however, took greater note of the changes. Such people kept tallies of individual loyalties, and it wasn't hard to spot the change in direction that was coming about. Among these elite members of society, reaction was highly mixed. Those whose loyalties toward Prince Ahmad were more a matter of convenience than conviction quickly began composing messages both subtle and blatant to Shammara, expressing their desire, in this time of upheaval, to work more closely with her for the good of Ravan. Thus did Shammara acquire more converts without having to court them.

Those officials who were dedicated to Prince Ahmad, who could not bring themselves to work with Shammara under any conditions, found themselves in awkward circumstances. They too could see the way the wind was shifting, and they guessed that their lives had been spared in the purge only because they did not occupy important enough positions to make their elimination urgent. That, however, did not mean they would always be spared. If Shammara ever considered them a threat in the future, they knew she'd deal with them as ruthlessly as she'd dealt with the others.

Those people found several ways of coping with their situation. Some of them abruptly decided to move to another land where their wealth and wisdom would gain them respect instead of a dagger in the throat. Others decided to resign their offices, hoping that would be sufficient to remove them from Shammara's consideration. Yet others decided to become inconspicuous and inoffensive so they would not come to Shammara's attention. All these people decided to wait for Prince Ahmad's return, hoping that his presence in Ravan would counterbalance Shammara's evil maneuvers.

Thus it was that most of Shammara's work was done for her without the need for further bloodshed. As she'd hoped, one dramatic gesture at the beginning of her coup had so frightened her opposition that additional gestures were unnecessary. One lesson for the wise sufficed.

With that much accomplished, Shammara waited. Soon, word would come from King Basir about Prince Ahmad's death upon the road at the hands of brigands, and then Shammara could put the remainder of her plan into operation. Once the prince was officially dead, not even his most loyal supporters could deny her son Haroun the throne, for his in-

ritance had been specified by King Shunnar on his death-
d. Thus would her triumph become complete and her
astery over Ravan become absolute.

Shammara waited patiently for a week, for it would take at
ast that long for messengers from the "brigands" to bring
e news to King Basir and for him to dispatch an official
voy to relay the news to Ravan.

After a week, though, the silence from Marakh continued.
s each day passed without the desired news, Shammara's im-
atience grew and her anger flamed. Her servants hid in cor-
ers when possible. Many felt the lash of her tongue and the
de of her hand in these fearsome days.

She'd known King Basir was weak and generally incom-
etent, but she'd felt she could at least trust him with a simple
mbush. His army, despite his inconsistent leadership, was
till one of the best in Parsina; they should have had no trouble
gainst a lightly armed wedding party whom they outnumbered four to one. Yet each passing day bespoke some trouble,
some unexplained foul-up that could endanger the smoothly
working plan she had so carefully arranged. Shammara did
not like to have her plans thwarted, and someone would end
up paying.

At the end of the second week a carrier pigeon arrived in
the special cage atop Shammara's tower. The pigeon-keeper
removed the sealed message and had it sent immediately to the
woman who ruled the palace. Shammara read it and flung it
angrily to the ground. She stormed around her room, breaking bottles and throwing objects to the floor in her frustration.
When she'd finally calmed down enough to present a civilized
front, she summoned the wali of police to discuss the matter
with him.

The wali, a man of great size and bulk, came instantly at
her command. He had a thin mustache, a sharply pointed
beard, and little piggy eyes that almost disappeared beneath
his shaggy black eyebrows. So great was his girth that even his
kaftan was tight across his midriff, giving him a slightly slov-
enly appearance even though his turban was impeccably
wrapped. His portly frame made his obeisance an awkward
gesture, but he tried his best as he said, "Salaam to thee, O my
noble queen."

Shammara, already in a foul mood, stiffened. "I have
never had the title 'queen' and I never will. That was reserved

for my late husband's first wife, and will belong to my so
wife, but never to me."

"You are queen of my soul, queen of my allegiance," sa
the wali, covering quickly, "I cannot think of you as any less

Shammara, clad only in a breezy thawb of bright yello
silk and no veil, looked at him for a moment. The corners
her mouth twitched in a quick smile despite herself. She re
pressed it by reminding herself of the serious situation the
faced. "Your explanation is accepted, but do not repeat th
mistake. Sit down. We have a problem."

The wali lowered himself awkwardly onto a plum
cushion on the tiled floor of the high-domed audience cham
ber while Shammara, as was her wont, reclined on her satin
covered diwan whose legs were carved in the semblance of
lion's claws. Despite her comfortable position there wa
nothing relaxed about her posture, and the wali—who wa
capable of reading such signs—braced himself for the worst

"I've just received word from one of my agents in Marakh," Shammara said without further prelude. "Prince
Ahmad escaped our ambush through some miraculous intervention and has gone into hiding somewhere. King Basir
doesn't know what to do, but is going to lie to us and say the
prince was killed as planned. Princess Oma will be sent here to
marry Haroun as soon as possible, to cement our relationship."

The wali scowled, making his thin mustache sag into his
face. "Can we trust an ally who lies to us this way?"

Shammara waved her hand idly. "Basir isn't much of a
problem. I'll deal with him in my own time. But right now
his incompetence has put us in some jeopardy." She looked
straight into the wali's eyes. "If Ahmad can raise an army, how
much trouble could he cause us?"

"Ravan has never been conquered in all its history," the
wali assured her. "Its walls are as strong as ever, its defenses as
secure. The armies of five kingdoms could not defeat us—and
if anyone tried, we have many allies to rally to our defense.
The Holy City would be defended by most of mankind if any
force, even Prince Ahmad, should attack it."

"And internally?" Shammara persisted, chewing lightly on
one well-manicured nail. "Could Ahmad spark an uprising
within the city to topple us?"

"My spies are always alert to the faintest signs of subver-on," the wali said. "The prince's strongest backers have been eutralized, and most of the common people don't care. Any prising he could stir would be weak and readily squashed. Je've planned too well to be easily toppled."

Shammara sat silently for several minutes, staring intently t the tapestry on the wall across from her. The blue, white, nd red floral designs soothed somewhat her troubled mind. At last she looked again at the wali. "According to the re-ports, Ahmad had some magical help in his escape. If he uses hat against us—"

"No magic can avail him against the walls of Ravan."

After another brief silence, Shammara said, "Then since there's little Ahmad can do against us, we can ignore him for the moment. Let's take Basir's word at face value and pretend we believe it. He'll be blissfully content to think he's fooled us, and it gives us a lever to use against him at some later date, should we need it."

"And if Ahmad should return to claim his throne?"

"We'll denounce him as an obvious impostor and kill him before he steps within the gates," Shammara said. "After all, we'll have the word of a king that the *real* Ahmad was mur-dered by thieves. I'm sure you can handle anyone who dis-putes our actions."

"Unquestionably." The wali smiled, stroking his thick beard with pleasure.

But Shammara still could not feel totally at ease and, after dismissing the wali, she paced the room like a caged tigress. Making a decision, she clapped her hands to summon a ser-vant, and commanded him to fetch Yusef bin Nard, her per-sonal astrologer—and acting high priest now that Umar bin Ibrahim was out of the city.

Yusef bin Nard came quickly at her summons; sweating, disheveled, breathless, he arrived within the hour. The priest was flabby, with soft, pasty skin; the white priestly robes and turban of his calling seemed somehow too large for him, swallowing him up in their folds and adding to the aura of ineffectualness he showed. Bin Nard was intellectually a eu-nuch, but he was Shammara's main tie into the priesthood— and he had other uses as well.

Although as acting high priest bin Nard possessed a gre
deal of nominal authority, he looked distinctly uncomfortab
in the presence of the woman who was the acknowledg
ruler of the Holy City. Shammara tried her best to put him
ease by wearing much more discreet and demure clothir
than she'd worn for the wali, and by keeping her tone lig
and conversational. "Sit down, O worthy priest, and ch
with me some moments about Oromasd's plans for the city
Ravan."

Yusef bin Nard moved awkwardly as he settled himse
cross-legged on a pillow in front of her diwan. "How may
help you, O gracious lady?" he asked.

"It's about the forecast you made for me a year ago,
Shammara said. "Do you remember it?"

"Oh yes, I remember being startled. The forecast said you
son would be the next king of Ravan. I've done as you askec
and not told anyone about the forecast; we didn't want tc
alarm anyone."

"Your discretion is to be commended," Shammara told
him. "At the time, of course, we were both shocked at the
thought that Prince Ahmad might not inherit the throne. But
now I have begun to wonder. There's been no news from Marakh, no word that the prince and his party arrived there safely,
and that reminded me of your forecast. It's frightening to
think how accurate you might be."

"The great lord Oromasd places the signs in the heavens,"
bin Nard said modestly. "It's we poor mortals who must read
them as best we can."

"I was wondering," Shammara said, "whether you could
elaborate a little more on that forecast. Could you read the
stars and tell what Prince Ahmad's destiny is to be? Will he
return safely to us with his new bride? Will there be any conflict between him and Haroun—or between him and me, for
that matter? I would hate the thought of bloodshed with the
Holy City."

"I shall draw the casts immediately and let you know upon
the morrow," bin Nard promised, and withdrew to his chambers to accomplish the task.

True to his word, he returned to Shammara the next day
with his forecasts. "As I believe I explained to you before," he
began, "we in Ravan live in an unusual situation. Because our
city is protected by the magical spells of Ali Maimun, any

eadings regarding the city are clouded by strange uncertainies. Prince Ahmad is now beyond the city, and all the signs I see say that the path of his life will never intersect with that of Ravan again. The heavens appear to be telling me that Prince Ahmad will never return. I cannot see further than that; he is beyond my scope, I'm afraid."

"And what of me and Haroun?" Shammara asked. "What will happen to us?"

"Again there are clouds, but it seems certain you will both live out your lives and die here in Ravan. Haroun will be the next king, and I see no signs of civil strife to mar his rule."

"If we are indeed to lose Prince Ahmad, then the rest of your forecast is welcome news," Shammara said. "I am in your debt, O noble Yusef. The Temple of the Faith is going through an exhaustive procedure right now, isn't it?"

Bin Nard nodded. "The thief who stole the reliquary urn polluted the Bahram fire. We're having to consecrate a new fire, and that can take more than a year."

"If there's anything I can do to facilitate your efforts, please feel free to call on me. As you know from our discussions, I've always felt that the priesthood must be well looked after in the Holy City."

Yusef bin Nard's greed showed through his fear as he expressed his appreciation of such religious devotion. With her usual caution Shammara masked her elation. Now that she had secured the priesthood with the bending of this weak man, she had completed the tripod of support she needed: priesthood, police, and civil bureaucracy.

She saw bin Nard to the door, then turned and smiled. Calling for her maids she went to her bath chuckling over the wali's slip of the tongue yesterday. While it was true she would never officially be queen, it was also true that few queens had ever held the power she was gathering—and none had ever attained it by her own hand as Shammara would do.

5

THE MISSION

BEYOND the Holy City of Ravan, stretching for many parasangs eastward, lay the vast wastes of Kholaj Desert. The Kholaj, bane of travelers, accursed of merchants, a portion of purgatory lying along one of the most important trade routes in all Parsina—the route from the eastern lands of Indi and Sinjin to the center of the world itself, Ravan. Each year untold millions of dinars worth of merchandise crossed through those forbidding tracts—and each year the tales grew of travelers who didn't complete the crossing. Many were the caravans that vanished entirely within the treacherous sands, and many more were the individual wayfarers who succumbed to the snakes, scorpions, and other vile creatures of Rimahn that plagued this barren land.

Near the center of the Kholaj Desert lay the oasis of Sarafiq. As one of half a dozen oases scattered throughout the vast wasteland, it was a popular stopover for travelers, a respite from the monotony of sand and oppressive heat. Here was abundant water for horses, camels, and men. Here was a major bazaar where merchants from more fertile lands surrounding the desert brought in food to sell at exorbitant prices to improvident travelers. Here were rich gardens whose many blossoms and delicate scents provided momentary beauty to ease the wanton defilement of the region by Rimahn. Here was quiet and peace, and breezes cooled by the splashing waters of the fountains.

Also in Sarafiq was a shrine, a place so holy that its imporance dwarfed all the oasis's other functions. The shrine dated back so far into history that no man could state its origin for certain. Some said it was founded by the great mage Ali Maimun shortly after the climactic battle between the forces of Rimahn and the forces of Oromasd at the beginning of this Cycle of the world. Other historians disagreed, saying the shrine had already been ancient in the days of King Shahriyan and the great battle.

The shrine of Sarafiq had a madrasa connected with it, noted for the quality of the students it turned out. Umar bin Ibrahim, high priest of Ravan, was a graduate of Sarafiq's madrasa; so was the wizard Akar just a decade later. If the shrine of Sarafiq had done nothing but turn out great scholars, its fame would have been secured.

But the shrine had even more than that, for at the shrine dwelled a prophet. There had always been a prophet at Sarafiq for as long as people could remember. Each prophet reigned for ten, twenty, thirty, sometimes even forty years or more before yielding to his successor with never a trace of a fight. The secret of how a prophet gained his powers, and how each prophet selected and trained his successor, was a total mystery to the outside world—but the system worked, and Sarafiq always had a prophet in residence.

The prophet of Sarafiq would grant to any man who came before him one vision of the future. The road to Sarafiq was arduous, and the path to the prophet himself was even more so—but so great was the reputation of the prophet of Sarafiq, and so accurate (if ambiguous) were his forecasts, that more people came to the oasis for his wisdom than for the life-giving water.

Eight years earlier, Umar bin Ibrahim had returned to Sarafiq seeking a vision—not for himself, but for the young and recently orphaned Prince Ahmad. At that time the prophet told him if Prince Ahmad ever left the city walls of Ravan before his coronation he would never return to rule there. For years Umar had jealousy guarded the prince, telling no one of the prophecy in hopes of thwarting it—but now, after the ambush by King Basir, it looked as though the prophet's words were to be proven accurate one more time.

Now, as an outcast from his home and his land, Prince Ahmad had come to Sarafiq to learn of his fate, accompanied

by his surviving guardsmen and servants. Here, too, ha
come Jafar al-Sharif, the storyteller from Durkhash who wa
pretending a claim to wizardry, hoping to learn the antidote t
Akar's curse so he could free his daughter Selima from it
effects.

And here it was that both men received the prophet's vi
sion for the two of them, that their destinies were intertwinec
and the fate of all Parsina rested upon their backs. And both
men accepted that burden, though with differing degrees of
willingness.

On the evening of the day he received the vision from the
prophet Muhmad, Prince Ahmad Khaled bin Shunnar el-Ravani, still a few months shy of his eighteenth birthday, assembled his guards and his servants in the sahn of the temple
of Sarafiq, under the open sky. It was summer and the sun was
late in setting; the sky ranged from dark blue in the east to
pinks and oranges in the west, and only the brightest stars
were making their appearance. The sky was free of clouds; it
was destined to be one of those nights when a person could
look straight up into the heavens and half expect to see the face
of lord Oromasd himself.

Prince Ahmad stood at the top of the alabaster minbar, a
tall, straight-backed young man with the rich beginnings of a
still-forming beard framing his broad, handsome face. His
black eyebrows grew together to form a single line across his
forehead, and the somber eyes below them showed a combination of determination and intelligence. Wearing his cloth-
of-gold kaftan and wine red zibun, he made a noble figure
standing above the group he was to address.

He looked out from his vantage point over the perplexed
faces of his followers, lit by the last rays of the setting sun and
the flickering light of torches around the sahn. Of the original
complement that had left Ravan with him on his ill-fated journey, less than half remained alive. These were his most loyal,
devoted subjects, and the message they were about to hear
was a particularly bitter one. Prince Ahmad tried to gauge
their love and dedication, knowing that this speech could well
be the most significant in his life.

Young Prince Ahmad was not an accomplished orator.
Though he'd studied speech and rhetoric at the madrasa in
Ravan, his skills had never been fully tested by reality. He

ayed now for Oromasd to make his words both moving and
ent, worthy of his royal heritage.

He took a deep breath, and inhaled with it the sweet scent
the flowers in the oasis's garden. For a brief instant his mind
ed with images of the royal gardens in Ravan, the most
autiful gardens in the world. The thought that he might
ver see them again almost made him waver in his resolve.
it he steeled himself, as a true prince should, and began the
eech he'd been rehearsing for an hour in his mind.

"My faithful servants, all of you," he said. "We sit here in
is peaceful oasis tonight largely because of you. You've
oven your loyalty through steel and blood—you and your
nfortunate comrades who fell in the forest at the hands of
ose brigands. You make me proud to number you in my
tinue, for no prince, no king, ever had a more honorable
llowing.

"Your valor makes it even harder to speak the words I
ust say, to tell you we have all been betrayed." He had to
ause here as a shocked murmur ran through the crowd.
hmad waited for it to die before continuing. "Betrayed not
y any of our number, but by treachery done against us from
hose we thought were our friends."

He repeated to them the story he'd extracted from the
Marakhi envoy Tabib abu Saar, of how Shammara and King
Basir had conspired against the peaceful wedding party and
set the ambush for them in the woods; of how Shammara had
planned a purge against all his loyal followers left behind in
Ravan so her son, Prince Haroun—married to Princess
Oma—could rule as king in Ravan; and of how only the miraculous intervention they witnessed kept them from being
slaughtered by King Basir's men.

"The gates of the Holy City are now closed to us," the
prince went on. "If we try to return, our small force will be
wiped out by Shammara's army. Some of you might slip in as
individuals in disguise—but as men known to be loyal to me
you would have to be careful, for discovery would surely
mean your deaths.

"Similarly, it is rumored that Shammara concluded deals
with most of the neighboring kingdoms that I and my party
be killed on sight if we seek protection there. I fear we will
find no sanctuary within a hundred parasangs of Ravan, other

than this holy shrine, which Shammara's treachery could subvert. It was for this reason I led you here after the ambu rather than to our original destination. I needed to confer w the prophet of Sarafiq and receive a vision of my destiny.

Prince Ahmad stood erect and proud on the minbar, jewels of his turban occasionally reflecting the last rays of setting sun. After their initial astonishment the men sat stunned silence, absorbing his words like bread soaking grease. Such heavy news took time to comprehend; it cou not be digested in a few seconds.

"I have now received that vision," the prince continue "and it is an onerous one. Ironically, the magical manifestatic that saved us from the brigands was Aeshma, king of th daevas, the personification of Rimahn on earth. He was r leased from the captivity in which he'd been held since h great battle with King Shahriyan many years ago; we suspe the thief who stole the urn from the Temple of the Faith es caped the city disguised as a member of our party. The blesse lord Oromasd himself must have been looking after us, for can think of no other reason why we were spared whe Aeshma destroyed our enemies.

"Regardless of how we escaped, we know that evil incarnate is loose upon the world. Aeshma will waste no time gathering the daevas into an army to eradicate humankind. As servants of Oromasd, it is our sacred duty to oppose the forces of Rimahn and defeat the tide of evil that threatens to overwhelm us."

The prince's handsome face took on an expression of solemn determination as he spoke. "The prophet's vision was that I and the wizard Jafar al-Sharif must recover the pieces of the Crystal of Oromasd and unite the armies of mankind to fight in the battle against Rimahn that is sure to come. This responsibility I accept, though the effort may be beyond me and I may die in the attempt.

"But the prophet's vision was for me. I speak now about the fate of you who have served me so faithfully. Though I carry the title of prince, I have no kingdom and can control no allegiances. I cannot and will not force any man to follow me to my fate. I hereby release you from any and all oaths of loyalty you made to me in happier times. No man of you is bound to the uncertain course of my destiny."

There was a long silence in the gathering twilight as the
n pondered the prince's pronouncement. Then one bold
vant spoke up from the back of the crowd near the
wara. "But we've lost our homes and families in Ravan,"
said, his voice choking with emotion. "If we lose you,
ere will we go, what will we do?"

"I have thought long and hard about your welfare," Prince
mad assured him. "It is not right for a master to discard
ch faithful and valued servants without suitable reward for
eir efforts. Oromasd has blessed me with the means for
ur reward. Ours was a wedding party, laden with gifts for
r treacherous host, King Basir. We carry with us enough
ealth in goods and coin to make each of you secure for many
ars. I shall see to it, before I depart on my own journey, that
e riches are divided fairly among you, and no man of my
rvice shall go wanting.

"As for where you will go—the world is wide and varied.
hough Ravan may be dangerous for you, there are many
ther places where honest and hardworking men like your-
elves can build their fortunes and will be eagerly welcomed.
hose of you with families in Ravan may be able to send for
hem and get them out of the city. Those of you free from
ncumbrances can build new and better lives for yourselves. I
hall send you forth with all my blessings and, I hope, with
Oromasd's as well. For those of you uncertain of direction,
the prophet Muhmad may give you guidance and counsel as
wise as he's given to me."

And, I hope, less ambiguous, the prince thought, but kept
that piece of doubt to himself.

As Prince Ahmad stood on the minbar, gazing down at the
confused and tearful faces, a man on the left stood up. In the
gloom the prince at first had difficulty recognizing him, but as
the man spoke Ahmad knew it was Nurredin al-Damasci,
captain of his guard. The soldier spoke loudly, with force and
fire in his voice.

"No," he said aloud. "I will not accept this decision. As
you said, the world is wide, and I have traveled widely
through it. I've served many masters through my years, but
never have I served one as fair, as just, and as righteous as
Prince Ahmad Khaled bin Shunnar el-Ravani. The prince
needs my help now more than ever. The journey he con-

templates will be long and dangerous, and the fight agair
the demon forces of Rimahn will be the hardest men have ev
waged. I would be less than a man if I did not keep my oath
him and fight at his side against the enemies of mankind."

"Your oath was made to the prince of Ravan," Ahma
said. "I am that no longer, and you are released from that oath
It is no shame on you not to fulfill it."

"Then I make a *new* oath, to the man and not the prince,
Nurredin al-Damasci persisted. "I vow by Oromasd and th
Bounteous Immortals, and by all my hopes of attaining th
House of Song, that I shall faithfully serve the wishes c
Ahmad Khaled bin Shunnar el-Ravani with all my breath, a
my strength, and all my soul, as long as life remains in m
body, and that I shall fight the lies of Rimahn and his legion o
evil servants."

The captain turned and looked at the rest of the men seatec
in the courtyard. "Thus have I pledged my life and my swore
to the defense and honor of my noble lord. All those among
you who would call yourselves men, I charge you now to give
your oath again."

And as a single man, the audience rose to its feet and began
cheering the name of Prince Ahmad Khaled bin Shunnar el-
Ravani, their chosen liege. The deafening chorus of their en-
thusiastic voices rang out over the still desert air and shook the
very walls of the shrine with the power and intensity of their
devotion.

Prince Ahmad stood on the minbar utterly speechless, gazing down at the emotional outpouring that threatened to overwhelm the oasis. His eyes were suddenly filled with tears at
the loyalty he inspired in these good men, and he vowed silently to Oromasd that he would not lead them astray. He
prayed for wisdom to do justice to these people who would
place their lives so trustingly in his hands, and for the maturity and composure to carry on with what must yet be said.
He made a mental note to thank his mentor, Umar bin
Ibrahim, for all his insistence on emotional discipline; that discipline now was what kept him going.

When, after several minutes, the cheering did not abate,
Prince Ahmad held up his hands for silence and slowly the
noise died away. The crowd in the sahn looked to him for their
new direction.

"I am no longer a prince, save in name, and I still feel I have no right to command you or accept your oaths," he said. As a few protests were shouted, he continued quickly and with more volume, "However, the prophet's vision has made me, not a prince, but a servant of Oromasd, pledged to fight the battle to restore the balance he ordains in the world. I shall accept your oaths on behalf of our lord Oromasd, creator of the world and all that is good; so long as I follow his path you shall be bound to my commands as I am to his. When the battle against Aeshma is over, I shall again release you from any loyalties and you'll be free to pursue your own destinies. In the meantime we shall all be vassals of Oromasd together."

This fine speech so inspired the men that the sahn was again filled with their cheers for several minutes. Prince Ahmad stood patiently until the noise had completely subsided and he could speak once more. They would not be nearly so happy about what he must tell them now, and he wanted to have their full attention.

"But whether you are sworn to me or not," he told them, "you cannot come with me on my journey. I have consulted with the high priest Umar bin Ibrahim and with the wizard Jafar al-Sharif, and we are in agreement that we must move quickly and as secretly as possible if we are to accomplish our appointed task. The three of us—with Jafar's poor spectral daughter as well—shall travel alone to the corners of Parsina. In this way we hope to remain inconspicuous as we go, threatening no one and not being threatened in turn. To travel with a larger party would not only slow us down but would also bring us to the notice of people who are allies of Aeshma, and to the notice of his servants, the djinni."

There was some grumbling in the ranks, and Nurredin al-Damasci called out, "But you'll need help—"

"Indeed I will," the prince interrupted before his captain could complete the sentence. "And I'll call upon all of you, everyone, under your oaths of allegiance, to give it to me. Part of the mission laid upon me by the prophet was to forge an alliance among the kings of Parsina, and to amass an army to counter the daevas Aeshma will lead against us. I cannot achieve this goal all on my own, since I must spend most of my time searching for the pieces of the Crystal of Oromasd. I therefore charge you all to complete this part of my mission for me—to act as ambassadors in the courts of Parsina and raise an army that will march against the demon hordes."

Prince Ahmad looked at his captain. "The warriors Damasc are renowned as being among the fiercest fighters the world," he said. "Can you convince the king of Damasc see the righteousness of our cause and enlist the Damasci arm on our side?"

"I'll do it, my lord, even if it takes the point of my swor to convince him," Nurredin al-Damasci said with convictior

Prince Ahmad shook his head. "Our allies must fight vo untarily or not at all," he said, "but your enthusiasm is com mendable. If you put the same energy into convincing othe kings, we're assured of converts to the cause."

He turned to examine the rest of his audience. "Others o you are also not native to Ravan. O Abban, I know you'r from Syron; you, O Kousar, come from Bann. You shall hav the mission of returning to your native lands and convincing your people to support us in the upcoming battle. All of you wherever you go, request or, if you must, demand an audienc with the king. Show him my seal on the scrolls I will prepare for you. Tell him the battle is coming, and that Oromasd requires his presence at the battlefield fifty parasangs south of Ravan in the Leewahr Plains by the time of the first floods next spring.

"I am not King Shahriyan, and I have no mighty heroes beside me; only with the combined armies of mankind do we stand a chance against the legions of Rimahn. If you would serve me and aid my cause, I beg you to carry the message throughout Parsina that mankind must mobilize against the powers of darkness."

Amid even more cheering, Prince Ahmad descended with stately bearing from the top of the minbar and walked out of the sahn to the side of the temple at the shrine of Sarafiq.

Jafar al-Sharif stood off to the side as the prince spoke to his men. The storyteller-cum-wizard was a tall man of forty-two years, with a handsome face and distinguished streaks of gray in his well-trimmed black beard. His clothing was tattered and ill-fitting, having been hurriedly taken off a dead jailor when he escaped from the dungeons of Ravan, but Jafar's dignified bearing made his garments seem almost inconsequential.

Accustomed to public speaking himself, though not on such a grand scale, he viewed the prince's performance with an analytical eye and found little to criticize. Physically the prince was a distinguished figure who looked born to command. His tone and words were perfectly fitted to the occasion. He managed to blend the proper balance of dignity, loyalty, and humility that would make him a leader beloved by his followers.

As the prince triumphantly descended from the minbar, Umar bin Ibrahim—once high priest of the Temple of the Faith in Ravan, now merely an exile like all the rest—stepped forward to embrace him. Just as the prince seemed naturally adapted to his royal role, Umar bin Ibrahim could have been born wearing the white robes and turban of a priest. He flowed in a stately swirl of white, enhanced by his long white beard. The beard and the lines of his face proclaimed him old, but the energy in his eyes was ageless.

The old man smiled, now, to look at his prize pupil. "A wonderful speech, Your Highness," he said. "Most effective."

"Quite," Jafar agreed. "Now more than ever I hope we succeed in our quest. You deserve to be king of *something*."

"I couldn't have dreamed of such a reaction," Ahmad said, still amazed at his own effectiveness. "I was sure of Nurredin and a few of the others, but to hold them all so completely—"

He reached forward suddenly and clasped his teacher, hands to forearms. "Thank you, Umar, for all your years of nagging me about my lessons. I couldn't have made this speech without your discipline behind me."

The old man's face was a fascinating study in emotions. The fatherly love was more than evident, as was the pride in having taught him those skills he'd shown today. But there was a wistful quality as well; Jafar's remark had emphasized the fact that Ahmad was a prince without a realm, and all the skills Umar had so patiently taught him might be wasted if he couldn't regain his throne.

Prince Ahmad finally pulled back from the embrace. "I'll leave to you, Umar, the task of apportioning our wealth among the men while I write the letters they must show to other kings. My servants have much traveling to do, and I'll not send them on their mission empty-handed. We ourselves should travel lightly. Several changes of clothing, food and water, two small tents, and a couple sacks of the gold coins

abu Saar was carrying back to his treacherous master; the gol
should help us buy anything we lack. Everything else shoul
be divided among the others—and if they can't take it, let th
priests here have it to sell for charity. I'd rather this wealth g
to the deserving poor than to feed the coffers of a scorpio
like King Basir."

He looked over to Jafar al-Sharif. "But you, O wizard
You cannot travel in such mean garments; they do no honor t
your exalted station, they command no respect. If we're t
convince people of our cause and get the pieces of the Crystal,
you must look the part."

Jafar was only too aware of his impoverished wardrobe,
but his life had been so hectic and confined in the past week
that there'd been no chance to acquire anything better. He
made a small salaam and, with a wave of his hands, said, "I
normally dress with more elegance, Your Highness, but the
magical duel with my archenemy Akar left me in reduced circumstances."

"I have in my train some suits made for my future father-
in-law," Prince Ahmad said. "They'll fit you well enough.
Take them with my compliments."

The next twenty-four hours were filled with the uninter-
rupted surge of activity battle-trained men can sustain. Umar
the priest consulted with Nurredin al-Damasci about the dis-
position of the treasure, and the captain agreed to divide the
wealth as was appropriate. Those with training in the quarter-
master's corps directed the others in the physical division.
That so much wealth, which had taken the servants of the
royal palace days to pack, could be sorted, weighed, and divided in a single day was a tribute to the skill and devotion of
the prince's men.

Prince Ahmad himself spent much of that time writing
letters. In his finest hand, with calligraphic skills honed at the
madrasa in Ravan, he explained the desperate situation that
confronted mankind and implored the royal personage who
would be reading the missive to aid in the coming battle in the
name of Oromasd, creator of the earth. He signed each letter
with his full name and title, and stamped each one with his
personal seal. The letters were then distributed to his men,
who swore to present them to as many kings as they could
reach in the upcoming months.

With Ahmad's mission being the most crucial, it was agreed that the prince's group would leave the oasis the next evening; his men would disperse on their own missions at their convenience. Umar also consulted with the scribes at the shrine, and obtained from them a series of maps detailing, as best they knew, the route the prince must take to visit the kingdom of Punjar, the citadel of Varyu, king of the winds, the sunken city of Atluri, and the interior of fiery Mount Denavan—the four corners of Parsina where the ancient mage Ali Maimun had distributed the shards of the Crystal of Oromasd.

True to his word, Prince Ahmad delivered to Jafar the clothing originally intended as gifts for King Basir. The storyteller went suddenly from having no suitable clothing to an overabundance, and the choice of what to take was a difficult one. He ordered his old clothes burned, ridding him of one more reminder of his painful night in the dungeons of Ravan.

Jafar's favorite of the outfits was a sky blue silken thawb, richly embroidered with gold thread, to wear over his Sadre. A yellow leather hizam circled his waist, holding both a khanjar and a gold-sheathed saif—traditional accessories to a court outfit, even for a wizard who shouldn't need such things. Jafar was by no means a fighter and didn't know how to use these weapons, but just having them at his side looked impressive and made him feel more important. His feet were shod in fur-lined boots of the same leather as his hizam, and over all this, if he chose, was a golden zibun that added to the rich effect. On his head was a fine silk turban the same shade as his thawb, wrapped with precision to lend an air of authority.

Jafar al-Sharif beheld himself in a full-length mirror and was pleased by what he saw. He particularly liked the way the full sleeves of his thawb swirled when he moved his arms in expansive gestures, as he often did when he was telling some exciting story or fable. When he straightened his shoulders and gazed imperiously outward, hands resting regally on his hips, he could easily be taken for the mighty wizard he claimed to be.

Thus attired, Jafar al-Sharif strode boldly into the courtyard of the oasis's caravanserai where the party was being housed. Amid the bustling servants preparing for their departure, Jafar spied his daughter Selima, standing to one side and looking lost and forlorn.

All the pride he'd just been feeling in his new clothes vanished, to be replaced by the terrible feeling of helplessness that overwhelmed him each time he looked at her. Akar's death curse had been meant for him—but because his slave, Cari the Jann, had shielded him from its effects, it was Selima who suffered from it. It was so frustrating to have Selima be there and yet not there, a smoky, translucent image of herself that could walk and talk and react to things and still neither touch nor be touched. Though Selima could stand or sit on solid objects and could not pass through walls, she could neither grab hold of things nor could anyone touch her. She was a mere wraith, an insubstantial half-entity in the land of living beings.

Selima said she could feel no pain—or any sensation, for that matter—but Jafar knew how her heart must be suffering from this cruel torture. Akar's curse guaranteed she would gradually fade away to nothingness until she passed altogether from the living world and ceased to be any more than a memory. The prophet Muhmad had said that only gathering the pieces of the Crystal of Oromasd could save Selima from this dreadful fate, which was why Jafar was undertaking such a perilous journey. But the prophet had also said Jafar would lose her anyway, though he'd gain more than he could possibly imagine. He wasn't sure what that was supposed to mean, but even a chance to save Selima was better than nothing.

And yet, despite her predicament, Selima was bravely determined to accompany her father, the prince, and the priest on their dangerous mission across the breadth of Parsina. Jafar marveled at how many wonderful qualities could be stored in a single fifteen-year-old girl—and how he, of all people, could have put them there. More than likely it was her mother's influence—and his heart twinged yet once more at the thought of his late beloved Amineh.

He saw so much of his wife reflected in their daughter—the clear, shining eyes, the lustrous olive-complected skin with the beauty mark just beside the left eye, the shining white teeth and the long brown hair. Her figure was supple and endowed with youthful grace, amply proportioned where a young girl needed such proportions yet slender enough to catch a man's eye. It was not merely a father's prejudice that made Jafar al-Sharif think his daughter was beautiful, and he knew it would be a tragedy if she were not permitted to live out a full and complete life.

Selima, who so loved beautiful clothes, would be the most plainly dressed of the group, wearing her blue niaal, blue sirwaal trousers, white Sadre, and red cotton sidaireeya with the yellow embroidery. To her great embarrassment she'd not been wearing a milfa when the wizard's curse struck her, and now she could don no other garments because of her insubstantial nature. Her face was naked to public view; it was to Prince Ahmad's credit that he was polite enough not to fuss over the matter. The prince treated Selima as an honored companion and ignored the implications the lack of a veil would have produced in other men.

Jafar al-Sharif put aside his feelings of pity and tried to act as brave as his daughter. "Well, Selima, how do I look? Better than some itinerant wordmonger, eh?"

Selima smiled when she saw him, and her eyes scanned his wardrobe approvingly. "At last you look as you should have always looked, O noblest of fathers," she said. "You could be the prince of storytellers or the shaykh of wizards, or anything else you care to be."

"To be your father is miracle enough. If only the world were as discerning as you, half our problems would have been solved long ago. But come, there are things to do and we must prepare for our journey."

Though in fact the prince's servants did most of the initial packing, Jafar made it a point to oversee their work so he'd know how to do it himself upon the road and also where everything was packed. They would be taking but four horses: Prince Ahmad's noble steed Churash, a horse each for Umar and Jafar al-Sharif, and a fourth horse to carry their packs and extra equipment. Selima, who weighed nothing in her present condition, would ride on this extra horse; since she couldn't hold the reins, her father would lead it for her.

By dusk the travelers were ready to depart. The priests at the shrine fixed them a final meal, a simple lamb stew and chelo, before they left. A short prayer service was held to ask Oromasd's blessing on their endeavors, and haoma was drunk to remind the travelers of their holy purpose.

Prince Ahmad bade an emotional farewell to his retainers and reminded them of their own important missions. He'd been hoping the prophet Muhmad would come out to see the party off, but the old priest remained secluded, merely sending word via one of his acolytes that his blessings would ride with the adventurers.

Jafar al-Sharif knelt beside the horse Selima was to ride and bent over. His daughter stepped upon his back and swung her leg over the saddle to mount the beast, and Jafar could feel no sensation of weight from her at all. Then the three men mounted their own horses and the party rode out of Sarafiq by the eastern gate, across the Kholaj Desert toward the far kingdom of Punjar.

Their first night's travel was uneventful as they rode under the starlit summer sky with the waxing crescent moon originally at their backs. The horses' gait was uneven across the shifting sands, and they traveled little more than five parasangs that night before calling a halt.

It was not until they were unpacking equipment to set up camp for the day that Jafar al-Sharif discovered the surprise awaiting him in his saddlebag.

6

THE JOURNAL

THE sun was just beginning to rise after their first night of traveling alone through the Kholaj Desert when Prince Ahmad and his party made ready to camp. Their arrangement was to use two tents—one for the prince and Umar bin Ibrahim, the other to shelter Jafar and his ghostly daughter. Since Selima took up little room, their water skins and other supplies would be kept in Jafar's tent, safe from the horses.

Although they hadn't yet reached the hot part of the day, they knew it would take them longer to set up camp than it would for more seasoned travelers. The hours just after sunup and just before sundown were considered best by desert wayfarers, but the prince and Umar were willing to forego them to avoid being caught in the midday summer sun without adequate protection. Many were the tales of men who died of heat under the relentless rays of the desert sun.

As they were reaching into their saddlebags to pull out the gear they'd need, Jafar al-Sharif felt something hard and unfamiliar. He'd watched the servants pack everything away very carefully, and could not remember anything like this going into his saddlebag. Reaching in curiously, he pulled out the intruding object.

It was a book. It was bound in rich, wine-red leather and embossed with gold lettering on the cover. The pages inside were of heavy vellum that was only starting to yellow with age, and the writing on them was done in a fine, spidery hand, precise and methodical. The manuscript was not illuminated, nor was there fancy goldwork on the edges of the pages. There were just sheets of writing, probably over a hundred pages—and all of it incomprehensible to Jafar al-Sharif, because he could neither read nor write.

Jafar turned the book over and over in his hands as though it were a Sinjinese puzzle box whose riddle he was trying to solve. Umar and Prince Ahmad were both preoccupied with their tasks and had not noticed his discovery; Jafar caught his daughter's eye and took her to one side. He showed her what he'd found and asked her opinion of it.

"It's a book," she said simply.

"I know it's a book. But what kind of a book is it, and what was it doing in my saddlebag? Who put it there, and why?"

"To know that, at least one of us should be able to read," Selima said with practicality. "Since we can't, we'll have to ask someone who can." She nodded in the direction where Umar and Prince Ahmad were struggling to erect their tent.

"But if I confess to them that I can't read, they'll know I'm not a mighty wizard."

"Surely my father, a man who can outwit a real wizard, is clever enough to solve this dilemma," Selima said with a smile.

"Your confidence in me is gratifying, if sometimes irksome," Jafar growled, but there was paternal affection in his tone that removed all the sting. He turned and looked back at the other two men, meanwhile fingering the book and wondering how to approach them.

At last, holding the book behind his back with one hand, he approached Umar, tapped him on the shoulder, and said quietly, "Something has happened that I'd like to discuss with you."

As the priest stepped aside with him, Jafar showed him the book. "I found this in my saddlebag just now as I was unpacking. I'd like to hear your opinion on it."

Umar took the book and fingered it curiously for a moment, then opened to the first page and began reading. His eyes widened in astonishment. "The journal of Ali Maimun!" he exclaimed softly. "How could it have ended up in your saddlebag?"

The journal of Ali Maimun! Though outwardly Jafar al-Sharif did not react, his heart skipped a beat as Umar identified the book. Ali Maimun, the greatest wizard who ever lived, the man who used the Crystal of Oromasd to defeat Aeshma and the legion of daevas, and who then broke the Crystal into the four pieces that Jafar now sought. The journal must contain secrets beyond anyone's dreaming, and would certainly tell them the way to go on their current quest to the ends of Parsina. This book could be their salvation—if only Jafar could read it!

"I have a few theories, of course, on how it came to be in my bag," Jafar said, taking the book back from Umar. "I was wanting to hear your suppositions, to see whether they agreed with mine."

Umar stroked his long white beard thoughtfully as he looked at the book Jafar now held in a tight grip. "Well, if you didn't have it before we reached Sarafiq—and you had no possessions with you when we found you—then it must have been acquired there. I'm certain it was not among the articles Prince Ahmad and I brought with us from Ravan. That means it must have been added in the shrine itself."

The old priest smiled. "But of course, that would only make sense. There are some stories that Ali Maimun founded the shrine of Sarafiq, and there's no question he at least visited there near the end of his life. The priests of Sarafiq have probably been repositories of the book since his death. It's only natural Muhmad would give the journal to you, since you're the man who must duplicate Ali Maimun's feat of using the Crystal to defeat Aeshma. He probably had one of his acolytes slip the volume into your pouch when no one was looking. There was so much bustle around the courtyard we would never have noticed."

Jafar al-Sharif nodded thoughtfully. "Your reasoning coincides with mine. Yes, that's exactly how it must have happened."

And silently he was thinking: *O great lord Oromasd, perverse indeed are thy gifts. First thou givest an altar cloth, branding an innocent storyteller first a thief and then a wizard. Now, when I face hardship and danger to save my daughter's life, thou givest me a valuable tool I can't even use. Thou hast woven the tapestry of my fate with a pattern of bizarre humor.*

But perhaps there was some way of tricking the priest into deciphering the book for him. "Since we are caught in the tangled webs of kismet together, O Umar, and since we seek the same goals, it would be terribly selfish of me to hold the book exclusively to myself. I propose we share it and study it together, the better to unravel the secrets it must contain."

Umar looked hungrily at the journal in Jafar's hands, a war of emotions playing across his face and behind his eyes. After a few seconds, though, he shook his head and said, "You tempt me greatly, O Jafar, with your noble and generous offer—but I'm afraid I must refuse. While we do travel to the same goal, you and I must each walk our separate roads."

"I don't understand your meaning," Jafar said.

"As a priest, mine is the way of the spirit; as a wizard, yours is the way of magic. I seek to transform the soul, while you transform the outward manifestations. The spiritual and the magical need not be enemies—Ali Maimun certainly worked his spells for the benefit of mankind and the glory of Oromasd—but neither can they ever be integrated. I have very definite tasks to perform in the world, and so do you. We must help each other along our travels, that much is ordained. But for us to mix our crafts would be a weakening of both. You could not help me in affairs of religion, and it's not right that I help you with affairs of magic."

"Do you think Prince Ahmad would like to help, then, since he's not a priest?"

Umar frowned. "Again, the division of the tasks would seem to rule against it. In the great battle, King Shahriyan led the forces of men and Ali Maimun led the forces of magic. To have shared those duties would have been to dilute the power of each. Each of us must concentrate fully on his own sphere and put all his energies in a single direction if we're to succeed against the powerful forces we shall face."

"Perhaps you're right," Jafar said, trying hard to hide his disappointment.

"I do thank you for your generous offer," Umar told him, "for I know how valuable the information in that journal must be. It's as hard for a wizard to share his secrets as for a miser to share his gold, and my esteem for you has risen greatly. I'm convinced now, more than ever, that Muhmad made the right choice. You are indeed a man worthy to use the Crystal of Oromasd."

"Thank you, O venerable priest," Jafar said, marveling at the irony that his act of deception should be interpreted as a noble and selfless gesture. But his problem still was not solved.

As he turned to walk back to where his daughter waited, Umar said after him, "I need hardly caution you to guard that journal carefully. You more than anyone know how little our lives would be worth if anyone learned we had that book. Its secrets are literally priceless."

A chill went down Jafar's spine as he suddenly thought of Akar, the blind wizard who'd traded his eyes for the knowledge of things' inner names. Akar was responsible for Selima's sorry state and would gladly kill Jafar for the deception that cost him the urn of Aeshma. To what limits would he not go, what price would he not pay, to steal this journal for himself? "I'll guard the book well," he pledged sincerely.

Jafar al-Sharif returned to his daughter and told her what had transpired. "So here I am with the world's most valuable knowledge in my hands and no way to read it. Oromasd must be playing a joke on the entire world and using me for the punchline."

"Why not summon the Jann Cari?" Selima asked. "She's lived two hundred years—perhaps she knows how to read."

Jafar looked at her with amazement. "There are times I feel like the stupidest man in the world, yet I know I can't be—no idiot could have sired such a brilliant, perceptive child. Unless—no, Amineh was too good to have ever lied to me." He looked at Selima tenderly. "Of course, it's already well established you got all your best features from her."

The storyteller looked to the ring on the middle finger of his left hand, the ring he'd stolen from Akar's storeroom. It was made of brass and inscribed with lettering Jafar could not read; set into it was a small piece of jasper. As jewelry it was unpretentious and trivial—but as power, it represented more than Jafar had ever expected to wield in all his life. It felt warm and alive on his finger and it fit perfectly, as though made to be worn by him.

He began rubbing the ring softly now with his right hand as he intoned the magical formula that would summon his slave. "By the ring that bears thy name, O Cari, I command thee to appear before me."

The exotic aroma of ylang-ylang tickled Jafar's nostrils as pinkish haze appeared in the clear desert air and began to take form in front of him. Within seconds, Cari the Jann had fully materialized. She had not been able to accompany them into Sarafiq because it was a place unsympathetic to magical creatures, but now she made a deep salaam to Jafar and said, come at your command, O my master." Then, looking u and seeing him in his new finery, she smiled and said, "At la you have raiment worthy of your noble self."

The Jann, as the lowest order of the djinni, were closest humans in ancestry and appearance. Though over two hur dred years old, Cari's most natural form was that of a your girl perhaps a few years older than Selima, wearing just whi sirwaal trousers and a lemon-colored sidaireeya with no shi beneath it, exposing what would have been considered an in modest display of her golden-fleshed bosom if she'd been human. She was barefoot and wore no veil, and her long blac hair was worn down her back to her shoulder blades. She ha an oval face, wide brown eyes flecked with gold and sparklir with intelligence, and a slender figure that could almost l called boyish.

"Thank you for the compliment and welcome to our de ert camp, O Jann," Jafar greeted her. "A lot has happene since we parted outside Sarafiq, and I'm afraid it will mea much work for you."

He detailed all the events that transpired since he dismisse her to her homeland just before entering the oasis at Sarafi Cari was stunned to learn that the young "merchant" they met in the desert and traveled with to the oasis was real Prince Ahmad of Ravan, and that his adviser was Umar b Ibrahim, high priest of the Temple of the Faith. When Jaf informed her that the prince was as homeless as he was, th Jann's eyes suddenly lit up.

"That must have been what Shammara and the wali we talking about when I eavesdropped, just before you wer brought in for questioning," she said. "Yes, they planned the coup well in advance. They were talking about how to mar age the transition, and that within a few hours after the prin left the city his supporters would be quietly eliminated. I fe Shammara may indeed be in complete control of Ravan b now."

This confirmation of what was already suspected did nothing to raise Jafar's spirits. He went on to tell Cari about his audience with the prophet Muhmad, and of the prophet's vision for him and Prince Ahmad. They had now begun their quest to the far corners of Parsina to reclaim the pieces of the Crystal of Oromasd to use in the upcoming struggle against the daevas and to cure Selima of the curse Akar had placed on her.

Since Selima was present, he didn't tell Cari about the ominous other portion of the prophet's vision—that even if Jafar succeeded in using the Crystal properly he would lose what he sought to gain, even though he would gain more than he ever dreamed possible. Only four people knew about that portion of the vision: the prophet, Jafar, Ahmad, and Umar. Jafar saw no reason to expand that circle. Selima was burdened with misery enough; he didn't want to load this additional bad news upon her.

As he closed his narrative, he showed Cari the journal of Ali Maimun, and the Jann was duly impressed. "With the aid of that book, you could rule the world," she said wide-eyed.

"Except that I can't read it," Jafar said. "I'm a storyteller, not a scribe. That's why I summoned you—to read it to me."

As Cari looked at him in openmouthed amazement, he asked her quickly, "You *can* read, can't you?"

Cari gulped and said, "Oh yes, I learned that skill some time ago. I'm just so overwhelmed by the thought that I, among the youngest of the righteous Jann, should be privileged to learn from the journal of Ali Maimun the mage, the greatest wizard of all time. This is an honor far beyond any I've earned. By all rights, such a privilege should go to the shaykh of the righteous Jann. He is much more qualified to deal with the material in that book than I am."

Jafar al-Sharif was becoming more than a little annoyed at all the polite refusals he was getting—and particularly from a slave who was supposed to obey all his commands.

"I don't want the shaykh of the righteous Jann to see this, or even know it exists," he growled. "I have no control over him; he could take the knowledge here and do whatever he wanted with it. This is a task that must be done in confidence between myself and my servant. From all I've seen, you're quite worthy of learning what's in here—at least as worthy as

I am. Now, will you obey my commands and read this to me?"

Cari, properly chastened, looked down meekly at her bare feet. "I must obey you, of course, O my master, and if that is your command I will do it without further hesitation." She paused and looked up at him again, struggling for the proper words. "But—if I may be so bold, O master—you did command me to give you advice when I felt you might be making a mistake or might be wrong. May I give you such advice now?"

Jafar al-Sharif took a deep breath and calmed himself down. "Forgive me, Cari; I just feel so frustrated that I lashed out at you improperly. You were only being modest—though even that, taken to extremes, is no virtue. Yes, by all means give me your advice. I said I valued your opinion, and I meant it."

Cari straightened her posture and looked into her master's face. "It occured to me, O my master, that you will be handicapping yourself if you merely let me read to you. I may be able to read Ali Maimun's words, and I may be able to explain their meaning to you—but what would you do if anything should happen to me? We're on a dangerous mission, and I could well die in your defense. You'd then be in the same unhappy position you're in right now."

"But what choice do I have, other than admitting my ignorance to Umar and Prince Ahmad? They'd immediately lose confidence in me if I proved to be a fraud, and it might ruin our entire mission."

"You could learn to read yourself," Cari said. "I could teach you."

Learn to read? The idea was a novel one, to say the least. Reading and writing were skills for the upper classes with much leisure time, or for scribes to whom it was their sole occupation. Very few of Jafar's acquaintances had ever mastered the art; the vast majority of people in Parsina were totally illiterate.

And yet, was the idea of reading any more novel than the thought of becoming a wizard? He'd assumed the mantle of sorcery with casual grace, and had managed to stumble his way through so far. Could reading be that much worse?

"No," he said aloud, shaking his head. "I'm too old to learn so difficult a skill. Maybe Selima could—"

Selima spoke up boldly. "When you told me the story of King Firkush's ass, Father, you said there was a possibility it might learn to talk. Are you not at least as clever as that royal ass? Is there not even the *possibility* that you might learn, for you to dismiss the idea so quickly?"

"Selima," Jafar began, looking into his daughter's face. There were so many things he wanted to tell her, so many reasons why he knew he couldn't do it. People spent years learning how to read and perfecting their knowledge of that mystical art. He didn't have years to spend in the pursuit. Besides, it was a well-known fact that a man's ability to learn diminished with age. How could he hope to master so difficult a skill?

But looking into his daughter's imploring face, the protests refused to come to his lips. He knew he had to try, just as he knew he had to use the Crystal of Oromasd even though he hadn't the faintest idea how to do it. As Umar had pointed out about their mission as a whole, he might fail if he tried, but he'd certainly fail if he didn't.

His voice softened as he said, "Will you take the lessons with me? You'll probably be better at it than I will, and that way at least one of us has a chance to be able to read the book."

Selima smiled. "I would be honored to study beside my illustrious father."

"But how can I go about learning lessons like a schoolboy in a madrasa? Umar and Ahmad will see me and know something is not as it should be."

Cari spoke up. "The three of us can sit apart and pretend to be studying the writings of Ali Maimun. Umar expects you to keep the material secret, so he won't think it odd if you withdraw to study the book. We can begin this evening after you've had a day's sleep, before we start traveling again."

And so, much against his own good sense, Jafar al-Sharif set his foot for the first step along the path to knowledge—a path that would prove longer and more arduous than his physical trek across the surface of Parsina.

7

THE WIDOW

N due course a rider arrived at the gates of Ravan with an urgent message for the regent from King Basir of Marakh. He was guided through the arched marble hallways of the royal palace into the presence of the regent, Kateb bin Salih, where he relayed his somber news. King Basir sent his greetings to the people of Ravan and explained that, when Prince Ahmad and the wedding party did not arrive in Marakh when they were expected, he had dispatched a troop of his finest guards to discover what the delay was. The soldiers found the prince's party slain down to the last man by a pack of brigands who had robbed them of all the treasure they'd been carrying.

King Basir naturally sent his condolences to the people of Ravan on the loss of their prince and future king and, to show his sympathy, he offered his daughter in marriage now to Prince Haroun, thus to solidify the feelings of unity between the two nations.

The news of Prince Ahmad's death, coming so soon on the heels of Shammara's purge, sent shock waves through the court of Ravan. Most of Shammara's followers had been kept in ignorance of the total plan, and were just as surprised as the rest of the populace, though they grieved much less. To those people who still harbored sympathies toward the prince, this was but the latest in a series of blows. Many had held the hope that, when Ahmad returned to Ravan with his bride, he'd be able to undo the damage Shammara had caused and set the government right again; now that hope was dashed, and they were left directionless and confused. A few refused to believe the reports. Of the majority who did, many nonetheless believed Shammara'd had some hand in his death, though no one had any proof and none dared speak such suspicions aloud.

Old Kateb bin Salih, feeble and ill as he was, wept openly at the news. He had loved the young prince as a cherished nephew, and had tried to the best of his ability to fulfill the late King Shunnar's request to govern righteously in the boy's name. Now he declared a month-long period of deep mourning for the late prince, as well as the full two years of court mourning. Then, as was his duty as regent, he declared Prince Haroun the new heir to the throne, to be installed on the date of his eighteenth birthday as the late King Shunnar had bidden.

The messenger from Marakh was dispatched back to King Basir with a message agreeing to the marriage between Prince Haroun and Princess Oma—but that, in the light of the current tragedy, Princess Oma must travel to Ravan for the ceremony. The regent was determined that Ravan would not lose two princes, and Shammara naturally backed him on the matter.

The people of Ravan were heartbroken at the news about Prince Ahmad. Women shrieked and wept in the streets, and men rent their garments in mourning for their fallen idol. Many shops closed in the bazaars, and merchants and housekeepers hung black flags of mourning on their doorways in tribute to the slain prince. While they could be indifferent to the machinations of the bureaucracy and the purge Shammara had instituted, Prince Ahmad had been a very personal symbol to them. He'd appeared at numerous public functions, spoken eloquently, and presented himself as a young man who cared about the affairs of his subjects and would govern them justly. He was handsome, dashing, and well mannered, and his death affected people like that of a favored son or brother.

In part, when the people mourned for Ahmad they may have been mourning for their own fate as well. While Prince Haroun was less well known to the general public, the people were aware he shared none of the qualities that had made his half-brother so well beloved. He was not of such handsome features, did not speak with the same eloquence, and it was widely rumored that the slave girls he bought did not live long in his service. Life in Ravan under the regime of Prince Haroun and his mother did not promise the same glory as it would have under the noble Prince Ahmad.

But before the news was made public, while there were still only a few top court officials who knew about the deaths, the task fell to Yusef bin Nard to inform Alhena, wife of Umar bin Ibrahim, about her husband's murder. As acting high priest he could have delegated the job to one of his subordinates, but he took his responsibility seriously enough to shoulder the task himself.

In his finest robes he appeared at the front entrance to bin Ibrahim's house. The high priest and his wife were granted a larger than normal residence beside the Temple of the Faith, and though Umar had often joked that it was larger than he needed, he maintained it for the dignity of his office. The high priest of Ravan could settle for no less.

Noura, the old maidservant who'd served Umar and Alhena for as long as bin Nard had known them, answered his knock at the gate. With a nod of recognition she led him into the house and down the turns of the passageway that led to the hosh. Here in this central courtyard Yusef bin Nard was told to wait and Alhena would join him.

The garden that Alhena kept was small compared to many in the finer houses of Ravan, but it was well tended and well loved. The lemon tree was perfectly pruned and hanging with ripe fruit; the flowers were arranged with precision in their beds. A narrow tiled path led from the various rooms that branched off this courtyard, wandering through the beauty of the garden and around the fountain that bubbled and splashed happily in the center. The afternoon breeze blowing through the fountain's spray brought a refreshing coolness to the entire house.

Yusef bin Nard sat down on a small stone bench beside the fountain, wondering what words he could use to tell Alhena the bitter news. The buzz of insects and the chirping of birds in the lemon tree reaffirmed life all around him. He could smell the appetizing aroma of bread being baked in the kitchen. This garden would not be the place to talk of death.

Alhena appeared on the path in front of him. She was a tall woman with kind eyes, and just the trace of graying hair at the corners of her temples. That was all he'd ever seen of her, for she always appeared modestly in public. Today she wore her black taraha and milfa with a dark gray thawb, and she moved quietly like a cloud floating through the garden.

"Welcome to my husband's house, O Yusef bin Nard," she said with the proper formality. "My servant says you wish to speak with me."

Her glacial calmness only made bin Nard more nervous in light of what he had to tell her. "May we go inside?" he asked.

"Certainly." Alhena turned and glided along the garden path toward the qa'a. Though bin Nard was her husband's immediate subordinate, the two men had never gotten along very well. Still, it was her place to offer the man hospitality, and no one would ever accuse Alhena of being less than a gracious hostess.

As the public entertaining room of the Royal Temple's high priest, the qa'a was suitably dignified. The rectangular room was both long and wide, with arched recesses in the walls for diwans. The paved leewan was covered with pale blue summer mats, while the tiles of the durqa formed a mosaic depicting fish, birds, and flowers in colors of blue, gold, white, and a few touches of amber. Overhead the ceiling and upper third of the walls were paneled in wooden screens, elaborately carved in a fine geometric pattern. The solid shutters were open and the cooling breeze moved through the room. Lower portions of the plaster walls held carved ivory plaques in which leafy vines intertwined with the designs of men and birds. The fountain in the center of the durqa splashed as playfully as the one in the garden.

Yusef bin Nard removed his zarabil and walked barefoot across the mats to sit down cross-legged on a mat beside the durqa. Alhena took off her own niaal and crossed the room to the other side of the durqa, where she sat facing him. She did not speak again, but sat watching him, waiting for him to begin speaking, as was mannerly for a woman.

Fumbling for words, his voice often faltering, Yusef bin Nard broke the news to Alhena as gently and considerately as he could. At first his babbling was so confused Alhena could only sit and look at him uncomprehendingly—but as she realized what he was saying her eyes became glassy and seemed to focus on some other world entirely. As his effusive condolences rolled on, her fingers trembled in her lap—but she wouldn't cry in front of bin Nard; she would uphold the dignity of Umar's house even in—especially in—this moment.

There was a long pause in bin Nard's monologue, and the air hung heavy with leaden emotions. At last the priest said, "I know you have no warm feelings for me, but please believe the sincerity of my grief. Your husband and I disagreed on many things, but we were both priests, both devoted to the cause of Oromasd in our different ways. He was a good and honest man, and I know that if he receives the judgment he deserves at the Bridge of Shinvar he'll be in the House of Song at this moment, awaiting us."

There was another silence, and then Alhena spoke up for the first time since entering this room. Her voice was coldly efficient, each word forced out with difficulty. "I presume you'll be named high priest now."

"That has yet to be decided," bin Nard said, embarrassed, "but since I'm next in rank they probably will so honor me. While I won't pretend I didn't want the position, I hope you'll believe me when I say that I certainly am not happy to get it under such clouded and tragic circumstances."

Alhena looked up at the walls around her. "This house will become yours, then. I'll prepare to move—"

"Oh now," bin Nard hastened to assure her. "I and my family manage quite well in our little house down the street. You may live here the rest of your days—and I'll see that the temple continues to provide for all your needs. Ravan owes you and Umar at least that much."

"You are very kind, and I appreciate your generosity." Alhena stood up and made it clear the meeting was over. "Will you excuse me now, please? I want to be alone for a while. There's so much to be done to prepare the house for the mourning period."

"Of course," bin Nard said, standing as well. "If I can be of any help to you in this time of sadness, please don't hesitate to call on me. I'll have special services scheduled for your husband and the others who died on the journey; I'll send a messenger around to let you know the time."

After one more round of condolences bin Nard departed, leaving Alhena standing quietly in the qa'a. Her eyes scanned the room, and everywhere they rested was some sign or remembrance of Umar. There on one shelf stood the enameled glass bottle—white with blue, brown, and green designs of horsemen and birds around the base and the thin neck, and blue arabesques on the sides. He'd bought her that bottle thirty years ago, after the birth of their first son. There on another shelf were the maroon glazed dishes with the gold inscriptions. He'd inherited those from his mother. There on the floor, on the low table, was the ebony and ivory chess set. He'd played many games on that board, matches with Prince Ahmad and his many other friends; once, even King Shunnar had played chess with him on that board.

Alhena turned away and walked from the room. She could not stay in the qa'a; there was too much of Umar in there.

She walked across the hosh and stopped in the doorway to the kitchen. Noura and the cook were arguing over the menu for supper. They stopped talking when they noticed Alhena in the doorway, and looked questioningly in her direction. Alhena merely waved her hand to indicate she had no instructions for them, and turned away again. The kitchen was no place for her, not today.

Her feet led her to the stairs, and she climbed with heavy steps to the second floor. The walls up here were bare plaster, the rooms were smaller and plainer. The ground floor, particularly the qa'a, had been decorated by the temple for semi-official functions, to maintain the dignity of the high priest. The private upper rooms more reflected the true man: simple and honest, unpretentious but with a basic strength to make them endurable. The plaques on the walls up here were of carved wood rather than ivory, though a few had touches of gilt. The niches held smaller, more personal mementos that Umar and Alhena had acquired during their life together, and most of them were so much a part of her that Alhena couldn't even remember where and when she'd gotten them.

Umar hadn't wanted to go on this trip, she remembered that distinctly. He'd told her about the prophet Muhmad's dire warnings of what might happen if the prince left the city before his coronation, and about his own fears for Ahmad's safety. He hadn't mentioned the fears for his own safety; Umar was the sort of man who never would. In the back of his mind he must have known the danger would be as great for him as it was for Ahmad, yet he hadn't let that influence his decision to go. Alhena remembered her own role in talking him into making the journey, telling him to trust in the

goodness of Oromasd to see him safely through his diffi-
culties. And now he was gone from her forever.

The house suddenly seemed strange to her. She'd always
thought of it as being just the perfect size for them, but now it
was cavernous. The rooms were too big, and each slight
sound echoed through the vast empty spaces. Umar had been
part of her life for thirty-three years of marriage. Now suddenly that part of her was gone. It was not just another human
being that had died, but a specially beloved segment of her
soul. She could see Umar in every corner of every room—
sitting here, standing there, eating there, talking everywhere.
The walls, the ceiling, the floor, all echoed with the tones of
his voice, the warmth of his smile. Umar was as much a part
of this house as he was a part of her. And now he was removed
from it, never to appear again.

She entered the bedroom and walked absently to the window that faced out onto the street. Through the close latticework of the carved wooden musharabiya she could watch
people walking past on their personal business, just as though
this were some ordinary day. The world moved on for everyone but Alhena; for her, everything had stopped.

She turned from the window and stood facing the carved
wooden closet inlaid with small diamond patterns of ivory.
She reached in and pulled out one of Umar's old robes. Fingering the cloth, she closed her eyes and hugged it tightly to
her, straining to capture the feel and scent of the man who'd
worn it. Thirty-three years of marriage included many things
they had said and done, but today all Alhena could think of
was those things she hadn't done for her Umar and those
words of love she'd left unsaid. Now they were gone beyond
redemption, and all chances to do or say were naught but
empty whispers on the winds of time.

The world was whirling around her. Alhena staggered
across the carpeted floor to the corner where the mattresses
had been rolled up out of the way for daytime. With legs no
longer able to support her, she knelt beside the mattresses.
Her pain and her loss overwhelmed her and, finally, Alhena
wept.

8

THE BADAWI

RINCE Ahmad's party had a simple meal that first morning on the trail. Lacking the materials to build a fire, they'd packed mostly preserved meat, nan-e lavash, and dried fruit to eat while they traveled through the desert. It would be an uninspired diet, but it would keep them alive for the week or so they needed to reach the eastern edge of the Kholaj.

They slept but fitfully in their tents through the summer's day. As the only one who didn't feel the heat, Selima slept soundest; the three men tossed and turned uncomfortably in the shade of their respective tents. Cari, who could go for long periods without sleep, food, or water, stood watch to see that no one disturbed their rest.

She awoke them, as instructed, when the sun was nearing the western horizon. The men would eat their evening meal of meat, bread, and fruit, then break camp and mount up to travel at night. They did not enjoy the inverted hours brought on by this nocturnal wayfaring, but until they were out of the desert they had little choice. Nighttime was cooler; a man caught unprepared in the midday sun could die within a few hours.

While they ate, Jafar and Selima sat apart from the other men and, with Cari's help, began their reading lessons. Cari found she had to start with the most basic of concepts. She explained to her pupils that there were certain symbols, letters, that represented the different sounds. Jafar and Selima had seen letters all their lives, but never paid attention to them because they didn't understand what they meant. Letters, in turn, were put together in the order of the sounds to form words. The words were then strung together to make sentences, which were then used to construct stories and books. Jafar understood the concept of building with words; it was how he'd made his living verbally all his life. It was the idea that words could be broken down into component sounds and represented graphically that excited him.

Cari started to open the journal of Ali Maimun to find examples of the letters when she discovered an interesting phenomenon. The first ten pages opened easily and turned without problem, but the pages at the back of the book seemed to be stuck together; no matter how hard Cari tried, she could not pry the leaves apart. Jafar also tried, with a similar lack of success. "Could they be glued together?" he wondered aloud. "What good is a book that you can't even open, let alone read?"

"This isn't glue," Cari said with a shake of her head. "It has the feel of magic about it."

"Is there anything in these first few pages to explain what's happening?" Jafar asked.

Much against her inclinations, Cari began reading the journal and found in the prologue the answer they sought. "To he who would glean the secrets of Ali Maimun," she read aloud. "Know ye that this journal has been protected by my power and my magic. For he who is not worthy, the book will not open at all. To he who does not need, those sections of the book will remain closed. Only to he who must know what is contained herein will those secrets be revealed."

Cari looked up at Jafar. "I think I understand. Ali Maimun placed a spell on this book. If you don't need to know something, the book won't open to those pages."

"Who decides whether we need to know it or not?" Jafar asked. "As far as I'm concerned, I need to know it all."

"When the mage created his spell he must have set up certain standards that aren't listed here," Cari told him. "Only when those conditions are met will the pages open."

"Just what we need," Jafar said. "A temperamental book."

"At least there's something positive," Selima said. "The fact that the book opens at all means you're meant to have it. The prophet Muhmad was right about that."

"But what good will it do us if we can't find out about the Crystals?" Jafar asked.

"It at least has enough examples of letters to teach you to read," Cari said. "Maybe at some later time the book will decide we need to know more and reveal more of its pages to us. In the meantime we'll use it as it is."

Cari had time to teach her pupils only one letter before they had to be on their way. She showed them the alif, the various ways it could look when written out, and the sounds it made in different contexts. She pointed to examples of it in the pages of Ali Maimun's journal until Jafar and Selima thought they were thoroughly familiar with it. They decided that was enough for one lesson and joined the others.

The party traveled slowly across the desert at night. The four horses jogged at a careful pace to conserve water, and every so often the riders would dismount and walk beside their steeds to give them a rest. Cari flew alongside them, sometimes soaring upward to scout the landscape for them and warn them of possible trouble.

The travelers talked among themselves as they rode. Prince Ahmad was not much for idle conversation. Although Umar could remember him just weeks ago as a jabbering teenager, his experiences along the road had matured him beyond his years. The prince was all too aware of the responsibility on his shoulders, and had become much more of an observer than a talker. He could still speak eloquently when the occasion demanded—but if he had nothing to say, he preferred to be silent.

Jafar al-Sharif was more than willing to take up the conversational slack. He could speak glibly on a multitude of subjects, whether he knew anything about them or not, but he was at his best when he was telling a story or emphasizing a point with a choice anecdote. At these times his arms would gesture broadly, his long, full sleeves would flap gracefully in the wind, and his voice would take on resonant tones that held his audience captive until he'd finished his piece. After a while the dry desert air took its toll, though, and he had to curtail some of his storytelling to avoid a sore throat.

As he did on the journey through the Kholaj Desert to the oasis at Sarafiq, Prince Ahmad spent a lot of time stealing glances back at Selima, who rode on the horse that trailed her father's. In the darkness her ghostly form was even harder to distinguish, which made him stare all the more. Selima rode quietly, quite used to her father's loquacity. She always listened attentively, but seldom added anything of her own to the conversation. She was very aware of her immodestly unveiled face, but there was little she could do except look away when she realized she was being watched. A couple of times the prince looked at her and cleared his throat as though about to speak, but whatever words he would have said died unborn before reaching his lips.

They rode through the desert night while all about them was in stillness. Some of the massive sand dunes towered many stories above their heads, but they saw no living creatures save a few insects and some hardy bushes that poked their way out of the sand. They knew there was more life than this on the desert floor, but it kept itself well hidden from them and they passed without incident.

Just as the sky was reddening in front of them with the dawn of a new day, Cari swooped down from one of her vigil flights to inform her master of some disturbing news. "There are riders headed this way from the north, about a dozen of them. They know you're here, they're coming straight for you."

Jafar al-Sharif looked quickly to Umar. The priest said, "They must be either Badawi or brigands." Upon further reflection he added, "They could be both. The question is, should we face them or flee?"

"They're more used to the desert than we are," Prince Ahmad reasoned, "and our horses are tired from traveling all night. If we fled they'd quickly catch us, and we would look cowardly. You've told me that most of the desert tribes respect valor. We'll stand our ground and face them. If it comes to a fight, we have three good swords, plus the magic of a wizard and a Jann."

Jafar al-Sharif noticed with dismay that the prince was counting him twice in that equation, both as a swordsman and as a wizard. In reality he was neither. "Cari," he said quietly, "make yourself invisible like you did when we escaped through the gates of Ravan. I may need you to provide a similar diversion here."

"Hearkening and obedience, O my master," Cari said, and vanished totally from view.

The travelers turned their horses to face north and nervously awaited the promised arrival of the horsemen. Ahmad sat astride Churash with his back upright and rigid, summoning his princely strength and courage. Umar was slightly worried, but still confident Oromasd would not cut short their mission so soon after it had begun. Cari steeled her courage to defend, if necessary, the life of her master Jafar al-Sharif, who sat in his saddle and tried to compose himself into a picture of wizardly dignity. Selima was not worried for herself, since nothing could harm her further, but she did fear for the safety of her father and the kindly priest and the handsome young prince who stared at her so often and so oddly.

In just a few minutes they saw the figures riding over the crest of the dunes and sliding effortlessly down the slopes to the desert floor. By the increasing glow of the dawn light they could see that the horsemen were wearing black kaftans that billowed around them in the wind from their horses' speed. They wore white turbans that wrapped down around their faces as well, covering nose and mouth to protect them from the desert sand and leaving only the eyes exposed. They rode their horses expertly across the treacherous dunes; as the prince had surmised, the travelers would have had little chance had they tried to flee such pursuit.

The horsemen pulled up to within a few cubits of the party and, at a gesture from one of the riders, surrounded the travelers. Like most men of the central region of Parsina the riders wore khanjars and saifs tucked in at their waists. The scabbards were plain leather and not studded with jewels, but those blades had probably seen more than their fair share of fighting.

The man who'd made the gesture for the others seemed to be the leader of the group. He was a big man with broad shoulders and piercing eyes, and he sat straight in his saddle as he looked the travelers over appraisingly. "Who dares transgress on the land of Nusair ibn Samman, shaykh of the Kholaj Badawi?" he said in a booming voice.

Prince Ahmad met his stare without flinching. "The Kholaj Desert belongs to no man," he said evenly, "and I do not treat with any man too cowardly to show me his face."

Most of the riders tensed at these inflammatory words, but the leader took the implied threat in stride. After a pause

he reached up and unfastened the cloth to reveal his face.
was very much a face of the desert: dark-complected an
leather tough, with thick lips and a nose like an eagle's beal
Nusair ibn Samman was grinning broadly as he replied, "Yo
are wrong, O yapping puppy—the Kholaj belongs to he wh
survives it. I, Nusair ibn Samman, lead my people across th
sands as have all the shaykhs before me. We live free and ca'
no man our master, and not even the desert winds can breal
our spirit. Now, since I have shown you my face, I ask agaii
who you are and what your business is on my desert."

Prince Ahmad sat up equally tall in his saddle, gathering
his dignity around him like an invisible cloak. "I am Ahmac
Khaled bin Shunnar el-Ravani, erstwhile prince of Ravan and
currently a pilgrim under the banner of Oromasd."

"A prince, eh?" Nusair ibn Samman's lips curled in a
smile; he clearly was not impressed. "Where is your royal reti-
nue? Do you carry treasure in your saddlebags for me and my
people?"

"There is naught there to interest you," the prince lied, for
some of the pouches were filled with gold, "and as you love
Oromasd and his truth you should let us go our way in peace.
We offer you no harm and no offense."

"As I love Oromasd," the shaykh repeated. "You speak
our lord's name very easily, O whelp. Do you presume to
speak on his behalf?"

"*I* do," Umar said. "I am Umar bin Ibrahim, high priest
of the Temple of the Faith in the holy city of Ravan. He who
would attack us would defy the messengers of Oromasd and
his commandment to treat all travelers hospitably, and must
prepare to answer for such actions at the Bridge of Shinvar."

Nusair's smile broadened. "Interesting," he said. "I see this
is a dawn for dignitaries." He turned to Jafar al-Sharif. "And
which are you, O silent one, prince or priest?"

"Neither," Jafar said, matching the dignity of his tone to
that of his fellow travelers. "I am Jafar al-Sharif, wizard of the
southern provinces and deflater of pompous egos. I am slow
to anger, but you must take care or I cannot answer for the
consequences."

"A brave talker, at least," the shaykh said. As his eyes traveled to the fourth member of the group they widened a little.
The semitransparent form of Selima surprised and unnerved

im slightly, though he was cagy enough not to let it show in his voice. "And what is this, some djinni queen?"

"She is my daughter, under a curse," Jafar said.

"Oh, under a curse. What a remarkable assortment we have here, O my comrades—though I fear our friend the wizard cannot be such a power as he claims if he can't even protect his own daughter from curses."

"Powerful enough to deal with idle braggarts," Jafar said. His own boldness astonished him, but he was caught up in the role of wizard and knew he dared not back down now.

"Indeed." Nusair ibn Samman leaned forward intently against the horn of his saddle. "Perhaps you will treat us to a demonstration."

"I prefer to use my powers sparingly, but since you entreat me so politely I'll see what can be arranged."

Jafar waved his arms before him in mystical gestures and intoned, "O magical powers at my command, take heed; unseat this nomad chieftain from his steed!"

Jafar was trusting Cari the Jann to be clever enough to know her cue, and he was not disappointed. The grinning Badawi shaykh was suddenly lifted off his saddle by an invisible force, pushed backward and tossed ungently to the ground.

Nusair ibn Samman landed with a rough bump on his posterior, where nothing was bruised but his dignity—but that might have been sufficient. His confident smile had turned to a twisted grimace of rage. He pulled his saif from its sheath and waved it threateningly at Jafar.

Prince Ahmad's hand flew instantly to the hilt of his own weapon, prepared to do final battle here among the dunes, but before he could draw his blade Jafar's hands were making other magical passes in the air.

As though with a life of its own, the shaykh's sword pulled itself free of his hand. It flew up in the air and came back down to his eye level, where it waved a couple of times in front of his face in the same threatening gesture he'd made toward Jafar. Then, in a defiant stroke, the sword plunged itself into the ground just a few fingers' breadth from Nusair's feet.

The other horsemen reached for the hilts of their own swords, ready to defend their shaykh from this supernatural attack. The tableau froze as all eyes went to Nusair ibn Samman, awaiting his reaction. Within seconds the air could be filled with flashing steel, and Jafar knew Cari could not be fast enough to protect him from a dozen swords at once.

Nusair ibn Samman stared at the sword in the ground before him, then looked up into the face of Jafar al-Sharif. Unexpectedly he threw back his head and laughed uproariously, revealing a set of teeth with a gap in the upper row where one had been knocked out in battle. His men relaxed their grips on their swords, but did not immediately take their hands from the hilts.

"A fine joke this is on old Nusair," laughed the shaykh. "My grandchildren will smile at the story of the wizard who taught their old ogre of a grandfather a lesson in hospitality."

He looked around at his men who still sat anxiously on their mounts. "Come, O my brothers, let's realize when we've been outplayed. We joked with these noble wayfarers, and they joked back at us even better. It's time now to remember how Oromasd would have us treat strangers, with kindness and courtesy."

Nusair ibn Samman walked up empty-handed just in front of the travelers' horses and opened his arms in a broad, all-enveloping gesture. "I beg you, O gentle wanderers, to accept the friendship of the Kholaj Badawi and to accompany us to our camp to share our meal. Let us prove to you that in all the world there is no hospitality to equal that of the people of the desert. In Oromasd's blessed name we welcome you to our bosom."

Prince Ahamad nodded toward Nusair. "We accept your offer, O gracious shaykh, and we pray for the blessings of Oromasd upon your head and your line and your entire tribe. The generosity of the Badawi is renowned throughout Parsina, and there are none who doubt its sincerity."

"Come then," Nusair ibn Samman cried lustily. "Let's return to the caravan before our poor women start bemoaning their widowhood." He walked back and pulled his sword from the ground, slid it deftly into its sheath, and mounted his horse with a springy step that belied his middle years. He turned his horse around and started back to the north whence he'd come. The other horsemen followed suit, guiding the party of travelers along with them.

Jafar, still a bit leery of this sudden turnabout in the shaykh's behavior, asked Umar privately if they were doing the right thing by returning to the Badawi camp.

"The moral code of the desert tribesmen is most rigorous," Umar assured him. "Having offered us hospitality and protection, Shaykh ibn Samman would die rather than let any harm befall us. We'll be as safe with him as we'd be anywhere in Parsina. Furthermore, it is here, in the desert or mountains, we can trust the support we'll almost certainly be offered in our ultimate mission. It isn't that the rural folk are without corruption or fault, but this is where the old ideals are still revered most highly.

"In many of our cities—yes even, perhaps especially, in the holy city of Ravan," Umar added, thinking of the treachery that began this quest, "lip service is paid to the principles of Oromasd—but real belief is more common here. These people live closer to death and punishment for breaking the rules and the law. They hold to it closely."

Jafar al-Sharif still knew, however, that if he and the others hadn't forced the desert shaykh to back down in the confrontation, their bodies would lie dying on the morning sands. He made a mental note to thank Cari for her quickness of thought in coming to his aid and preventing their massacre.

9

THE SAND JINN

IT has been said that the Badawi came into being at the same moment as the deserts themselves, and that the two have coexisted throughout all of history. Certainly it is true that the Badawi tribes have one of the oldest lineages in all Parsina—as well as one of the most paradoxical. For the Badawi have always been a study in contrasts, and no outsider has ever been able to fully comprehend the strange twists and turns of their unique culture.

To the casual observer they appear to be simple nomads, leading their caravans across the deserts of the world from oasis to oasis, border town to border town. They dress in a style that hasn't changed in thousands of years and use but the crudest of implements—except for their weapons, which are as well made as any modern warrior could ask. They have little regard for money and have no currency system of their own; they prefer to barter with outsiders for the goods they need—food, cloth, horses, camels, jewelry, and weapons—and treat most things within the tribe as community property. Aside from having the most respected tribesman serve as shaykh, they seem to have no social order or hierarchical structure whatsoever, yet everyone knows his place and internal arguments within a tribe are few.

For all their apparent simplicity, though, the Badawi have been eking a living from the deserts and wastelands of the world for countless millennia. Badawi, so the saying goes, can smell water five parasangs away and half a parasang under-round. Whether that is true or not, they certainly know the location of every oasis, every spring, every wadi that might contain water within their region of the desert. Countless are the tales of merchants' caravans that have been saved from thirst by friendly Badawi—and just as numerous are the stories of merchants who have spurned the Badawi and wandered off into the desert, only to die of thirst lost on the desert sands.

If they had to, the Badawi could live entirely off the ecology of the desert, but they seldom choose to do so. More often, either for a fee or a percentage of the profits, they will transport goods across the desert for some merchant who hesitates to make the journey himself. Badawi have been known to raid other caravans, looting and murdering at their whim. Sometimes they've carried their thieving ways into the towns they visit, creating ill feeling between themselves and the more "civilized" townsfolk. The Badawi are viewed by the settled villagers as a necessary evil, with the quality of relations depending on whether the accent was more on "necessary" or on "evil" at any given moment.

But whether they are hated or merely tolerated, the Badawi are always respected by everyone who comes in contact with them. They are known as fearless warriors, and their fierce battle cries alone have been known to send many enemies fleeing in terror. They are devout worshippers of Oromasd and strong supporters of family ties and traditional values. They laugh loudly and have coarse, vulgar senses of humor—but as Prince Ahmad remarked, they are also known on occasion for their overwhelming hospitality and kindness.

The Badawi are, in short, like the very desert they cross with such ease: simple on the surface, yet ever shifting and capable of treachery; constant, yet always in motion; calm, yet deadly turbulent; open, yet possessing inner secrets no stranger will ever fathom. Above all, they are as eternal as the desert and as stable as the sands. Some claim Badawi are the very heart of Parsina, for from them did all other cultures spring and grow.

The Badawi seldom care about definitions. They take their caravans across the desert wastes and let others argue about such things. They are the Badawi, and they do what they do.

The body of the Badawi caravan was only half a parasang from the spot of the travelers' encounter with Nusair ibn Sam-

man and his men. It was a scraggly sight to come upon in th
midst of a desert dawn, a mixture of loud noise and colorf
fabric. There were more than a score of tents, all low to th
ground and many going threadbare from constant use and th
merciless rays of the desert sun. The tents had enough color
to make up several rainbows; when the Badawi bought new
fabric to replace their old tents, they took whatever was a
hand in whichever village they were in at the time. When the
Badawi set up their camp there was no way they could disguise it from enemy sight, but they were philosopical. "Wher
Oromasd wants to find us, he'll know just where to look,"
ran the old Badawi proverb. As for enemies, the Badawi relied
on their own strength; the only people who could follow
them into the desert to fight were other Badawi tribes. Intertribal feuds were the exception rather than the rule; there was
just too much desert for them to quibble over parts of it.

This colorful spectacle was enhanced by the apparent
chaos throughout the camp. Everywhere one looked, people
were in motion. Teenage boys and the older men who hadn't
accompanied Nusair ibn Samman were all busy unloading the
bales from the small herd of camels tethered to one side of the
camp. The camels were braying loudly and complaining
about the treatment from their handlers; the men, in turn,
were cursing the stubborn beasts or coaxing them to cooperate—or sometimes a combination of both. One camel, more
balky than the rest, kept threatening to bolt the area, bales and
all, and several men kept surrounding it and herding it back in
with the group. The bales that were taken from the camels'
backs were stored either in a large open tent of broad green
and white stripes beside the tethering area, or else out on the
open ground under the cloudless sky. These items were either
the caravan's own gear or else merchandise the Badawi had
contracted to carry across the desert for some businessman.
Beside the camel area was a small herd of goats that the
Badawi kept mostly as a dairy.

The tents toward the center of the camp belonged to the
women, and it was here that the morning meal was being
prepared. Unlike their men, the Badawi women wore
clothing as colorful as the caravan's tents, long flowing thawbs
embroidered with fancy stitchery and often having coins or
bells or other tiny trinkets sewn onto them to give an individ-
ualistic appearance. Though they would normally wear a

burga when in town to shield their faces from the sight of strangers, within the caravan itself the women did not veil their faces.

The women stood and moved about the camp fire, chatting and laughing as they worked. Around them, young children and toddlers ran and played in the sand, wearing loose-fitting robes that could fit a multitude of sizes and going barefoot on the warm ground. One of the children looked up and saw the returning party. She yelled and pointed, attracting the attention of the others.

When the women saw strange men in the approaching group they stopped their work momentarily to dash into their tents and don their burgas. These were usually stiff and black, but each one had an individual pattern of embroidery and embellishment to identify each particular wearer. The women reappeared, fully covered, by the time the riders reached the camp, and they flocked around the shaykh and the visitors, curious to learn more about this deviation from their normal life pattern.

Nusair ibn Samman stood up in his saddle and bellowed a hearty greeting to his people that brought everyone around to him. He gave a bravado account of the meeting in the desert, claiming he'd recognized the nobility of these travelers all along but had wanted to test their valor against his own. A prince, a priest, and a wizard were all rare occurrences, and any one of them would have been an object of curiosity among the tribe; all together they drew unabashed stares from the nomads—and the ghostly form of poor Selima drew the most curious glances of all. Jafar's daughter was sorely embarrassed to be stared at by these strange people when her face was bare and the Badawi women were so completely covered, but there was nowhere she could hide or even turn away; the horses were completely surrounded by curious Badawi.

One of the older women, noticing Selima's embarrassment, went up to her horse, took it by the reins, and firmly guided it over to one of the women's tents. Selima thanked her, jumped down from her mount and ran inside, where she could be out of public attention. Several of the other women followed her inside, eager for the chance to question this curious ghost-girl and find out her story for themselves.

Nusair ibn Samman insisted that his male visitors share his own tent with him. He led them to a large purple tent, the largest tent in the camp, and escorted them inside. Most of the tents were low to the ground, but this one was large enough to stand up in, with many poles holding up its top. The tent was barren of furnishings except for a once-elegant, but now faded, carpet laid on the ground in the center. The morning sun was already blazing hot, but the tent gave cool shade to the travelers and they gladly accepted the shaykh's hospitality. Cari whispered in Jafar's ear that she would remain invisibly beside him, to protect him in case of trouble. Jafar nodded, glad that she was being so helpful.

The men sat down on the carpet and several women came in to serve them. The shaykh's older wife sprinkled droplets of perfume around the tent to rid it of the worst smell of camel, while other women brought in the food—a heaping bowl of pilau and a plate filled with nan-e lavash. Moving silently the women placed the dishes in the center of the carpet and departed to leave the men in peace. Compared to their own meals of cured meat and dried fruit, this looked like a feast to the three travelers; they crowded around and reached with their right hands into the bowls, sampling the women's cooking and pronouncing it good. Nusair called for a skin of wine, and the foursome ate and drank more heartily than the travelers would have expected possible in those surroundings.

During and after the meal, Nusair ibn Samman questioned the group closely about their destination and ultimate objectives. At first they were cautious, merely telling the shaykh they were headed east past the Kholaj Desert, but under his persistent and friendly questioning they opened up more about themselves and their mission. Prince Ahmad explained how his throne had been usurped and, more importantly, how the urn of Aeshma had been stolen and opened, loosing evil incarnate upon the unsuspecting world. He told the shaykh about Muhmad's vision, that Prince Ahmad must unite the armies of the world to fight against the onslaught of Rimahn's legions, and that they must also find the four pieces of the Crystal of Oromasd so the wizard Jafar al-Sharif could use its powers to counter the magic Aeshma would use against them.

Much to their surprise, Nusair ibn Samman reacted most enthusiastically to the prince's words. "In this coming struggle," he pledged, "you will have the help of the Badawi. The sharpness of our swords and the courage of our fighters are renowned throughout Parsina."

"Indeed they are," Prince Ahmad said, "I saw but twelve fighters today and no more here at your camp, but all good men will be welcomed in the fight against Rimahn."

"We are a small tribe," ibn Samman admitted, "but I will deliver you far more than a dozen swords. At the end of summer, all the tribes of the Badawi will gather for our annual council. There will I repeat your message, and there will the Badawi rise up as with one voice to fight with me at your side in the great battle that is to come."

"How can you be so sure?" Jafar asked. "You scarcely know us, and the other tribes don't know us at all. Why are you so willing to fight in a cause so remote from your daily life?"

"You may be strangers," said ibn Samman, "but our lord Oromasd is not. We, the Badawi, are the specially favored children of Oromasd. The farmers who tend their fields and their flocks, the city dwellers who run their commerce, none of them know Oromasd the way the Badawi do. They are caged up inside their concerns, and they think of Oromasd as something apart from themselves, something distant and special. We see Oromasd every day in the world about us, we travel constantly through the land he made. We feel the coolness of his breezes and the warmth of his sun and the sweetness of his water. He is most truly our father—and is it not written that a son shall defend his father's honor?

"You say the cause is so remote from our daily life, O wizard, yet the cause is here all about us. Each day we battle Rimahn's creatures, the flies and the scorpions and the snakes. Each day we traverse the wastes that Rimahn brought to the fair world Oromasd created. Each day we fight the harshness Rimahn brought to Oromasd's sweet gift of life."

The shaykh folded his arms across his chest. "We could live in the cities, O wizard. We could give up our ways and become as other men, but then we would lose our special closeness with Oromasd. There is no glory in living the easy life and worshipping once a week in the temples. Here is where we do the work Oromasd has planned for us. To live against the worst ravages Rimahn can deliver, to fly in the teeth of all his evil—this is the ultimate proof of a man, the proof that we are indeed the weapons of Oromasd to defeat evil for all time. As long as the Badawi travel the desert, as long as the Badawi survive against the tortures of Rimahn, then Oromasd is victorious. This is why we can and why we must fight in your war against Rimahn. The Badawi, children of Oromasd, will rise to wipe evil from the face of the earth."

Having finished his piece, Nusair ibn Samman looked around the tent at the faces of his visitors, as though challenging any of them to dispute his position. None of them did, not even the normally voluble Jafar al-Sharif. Finally Prince Ahmad nodded and said, "Then welcome to the army of Oromasd, O noble shaykh, you and your Badawi brethren. May we all prove worthy of our master Oromasd and bring to him the victory he so richly deserves."

Selima spent that day in the women's tent, for even though she was but a ghost it was not considered seemly for her to sleep in the company of men. She told her story to the women of the caravan who sat around her, fascinated. One black-haired, black-eyed beauty was particularly interested in the tale. This was Murrah, daughter of Nusair ibn Samman and only a couple of years younger than Selima herself. Murrah politely pestered Selima with questions until finally her mother told her to get some sleep during what little remained of the day. Selima slept with the women while the men stayed in the cool purple tent of Nusair ibn Samman, resting in the shade.

Cari the Jann remained invisible and awake, keeping watch near the sleeping form of Jafar al-Sharif in case of treachery. She watched him as he slept, memorizing every trace and curve of his handsome features. She'd only had two masters in her life—Akar the wizard who'd captured her soul and enslaved her to the brass ring, and Jafar al-Sharif who'd stolen the ring from Akar. The two men were as different as sea and mountain. Akar she obeyed because she had no choice, even when his orders threatened her very life; Jafar she obeyed beyond the limits of his orders because he was a gentle, kind man whom she respected. Akar made her feel like a slave; Jafar treated her as a servant or a paid employee. Perhaps she respected Jafar so much because, in the final analysis, he respected her.

As the sun was lowering in the west the camp began to stir again. The older children got up and started on their chores of tending the goats, camels and horses. The women started cooking the pilau and making the bread for their evening meal, while the men began the exhausting task of loading the bales back on the camels, who resisted the process with every bit of stubbornness those contrary creatures possessed.

As the travelers were to discover, nan-e lavash and pilau were the standard fare of these desert nomads—but this diet of flatbread and rise was so flavorful and filling that it never grew boring. The usual meals were served with water rather than with wine as it had been on the first morning, but Prince Ahmad and his companions never complained about the simple menu.

After the evening meal the Badawi broke camp and prepared for another night's travel. Jafar al-Sharif was astonished at how quickly these colorful tents could be taken down and packed away on the camels, but this was a way of life the desert nomads had practiced for centuries and it was as natural for them as bargaining in a city bazaar was for Jafar.

The caravan moved slowly through the desert, as most of the Badawi traveled on foot. Only about a third of the men— Nusair ibn Samman's finest fighters—and none of the women rode horses, and no one rode the camels; those beasts were too valuable for carrying cargo. The Badawi thought it odd that Selima was allowed to ride on her pack horse, but no one made any comments aloud. Selima was, after all, the daughter of a wizard and few would risk Jafar's wrath. Murrah would occasionally walk beside Selima's horse, and the two girls became firm friends.

The adult men who didn't ride walked beside the camels, guiding and prodding them; the women and children walked behind the camels scooping up the dung that was dropped and collecting it in simple sacks. The dung would later be dried in the sun and used as fuel on the fires.

The caravan traveled mostly single file as it moved through the moonlit desert landscape. Even in those hours when the moon was not in the sky, the pitch-soaked torches the leaders carried provided enough light to travel by. Some of the women sang traditional songs as they walked, and the whole caravan took on a festive air. Far from being somber and serious, the Badawi seemed to treat living on the edge of survival as a grand experience to be thoroughly enjoyed.

Ahmad and Umar found the shaykh to be a mine of information about desert conditions and desert warfare. Though there had been peace in the desert for many years, this had not always been so, and Nusair ibn Samman could remember times as a young man when he accompanied war parties on raids against oases that had treated the Badawi unfairly, or against soldiers and caravans from countries that had cheated or fought with the nomads. The shaykh's tales of Badawi fighting prowess could have been dismissed as simple bragging except that Umar had heard similar stories confirmed by the Badawi's enemies. The desert wanderers were tough, stubborn fighters whose ferocity was matched only by their pride. If Nusair ibn Samman could indeed convince the other tribes to join Ahmad in the upcoming battle against Rimahn, they would prove to be invaluable allies.

As for Jafar al-Sharif, he cared little for the details of battles. He quickly discovered who among the tribe was the primary historian and storyteller, and spent most of his time in that fellow's company. He gave the old man a few stories of his own, but mostly he listened. The Badawi tale spinner was an ancient but active man who walked beside the camels; in tribute to him, Jafar al-Sharif dismounted and walked along with him, leading his own horse and Selima's. The older man was delighted to have a new audience for his stories, and Jafar listened without interrupting. Many of the stories he had heard before in other forms with other names, but some of them were truly new and surprising. Jafar al-Sharif swallowed them avidly, his retentive memory digesting them and adding them to his already considerable repertoire. A new story was always a banquet to a man who relished words.

When the caravan stopped that morning, Jafar's legs were aching from the unaccustomed exertion, but he was otherwise exhilarated. While the Badawi were busy with their usual routine of setting up their camp for the day, Jafar decided it would be a good time for his and Selima's second lesson in reading. To do that, it would be best if Cari made herself visible, so she could point to letters and give examples.

He debated with himself whether to allow that. If the Badawi saw Cari appear from nothing, they might realize that it was the invisible Jann that had caused the manifestations yesterday, not Jafar's own powers. But then his mind was eased with the thought that there would be no apparent connection between the two events, and that having a Jann as his servant would only make him appear more powerful rather than less. He therefore made an elaborate show of commanding Cari to appear before him, and the Badawi were indeed impressed with his skills at wizardry.

Jafar, his daughter, and his slave went off to one side to study the journal of Ali Maimun in private. To their consternation they found the book still would not open any further than it had before, but there was still enough of the text to provide examples for the students. Cari began with a review of the alif, and when she was satisfied her pupils knew that she moved on to ba. She drilled father and daughter on the letter's appearance until she was sure they knew it as well, then started them memorizing the names and order of the letters in a little singsong chant. With his training, Jafar learned this rote in moments, and Selima managed to learn more than half. Cari said she'd been taught this way herself. The twenty-eight letters seemed a small number to Jafar. All the thousands of words that built tens of thousands of stories, relating millions of ideas—all could be built onto paper with only twenty-eight letters. This was certainly as big a miracle as having a Jann do his bidding.

All this learning was very exciting, and it made Jafar al-Sharif feel like a youngster again, fresh with the hope of a new world awaiting his discovery. Even the dismal fortune foretold in the prophet's vision seemed distant and conquerable, and after the lesson Jafar ate the simple morning meal of pilau and nan-e lavash with great gusto. He slept in the shaykh's tent again, content in the knowledge that he was making progress in his studies.

He awoke late in the afternoon to the sound of thunder. Rising from the carpet, he went to the opening and stared out at the desert sky. High, dark clouds had gathered rapidly, and to all appearances a storm was in progress. Lightning forked and thunder rolled, and curtains of rain could be seen pouring down from the clouds—but none of it reached the surface of the desert. The air on the ground remained dry and hot, as though the water were being caught in some invisible basin before it could reach the earth.

Jafar al-Sharif stood at the tent door for several minutes marveling at this paradox when suddenly a heavy hand clapped on his shoulder. "So," said the shaykh behind him with a hearty laugh, "does the great wizard have an answer to that riddle?"

"No," Jafar said honestly. "I've never seen anything like that before. It should either rain or not, but to have it rain and not rain at the same time is a mystery I cannot solve."

"I've seen it happen many times," said ibn Samman. "My people know it is one of the cruel tricks of the desert, obviously the work of Rimahn. It's like the mirage lakes and oases that appear and vanish without warning. Such illusions could only come from Rimahn, the father of lies."

"So you can't solve the riddle, either?"

"My people have said it's the work of the Afrits of the air," ibn Samman replied jovially. "When they get thirsty they make it rain, and then drink up all the water themselves before it can reach the ground. In this way does Rimahn keep the deserts barren and thwart the plan of Oromasd."

Despite the afternoon heat, Jafar suddenly shivered. He remembered all too well his encounter with the tall, powerful Afrits of the air, and how they had taunted him and knocked him from the flying carpet he'd stolen from Akar. They were cruel and mighty djinni who would easily have killed him if they'd thought he was the least bit significant. Even a passing reference to them was enough to frighten him.

But he could not allow his fear to show, so he controlled his voice as he told the shaykh, "I deal with djinni all the time. The next time I talk to an Afrit, I must ask him the truth of this riddle."

Later that evening, as the Badawi awoke and prepared to set off once more on their nightly travels, Jafar and Selima had time to sneak off for another short reading lesson from Cari; in that respect this second night's travel with the nomads began much as the first had done.

Midway through the night, Prince Ahmad—who had been making his customary glances in Selima's direction—finally excused himself from the company of Nusair ibn Samman and rode over to where Jafar al-Sharif was walking beside the Badawi storyteller. Ahmad asked if he could unburden Jafar by taking the reins to Selima's horse, that he might lead it for a while, and Jafar was so engrossed in his colleague's tale that he handed the reins to the prince without so much as a second thought.

The prince and Selima rode for a while, side by side in silence. Finally Prince Ahmad broke the stillness between them. "I hope your sad condition does not cause you too much pain, O Selima," he said formally.

"None at all, Your Highness," she replied just as stiffly. She found herself in an awkward position: courtesy demanded she look at him when she spoke, but her modesty and the shame of being unveiled—even after all this time—made her want to look away. She compromised by looking straight ahead at her horse's mane. "Indeed, I feel nothing at all—no heat, no cold, no hunger or thirst. Were it not for the fact that I can't touch anything and will soon fade away to nothingness, it might almost be an ideal state."

"Do you feel bitter, then?"

"Do you feel bitter for losing your kingdom?" she retorted, but still could not bring herself to look at him. "I was caught in the web of kismet, as are we all. We play our roles in Oromasd's battle with Rimahn, and who is to say what role is better than another? I know I've lived a good life, I know I'll reach the House of Song. Does it matter whether I get there sooner or later?"

"So well spoken for one so young," Prince Ahmad marveled. "I've had teachers in the madrasa who couldn't make a point so eloquently and succinctly."

Selima blushed. "I think I inherited my father's tongue."

"Well, certainly his wit. But I'm at least glad you feel nothing in your condition."

"But I do," Selima told him.

"But you just said—"

"I said I felt no pain. But I do feel many things. I feel regret at having to leave this life, however imperfect it is, so soon, without having a chance to sample some of the better things it has to offer. I feel sad that my poor, dear father blames himself for my condition. I feel frightened that he and you are risking your own lives on this quest for the Crystal of Oromasd. And . . . and I feel hopeful that perhaps you can make it after all and defeat the powers of Rimahn before they overwhelm the earth. I may not be able to touch the physical world, but the world can still touch my heart."

Prince Ahmad recalled the prophet's vision regarding poor Selima, and his heart was burdened with sadness. How tragic it was that a young woman so beautiful, so intelligent, so obviously trained for greatness, should meet such an ignoble fate. So overcome with grief was he for her condition that he could bear to speak to her no longer. After riding in more silence for a while, he handed the reins back to Jafar and returned to his less emotionally demanding conversation with Nusair ibn Samman.

Selima, too, felt relieved at the departure, for it meant the end of the curious hollow sensation in the back of her mind and the pit of her soul. Normally she was a well-spoken and sensible young lady, but when Prince Ahmad was near her those senses became confused and she felt inadequate to deal with the situation. The only cause, she reasoned, was that he was a prince and she was a commoner, daughter of a good but plebeian storyteller. The social gap between them was almost as great as the gap that separated her from the world of living people, and she knew not how to bridge either one.

The caravan traveled thus for five days through the Kholaj Desert at a slow but peaceful pace. Life in the desert was a simple matter of survival against the heat and the dryness, and the dunes all around them became their world in miniature. The problems of the outside world did not intrude in this microcosm; the only reminders of those problems were Selima's ghostly state and the journal of Ali Maimun that Jafar al-Sharif kept well hidden in his saddle pouch when he and Selima weren't taking reading lessons from Cari. But for those things it would be easy to imagine that the mission on which they'd been sent was but a dream, an unpleasant memory that would fade with time.

As the caravan moved eastward it passed between giant dunes many stories high, mountains of sand that towered over the puny human figures. The Badawi took this spectacle for granted, having lived with it all their lives, but it was an impressive sight to the travelers from Ravan.

They were now just a couple days' travel out from Tannakesh, a town on the eastern edge of the Kholaj Desert. It was there the Badawi were to sell the wares they were carrying with them and—it was to be hoped—where they would pick up new merchandise to carry westward again through the summer wastes. It was here, also, that Prince Ahmad's party would take leave of the Badawi's hospitality, for their path carried them yet further eastward. Tannakesh was south of Marakh's borders and far enough from Ravan that there was a good chance Shammara's alliance had not reached it. If the royal party was not welcomed with open arms, at least they would probably not be killed on sight, either.

It was early in the morning and the caravan was just about to make its stop for the day when suddenly the ground exploded beneath them. Sand went spraying in all directions and a sulfurous stench belched out into the clean desert air. A hot wind blew through the caravan, like the heat from a blacksmith's furnace, and the sound of the rushing air all but drowned the frightened cries of the animals and people.

Jafar al-Sharif grasped tightly to the reins and threw his arms around his horse's neck as the beast reared in panic. Around him other horses were rearing as well and some riders, their reflexes not as quick, were tossed to the ground. Selima, who couldn't hold onto her mount, was thrown to the sand and might have been trampled under her horse's feet but for the fact that the hooves went right through her insubstantial body. Elsewhere in the caravan the camels bolted away from their handlers, running randomly through the desert to escape the sudden storm that had come into their midst. Bales of merchandise were thrown every which way as the creatures shook themselves to rid their backs of their burdens and allow them to run faster.

Through the swirling sand a shape could be seen, faint and indistinct but towering many cubits above the ground. Its very obscurity made it all the more terrifying as it threw back its head and laughed at the plight of the scurrying humans and animals. It strode calmly through the center of the sandstorm it had caused, casually knocking aside anything—man, horse, or camel—that blocked its path. In a sudden motion it stooped down and picked up something that could not be easily recognized through the blowing sand and dust. With its prize securely in its grip, the shape took off flying into the air, where none could look up and follow its flight for fear of getting sand in the eyes.

With the creature's departure, the air slowly returned to normal. The hot winds abated and the sand that had been stirred by the whirlwind slowly sifted back down to the earth. Even the experienced Badawi were left coughing and rubbing the grit from their reddened eyes in the aftermath of this catastrophe. The horses were still rearing and needed soothing, and it would take at least a couple of hours to track down and retrieve the camels and their merchandise.

"What was that?" Prince Ahmad asked when he could clear his lungs enough to speak.

Nusair ibn Samman shook his head sadly. "That was Estanash, the Jinn of the Kholaj wastes. He is said to dwell in the eastern region of the Kholaj and sometimes he attacks caravans coming by. There's no way to avoid him, but if you're lucky you can get past without his bothering you." He spat into the sand at his feet. "Today we were not lucky."

"Aiyee!" The cry went up suddenly from the rear of the caravan and the shaykh, recognizing the voice of his first wife, turned in that direction. Getting his mount firmly under control he rode quickly to her side to learn what was wrong. The others followed closely behind him.

It didn't take long to find out what the matter was. The shaykh's thirteen-year-old daughter Murrah was missing. It must have been her that the Jinn took with him when he ascended into the sky, leaving the caravan to flounder in his wake.

"What would he want with your daughter?" Umar asked.

Nusair ibn Samman looked up and met the priest's gaze with eyes now reddened by tears as well as sand. His voice had a dead quality to it as he said, "He will eat her."

"That's barbaric," Prince Ahmad said. "We must do something."

Nusair ibn Samman dismounted from his horse and put his arms around his wife to comfort her cries. His shoulders were slumped and he looked like a beaten man. To the others, who were accustomed to seeing him full of life and vitality, it was a startling transformation.

"There's nothing that can be done," the shaykh said hollowly. "You saw him and what he can do. Not even Badawi fighters can stand against him."

"That's because he took us by surprise," Prince Ahmad insisted. "When we know what we're fighting—"

"You don't understand," said Nusair ibn Samman with a sad shake of his head. "Estanash is immortal. All who fight him die and none can kill him."

"All djinni are mortal; they're partially descended from humans," Jafar al-Sharif spoke up. He surprised himself by intruding into this conversation, and he knew he'd end up regretting it.

"Perhaps, but Estanash might as well be immortal," the shaykh replied. "Many years ago my people consulted a mage to learn how to rid ourselves of this terrible Jinn. The mage told us many things about Estanash. He lives by himself in a cave beneath the earth. There is a magical entrance through which he comes and goes, but for strangers there is only one narrow entrance, and it is guarded by a two-headed lion that strikes so quickly no one can get past it. Estanash sleeps during the day, and when he eats—which is only once or twice a month—he dines only on living human flesh right after sunset. He likes to capture his food before he goes to sleep, so it will be ready for him as soon as he wakes up. The mage assured us that Estanash could only be killed by the use of a particular magical sword—and Estanash, knowing that, has found the sword and stored it safely in his own cave, where he carefully guards it from anyone who might use it against him. So you see, the fight would be hopeless."

"You forget we now have a wizard of our own," Prince Ahmad said, "a man familiar with the ways of djinni. He will help us find a way to rid your people of this pestilence."

Jafar al-Sharif froze in cold fear. "Your Highness is very generous in his praise," he said, adding to himself, *and very quick to volunteer me in a cause*. "Ordinarily there is nothing I would like better than to rescue the daughter of our gracious host from the grasp of this monster. But you forget how handicapped I am at the moment. Were I back at my citadel, surrounded by my talismans and amulets and tools and symbols of power, this would be a routine task—but here and now my abilities are somewhat limited and I can't guarantee a successful outcome."

"I understand," Nusair ibn Samman said weakly. "Even the mage to whom we paid good money refused the task, saying it would be too difficult. In a way I suppose we've been fortunate. Estanash has been known to slaughter whole caravans and steal all their possessions, leaving their bones to bleach in the desert sun. He must have decided we were too poor and not worth the trouble. All he took from us was one young girl for his dinner. Right now he's probably sleeping in his cave, and at sunset he will eat my Murrah."

He let out a deep sigh. "The task is hopeless," he said with finality. "My family and I must begin our period of mourning. May I ask you, O priest, to help us with the prayers for our daughter's soul?"

"Certainly," Umar said, his voice heavy with grief.

Jafar al-Sharif continued to look at Nusair ibn Samman, this once-proud man now broken in spirit by the loss of his child. And Jafar remembered his own feelings when he'd learned of Selima's fate. For a father to lose a child was a terrible thing, a negation of his manhood and all the love he had put into raising the baby to near-adulthood. Jafar's heart went out to this other father faced with the loss of his daughter, and knew there'd been too much death and tragedy surrounding this quest. A line had to be drawn somewhere, a stand had to be taken.

"Nothing is hopeless," Jafar al-Sharif said aloud. "In Oromasd's grace there's always hope. Give me but some time to dwell on the matter and let me see what solution occurs to me."

"Not too much time, I hope," said Nusair ibn Samman. "Murrah will only live until sunset."

Jafar al-Sharif turned his back to the group and walked some paces into the desert to think. *O great and powerful lord Oromasd*, he prayed, *thou hast seen fit to deliver miracles into my hands when I needed them before. Is it too much to ask for one more?*

10

THE SAND JINN'S CAVE

JAFAR al-Sharif sat down cross-legged on the warm sand and called for Cari to materialize before him. She appeared in her normal shape, sad-eyed and somber, and made a formal salaam. "I am here, O master."

"Have you been listening to the conversation?"

"Yes, I have."

"Do you have any knowledge of this Jinn named Estanash?"

"Just general things that confirm everything Nusair ibn Samman told you. From the brief bit I saw of him, he is a powerful Jinn with magical abilities far beyond my own meager talents. I would be no match for him in a fight, if that's what you were thinking."

"I was afraid of that."

"I'm sorry I disappoint you so greatly, O master."

Jafar al-Sharif shook his head. "You're no disappointment. Quite the reverse. It's just that where our physical powers are limited, we'll have to use our brains instead." He rubbed at his forehead with his right hand as though trying to press an idea into his thoughts.

"Let's see, the first step, I suppose, is to find this Jinn. Could you do that much for me?"

"If his cave is anywhere within a hundred parasangs of here, I'll find it, O master," Cari vowed.

"Could you also go into it and steal the magical sword we need to kill him? That'll put us a good step on the road to success."

Cari hesitated. "That would be harder. If he's in his cave, even if he's asleep, he would sense me and know I was there. He might even kill me before I could get away."

"Even when you're invisible?"

"Djinni can make themselves invisible to humans, but not to other djinni. We can always see one another no matter how immaterial we are to human eyes."

"I see," Jafar said. "Well, I can't let him kill you, you're too valuable to me. I order you to find Estanash's cave and scout it out as thoroughly as possible without incurring any risk to yourself. If the Jinn isn't there, free Nusair's daughter and bring her back, or at least the magical sword—but if you run into any trouble, return immediately and tell me what you've learned."

"Hearkening and obedience," Cari said.

While she was off on her task, Jafar al-Sharif continued to sit and ponder the problem. He remembered how he, Selima and Cari had defeated the djinni who tried to block them from leaving Akar's castle; while big and ferocious, djinni were vulnerable to someone with speed, strength, and valor. Of course, those had been tame, household djinni, perhaps softened by years of duty in Akar's service. Estanash looked bigger and more formidable—though again Jafar reminded himself that the Jinn had created the situation of confusion with the sandstorm all around him, giving the impression he was less vulnerable than he really might be. The heroes of old were certainly able to kill djinni; Jafar knew plenty of stories attesting to that. This would be a good early test of Prince Ahmad's worthiness to lead the armies of mankind; if he could stand up to this Jinn, perhaps he could indeed become as worthy a hero as the men of legend.

Cari returned within half an hour. "I've found Estanash's cave, O my master," she said as she materialized and made her salaam. "It's but four parasangs from here. The entrance is at the bottom of a deep wadi."

"What about Murrah?" Jafar asked. "Is she safe? Did you see the sword?"

"Alas, I couldn't get in," Cari confessed. "Estanash has ringed the entrance with spells against trespassing by other djinni. Had I entered the cave he'd have awakened instantly and come after me."

"What about humans? Could people enter without setting off an alarm?"

"Not easily," Cari reported. "The spells might not detect them—magic is at its most effective against other magic—but as Nusair ibn Samman told you, there is a fierce two-headed lion guarding the entrance inside the cave. I've heard about those beasts. They can move faster than any man and will attack anything they see."

"Anything they see?" Jafar repeated.

"Yes, O master. Even were an army to attack one, it could rush from man to man, killing them all so fast they would have trouble dispatching it—and even if one man finally did kill it, the noise it would have made in the meantime would surely wake the sleeping Jinn."

Jafar al-Sharif stared at the far desert horizon for several minutes. At last he took a deep breath and exhaled it slowly. "Well, I may have a plan. Have you ever heard the tale of Shiratz and the archer Follaz?"

"I don't think so," Carl replied.

"Follaz was the fastest and most accurate archer in the world. He never slept, and he guarded the entrance to the castle that Shiratz needed to attack. No man could sneak past without taking one of his shafts in the chest or throat. In desperation, Shiratz built a man out of a thick pile of straw, dressed it in his own clothes, and raced in the doorway behind it. Follaz wasted all his arrows shooting the straw man, and Shiratz beheaded him with one sweep of his blade."

Jafar paused and looked at Cari quizzically. "How could you have lived more than two hundred years and not heard that old story?"

"The righteous Jann have other things to do with their lives than listening to the tales of men and their heroes," Cari said a bit testily.

Jafar shrugged. "Well, then, let's hope Estanash the Jinn hasn't heard the story, either."

With Cari flying on ahead as guide, Jafar al-Sharif took Prince Ahmad, Umar, Selima, and a party of Badawi warriors to the wadi where the entrance to the evil Jinn's cavern lay. They pulled to a halt several dozen cubits from the edge of the channel as Jafar explained, "Most of us can go no further until we hear the signal that the way is clear. This is more a job for stealth than strength."

He turned to Prince Ahmad and Selima and spoke low to them so only they could hear. "Cari will guide you to the entrance, and after that you'll be on your own. You know what you must do. May the blessings of Oromasd go with you on your mission."

He particularly looked at his daughter and wondered at her courage. Intellectually he knew that nothing of this world, not even an evil Jinn, could harm her further—but his father's heart told him he was sending his child into mortal danger from which she might never return.

The prince nodded as he accepted Jafar's blessing, while Selima smiled and blew her father a kiss. Then the two young people dismounted their horses and followed Cari to the edge of the wadi.

The gulch was deep and its sides were steep. It had been cut into the ground by centuries of flash floods that occasionally swept through the desert floor during infrequent storms. The wadi ran a twisting, curving course through the landscape, and extended to a depth of more than a dozen cubits. The Badawi called such features "the rivers of the desert," and in fact they were often harder to cross than real rivers, for ferries could not float across them. In some places bridges had been built, but that was usually a futile endeavor; when the next storm came, the floods would carry away even the sturdiest bridge as though it were made of spiderwebs. More often than not, the Badawi and other travelers found ways around these clefts in the earth.

Prince Ahmad and Selima looked down into the wadi. The prince was carrying a spear given him by Nusair ibn Samman, in addition to the saif in his belt, and he did not relish the thought of a climb down the steep sides of the ravine. The dirt that packed the walls was loose and crumbly, and a fall from this height could risk serious injury or even death.

"It won't be easy getting down there," he commented to Selima.

The girl smiled. "For me it is." And before the prince could say another word, she jumped off the edge of the wadi and fell to the bottom. Selima landed on her knees and fell forward, but then rose to her feet none the worse for the experience.

Everyone at the top of the wadi gasped when she jumped, but then quickly realized Selima wouldn't be hurt by the action. That method wouldn't work for the prince, however, and he was contemplating the awkward descent when Cari suddenly said, "By your leave, Your Highness." Placing her hands under his arms she lifted him into the air and flew gently to the bottom of the wadi to set him on the ground beside Selima.

As he recovered from his surprise, Prince Ahmad said, "Thank you, O Jann," and checked himself over once more to make sure he was ready for the ordeal that was to come.

"Follow me," Cari said and began walking ahead of them through the cleft of the wadi toward the sand Jinn's cave.

The wadi was wide, with room for eight people to walk abreast without touching the sides. The floor was level and gravelly, with a few hardy bushes poking their way up here and there through the sand. The walls towered several stories above their heads and were pockmarked with many holes of differing sizes. The reddish clay was moister than the dry sand on top of the desert, and provided a home for many colonies of insects, as well as birds and small rodents. Plants, too, were more abundant clinging to the sides of the wadi, and rootlets could be seen sticking out of the soil most of the way up the walls.

It was near noon and the heat of the summer sun was becoming oppressive. Down in the wadi, though, there were some shadowed places where the high walls kept out the direct sunlight. The trio marching toward the Jinn's cave stayed in the shady patches as much as possible, trying not to make any noises that would alert the Jinn to their presence.

After a few minutes' walk they came to the cave entrance. This was merely a ragged hole at the base of the left-hand wall, only a couple of cubits high and three times that in breadth. It would be wide enough for two people to enter side by side, but they'd have to crawl on hands and knees into the darkness beyond the opening.

"I must wait for you here," Cari told her companions. "If I go with you any further, it could set off the spells the Jinn has placed around his cave."

Prince Ahmad stood silently for a moment, contemplating the cave opening and the perils that lay in the darkness beyond. Then, steeling his resolve, he thanked the Jann for leading him this far, walked to the edge of the cave mouth, and got down on hands and knees. Beside him, Selima was doing the same.

Cari stood in the wadi and watched her companions crawl through the entrance until they disappeared from her view. Her spirit was troubled, for she knew so many things could go wrong. Prince Ahmad was a brave and skilled young man, but what if he couldn't stand up to the Jinn's strength? Selima, in her insubstantial form, should be as safe in there as anywhere else, but what if Estanash—far older and wiser than Cari—knew some way of hurting her further? There were so many unknown dangers, and if anything bad happened she'd feel unbearably guilty at having failed her master Jafar.

Meanwhile, unaware of the Jann's anguish, Prince Ahmad and Selima crawled on the ground past the opening of the cave. The ground here was actually cool and slightly moist, and the gritty sand rubbed roughly on Ahmad's hands and knees as he crept along.

"I hope the cave doesn't go on like this," the prince whispered to the girl beside him. "I can't fight the lion in this position, in the dark."

As the pool of light from the entrance fell behind them the darkness of the cavern enveloped them. The ceiling, walls, and floor were of hard-packed earth rather than rock, and Prince Ahmad knew a slight moment of claustrophobia, fearing the tunnel might collapse around him. The moisture in the air gave it the dank smell of wet clay, but at least it was blessedly cooler than the heat of the desert outside.

After they'd been crawling for several minutes the ceiling of the cave rose enough for them to stand. They could not see one another in the total darkness that now surrounded them, nor could the prince reach out to grasp Selima's hand. They whispered very cautiously to one another until they located themselves, and then Prince Ahmad started moving slowly ahead again. The floor began sloping steeply downward and they went one cautious step at a time into the darkness, wary of traps and pitfalls that the Jinn may have set for unwanted intruders.

After a few more minutes they began to detect a faint light ahead of them, which grew brighter as they approached. Now they slowed their pace even more, for they were nearing the opening of the Jinn's large interior cavern and would soon encounter the two-headed lion that guarded his threshold. Prince Ahmad placed his back tightly against the left-hand wall of the tunnel and edged carefully down the passageway. The spear was ready in his right hand in case of trouble.

In this dim light Selima was virtually invisible; Prince Ahmad had to take it on faith that she was beside him. As they reached a slight bend in the passage where the light increased, Prince Ahmad whispered, "It's time for you to go on ahead of me. If you're afraid, just say so and I'll—"

"Nothing more can harm me," Selima replied softly. "Thank you for your concern, but I'll be fine."

"May Oromasd guide your steps," the prince whispered after her as she started down the path ahead of him.

Prince Ahmad continued to edge his way forward, clinging tightly to the wall at his back to hide himself as much as possible, while Selima strode boldly down the center of the passage into the light. The prince still felt a twinge of conscience about the wizard's plan, thinking there was something cowardly about it—but since he could not propose a better scheme, he was stuck with this one. It still did not seem right, though, that he should follow a woman into a place of danger.

Selima walked brazenly into the Jinn's cavern, making no attempt to disguise her presence other than being quiet to avoid waking the Jinn. The light around her came mostly from a set of torches Estanash kept burning on the far side of the cave, as well as from natural phosphorescence in some of the rocks themselves. It was a muted orange glow, but it seemed bright after coming through the totally black caverns.

Suddenly Selima heard a loud snarl behind her. Turning, she saw a horrible beast crouched on an outcrop of rock that overhung the entrance from the tunnel into the cavern. It was an enormous lion with two heads, each mouth open and baring fangs that gleamed in the cavern's dim light. The lion's tawny body was three times as long as her own, and even on all fours it stood taller than she did. The beast sprang from its crouch, its claws set to dispatch instant death, and Selima instinctively pulled back to get out of its way.

But the beast was in for a major surprise as it reached the object of its fury. Its graceful body, soaring through the air, sailed right through Selima's insubstantial form. The sharpness of its claws and its two sets of teeth took no toll on the girl as she flinched but did not run away.

The lion had calculated its leap to intercept the human figure and instead flew on through it, landing awkwardly on the ground some few cubits past Selima. It scrambled to its feet, its two heads snarling in confusion and fury as it turned to attack once more.

This time the lion did not leap, but instead ran to where the girl was standing and swiped at her with one powerful front paw. Selima stood her ground and the vicious claws went right through the space where her throat should have been. The lion snarled and bit at her with each of its heads, but its teeth closed only on empty air.

Selima danced around on the ground and the lion, even more enraged by its failure to kill the figure it saw so plainly, leaped after her, moving back and forth in the direction Selima led it. The confused beast hissed and spat, but it could have no effect on the girl who was now chuckling playfully at its pathetic efforts.

As the lion's back was turned to the cave entrance, Prince Ahmad stepped forward cautiously with his spear. He'd been trained in the use of all kinds of arms, and his skill with a spear was undisputed—but it was one thing to aim at a target on a practice field and quite another to face a rapidly moving adversary in the dim light of a cave. He would have only one chance with his spear; if he missed, the lion could well be upon him before he had a chance to draw his sword from its sheath. Everything would have to be perfect the first time.

Perhaps he made some slight sound as he stepped forward out of the passageway, or perhaps even this minor motion registered in a corner of the lion's eyes—for as Prince Ahmad readied his spear the beast turned suddenly from its futile pursuit of Selima to face him squarely. Frustrated by its first quarry, the lion was eager to vent its fury on this new intruder.

Prince Ahmad stood as if paralyzed for a split second, staring into the raging faces of this two-headed beast. Faster than he would have believed possible the lion turned its body toward him and crouched to leap in his direction. He could see every taut band of muscle beneath the beast's tawny hide and every fleck of saliva dripping from those eager jaws. Four glowing yellow eyes were focused entirely on him with a bloodlust of animal ferocity. In that moment—more so even than when he was fighting the brigands who'd attacked him in the forest—Prince Ahmad knew the burning feel of fear devouring his insides.

Then the lion sprang at him, and the spell was broken. Without further hesitation, Prince Ahmad flung his spear at the creature's throat where the two necks joined the body. The spear flew through the air with all the strength and accuracy the young man could impart to it—and the force of the throw was more than matched by the force of the oncoming lion. The spear point went through the beast's throat, causing it to yell a garbled roar of pain.

Prince Ahmad tried to step back out of the way, but even so the body of the big cat hit him squarely and knocked him off his feet. The animal's body jerked in a frenzy of pain on top of him and the teeth gnashed ferociously in the death throes, and then quite suddenly the beast was still. The prince realized only too well how quickly he would have been killed had not his aim been perfect, and he shivered for a moment before pushing the heavy body of the dead lion off his own bruised body and climbing slowly to his feet again.

For the first time he had a chance to examine his surroundings closely. The passageway he'd come through opened into a much larger cave whose ceiling rose some three stories above him and could only be seen by the dim shadows that danced across it from the light of the flickering torches. The walls were bare rock and limestone, dull gray and roughly hewn, with droplets of moisture glittering on them. The floor was strewn with stalagmites of different sizes, some coming up higher than waist level and others joining with stalactites to form natural pillars that held up the arched ceiling of the cave. In one corner of the cavern was a pile of human bones, all that remained of Estanash's previous victims.

In a large niche toward the right-hand side of the opposite wall lay the Jinn named Estanash, sprawled out asleep. His tall body, grossly overweight, was a deep golden brown and totally devoid of hair. He wore just a loose-fitting loincloth and had no turban on his bald head. He had sharply pointed ears and a nose that was pressed flat against his face, and fangs that showed even when his mouth was closed in sleep. His massive hands had long, slender fingers that ended in nails sharper than an assassin's dagger. His snores were so loud they caused a low rumbling throughout the spacious cavern.

It seemed miraculous to Prince Ahmad that the Jinn hadn't wakened at the sound of the lion's roars, which had seemed deafening at the time—but perhaps Estanash was used to such noises, or perhaps the sound of his own snoring had covered them from his ears. In any event, his luck was holding and Prince Ahmad was not going to question such a blessing any further.

Chained against the wall behind Estanash was Murrah. Her body sagged and her head was down, and at first Prince Ahmad feared he was too late to save her from death—but then he saw the slight movement of her chest as she breathed, and realized she was merely unconscious. He couldn't tell whether she was drugged, or whether she'd fainted from fear, or whether she'd succumbed to fatigue after screaming herself hoarse in her captivity—but while she still breathed, there was a chance to save her.

Most of the cavern was bare of furnishings, but against the far wall was scattered an enormous array of stuff, loot gathered from the Jinn's centuries of pillaging and robbing desert caravans. Chests and sacks filled with coins and jewels were piled haphazardly about, while other objects whose natures could not be determined from a casual glance lay scattered among the piles. This cave was a treasure trove whose wealth would have rivaled that of many kingdoms.

Selima raced over to Ahmad as he pulled himself free of the lion's dead body, and the silent question in her eyes asked whether he was all right. He nodded to her and gestured that they should move quietly to the far wall and begin sifting through the treasure heaped so carelessly there. They had to find the magical sword that could kill Estanash, or all their efforts so far would have been in vain.

There was so much loot heaped haphazardly that it was difficult to spot any single item within it. Selima could only look through the piles of precious relics for anything that might resemble a sword, and even Prince Ahmad dared not disturb the piles too much for fear of sending all the treasure tumbling to the ground with a clatter that was sure to wake the sleeping Jinn. The prince and Selima split up so they might search the piles and find the sword more quickly.

It was Selima who found the sword after five minutes of searching, though it was difficult to recognize as such. Only the tip of its hilt projected outward from beneath a massive pile of jeweled chests; the sword was noticeable only because it seemed so plain compared to its surroundings. Selima beckoned her companion over and the prince looked at the sword dubiously. It did not appear particularly impressive—his own sword was much fancier and better forged but it was the only sword in the cavern, so it must be the one the mage had foretold.

The trick would be to take it from its surroundings, buried as it was beneath a mountain of loot. Prince Ahmad tried tentatively to pull it out, but the weight of the pile on top of it wedged it firmly in place. Slowly he began unstacking some of the treasure so he might pull it out more easily.

All went well until he came to one large chest. It was far heavier than it looked, and the prince staggered backward under its load. His foot slipped on a loose gemstone and he went toppling over. The chest slipped from his grasp and went crashing to the floor with a loud bang that resounded through the cavern like a peal of thunder.

Estanash stirred and began to open his eyes. He was facing away from the prince at the moment, but in another second he would turn his head and see the young man sprawled out dazed on the ground. Before Prince Ahmad would have a chance to retrieve the magical sword, or even to draw his own, the Jinn would be upon him and tear him apart with his murderous claws.

Realizing she could not let this happen, Selima dashed out into the Jinn's view as though she were responsible for the noise. "O thou son of a sandworm, more insignificant than a scorpion's spit," she yelled at Estanash. "Prepare this day to meet thy doom."

As she'd hoped, the Jinn turned all his attention on her and did not notice Prince Ahmad. Estanash had eyes with the vertical pupils of a cat, bright yellow and gleaming with the light of evil. "Who art thou, foolish mortal, to dare invade my cave?"

"I am Selima, daughter of Jafar al-Sharif, the greatest wizard of our age, and I am come to kill thee."

Estanash laughed, a deep, thunderous tone that rumbled through the cavern and shook the very walls. Then the Jinn rose and Selima's eyes widened. It had been hard to judge his height when he was lying down, but standing his head nearly touched the high ceiling of this cave. The fat of his belly and his ponderous breasts hung flabbily, but his apelike hairless arms gave him a broad reach.

"Daughter of a wizard?" the Jinn laughed, and his breath smelled of carrion carried on the hot desert wind. "Is he too cowardly to fight me himself?"

"He had more important things to do," Selima replied. "He knew a girl was more than enough to deal with camel dung like thee."

"Thou art not even there," the Jinn observed. "Thou art merely a phantom and not worth the effort to kill."

"This is but a simple spell to confound thee," Selima jeered. "All thy power and all thy magic are for naught now in this hour of thy death."

Estanash roared with anger and swiped at Selina with one monstrous claw. The girl boldly stood her ground and the Jinn's hand passed harmlessly through her insubstantial body. As the Jinn looked startled it was Selima's turn to laugh.

"See how helpless thou art before my powers, O impotent son of a thousand beardless fathers," she taunted. "Now shalt thou pay for thy ravishing of innocent wayfarers, for today the judgment of Oromasd comes upon thee." She took a few steps backward and, as she'd hoped, the Jinn followed after her, ignoring what was happening behind him in the cave.

As he watched Selima dart out to distract the Jinn, Prince Ahmad paused a moment to regain his bearings, then scrambled to his feet and raced to the magical sword jutting from beneath the pile of treasure. The sword was still stuck firmly in place, but Prince Ahmad gave it a mighty heave and pulled it loose from its sheath. Now that he held the blade out in the air he could feel the power of the magical spell it contained, vibrating with a strong but subtle hum. The prince knew this was truly a sword to be used for marvelous deeds.

Estanash's attention was still riveted on Selima, as the Jinn proclaimed, "Rimahn shall protect me from the judgment of Oromasd, and I can protect myself well enough from a phantom girl."

"But there is no protection from me!" yelled Prince Ahmad, waving the enchanted sword above his head and announcing his presence for the first time.

Estanash turned his head and spotted the prince. "So there are two clever mice in my pantry. No matter. I fear no man's sword."

Prince Ahmad raced forward toward the giant Jinn, sword above his head. Estanash reached down to grab him, but the prince sidestepped the large hand and swung the sword with all his strength at Jinn's right leg, severing the Achilles tendon

Estanash roared with pain; his leg buckled and he staggered forward, just barely managing to brace himself against the far wall of the cave before falling completely.

"This is no man's sword, but thine own, taken from thine own treasure hoard," Ahmad yelled in defiance. "It is the very sword thou hast provided me to spell thy doom."

Estanash's expression changed as he realized which sword the prince meant. He could feel the magic radiating from the blade; he could feel the pain its sting had caused. This was the sword that had been prophesied for his death, the sword he'd stolen and guarded so zealously all these centuries.

As the look of horror swept across his face, Selima laughed. "Dost thou know fear now, O pompous murderer of virgins and innocent travelers? Then feel the full terror thou has caused in others, knowing thou art helpless before thy fate."

Estanash's lips curled into a snarl of rage as he faced the two young people. "Fear? You'll be the ones to fear. You'll both wish you'd only died by the time I'm through with you."

The hesitation Prince Ahmad had felt while facing the lion was now totally gone; in its place was the cold determination to do that which needed to be done. He strode purposefully forward against his foe, with neither haste nor fear in his step. He held the magical sword in neither hand and the blade became a part of himself, transforming him into something greater than he was.

Snarling his hatred, Estanash reached down with his left hand to grab the offending human, but Prince Ahmad was not to be so easily taken. The young warrior swung his blade once more, and the naked steel carved through the Jinn's flesh like a meteor through the night sky, severing three of the enormous fingers and causing the creature to howl once more in pain. Trying to stay out of the prince's way so she wouldn't distract him. Selima withdrew to Murrah's side and breathlessly watched the struggle from there.

Prince Ahmad, meanwhile, raced around to the Jinn's back and struck at the Achilles tendon of his left foot as well. Unable to stand, now, the Jinn fell forward onto the hard stone floor of the cave, and Prince Ahmad leaped on top of his prone body. Taking the hilt of his sword with both hands, he plunged the blade with all his might into the Jinn's broad back and felt it enter with a satisfying thud.

As the sword stuck in Estanash's flesh, it began to shine with a life of its own. Within seconds the hilt was too hot for Prince Ahmad to hold and he let go in astonishment, tumbling backward off the body of the dying Jinn to fall on the cave floor once again.

The glow of the sword quickly spread to the body it was lodged in, and in less than a minute both sword and Jinn were consumed by a flickering blue flame. Standing only a cubit away Prince Ahmad could feel no heat, yet he could not bring himself to touch the body of Estanash. The blue flame flickered, then suddenly exploded in a flash of brilliant white light.

Prince Ahmad and Selima both looked away, blinded momentarily by the brilliance of the flare. When at last they could look back they found the space before them empty; there was no sign of the Jinn Estanash or of the magical sword that had slain him. Selima and the prince were alone in the cavern with the Jinn's treasure and the unconcious but otherwise unharmed daughter of the Badawi shaykh.

The death of Estanash the Jinn caused a small disturbance on the magical web of the world. High up in Shahdur Castle the wizard Akar, preparing for his showdown with Aeshma, felt the tremor but dismissed it as insignificant compared to his own endeavors. In the desert south of Sudarr, Aeshma felt the vibrations; but he too dismissed the event merely as the death of a minor djinn, not worth bothering about.

Only in Sarafiq, where the prophet Muhmad sat in silent meditation, was the event recognized for what it was. Prince Ahmad had taken another step on his path toward maturation. Jafar al-Sharif would soon have more tools at his disposal. Muhmad smiled contentedly and returned to his plans regarding his upcoming death and the destruction of his beloved shrine.

11

THE TEMPLE OF
THE ASSASSINS

I N the long ago days when the world was new, when Oromasd was just beginning his plan to defeat the evil of Rimahn and rescue all of creation from darkness, Goush, the Bull, and Gayomar, the Man, were set upon the earth to appreciate the loveliness of Oromasd's creation. Rimahn, seeking to end his rival's perfection, sent his daevas to murder the Bull, which they did—but from the blood of Goush came the seeds for all the plants, flowers, and trees on Parsina, and from the flesh of his dying body did emerge all the good and clean animals that populated the world.

In a further attempt to corrupt creation, Rimahn sent the Great Harlot, Jahi, to seduce and murder Gayomar. Jahi fulfilled her purpose, but again Rimahn's will was to be thwarted—for from Gayomar's blood sprang the seeds of the haoma plant used for the holiest ceremonies, and from Gayomar's dead body sprang the plant that blossomed into the man and woman who begat the human race. At this point did the first great Cycle of the world, the Cycle of Creation, draw to a close and the next Cycle began.

The first man and woman came from the plant that grew from Gayomar's body and when they were mature they fell off and began living upon the earth. But because it was part of Oromasd's great plan that they should start out simple and

grow into knowledge, they were imperfect and ignorant creatures, and Rimahn took great advantage of their ignorance.
The lord of lies confused and seduced their senses until they
believed that he, not Oromasd, was the creator of all they saw
around them. They bowed down and worshiped Rimahn, de-
claring him to be their lord, and they began the practice of
eating animals, and indulged in many sins and committed
many wrong acts in the name of their supposed creator. Not
until the yazatas came down from the heavens and taught
Oromasd's ways of good thoughts, good words, and good
deeds did they and their children realize their errors.

But the descendents of these men and women were still
imperfect, and Rimahn continued to take advantage of their
ignorance. No matter how self-evident were the beauties of
Oromasd's creation, there were those people who would always turn to the path of Rimahn and perform evil deeds,
speak evil words, and think evil thoughts. And Rimahn
looked at the numbers of those people and was comforted into
thinking he was winning his ages-long battle with Oromasd.

The majority of these people slipped into their evil ways
through ignorance, convenience, or sheer laziness. Neither
Shammara nor Hakem Rafi the thief, for example, were worshippers of Rimahn. Both of them had been raised in the faith
of Oromasd, and though each had turned from that faith it
was not through opposing convictions. They simply convinced themselves that what was right for them was right for
the world, and the rules of Oromasd need not apply to their
special cases. Within their own perceptions they thought they
were doing the right thing—and Rimahn was only too happy
to support them in their delusions.

But there were some few people who, through a perverse
defect in their natures, were completely seduced by the lies of
Rimahn. These people turned their backs completely on the
goodness of Oromasd and proclaimed Rimahm to be the
greatest power in the world. They reveled in their evil
thoughts, evil words, and evil deeds; they prided themselves
in their superiority to the people around them; and they paid
no attention to the fate that awaited them at the Bridge of
Shinvar. And, as creatures of Oromasd, even these people un-
knowingly played their role in the great plan of the lord of
creation. All the world was created as a snare for the father of

lies, so that he might become enmeshed in it and sap his power for the true fight that was to come.

At first these rimahniya—as these evil people were called—practiced their perversions publicly, where all good and righteous people could see them and be repelled. But as their worship became more and more extreme, the rimahniya became ever less acceptable to the good citizens of their community. They were shunned, outlawed, banished from the haunts of decent people, but still they persisted in their abominations, and even flourished because of their persecution.

And their lord Rimahn rewarded their dedication by teaching them the skills of deceit and treachery. The rimahniya learned to disguise themselves and their practices so they could walk among ordinary men without attracting attention. They learned to lie and plot and sow dissension among the cities and nations of Parsina. They learned to coax and persuade and convert the weaker willed of Oromasd's flock to their religion. They learned to swindle and rob and murder with an adroitness few ordinary people have ever mastered. The rimahniya became synonymous with evil in the world.

With time and determination, the rimahniya spread like a plague throughout Parsina. Starting as isolated colonies and clusters hidden within different cities, they began to grow, to organize, to unite into one worldwide network until at last there was no nation that did not have a knot of believers festering within it, and no city was free of their evil influence.

Even the holy city of Ravan was not safe from their intrusion. The spells placed upon the city's walls by the great mage Ali Maimun kept out all harmful daevas, djinni, and wizards, but they could not stop evil men from passing unmolested. Perhaps, though, there was some residual effect, for in all those centuries the rimahniya had never been able to establish a strong base or a temple of their own within the Holy City. Each time they tried, the priests of Ravan would ferret them out and lead the forces of decency to rout them from their hiding places. They had to settle for placing their central temple, their holiest shrine, in the Tirghiz Mountains, some distance from Ravan. From thence did their leaders plot their mischief upon the world.

While the rimahniya were officially reviled by ordinary human society, there were those who nonetheless found them useful as spies and assassins. The rimahniya encouraged this and hired themselves out in these capacities because it helped promote chaos and evil within the world, thus fulfilling Rimahn's goals. Their reputation grew, and they were always in demand by kings and courtiers to further their private ambitions.

Because they were so widespread, it was usually not a difficult matter to contact the rimahniya and arrange for them to perform a given service. In some matters of the highest importance, however, the bargaining couldn't be handled by local members. In such circumstances the petitioner would have no choice but to travel to the temple of the rimahniya and speak directly to the high priest of Rimahn. Only he could make such decisions, and the price he demanded was always a steep one.

Shammara had used the aid of the rimahniya on a number of occasions in the past, and on two of those she'd made the journey to their temple in the mountains. She knew it was not a trek to be taken lightly, but now—even though her coup was an apparent success—it was a trip she was determined to make.

It was three days since the general announcement had been made in Ravan that Prince Ahmad had died on the road to Marakh at the hands of brigands. The weeping and wailing and official orations had all been done, and Shammara judged her presence would not be required immediately. She knew she was taking a major risk; with her coup this recent, any absence from Ravan might be taken as a sign for her enemies to stage a counterstroke against her. Only the opposition's disorganized state emboldened her to take this move.

Only six people in the palace knew she was making this journey: the three most trusted retainers who would accompany her along the way and the other three trusted servants who would guard her chambers and admit no one during her absence, making apologies and claiming she was feeling unwell. Not even her son or the wali of police were told she was leaving the city; although neither of them was ambitious or smart enough to replace her, either might make some foolish grab for excess power that would bring trouble to them all. If they merely thought she was indisposed for a few days, they would take no precipitate action.

Shammara dressed so no one seeing her would recognize her as the most important woman in Ravan. She wore a plain black cotton thawb with no adornment, and over her head she wore a black silk burqa whose front panel was simple black-dyed leather. The only holes were two narrow slits for her to see out of, and no one could see in. On her feet she wore plain black leather zarabil. Aside from a slight swishing of her thawb she made no sound as she moved.

In the dead of night, when most in the palace were asleep, Shammara and her servants slipped out of the women's quarters and down a secret stone stairway leading to a hidden passage. This underground tunnel led straight on, seemingly forever, in a westerly direction under the fabled walls of Ravan. The only light was cast by the torches of her three servants, a flickering glow that was gobbled up by the darkness before and behind, making the corridor seem like an endless stretch of *now*, constant and unchanging. The walls were gray stone with wooden supports at intervals to hold up the low, uneven ceiling. The rough-hewn floor was thick with dust, and even the dignified Shammara had to cough as her feet raised the dust into the air. She could only suffer it because no cleaning crew could be trusted with the secret of this entrance.

Even this long tunnel came to an end, though, exiting from a hill a few hundred cubits west of the city walls. The heavy wooden door at the end was locked, but Shammara had one of the few keys in existence. She carefully looked through the view holes to be certain no one happened to be near, then unlocked the door. The key squealed noisily as it turned in the seldom-used latch, and the door groaned on its iron hinges as it was pushed outward and the small party emerged into the open air. They doused their torches and set them by the doorway inside the tunnel for the return trip, then closed the heavy oaken door behind them. Shammara locked it once more from the outside to keep the passage safe from any nosy interlopers who might find it behind its screen of dense bushes.

The sky was clear and a gibbous moon provided all the light the travelers needed as they walked westward along a narrow path from the tunnel door down to the banks of the

Zaind River. Further to the south were rows of houses that bordered the official road from River Gate to the river itself. Fishermen, sailors, and others who made their living from river commerce lived in the shanty town outside the city walls; but up here on this lonely trail that few people ever traveled, the land was clear and empty. No witnesses saw Shammara and her companions walk down the narrow path to the river's edge.

As the rimahniya had promised, a boat was moored at an inconspicuous little dock, awaiting their arrival. It was a tiny craft, barely large enough to hold Shammara and the other passengers in addition to its sole boatman, who nodded silently to the group from the palace as they arrived. Shammara and her companions seated themselves as comfortably as they could on the unpadded seats of the small wooden vessel, and the boatman pushed off from the dock with his pole.

The boatman was almost certain to be a member of the rimahniya, and Shammara's servants were a little nervous sitting in such close confinement with one of these notorious killers, completely at his mercy. Shammara, however, remained calm and sat with her back erect and proud. The rimahniya would gain nothing by killing her here and now; their high priest would certainly want to hear her proposal before making any rash decisions. She did not believe this to be the hour of her death, so she did not worry about it.

They were traveling northward along the river, against the current, so they stayed close to the riverbank to avoid the strongest flow in the center. The boatman was a powerfully muscled man with a black mustache and no beard. He wore nothing more than a loincloth and a turban as he worked; any more clothing would have hampered his efforts. He knew the vagaries of the river well, however, and poled efficiently to propel the small boat along its way. Occasionally he could be heard humming to himself, but otherwise he did not speak as the craft moved upriver.

Daybreak found them still on the river, leaving the gentle plains behind them and starting up into the Tirghiz Mountains that were the river's source. The waters became more uncertain here, the current faster and more treacherous, and before the sun was two hours above the horizon the boatman docked the boat at another inconspicuous landing and the group set out into the mountains on horses that were tethered and waiting.

The trek continued through a small forest and then up a steep and narrow trail through the rocks. The group stopped once to eat a breakfast of the provisions they'd brought with them, then continued on their way. The travelers were tired, but sleep was unthinkable just yet; they had to reach their destination first.

Shortly after noon they spotted their goal: an enormous cave opening in the face of the mountain itself, a hole so huge that two score horsemen could have ridden through it abreast without touching the sides, and so high that the tallest tower in the royal palace of Ravan could have stood inside and barely scraped the ceiling. Even though Shammara had seen it before, she nonetheless felt moved by this inspiring sight. It was an impressive entrance, as it was intended to be.

They were greeted inside the cave entrance by a group of men in dark blue robes who took their horses and led Shammara's party to temporary quarters where they could freshen up. The travelers were fed a simple meal and Shammara, tired after her lengthy journey, slept in preparation for her appointment this evening. Her companions stood guard around her while she slept; they would sleep later, while she was conducting her business with the high priest of this evil cult.

Her servants awakened her shortly before sunset and Shammara prepared for her interview by donning one of the finest—and warmest—outfits she had. Her heavy thawb was of black velvet embroidered with thread of silver and burgundy, while her black headpiece of shayla and gnaa had appliquéd silver triangles and squares, and burgundy tassels that dangled at the sides of her head. She wore black zarabil embroidered with silver on her feet and her finest black milfa with silver stitching around the edge. Thus clad she was ready for her appointment.

Leaving her servants behind to sleep, she was guided by a group of women from the caves through a labyrinth of corridors and tunnels; the route they took was so complicated that even she, clever as she was, could not have retraced her steps without assistance. After half an hour of walking they reached her final destination: the vast cavern that served as the temple of the rimahniya.

It was as though Rimahn, lord of lies, had grown jealous of the Temple of the Faith in Ravan and created his own place of worship here within the heart of a mountain. The roof of the cavern was so high it could not be seen without bending one's head all the way back—and even then the lights from the torches barely reached it, giving the ceiling a shadowy twilight effect. The broad, open floor rivaled in size the enormous audience chamber of the palace in Ravan, and the natural stone walls of dark rock were lined with hundreds upon hundreds of torches, their light so bright it made the cavern seem as though lit by daylight. Despite the torches, though, the air was bitingly cold and patches of ice within the cavern walls glistened in the light like diamonds.

The floor of this huge cave was covered with the kneeling forms of perhaps a thousand rimahniya—the worshipers of Rimahn, all dedicated to the god of death and the powers of darkness. They paid no attention to Shammara, but faced instead to the front of the cavern, to a large electrum altar on which a calf was about to be sacrificed. Calves, sheep, goats, and chickens were not the only creatures to be sacrificed upon that splendid altar; throughout the ages many people had gone to their deaths as a tribute to the powers of Rimahn and his fanatic followers.

Serving as backdrop for this scene, the entire rear wall of the cave was a massive sheet of ice from floor to ceiling, sparkling and gleaming in the torchlight as a cold antithesis to the fires that signified Oromasd. Even though the torch fires were necessary in the cave for seeing, the torches were coated with copper-impregnated pitch and impure materials to defile the sacredness of the flames they harbored and make them burn an icy blue. No respect was given here to the lord of light and truth; the temple of the rimahniya was a tribute to the cold, heartless powers of evil.

Standing on the dais before the kneeling faithful was the high priest of Rimahn, Abdel ibn Zaid. He was a tall man in his late forties, powerfully built, with a brown beard down to his chest and blue eyes that gleamed with fanaticism. His long robes were brilliant indigo, and an enormous diamond was sewn into the center of his indigo turban. With both hands he held a gleaming obsidian-handled dagger over his head. He looked down at the bleating calf and intoned his long prayer to Rimahn. At the climactic moment he brought the blade down with full force into the calf's neck, ripping it open cleanly. Blood streamed down the side of the electrum altar and onto the floor, where it seeped slowly into the porous rock to join the blood from other victims and other times.

Shammara watched impassively as the followers of Rimahn went into ecstatic howls at the death of the calf, shrieking and crying their loyalty to Rimahn and the forces of the lie. They swayed back and forth independent of one another as their ecstasy gripped them, making the cavern floor appear as a restless sea of human bodies. At the altar, Abdel ibn Zaid waited, too, for the frenzy to abate, then led the service in the concluding prayers.

At last the ceremony was over and the followers rose awkwardly after kneeling so long on the hard stone floor. They walked from the temple, filing past Shammara with a look of dreams and nightmares frozen in their faces. Shammara waited for them all to leave, then walked boldly to the front where Abdel ibn Zaid stood waiting for her before the wall of ice.

The ice wall was not the only cold presence here by the altar; for all the human feeling he possessed, Abdel ibn Zaid might as well have been cut and carved from that same material. He stood on the raised platform with the altar, staring down at her from a mountainous height with eyes as blue and as cold as the ice. His hands were constantly clenching and unclenching in barely restrained power. Even Shammara, who inspired fear in her subordinates, felt uneasy in his presence.

"Speak!" he commanded, and his voice echoed through the empty cave like thunder. "Why have you come to the temple of Rimahn?"

He knew the reason, of course; she'd already discussed it with his emissaries when she arranged for her passage to this mountain hideout. He was merely emphasizing his position of power by placing her in the role of supplicant.

The coldness of the ice, and of ibn Zaid's stare, made Shammara shiver despite her best intentions of seeming impassive. "Prince Ahmad must die," she said evenly.

"But Ravan mourns his death already," the high priest said. "Would you pay the rimahniya to do what's already been done?" The corners of his mouth, mostly hidden by his bushy beard, still gave enough hint of a cruel smile to tell Shammara he already knew the truth. The rimahniya had agents everywhere—and she knew of one herself who was in a position to know the ambush had really failed.

"Surely you, of all people, appreciate the value of a well-placed lie," Shammara said. "The truth is that I trusted the work to amateurs and they bungled it. Now I want the job done right." She paused. "Although your own people have been less than successful in this matter themselves."

The fires of rage sparked in the eyes of Abdel ibn Zaid. As a giant blue eagle stooping upon its prey he leaped from his place beside the altar, indigo robes flying, to land on the floor beside Shammara. Even though she was a tall woman, the high priest of evil towered more than a head taller, staring down at her with barely contained fury. His hands went to her throat, massive hands, strong, calloused hands that had known a lifetime of killing. He pressed his thumbs tightly against her windpipe as he said, "Would you like a firsthand experience of rimahniya success?"

Shammara was not a woman to frighten easily, but even she knew fear at this moment. She and her plans meant little to ibn Zaid, even though they would help him in the long run. He was a fanatic, and could not always be counted on to do the sensible thing. He could kill her as a sacrifice to Rimahn and consider it a gracious act. It took all the courage she had to remain utterly still, for she knew that if she cried out, or struggled, or tried to flee, this man would erase her life in an instant.

"Your people only failed because Prince Ahmad was held in the center of Oromasd's stronghold, with priests around him who protected him with their lives," she said with feigned calmness. "Were that not the case, they would have performed as admirably as your agent for me in Marakh."

Abdel ibn Zaid relaxed his grip, but didn't take his hands immediately from her throat. The two people locked their gazes in a test of wills. Shammara, knowing she must win this struggle or die, stared her opponent down and after a few more moments ibn Zaid removed his hands from her neck.

Relief flooded Shammara's body, but she dared not show it. "This time," she continued, "I'm sure there will be no such problems. The prince is beyond the protection of the Royal Temple, with no more than a few dozen men to guard him. To ensure success, I want you to handle this matter personally.

Bring me his head or your sworn assurance he is dead and the rimahniya will be well rewarded."

Abdel ibn Zaid smiled, a cold, cruel smile even more threatening than his glare. "For such perfection I may choose a band of my followers to accompany me," he said, "and for my personal involvement, the cost will be high. The price will be one hundred thousand dinars "

Shammara knew better than to bargain with the rimahniya; the price set by ibn Zaid was the price that would be paid, not a fal less, even though it represented ten years of a successful merchant's income. She did not even blink as she said, "Done. The first half of the money will await your emissary as soon as I return to Ravan." The high priest would know he could trust her; no one cheated the rimahniya.

She paused. "The other fifty thousand will be held until the job is completed, as is our standard arrangement. In addition, I want your oath that you will accept no other assignments until mine is completed."

Abdel ibn Zaid turned abruptly from her and moved with crisp steps to the altar. Kneeling before it, he bowed his head and intoned, "I swear in the name of Rimahn, lord of the darkness, that I and my companions will pursue the death of Prince Ahamad; that he will die at the hands of the rimahniya unless kismet decrees him some other death first; that I will accept no other assignments until this one is completed; and that I will die by my own hand should my missio prove a failure."

Shammara nodded as he stood again. The oath of the rimahniya was known to be binding. "As an added incentive," she said, "if you are successful within a year's time I will help you establish a temple of your own within the walls of Ravan. No more will the rimahniya be outcasts in the mountains; you can reach for the glory that is your rightful due."

The fanatic gleam glowed ever brighter in ibn Zaid's eyes. "Prince Ahmad's head will grace your tower post by the end of next spring's rains," he promised solemnly.

Thus did each of the bargainers achieve what they wanted. Even though Yusef bin Nard had predicted that Prince Ahmad would not return to Ravan to disturb her rule, Shammara would not rely solely on that to keep her safe. She believed firmly in doing what could be done to ensure that prophecies occurred as predicted—and perhaps the prediction would come true *because* she was taking this action. Her deal with the rimahniya guaranteed her safe rule in Ravan, and she could now turn all her attention to the next item on her agenda—the marriage of Princess Oma to her son, Prince Haroun.

And for Abel ibn Zaid, the bargain promised much money in the rimahniya coffers—but more importantly, it promised a foothold at last in the world's greatest city. With that as a beginning, Parsina would soon be as it should be—under Rimahn's rule . . . and his.

12

THE KING OF KHMERIA

HILE Prince Ahmad stayed in Estanash's cave to guard the unconscious Murrah against any other hazards lurking there, Selima raced back to the entrance to tell Cari of their triumph. The Jann had already sensed the dissolution of the spells protecting the cave, and was flying toward her. They met in the cramped, dusty passageway and Selima told Cari of the victory. The Jann then sped off to tell Jafar al-Sharif and the waiting Badawi warriors to come ahead and share in the loot of the deceased Jinn. Jafar and the Badawi descended into the wadi, crept through the narrow cave opening, and followed Selima to the late Jinn's cave.

Nusair ibn Samman's eyes widened at the sight that greeted them. There was no sign of the evil Estanash who'd so plagued the Badawi for ages—but there was Murrah, apparently unharmed by her captor except for chafed wrists and ankles and total exhaustion. And there was treasure, mountains of it piled against the wall, its sum surpassing even the greediest dreams of a desert nomad. It gleamed and glittered in the torchlight—coins and jewels and beautiful objects made from precious materials, as well as packs of exotic fabrics, decanters of wine, boxes of dates and figs, and bottles of precious olive oil that were sealed as fresh as new.

Prince Ahmad welcomed the Badawi to the cave with a formal bow. "Estanash, your enemy, is dead," he proclaimed.

"His treasure is mine by right of conquest. Since I have all the money I need for now I bestow this treasure on you, O shaykh, in repayment for your gracious hospitality to strangers traveling through the desert."

Nusair ibn Samman's men raced forward unbelieving to run their hands through the treasure for themselves, laughing like children with new toys. The shaykh himself walked more slowly over to the side of his daughter Murrah, bent over her to see that she was unharmed, then wept openly at the joy of her return to him as he began to strike off the chains that held her to the stone niche. Jafar al-Sharif watched him with bittersweet envy; his own daughter was still as far from life and safety as ever, even though her presence stood lovingly at his side.

A rider was dispatched back to the caravan to tell them all was well, and the rest of the afternoon was spent sorting through the piles of loot the rapacious Jinn had accumulated over the ages. The nature of most items was readily apparent, but there were three things that puzzled the Badawi. Nusair ibn Samman brought them over to Umar and Jafar for their inspection.

The first item was a strange cap made of some shiny, silvery material that was as light as cloth yet glittered as though it were metal. The second object was a heavy wooden staff, knobby and thick at one end tapering almost to a point at the other. There was some writing embroidered around the rim of the cap and carved onto the staff to identify those items.

The third object was the most mysterious. It looked as though it might be a key, but the end that should have been notched to turn the tumblers in some lock was perfectly smooth and cylindrical. It was half a cubit long and solid brass, and it had no writing on it to explain its purpose. The only marking was a pair of wings etched into the middle in a peculiar design.

Umar examined all three objects carefully, then handed them over to Jafar. "Since these are objects of magic, they rightfully fall into your domain," he said. "At least, the first two are magical; this third," and he turned the almost-key over again in his hands, "is a mystery I can't fathom. Perhaps with your knowledge of the arcane arts you can solve its riddle."

"Perhaps," Jafar nodded solemnly. He took the items from Umar and examined them closely. He could recognize some of the letters in the writing by this time, but the words they formed still eluded him. He made a great show of studying the objects, then tucked them away saying, "The study of these must wait until a leisure moment when I can devote my full attention to them. Right now I, for one, would be grateful if you'd lead us in a prayer of gratitude to Oromasd for giving us the victory this day." Prince Ahmad and the Badawi warriors echoed that sentiment, and Umar gladly recited an impromptu thanks to the creator for helping the prince and Selima overcome their powerful foe.

By this time it was nearly nightfall and the Badawi were anxious to return to camp with their loot. They could not carry it all, and Nusair ibn Samman wisely decided not to try. If his tribe suddenly became too wealthy, it would incur the suspicion and jealousy of all the other Badawi tribes. Better far, he reasoned, to keep this stash in reserve and draw on it a little at a time; that would keep his people prosperous and free from want, but also free of intertribal enmities. They took enough coins to buy all the things they would need at the next bazaar, about a fourth of the food (as much as they could eat—no, feast on—in the upcoming trip and still have just enough normal left over to trade in Tannakesh), and a few gaudy trinkets for the women, including several special pieces for Murrah; the rest they left there in the cave for the future. Even though every place in the desert looked the same to Jafar, the nomad shaykh assured him the tribe could find this cave again when they needed to.

They ran into an unexpected problem getting out. The men and Murrah could, with some difficulty, climb out of the wadi but Selima, unable to grab hold of objects, could not scale the sides. After a few moments' thought, the answer occurred to Jafar. Since she could stand and sit on objects, he had Selima sit on top of one of the trunks from the Jinn's cave, and two husky Badawi pulled the trunk out of the wadi on ropes. Selima mounted her horse in her usual manner and the party rode back to camp.

There would be no traveling this night. This was a night for celebration and gaiety, for good food and a sampling of the wine and fruit they'd taken from the sand Jinn's cave. It was a night for singing and whistling and clapping of hands, for dancing around the sand until the dancer collapsed happily from exhaustion. Even though the Badawi hadn't slept during the day, they found reserves of energy to continue their revel late into the night.

After the first half hour of celebration, Jafar al-Sharif walked off by himself to ponder the three magical objects he'd been given this afternoon. He summoned Cari to him and they looked over the cap, the staff, and the strange keylike object. Cari examined each of the items in turn before giving her diagnosis.

"The embroidered lettering around the base of the cap," she explained, "says it is a magical cap of truth. When placed on someone's head, that person must answer as many as three questions truthfully. I suppose that could be useful to us someday; we should definitely bring it along with us.

"The wooden staff has a legend engraved on it: 'This is the staff of Achmet the terrifying who, with the aid of its mystical powers, can call down the lightning from the clouds.' I assume that means it's a tool you could use to direct lightning out of the sky to strike down your enemies."

"That could be *very* useful," Jafar said. "I'll definitely want to keep that. Am I right in assuming I'd use it the same way I used the carpet?"

"I'm not highly schooled in wizardry, but it seems logical," Cari said. "If you used the staff to focus your will, you could draw down the lightning and direct it where you wanted it by pointing the staff."

"Is there any special magical word that must be used?"

Cari looked the staff over carefully again from top to bottom. "If there is, it isn't written here—and it would be impossible to guess."

"Then we'll just have to hope there isn't a special word needed," Jafar said. He picked up the mysterious almost-key and held it before his face; the shiny brass gleamed in the camp's firelight. "And what is this?" he continued. "Have you any ideas at all?"

"None I'm afraid, O my master," Cari said. "I've never seen anything like it and it has no writing on it to give me a clue to its purpose—just that strange design of the two wings, and I've never seen anything like that before, either. It looks like it should be inserted in something and turned, but the details are beyond me. It is a total mystery."

Jafar al-Sharif continued to stare with fascination at the metal key. He did not want to become burdened down with things he couldn't use and was tempted to throw it away, but some instinct refused to let him do that. "Estanash the Jinn collected many things," he mused in a low voice. "His cave was heaped with loot, yet nowhere in there did I see anything that was not valuable. He must have had discerning taste, to separate out all the trash that would accumulate during the centuries. And yet he kept this key that has no apparent use, this key that fits nothing in his cavern. He could easily have tossed it into the desert sands, yet he kept it in his collection even as he kept the cap and the staff. I'm tempted to believe it must do *something*, even if we don't know yet what that is."

"But just because it does something doesn't mean it'll do *us* any good," Cari pointed out. "For all we know, it may open the door to a treasure room in some faraway castle we'll never visit. It could be very valuable and still be of no use to us."

Jafar pondered some more. "Kismet has been playing tricks on us since our whole adventure started," he said. "It weaves our destiny in bizarre patterns as we travel the road the prophet Muhmad foretold. You rescued me from the dungeons when I had no right to expect any help, and I rescued you from service to Akar. It took us to Sarafiq to meet Prince Ahmad, even though we each came by separate routes that should never have intersected. Who are we to say, then, that this key will never come in handy to us? Mysterious indeed are the workings of Oromasd, and far be it from me to doubt his powers. If he wants us to use this key, he'll find a way to make it happen. In the meantime it is light and easy enough to carry. I'll ask if Nusair ibn Samman has a thong I can borrow; I'll tie the key to that and wear it around my neck until I find some use to put it to."

Elsewhere in the camp, Prince Ahmad also wandered away from the revelry. His body was stiff and sore from the ordeal he'd undergone in the Jinn's cave that afternoon, and though he was elated by his triumph he was too tired to celebrate with the others. He stood by himself looking up at the stars through the clear nighttime sky until a slight movement attracted his attention out of the corner of his eye. He turned quickly, not being sure what to expect.

At first he saw nothing there and thought he must have imagined the movement—and then he made out the faint form of Selima standing a short distance away, barely visible in firelight that came from the other side of the camp. She too had walked away from the festivities and was observing the desert sky. She did not seem to have noticed him, but stood alone and pensive in the night.

Prince Ahmad took a moment to decide what to do, then walked over to her side. She must have seen him coming, but she made no move either to turn away or greet him; she simply stood staring at the southern horizon as though it held some great and timeless mystery for her to unravel.

"My finest compliments to you, O brave Selima," the prince greeted her. "Your quick actions this afternoon saved me from both the lion and the Jinn."

"It's easy to be brave when you know you're dead anyway," Selima replied in a near monotone. "I'm glad I could save you, of course, but I did nothing extraordinary."

"Very few would have thought quickly enough to distract the Jinn and give me time to get the sword," Prince Ahmad persisted. "That was you alone deserving of credit."

"Very well, I'll accept that," she said absently.

The prince took a deep breath and let it out slowly. "You're not very happy, are you?"

"I see I can have no secrets from you, can I?" she snapped, then immediately apologized. "Oh, Your Highness, I'm sorry, I didn't mean to be rude. It's just that everyone else seems to be cheerful and I just can't share in it."

"Why not? What's wrong?"

"Nothing—at least, nothing that hasn't been wrong all along. We saved young Murrah from death today. That's wonderful, I'm delighted for her—but who is there to save me? Nothing's changed. I'm still half in the world of the living, half in the grip of death. Rescuing Murrah only makes it more obvious how precarious my own life is."

"Your father's trying very hard to fulfill the prophet's vision," Prince Ahmad said. "He's a mighty wizard, he should be able to do it." Even as he said this he felt an inner sense of guilt, knowing that Muhmad had said Jafar would lose his daughter even if he succeeded with the Crystal of Oromasd—but he had to do what he could to keep the girl's spirits up.

Selima gave a half smile, as though at some private joke, but all she said was, "Even mighty wizards aren't infallible."

"I'll be helping him," the prince continued. "I know no magic, but I'll fight at his side to get him the pieces of the Crystal he needs to fulfill Muhmad's prophecy."

"You'll do what you can to save Parsina from Rimahn's clutches, I'm sure of that," Selima said.

"I have my duty to Oromasd, of course," Prince Ahmad said, "but I won't be doing it for Oromasd alone."

Selima blinked and, for the first time, looked directly into his face. "What do you mean?"

It was Prince Ahmad, this time, who looked quickly away. He was regretting his rigorous, masculine-dominated up-bringing that had kept him from learning how to talk to women, especially young, pretty ones. "Well, you are a very special lady, intelligent and brave. If there is any justice in this world, Oromasd will help your father and me save you from your horrible fate."

"You are very kind and noble, as a good prince ought to be," she said. "It was your kindness and nobility that led you to rescue Murrah; selfishly, I can hope you'll be able to do the same for me."

She looked at him and rallied her spirits enough to smile. "On this night, then, I'll allow myself a little hope, even though I know it'll bring me pain in the morning when my condition is unchanged. Thank you, Your Highness, for your civility to the daughter of a humble stor—sorcerer."

She turned abruptly and went back to the camp fire where the revels were still going on. Prince Ahmad, though, stood out alone in the desert yet another hour before wandering back.

The celebration lasted well past midnight, by which time everyone was ready to collapse from exhaustion. Most people slept past noon the next day, and then there was a bustle of activity even in the midday heat as there were animals to be watered and fed.

Jafar and Selima, waking in late afternoon, took an extra long reading lesson from Cari. Jafar was encouraged at how well he and his daughter were doing, and commented on it to Cari. The Jann merely nodded and said, "It's as I suspected it would be. The hardest part of learning to read is developing a vocabulary. This is why a child takes years to read well. Both of you—and particularly you, O master—are already well skilled with words; you know what they mean and how to use them. You simply can't recognize them in written form. Once you learn how to connect the written symbols with the sounds of the words themselves, you'll be fine readers."

The Badawi caravan spent another three nights traveling across the Kholaj Desert until they reached the town of Tannakesh. Here they disposed of the goods they'd been paid to deliver across the desert and here, in the modest bazaar, they spent some of the treasure from the sand Jinn's cave to replace their supplies that were running low. Here, too, was where they parted company with Prince Ahmad's group, whose destiny lay further to the east.

There were embraces and fond words of farewell as the two groups parted. Even though they'd known each other little more than a week, strong bonds of friendship had been formed between the people of such different worlds—and Prince Ahmad's daring rescue of Murrah had cemented the friendship for all time. The tribe was now rich because of that, and the Badawi prided themselves on honoring their debts.

Before the final parting, Nusair ibn Samman reiterated his pledge to speak on Prince Ahmad's behalf at the upcoming Badawi council, and to convince the other tribes to join in the approaching war against the forces of Rimahn. "I guarantee they will join in the fight, or else be branded cowards and traitors for all time," the shaykh said. "We will assemble, as I've pledged, on the Leewahr Plains fifty parasangs south of Ravan by the first floods of spring, and there will the Badawi show their strength and dedication to Oromasd."

Whatever doubts Nusair ibn Samman may have held about the sanity and identity of his guests had been left in the cave of Estanash. All his influence, and decades of favors, would be used to gather these tribes for Oromasd, and for these brave new friends.

With that pledge renewed they parted company, and Prince Ahmad's party left Tannakesh early the next morning, heading east. Now that they were out of the desert and no longer worried about the scorching heat of the midday sun they could return to the normal schedule of traveling during the day and resting at night. Being able to see clearly where they were going and moving over solid ground instead of shifting sands, they made much better time than they'd made while traveling through the Kholaj Desert.

The way from Tannakesh through Kandestan into Indi was a well-traveled route, and their journeying was far easier than it had been through the desert. The roads were clear and well marked, traveling through fields and forests and broad, open plains. The maps they'd been given in Sarafiq stood them in good stead through this portion of their journey and they were able to move without incident.

They were even saved the bother of camping out, for caravanserais had been erected along the road, each one-day's travel away from the next. Historically these way stations catered to all travelers, and would have lodged the prince's group for free if they'd been destitute. With plenty of money to spend, however, the travelers paid a fair price for the lodgings and meals the caravanserais provided.

As always, Selima was a problem, for she would draw attention to them wherever they went. To solve the problem, Cari would materialize as they neared a caravanserai and modestly wrap herself and Selima's ghostly form within a large black cloak. Thus covered head to toe, the two women would walk as one through the courtyard—and though their gait looked a bit odd, no one commented much about it, and certainly not as much as they would have commented had they seen Selima. Jafar's daughter would then stay hidden in his room while the men went out to have their meals in the communal dining room. Food would be sent to Cari, as the woman who kept modestly hidden, to complete the deception.

Their route led them to fords where they could easily cross the smaller streams and rivers, and they hired ferries to carry them across the expanse of the mighty Harrud and Meshkal rivers. By taking this route they were traveling well to the south of Marakh and, they hoped, out of danger from its treacherous King Basir.

They talked as they rode and came to know one another better. Jafar al-Sharif had a chance to practice many of his favorite old stories, and some of the less well known ones he adapted and changed to describe his own wizardly exploits.

Sometimes, too, Umar continued Prince Ahmad's lessons as he'd sworn to do before they left Ravan—and even Jafar and Selima, listening in, managed to learn some new things.

The more private reading lessons that Jafar and Selima were taking from Cari the Jann continued apace. Letter by letter Jafar was mastering the alphabet and he was fascinated by how the letters, alone and in blends easily learned, represented the sounds he was so skilled with. Already he could go through the opening pages of Ali Maimun's journal and pick out some of the simpler words that used only the letters he'd learned to date; he could also guess at other words that used only a few unknown letters by their context in this classically formed introduction, so like those in the stories he'd told for years. He was quite proud of his progress. Selima was equally quick to learn, and Jafar commented that they would represent the first two generations of his family, for as far back as anyone could remember, who would know how to read.

The one discouraging fact was that the journal of Ali Maimun would not open for them any more than it had on the day they'd first found it. They were drawing closer to Punjar all the time, the place where the first piece of the Crystal of Oromasd was supposedly hidden, and they still had no idea of where in that country the Crystal was to be found. Jafar al-Sharif could only hope the book would be more cooperative once they reached their destination.

They entered the vast tropical area known as Indi, and Umar bin Ibrahim suggested they stop in the kingdom of Khmeria, which was along their route to Punjar. Umar had some contacts among the clergy there, so they could be guaranteed of a safe reception—and the king of Khmeria had a reputation for righteousness that made Umar doubt he would ever be in league with Shammara.

None of the travelers, except for Cari, had ever been in a tropical climate before. Rain sometimes fell in the summer, a soft warm mist that lightly soaked them to their skin—and even when it wasn't raining the hot, sticky weather made them all uncomfortable. The smell of the verdant area, though, refreshed the travelers, who'd felt dessicated by the desert; the land in between had hardly touched the feeling. Here, the proliferation of flowers and the richness of their color often led Umar to praise the beauty of Oromasd's creation, though in the next breath he cursed Rimahn's allies, the midges, mosquitos, and flies. For once Selima was glad she could feel none of the effects of the weather and the insects.

The fields around them grew green with crops even Umar, with all his knowledge, couldn't identify. The rain forests through which the trail led them could almost be called jungles, with the broad green leaves of the trees so dense overhead they often shut out all sight of the sun. Umar cautioned that these forests were reputed to be the home of strange and ferocious beasts, but Cari kept on watch for them and none ever crossed their path. The caravanserais along this portion of the route were older, more delapidated, less used than they'd encountered elsewhere. Most commercial traffic these days took a more northerly path through Marakh, something Prince Ahmad could not afford to do, so the travelers received a generous welcome at these places. If it were not for the urgency of their mission it would have been a delightful journey. Jafar al-Sharif took advantage of the inns to do a little storytelling, telling his comrades it was one of a wizard's minor talents. He enjoyed the familiar power over the audiences, and it gave him some added self-confidence.

More than two weeks after leaving Tannakesh, several hours past sunup, the travelers topped a hill and looked down into the peaceful green valley that held the capital city of Khmeria. They'd all heard of it before, and they stopped in awe to look at this historic site.

Khmeria, the hub of Indi, had been ancient long before King Shahriyan decided to build Ravan. Its origins ran well back into mythic times, and Jafar al-Sharif was quite familiar with the tale of how the first Khmeri king, Kushtan, cheated the river Jinn into ceding him the land on which the ancient city was built. Five different dynasties thrived on this site over the millennia, and Khmeria's fortunes rose and fell like a predictable tide. Wars had scarred the land and peace had healed it, repeating in endless cycles. Ferocious battles had raged up and down the length of this river valley that now looked so peaceful in the morning sunlight. Jafar al-Sharif knew there were whole sagas of the Khmeri heroes and their marvelous exploits, of which he only knew highlights and fragments. Khmeria was a land out of legend, one of those faraway places he'd often talked about but never expected to see with his own eyes.

Looking down into this valley, the travelers could see the Induri River wending its way to the south. The river was broad and deceptively still. On a large island directly in the center sat the ancient city of Khmeria. The travelers, looking at it, had to agree that few cities, even blessed Ravan, were as favored and impressive as the spectacle they now beheld.

The city was built in the shape of an enormous rectangle, several parasangs in length and breadth, with high stone walls defending it from attack. The river acted like a natural moat around the island, breached only on the east and west by bridges spanning the narrow forks and leading into the city's two large gates. Khmeria was a city of high towers, each topped with the bulbous shape of a lotus blossom; the entire municipal area looked like an enormous field of stone flowers. Even the traditional minarets with their constant flames bearing the welcome of Oromasd echoed the lotus decor. The city was so vast that two Ravans could have fit quite comfortably within its walls, though feature for feature Khmeria could not begin to compare with the beauty of the Holy City.

"Here is where our mission truly starts," Umar said to break the group's long silence. "If we can convince the Khmeri king to follow our cause, the rest of Indi will fall in line and we'll have the southeast quadrant of Parsina behind us. King Armandor is noted for his fair and just rule. We can hope he'll give us his heart as well as his ear."

They rode down the hillside toward the river with Cari flying invisibly beside the horses as usual. Distances were deceiving here, and it took longer to reach the city than they thought—which made its size even more impressive when they finally came up to it. They reached the western gate by late morning, declared themselves to be peaceful travelers on a pilgrimage, and were admitted to this fabled city.

Khmeria was a city of crowds. None of the travelers had ever seen so many people living in such cramped conditions in all their lives. People jammed the streets, people mobbed the bazaars, people thronged through every space available to put them. Even in this huge city there weren't enough houses for everyone, and many people simply lived out in the streets where the wind and the weather took their toll. It was impossible to get through the surging crowds on horseback; the travelers, except for Selima, had to dismount and lead their horses on foot to make any progress.

Many of the men here were thin and bony, and dressed in simple dhotis; even those who were rich enough to wear full kaftans wore ones of simple cotton with basic embroidery. There were more women on the street here than in Ravan, dressed in colorful cotton saris and shawls over their heads, but their faces were left uncovered in public. Almost everyone walked barefoot, but a few wore sandals. Men's turbans were ~~tied~~ differently here, wrapped in a much looser and infor- manner.

The streets smelled oddly of sweat and strange spices, and noise from all these people, hawking their wares or talking their friends, was a deafening babble; the travelers won-ed how anyone managed to stay sane within this constant n. Bright colors were rampant here, providing a din for the eyes as well. It was the fashion to hang brightly colored tapes-tries from the roofs of most houses down the side walls, giv-ing a festive appearance; perhaps the inhabitants felt this eased the feeling of crowded conditions within their city.

The travelers attracted many stares as they led their horses through the streets of Khmeria—the men because they were wearing such fine clothes of a foreign cut, and Selima because of her ghostly nature. No one hindered them, though; in a city as crowded as Khmeria, people learned to respect one another's privacy. Umar asked directions of people he met, though it was difficult to understand the replies because the Khmeri spoke in a lilting, singsong style that was alien to the travelers' ears. At last, by asking enough people, the group was able to make its way through the crowded streets to Khmeria's main temple.

The Khmeri temple was old, far older than the Temple of the Faith in Ravan, but was still laid out in the traditional rectangular pattern of outer and inner walls around a central courtyard. The walls were of bare stone, weathered by the rains and winds of tropical centuries; moss and weeds were even growing between some of the stones of the outer walls. Unlike temples in the less humid parts of Parsina, the sahn here was covered by a roof to protect the worshipers from the elements during services.

Umar bin Ibrahim had long been in correspondence with the high priest of Khmeria, a devoted man named Sarojin Fadakir. When Umar gave his name to one of the young priests who questioned him at the temple door, he was quickly escorted into Fadakir's chambers while the others of his party waited in the riwaq. Fadakir was delighted to finally meet his illustrious compatriot face-to-face, and asked what had occasioned this surprise visit. Umar temporized, not wanting to tell too much of the story now, and instead asked Fadakir if he could get Umar and his companions an audience with the king on a matter of utmost urgency. Sarojin Fadakir promised to do what he could.

The priest was as good as his word, and by midafternoon the travelers were ushered into the presence of King Armandor, monarch of all Khmeria. King Armandor was a man in his sixties who dressed with simple dignity; he eschewed the fine silks and satins that many monarchs wore, preferring the simple cotton fabrics instead. His robes and his turban were finely tailored, but of common cloth; his visitors were all dressed more splendidly.

But King Armandor's regal nature was revealed by much more than his clothes. He was a king, and had reigned for over thirty years. He was renowned far and wide as a just ruler beloved by his people, and this reputation was reflected in his countenance. He was a man who could be both stern and compassionate, decisive and caring. His eyes missed no detail as he watched his visitors approach down the long hall to his dais.

The audience hall of the Khmeri palace was less than half the size of the one in the palace of Ravan, and far less well appointed. The tile floor had been worn through the glazing in the main aisles and been replaced in different places by slightly different colors. The whole floor was now a tone-on-tone crisscrossing of rich gray and gold arabesque patterned tile. In such humble detail did the majesty of this ancient building speak to the visitors.

The pillars supporting the arches of the ceiling were of brick and stone, and the bare stone walls were hung with fine and ancient tapestries to give a feeling of warmth. A brazier burning rose petal incense stood to the right of the throne while one of King Armandor's fine hunting cheetahs, imported all the way from Fricaz, lolled at the monarch's feet. The courtiers in attendance were clustered much more closely about the king than was common in Ravan.

Sarojin Fadakir introduced Umar bin Ibrahim to the king. King Armandor stroked the pet mongoose seated in his lap nodded graciously and said, "Welcome to Khmeria, O il-lustrious priest. The doors of my palace are always open to a holy man from the Holy City. Sarojin tells me you wish to speak on a matter of great urgency. It must be urgent indeed to bring you all this distance. Please tell me what the matter is."

Umar gave a formal salaam. "Your Majesty, may you live forever, I have the honor of presenting to you His Highness Prince Ahmad Khaled bin Shunnar el-Ravani, prince of Ravan."

The prince stepped forward and made his own salaam. He had chosen for this occasion to wear the same spectacular out-fit he'd worn on his departure from Ravan: a Sadre and white silk sirwaal trousers tucked into calfskin leather boots, over which he wore his light blue zibun embroidered in silver thread and fastened at the waist with a silver sash. His white turban was set with a sapphire the size of a hen's egg, and rings of silver and turquoise circled his fingers. These were clothes to command respect, and the court of Khmeria was duly impressed with the handsome young man they saw.

King Armandor's eyes widened ever so slightly, but that was his only visible reaction to this stalwart stranger. He con-tinued stroking the mongoose and his voice was formally po-lite as he said, "Your Highness does me great honor by this unexpected visit. Had I more warning I could have prepared a welcome more in keeping with your station."

"None of us are getting much warning of things these days, Your Majesty," Ahmad said, "but I bring you news that may yet avert a worldwide calamity."

King Armandor wrinkled his brow; he did not like riddles. "What do you mean?"

Prince Ahmad related to him the story of how he'd been betrayed and cast out from the city he was meant to rule. The king listened to the tale with growing fury on his face. "You will find safe haven in Khmeria, I assure you," he declared. "Fifteen years ago I had cause to visit the Holy City and your father treated me with fine hospitality. I doubt you remember it, you were only a child, barely walking. King Shunnar was a good man, and in his memory I offer you the safety and pro-tection of Khmeria, however you require it."

"Your Majesty is most noble and generous," said the prince, "but I don't come here seeking refuge. Indeed,

Khmeria is but one stop along the path I must travel, albeit an important one. My exile from Ravan is of but minor significance compared to the true tragedy that may befall mankind."

Prince Ahmad went on to describe the vision given him by Muhmad the prophet, and how he was to rally the armies of mankind to oppose the forces of Aeshma that would soon be massing. He introduced the mighty wizard Jafar al-Sharif whose duty was to gather the pieces of the Crystal of Oromasd and use their power to defeat the daevas. King Armandor and his advisers listened in silence and growing apprehension to the story, and when the prince was finished speaking the advisers crowded around the throne to give their opinions of what was needed.

"I urge caution," the first wazir said. "It sounds to me as though this landless prince is asking nothing less than full control of your army for his own purposes."

"He'll get the army, but not full control," King Armandor said. "I myself shall lead the army of Khmeria into this battle."

"But Your Majesty, your age—"

"If we fight in the name of Oromasd, then Oromasd will grant me the strength of youth."

Then, brushing aside his advisers, King Armandor placed his mongoose gently upon the ground, stepped down from his throne and walked forward to embrace Prince Ahmad personally. "In memory of your late father," he said, "I greet you as I would my own son, and I swear to you that your battle will become my battle. The wisdom of the prophet Muhmad is widely known and respected; if he tells you to fight in the name of Oromasd, then the armies of Khmeria will fight with you. I myself will lead my men into the battle."

"Your Majesty honors me with his faith," said Prince Ahmad humbly; and then, echoing the king's own wazirs, he added, "But at your age do you think it's wise—?"

King Armandor brushed aside the objections as he'd done to his counselors. "In the last great battle when men faced the legion of daevas, the armies of Khmeria and all of Indi marched at the right hand of King Shahriyan and distinguished themselves proudly on the field. My ancestor, King Devodar, fell in that battle, and King Shahriyan honored his memory with a golden plaque that hangs elsewhere in this palace. The fighting men of Khmeria today are no less valiant, no less devoted to their creator. It will be our sacred duty to fight at your side against this menace to all mankind. If I were asked on the Bridge of Shinvar why I shirked my sacred duty, could I make the excuse that I was too old to serve Oromasd? What a cowardly response that would be!

"Furthermore, all the other kings of Indi are my firm allies, as are many of the kings in Sinjin. I shall apprise them of your message and exhort them to rally to our cause as well. When you come to that battlefield next spring, the east will be well represented, that I swear to you.

"But enough of solemn talk for now," he said as his mood brightened. "You and your honorable companions must be weary after so many days of travel on the road. You must relax and enjoy the civilized pleasures again—good food, wine, music. Stay with me a week and accept my hospitality, and then be on your way with the blessings of Oromasd."

"A week we cannot spare," the prince said, "much though your invitation tempts me. Each day we delay gives the forces of Rimahn that much longer to gather their strength, and we're already far behind the pace we should be setting if we're to circle Parsina before spring. Still, our spirits and our bodies could use some respite from the grueling regimen of the trail. Can we compromise on one night's hospitality before we must be on our way to Punjar?"

King Armandor's eyes widened. "Punjar? You travel to Punjar?"

"Yes, why? What's the matter?" asked Prince Ahmad.

King Armandor shook his head. "We don't have many dealings with Punjar. Few people do. King Zargov is reputed to be—well, bizarre, and not a little dangerous. Were you going anywhere else in the east I could give you a passport under my personal seal and guarantee your safety in any land—but my word means nothing in Punjar. King Zargov has been quiet for many years, making no trouble for his neighbors, but he is not very stable. If you travel there you may be in peril."

"We have no choice but to go there," Prince Ahmad said. "Peril or not, Muhmad's vision drives us onward."

King Armandor sighed. "Then my hospitality must be even greater to honor your courage and dedication. For this night, the city of Khmeria will open to your every need, and after that—after that, we must pray Oromasd will open King Zargov's eyes to goodness and spare you pain in the land of Punjar."

13

THE DUEL OF SORCERY

 HE weeks since he'd come to the palace of Rashwenath passed in a monotonous blur for Hakem Rafi the thief. As Aeshma had promised, the palace was restored to its former grandeur; never since the far-off days of Rashwenath himself had spendor such as this been seen in Parsina, not even in the golden city of Ravan.

The walls of the palace were of alabaster that gleamed as though it were alive, and of marble so polished it reflected like a mirror. Inlaid mosaics pleased the observer's eye, and jewels set in the walls sparkled with unearthly brilliance. Tapestries from all corners of Parsina, each of different colors and designs, hung against the walls of the smaller rooms, and these rooms were of numbers beyond counting. Doorways were carved in exquisite pointed arches, and domed ceilings soared high above the floors. Each room had at least one fountain and many had several, all spraying water and allowing the breezes that blew through the palace to cool the air.

Those breezes stirred the tapestries that gave the themes to the different rooms. Hakem Rafi's bedrooms had erotic tapestries depicting every possible, and some impossible, sex act. The rooms containing his hawks showed scenes of them hunting. In niches and beside doorways were ornaments of every kind: elaborately carved plaques of ivory from Indi, Sinjinese jade statuettes, rare Fricazi woods, and jewel-encrusted precious metal plates. Most of these depicted beautiful women, while a few showed scenes from myths and history. Tables in many rooms were finely detailed and held embossed brass samovars or dishes of fruit and other snack food.

The floor plan of the palace was designed so there was at least a small hosh within a few hundred cubits of any spot, as well as vast courtyards planted with flowers and trees. Exotic birds hung in cages against the walls singing pleasantly all the day and brightening the atmosphere with their colorful plumage. Baskets of flower petals, picked fresh each day from the extensive gardens, scented the rooms with the natural smells of floral perfume, while other rooms were scented with delicious incense or the smells of fresh-cooked food.

A palace this huge required constant attention, and Aeshma provided the necessary staff. Each hosh had its own gardener, and there was an additional army of gardeners to care for the spacious courtyards. Still more servants were constantly bustling about feeding the birds, polishing the walls and floor, beating dust from tapestries, polishing the silver and gold ornaments, washing clothes and dishes, and in every way keeping the palace clean and functioning. Musicians roamed constantly through the corridors, and the halls were alive with the sound of music. In addition to these were the dozens of servants required just to wait on Hakem Rafi's personal needs.

Hakem Rafi had never dressed so well in his life, nor had he ever heard of anyone who had. He had turbans of every color in the rainbow, and so many changes of clothing he could have worn three different outfits a day for a month and still not have repeated himself or exhausted the possibilities. He wore the softest leathers, the sheerest silks, the smoothest satins, the richest cloth-of-gold. There would be no more cheap, coarse materials scratching his skin; only the softest, most luxurious fabrics caressed his bony body. His fingers were covered with rings holding only the finest gems—diamonds and sapphires, emeralds and rubies all sparkled, each stone perfect, each larger than the richest merchant in Ravan could have dreamed of owning. His turbans, too, sported large gems that flashed in the light and made him feel like an emperor.

His body was given pampered treatment. Hakem Rafi had his own private hammam where he bathed at least once, and often two or three times, a day and where a skilled servant massaged his body with fragrant oils. Another servant trimmed his hair and beard daily and gave him manicures and pedicures. No fleas, flies, mites, or mosquitos came near his person. Never had Hakem Rafi felt in finer shape.

Aeshma had assembled skilled cooks from all parts of Parsina to prepare Hakem Rafi's meals, and each cook brought with him the knowledge of his native cuisine. Each meal was different, each dish an adventure. Hakem Rafi made culinary travels to Indi for curried dishes, to Sinjin for stir-fried marvels, to Norgeland for smoked fish, to Nikhrash for stuffed grape leaves, to Fricaz for fried insects. Each meal seemed finer than the one before, each dish brought new taste sensations to be experienced and savored. Hakem Rafi ate better in one average day than he'd previously eaten in an average week, and he gained weight accordingly. While no amount of overeating would ever turn his spare frame to fat, the extra weight did fill out the exaggerated leanness in his limbs and in his face that came from many years of starvation and malnutrition. His cheeks were no longer cadaverous and his bones acquired a bit of flesh.

With adequate shelter, adequate clothing, and adequate food—three commodities he'd always considered the greatest luxuries, and had seldom possessed all at the same time—Hakem Rafi's thoughts turned next to women. Once again, Aeshma catered to his needs with abundance. The king of the daevas scoured the world for beauties to add to his master's harem—doe-eyed, brown-skinned ladies from Indi, strapping and muscular black women from Fricaz, statuesque fair-skinned blonds from the northern reaches of Norgeland, delicate yet strong women from the mysterious climes of Sinjin . . . all manner, shape, and color of women, each in her own way trembling with desire for the feel of Hakem Rafi's body against her. The thief was so inundated with the sight and scent and sensation of female flesh that his spirits grew quite jaded. He was not impotent—Aeshma provided him with elixirs to stave off that worry—but his mind was so overwhelmed by the constant experience of female desire that he soon went beyond caring. He tried some slender young catamites in search of diversion, but quickly tired of that sport, too. Eventually he reached a stage where he would visit his harem for sheer physical release as casually as another man might visit the hammam, then left the women there while he went off on other pursuits.

Hakem Rafi had always been a man with a petty, vindictive mind—and now that he was free to indulge even his slightest whim, that mind took a particularly vicious turn. He'd spent many long, hungry nights cataloging the wrongs done to him over the years by one person or another; some of these offenses were quite real, while others were merely products of his fevered imagination. But now that the power was his, he vowed to avenge every slight ever done to him, and he set about doing so in spectacular fashion.

He would order Aeshma to bring each offender before him to face his wrath. One time it might be the former partner in crime who'd cheated him out of some loot; another time it might be the sadistic policeman who beat him before accepting a bribe not to arrest him; still another time it might be the woman innkeeper who slammed the door in his face while he was fleeing the police, forcing him to seek shelter elsewhere.

One after another he had them brought to face him as he sat upon a jeweled throne in the main hall of his magnificent palace, and he would recite to them the crimes of which he'd already convicted them. When the miscreants looked around and saw the power of life and death he held over them, they invariably knelt and wept and begged for his mercy. Occasionally, if the offense was slight enough, the groveling might suffice to appease his anger and he would let the offender go— but in most cases nothing would soothe Hakem Rafi's feelings except full retribution for the injury he'd suffered. Those whom Aeshma did return were spellbound never to talk of this but, in one of Hakem Rafi's cruelest inspirations, they were forced to dream, once a fortnight, of the punishment they'd escaped. Many went mad.

One thing Hakem Rafi the blackhearted never tired of was hearing the cries of his enemies as they suffered the tortures his ingenious mind devised for them. He would sometimes have as many as ten enemies suffering in rings around him at one time, and each one's screams would set off the next, amplifying their terror. His enemies died slowly and painfully under the ministration of the torturers Aeshma provided— but eventually they did die. There was only so much abuse the human body could withstand, and even expert torturers could not keep people alive indefinitely when their spirit decided to depart. Though his list was a long one, counting every slight he'd received down through his childhood, Hakem Rafi at last ran out of enemies to torture. He tried a couple of times with strangers, but he could never invest the same emotional energy into their torture as he could into the people who'd wronged him. Eventually this pastime, too, faded into nothingness.

Seeking other sensory experiences, Hakem Rafi drank exotic wines provided by the ever-obliging Aeshma—wines from the different corners of Parsina, each with its own subtle bouquet and flavor. Hakem Rafi's palate was not sophisticated enough, in most cases, to distinguish between the different kinds, but the wines did allow him to drink himself into a stupor and awake without a trace of a hangover.

Aeshma also provided his master with massive quantities of drugs to make the cares of reality seem less important. Every room held at least one delicate hookah and a box containing the finest hashish compounds: blond from Nikhrash, mixed with the sweet pollen of the plant: rich, black, tarry hashish mixed with opium from Ventina; and the finest upper leaves and buds that had been dried, then dipped again and again in the deep sienna most prized among users of this drug. It was this last that the women of his harem most enjoyed, and Hakem Rafi came to believe the sweet exotic scent was that of women themselves, so heavily did it hang about their rooms as they fought off the boredom in this isolated place with only hashish and one another's company. Aeshma knew that as the weeks wore on and the thrill of possessing the ultimate power wore off, Hakem Rafi would spend more and more of his time with drink and drugs to while away the long, empty days.

This was just fine with Aeshma. A quiescent master was the best master—if one had to have a master at all. The daeva was worried about the Marids who'd come around to spy on him one day, knowing they must have been sent by some powerful wizard—but as time passed and no threat came, he relaxed his guard ever so slightly.

Then one day an enormous eagle flew through the sky from out of the northeast, landing within the outer wall of the palace. The huge bird alit in the outer courtyard beside the ornate flowing fountain, surrounded by pomegranate trees laden with their ripe fruit. A man dismounted from the bird's back—a man dressed in black robes with a black turban, and with black patches over both his eyes. When this man stood firmly on the ground facing the palace, he gave a slight wave of his hand; then the eagle that had borne him flew off again into the clouds and out of sight.

"I am Akar," said the man simply, and although he spoke in level tones his voice carried throughout the grounds. "I come to speak with the master of this palace."

Hakem Rafi, who'd been alerted by Aeshma to the arrival of this intruder, stood at a second story window in the front of his palace and looked down into the courtyard at his visitor. "What should I do?" he asked the daeva.

"You have but to say the word, O my master, and I'll destroy this insolent intruder where he stands," Aeshma replied, unhappy that a random factor should enter his carefully orchestrated plans.

But this was the most interesting thing to happen in many days, and Haken Rafi was not about to let it pass without learning what it was about. "There can be no harm in talking to him," he said, "as long as you remain ready to protect me in case of trouble."

"I'm here to protect you as I swore upon my oath to do, O noble master."

Thus assured, the thief leaned out the window and yelled to the figure below him, "I, Hakem Rafi, am master of this palace. What business brings you to trespass on my grounds?"

"I come on a matter of greatest urgency, O Hakem Rafi: the matter of Aeshma, chiefest of the daevas and satrap of the demons of the Pits of Torment."

Hakem Rafi was immediately defensive. "What do you know of such things?"

"I know he is with you and that you make use of his power," Akar said. "I also know that, as personification of the inventor of lies, Aeshma is the most skilled and powerful liar on the face of Parsina. While you have some control over him, he will find a way to destroy you and then work his evil upon the world."

"I cannot break my oath to protect you and save you from harm," Aeshma insisted with a harsh whisper in Hakem Rafi's ear.

"He is sworn in Rimahn's name to protect and obey me," Hakem Rafi repeated to Akar. "If you came merely to warn me, you traveled in vain."

"I came to offer you a partnership," Akar replied.

"What do you have to offer?"

Akar spread his hands and lightning flashed across the cloudless sky behind him. "Know you that I am Akar, the world's most powerful wizard. Know, too, that no untrained mortal can control the powers of Aeshma for very long. Soon, no matter what he has sworn to you, he will burst the bonds you've set for him and pursue his own ends. Only I, of all the people in the world, have both the knowledge and the power to chain him against his will and turn his abilities to profitable use."

Hakem Rafi knew a moment of doubt. He'd seen the power and abilities of Aeshma, and knew how strong the daeva was; but this strange wizard had a confidence that also bespoke power. What if Akar's claims were true, that he could overcome Aeshma? What, then, would happen to Hakem Rafi?

"To what 'profitable use' would you put him?" he asked the wizard in the courtyard.

"With his power added to mine, I would rule the world," Akar said with no trace of idle boastfulness. "All the petty princes and quarrelsome kings would fall before my advance. The world would be united in one kingdom under a single regime of justice."

"And what about me?" Hakem Rafi asked. "What am I supposed to get out of this?"

"You would be my wazir, receiving the full honors due the man who discovered Aeshma," Akar said. "You would have fame, wealth, respect—everything a man could wish. You have but to deliver Aeshma into my hands to make it all yours."

Aeshma had been closely watching this wizard standing by the fountain, and did not like what he saw. Hakem Rafi was a weak-willed fool, easily misled by gaudy trinkets, easily guided by the winsome words of someone cleverer than he. This Akar was none of these. He had the aura about him of a man much practiced in magic, a man who knew what he wanted and how to obtain it. Aeshma's powers were great, but he'd been confined for thousands of years in a small urn and he'd not yet recovered his full strength. In a test of magics and wills Aeshma felt he'd probably win—but the battle would be more trying than he'd care to think about.

"The man offers you nothing, O master," Aeshma whispered seductively in Hakem Rafi's ear. "You already have wealth beyond men's dreams, servants at your beck and call, revenge against all who would oppose you. You have wine, women, and hashish. If you want political power, you have but to ask. You need be no man's wazir. *You* could be the man to rule the world, with armies so vast they stretch beyond the horizon; let this boastful Akar serve as *your* wazir if he craves power so much."

Hakem Rafi thought on the daeva's words, then yelled down to Akar, "You promise me nothing I don't already have. I'm the one who controls Aeshma. The ultimate power in the world is mine to decide what to do with."

"I warn you, O Hakem Rafi, do not try my patience," Akar said in icy tones. "I can be openhanded to my allies, and my offer was made in such a spirit of generosity. But don't mistake generosity for weakness, for I am merciless toward those who oppose me. I will bring Aeshma under my control, and if you deny me what is my due you will die because of it. Let prudence be your guide, or you will die a needless death."

Hakem Rafi was trembling from both fear and rage. "I won't let anyone threaten me, never again," he declared. "Kill him, O Aeshma. I command it!"

"I hear and I obey," Aeshma said. While he would have prefered to avoid this battle altogether—and certainly so soon after his release from the urn—he felt reasonably competent here on his home ground, where he knew the territory.

In the twinkling of an eye the daeva transformed from his normal hideous self into the semblance of a huge lion, five times the length of the tallest man. His golden fur was sleek, his sharp fangs gleamed in the afternoon light, and his claws were like razors ready to slash at the unarmed man standing in the courtyard below. With a snarl of rage that roared through the still desert air all the way to the nearby mountains he leaped out of the window, plunging downward toward the ground, then bounded across the open courtyard to where Akar stood waiting.

The wizard may have been blind, but he had some senses that reached beyond the visual. Feeling the approach of Aeshma, he called upon the power of the spells and talismans he'd placed in the small bag he wore around his neck. Those spells, prepared in advance when he could concentrate more fully, gave him great control over himself and his surroundings. It was that control he now needed to draw upon quickly in this duel of magic.

Reaching up under the turban, Akar plucked a single black hair from his head. Holding the hair up to the sky, he uttered a short incantation and, to the astonishment of the watching Hakem Rafi, the hair became a scimitar of glistening edge and jeweled handle. As the lion came charging down upon him with its hot breath blowing in his face. Akar swung the scimitar with uncanny accuracy, slicing the beast cleanly down the middle lengthwise and remaining unharmed as the two halves sailed past him.

Hakem Rafi gasped in horror at the thought that his powerful servant could be defeated this easily, but this turned out to be only the first blow in a long battle. The two halves of the lion went flying through the air; one half simply burned itself into nothingness, as a stray spark escaping from a brazier. The half containing the head, however, began contorting in the air and changing its form even as it flew, until it became an enormous scorpion the size of a horse. Its pincers glowed with red hot fire, and its huge tail was raised high in the air, poised to deliver a fatal sting. As it landed on the ground past the point where Akar stood, it began scuttling back toward the wizard.

Akar turned instinctively to face the oncoming foe, and as he did so he called once more upon the magic in his bag to make his own body change as well. His shape grew more slender, more elongated, and his skin darkened until he became an enormous cobra bigger even than the scorpion attacking him. The scales on his back glistened like black rainbows and his eye sockets were empty, but he knew where to face to strike at the daeva. His mouth was open showing enormous curved fangs, holding poison every bit as deadly as the scorpion's sting.

The two enemies maneuvered around the open courtyard, striking and falling back without ever quite delivering a fatal blow to the other. After half an hour of parrying, the snake made a lunge and wrapped its body around that of the scorpion in such a way that the scorpion's tail couldn't reach it to sting.

The two creatures writhed and squirmed on the ground for some time until it again looked as though the Akar/cobra would defeat the Aeshma/scorpion. Then, at the point of defeat, the scorpion began to shift its shape again, becoming a vulture of curved beak and rapacious eyes. Its new, smaller shape was harder for the serpent to hold, and it wriggled free of the cobra's grasp and flew up into the skies.

Not to be outdone, Akar again summoned the power of the spells he'd brought with him and transformed himself into a large black hawk. This blind bird, with feathers the color of purest ebony and talons as sharp as a barber's razor, flew up into the sky in pursuit of its escaping prey.

The vulture suddenly wheeled in its flight and came back toward its pursuer. The two birds flew fiercely at one another, tearing with their talons and ripping with their pointed beaks. First one bird would lunge and seem victorious and the other would fly away, only to wheel suddenly and attack in its turn. After an hour of this duel, with the desert sky being rent by the sound of the birds' shrieking, the hawk landed a blow with its talon against the throat of the vulture. The vulture came plummeting to earth with a hideous cry, and the black, sightless hawk swooped triumphantly after it.

Just before reaching the ground, however, the vulture changed once again, this time into a wolf twice the size of a man, with pointed snout and ferocious snapping jaws. Its shaggy fur was steel gray and its eyes gleamed with the fiery glow of the Pits of Torment. It landed squarely on all four paws, turned, and leaped upward with jaws open and fangs bared to snatch the descending hawk from the sky.

Sensing the threat, the hawk swerved from its dive and changed its own form yet again. This time it became a black panther, its fur short and sleek and its yellow eyes clouded and sightless. Baring its own teeth, it leaped into combat with the wolf and the two ferocious animals sparred in the courtyard, snapping and biting at one another. Finally, with the tide of battle starting to turn, the gray wolf managed to get a stranglehold on the panther's throat. Jaws tightly clamped, the wolf shook the body of his opponent until the panther was near unto death.

At that point the panther suddenly vanished, leaving the wolf standing bewildered for a second in the courtyard. Then, looking around, he saw that the panther had transformed itself into a tiny black worm and was busy crawling into a pomegranate that had fallen from one of the trees around the fountain. With an angry cry the wolf transformed itself into a cock with brightly colored tail feathers waving in the air. Running over to the pomegranate the cock began attacking it with his beak to kill the worm inside.

The overripe fruit split open with the force of the cock's attack, and the seeds scattered all over the courtyard. One seed in particular rolled under the lip of the fountain and was momentarily hidden from view.

The cock meanwhile raced around the yard, gobbling up every pomegranate seed it could find. It looked up toward the window where Hakem Rafi stood watching this bizarre spectacle, and spread its wings as though to ask, "Are there any seeds left?" But Hakem Rafi was frozen in awe at this magical duel he was witnessing and either did not understand the cock's signal or else could not bring himself to point.

At last the cock spotted the single remaining seed and raced to it—but just before reaching it, the seed changed shape and became a large eyeless black carp with scales glistening like diamonds, and leaped off the ground to splash into the fountain beside it.

The cock flapped its wings and crowed angrily, then transformed itself into a giant blue fish and dived into the fountain after the blind black one. The two antagonists swam and bit at one another so furiously that the water frothed and foamed at their actions and the peaceful fountain became a whirlpool of violence. The water churned so ferociously that Hakem Rafi, looking down from his window, could not see which fish was doing what or who was winning the battle.

Then, as more and more water splashed out of the fountain and it seemed about to go dry, a spout of black flame erupted from the basin, leaping high into the air. Beside it, a second pillar of blue flame emerged from the water, and the two flames seemed to compete to see which could rise higher. Both were already taller than the roof of the palace, and Hakem Rafi had to lean out his window to see their tops. The black and blue flames flickered and danced, and started twining around one another, each seeking ultimate control. Wherever the two flames touched they threw off myriads of sparks that flew in all directions.

Some of the sparks landed in the gardens, others landed in the desert, and still others on the walls or the roofs of the palace itself. The sparks that landed on sand merely sizzled and went out in a small wisp of smoke, but those that landed in the garden or on the palace began to burn brightly. As more and more sparks flew from the combatants, the fires that they caused burned hotter and covered more area.

Now half the palace grounds and most of the roof were ablaze, and still the battle in the courtyard showed no signs of abating. Servants ran screaming from the palace, their clothing in flames; even stone and marble were burning in the magical fire that consumed everything before it. The palace of Rashwenath, which had stood here in the desert for millennia as a tribute to the genius of its builder, was in imminent danger of burning to the ground.

The pillars of blue and black fire blazed, interweaving in their attempts to strangle one another and oblivious to the devastation being wrought around them. The sparks were flying now at such a rate that they looked like a fiery hailstorm, driving so hard it was impossible to see through. Thick black smoke was coming from the fires in the palace as the roof, walls, and furnishings blazed away.

Hakem Rafi began coughing and held his hand over his face to keep out the flames. The heat was becoming oppressive and he could no longer see the two combatants who had caused all this conflagration.

"Aeshma!" he called between coughs. "Save me!"

"I hear and I obey," came the daeva's deep voice, and he broke off his battle instantly. Hakem Rafi was coughing so heavily now he could barely stand, but from out of the thick black smoke came the strong, reassuring arms of Aeshma to grab him up and fly him away from the palace that was now a solid wall of flames.

14

THE PITS OF PUNJAR

FTER hearing Prince Ahmad's story and pledging his support in the upcoming battle, King Armandor of Khmeria sent an order to his staff that a feast should be prepared in honor of his visitors. This sent the kitchens into an immediate uproar. The head cook sent a messenger to tell the yardsmen to butcher two kids and two lambs, and was grateful for the nannies and ewes who'd dropped them late in the season. Assistants were sent to cellar storerooms for the spices and root vegetables waiting there. Every saucepan, rice pot, and spit was in use before the hour was up, while servants in the dining hall polished the finest gold and imported porcelain dishes.

The result of all this furor was a gracious banquet, an unbelievable feast after the simple trail rations and cheap caravanserai food the travelers had been eating of late. The kids had been disjointed and simmered in sweet and hot curry sauce until the meat nearly fell off the bones. This meat became the center of a curry of a hundred dishes: fruit relishes, hot, sweet, and pungent; pickles of several sorts; many vegetables, raw and steamed; fresh fruits and nuts, dozens of each. And all of these were arranged to form a tapestry of color around the huge bowl of saffron rice.

The lambs had been butchered and then each whole carcass was stuffed with citrus, garlic, and spices, sewn closed, and then turned on spits until the meat was pale pink and perfumed with the stuffing and the garlic oil it had been basted in. Eggs were served in many styles, both as dishes and as garnish. Whole fish, live from the ponds they were stored in behind the kitchen, had been prepared too many ways to list. With each were flatbreads and butter, sweets of every kind, and rich tea that compared in complexity to the finest wines.

The chef apologized again and again for the poor meal, complaining about the lack of notice. Jafar al-Sharif, expert storyteller, recognized another expert when he saw one, however, and spotted the gleam of pride within the man's eye. As he saw the table groan in front of him, he knew that pride was justified.

The travelers ate seated in chairs around a table, rather than sitting on the floor and reaching into the communal dishes as they were used to. Because there were so many different foods to be sampled, an army of servants ran back and forth around the long teakwood table, dishing up portions of each dish for the guests to taste.

Umar bin Ibrahim sat next to his counterpart, Sarojin Fadakir, throughout the meal, and the two priests spent much time talking about the religious consequences of the upcoming holy war. The high priest of Khmeria also agreed to do a favor for his colleague from Ravan. Along the trail, in spare moments, Umar had composed a letter to his wife Alhena, letting her know he was still alive and well and telling her why he could not return to her at this time. This letter was written with all the outpouring of love Umar could put into ink, for he knew by now she'd been told he was dead and he knew she must be suffering.

Sarojin Fadakir promised to dispatch his most trustworthy priest to carry this letter to the Holy City. The priest would be given strict instructions that this letter was to be delivered *only* to Alhena, and to no one else who might claim to represent her. Umar knew that Yusef bin Nard would by now have been appointed high priest of the Royal Temple, and bin Nard couldn't be trusted not to relay this information directly to Shammara. Umar wanted to put his wife's troubled mind at ease, but not at the cost of telling his archenemy what he was up to.

The travelers—with the exceptions of Selima, who remained back at the Khmeri temple, and Cari, who hovered invisibly near Jafar to protect him—ate and drank to the bursting point, continually praising their host for his kindness and generosity. Jafar al-Sharif, sitting near the head of the table with Prince Ahmad and King Armandor, enlivened the dinner conversation by relating the story of their adventures in the desert with the Badawi and fighting the evil Jinn Estanash; he omitted only the part about the Jinn's treasure, as he did not want to make trouble for Nusair ibn Samman by stirring up other people's jealousy against his tribe.

After the enormous dinner the travelers, barely able to stay awake, excused themselves with the fatigue of their journey and begged the chance to rest. It was decided that Selima could stay in the safety of the temple, while each of the men was given a private room near the king's own chambers here in the palace.

For the first time in his life, Jafar al-Sharif knew what it was to sleep in regal splendor. He was given a room with a large canopied bed, its posts carved in the exquisite likenesses of birds and animals. The sheets were of the finest silk, seductive to the touch after so many nights on lumpy mattresses in caravanserais. An incense of gentle spices scented the room with pleasant associations. And all of this luxury was wasted on the storyteller, for he was so tired after the day's activities and the large meal that he fell almost instantly asleep.

In the middle of the night, though, Jafar al-Sharif was awakened by the sound of someone entering his room. "Who's there?" he whispered. He sat up suddenly and reached for the khanjar he'd placed on the floor beside the bed before going to sleep, then realized that wouldn't be necessary; Cari would be in the room guarding him against danger. She would protect him if this intruder proved to be a threat.

"Fear not, O illustrious wizard," came the intruder's response. "It is I, King Armandor. I merely wish a word with you in private."

Jafar al-Sharif tried to shake the cobwebs of sleep from his mind. Despite all he'd experienced so far on this journey, he still was not used to the idea that a king might slip secretly into his room at night to speak privately with him. "I am your servant, O noble king. My ear is yours at any hour."

King Armandor, barely a silhouette in the darkness, sat down beside him on the bed. "Umar bin Ibrahim is a man of Oromasd, wise and dedicated but perhaps a little too dogmatic. Prince Ahmad has the shadows of his father in him, but is yet a little callow and untried. That's why I come to you, a wizard and a man who's traveled widely in the world."

"I've seen much and heard more," Jafar admitted cautiously.

"Must you go to Punjar?" the king asked abruptly. "I fear greatly for the safety of your mission if you travel into the lands of King Zargov. The man has no respect for the laws of Oromasd and has not been known to deal hospitably with strangers."

"Thank you for the warning, Your Majesty, but I'm afraid we have little choice in the matter," Jafar replied. "We must obtain the pieces of the Crystal of Oromasd, and Muhmad told us that the first piece is hidden somewhere in the land of Punjar. Like it or not, we must go there and risk Zargov's wrath."

"They say Zargov knows some magic himself, that he has some djinni blood in his ancestry. You could face a duel of magic, and by your very story tonight you admit being ill-prepared for such a duel."

"I've faced magic before and survived," Jafar said haughtily, though his heart felt less confident than his words proclaimed.

King Armandor was silent for several minutes, and Jafar al-Sharif had to fight to stifle a yawn and keep himself awake in the royal presence. Finally the king said, "Well, if it is kismet that you shall journey to Punjar, neither I nor anyone can stop it. But let me present you with a gift that may help along the way."

He held something out and Jafar reached over to take it. It was a heavy piece of fabric folded over several times, but Jafar couldn't tell in this dim light precisely what it was. "I'm grateful for Your Majesty's favor," he said, "but I admit I'm not sure what you've given me."

"Many decades ago my great-great-great-great-grandfather, a king named Panadur, befriended a wizard and, as a reward for that friendship, received a magical cloak. The magic of this cloak is that when the owner dons it and utters

the magical word 'Decibah,' he and the cloak and everything
he carries become invisible to all eyes, human or djinni, until
he removes it again. The cloak has remained a secret within
my family down through the generations, but put to little
good use. I myself have used it merely for minor amusement,
to spy on my counselors to make sure they're loyal or to peer
into my harem unnoticed and watch the women in their daily
conceits. Such uses are trivial when I compare them to your
mission, and I feel you should have the cloak to help you
along your way."

"I'm at a loss for words, O generous king," Jafar said, and
genuinely meant it. "This is a gift beyond price, and I'll treasure it among my finest possessions."

"The price I ask is that you succeed in your mission and
use the Crystal of Oromasd to defeat the legion of the
daevas," King Armandor said. "If you accomplish that I'll
consider myself well recompensed."

"A bargain made and struck, Your Majesty," Jafar al-Sharif
promised, even though he still had no idea how he would go
about it.

After the king had gone once more, Jafar al-Sharif called
upon Cari to materialize in his room and light one of the
lamps in the niches of the walls. The Jann had watched all that
passed between her master and the king, and was eager for
him to try out his new acquisition. Putting the cloak around
his shoulders, Jafar said the magical word, "Decibah," and, as
King Armandor had promised, he promptly became invisible
even to the Jann's sharp eyes. He found, however, that he
could not become intangible the way she could, and still had
to open doors to go through them—nor was he inaudible unless he moved very quietly and took special effort not to make
any sounds.

"I'm acquiring quite an arsenal," Jafar commented as he
removed the cloak and folded it neatly. In the light of the lamp
he could see the fabric was of cloth-of-gold heavily embroidered with purple thread—a striking garment in and of itself,
even without its magical powers.

"I've got this cloak," he continued, "plus the lightning
staff of Achmet the terrifying, the truth cap, and the mysterious key we captured from Estanash's cave. And there's you
yourself, which I consider my greatest magical treasure."

"Don't forget the book," Cari reminded him, even as she tried to hide the little smile of pleasure at his assessment.

"Ah yes, the secretive journal of Ali Maimun the mage," Jafar said. He tucked the cloak of invisibility neatly away in his saddle pouch and pulled out the ancient leather-bound volume he always kept near at hand. Holding it up and examining it anew, he continued, "I'd consider this a little more valuable if it proved to be a little more helpful. But here we are, almost to Punjar, and it still hasn't told us anything about the first piece of the Crystal. What good is even the greatest source of knowledge if it won't divulge its secrets?"

In annoyance he tossed the book lightly onto the bed. To his great surprise, the volume fell open to a page that had never been opened before, a little farther into the back than they'd gone. Jafar stared, unbelieving, for a moment, then slowly walked over to the bed and squinted painfully at the page to decipher its meaning. Picking the book up again, he turned and carried it back to where Cari was also staring in wonderment.

"It seems the book has decided we need to know a little more," Jafar said. "I've come a long way in my reading lessons, many thanks to you, but I still can only pick out the simplest words. I know you didn't want to know all of Ali Maimun's secrets, but we don't have time for me to learn to read well enough to find out where the Crystal is. Could you at least look through this new section and tell me what it says? Maybe this way we can find the piece we need without having to tear apart the entire country of Punjar."

Cari nodded and set to work skimming through the newly opened leaves of the book. There were six pages now available to her that weren't open before. She read quickly through the first few until she came to passages where she had to read everything with a careful eye. After reading this section twice through she shook her head and looked up sadly into her master's face.

"I'm sorry, O my master, but the book is not much help," she said. "The first few pages just tell about the path Ali Maimun took to reach Punjar. Then he describes Punjar itself; he calls it 'a blighted land where the power of Rimahn is great. Its people are unenlightened and selfish, and live lives of quiet deprivation. They do little farming, preferring to eat roots, bark, tubers, and insects. They scavenge fruits and nuts and occasionally will hunt a small animal. The natives dwell in caves that honeycomb the mountains of their land; they are small and scrawny, ill-fed and ill-clothed, and they stink from the closed-in odors of their tunnels.'"

Cari turned the page, "Ali Maimun continued, 'I arrived and was granted an audience before King Durrego of the lame foot. To him did I give the first quarter of the Crystal of Oromasd, a piece slightly larger than a man's fist, and told him to hide it somewhere within the earth. He accepted it in trust, and assured me the Crystal would be a treasure of his household for future generations until the one who needed it came again to claim it. He then offered me what meager accommodations he could afford, and after two days I departed to the northwest to visit the castle of Varyu, king of the winds.'"

Cari looked up and closed the book. "That's as far as his record goes on this matter. Pages of the book beyond that point still refuse to open. There's no record of what this King Durrego did with the Crystal, nor does Ali Maimun tell us how to retrieve it."

Jafar brooded. "So the Crystal was hidden somewhere in the earth many ages ago by a long-dead king, and we don't know where it is. Maybe King Zargov doesn't even know where it is. Maybe he doesn't even know it's there!" He beat his fist against his palm. "I know it's blasphemy to curse a holy man, but at times like this I have little love for that wretched prophet Muhmad and his smug little ill-defined visions."

In the morning the travelers were treated to a hearty breakfast of rice porridge with ghee and honey, bowls of fresh fruit, and baked quails glazed with honey and stuffed with hard-boiled quail's eggs. After finishing this sumptuous repast they made their plans to depart and thanked King Armandor for his gracious hospitality. They found, however, that the king would not let them go that easily. First he pleaded with them to stay for several days to recover from the rigors of the trail, and offered as inducement a series of festivities and sports in their honor. This was a tempting offer, for they *were* tired of traveling, but they steadfastly refused.

King Armandor next offered to send them along the trail to Punjar with a full escort of his finest soldiers, including fifty horsemen and four elephants in their finest regalia. Prince

Ahmad and Umar, who wanted to keep their party small and inconspicuous, were appalled at this suggestion and politely demurred on the grounds that they wanted to move quickly. Not to be denied, King Armandor insisted that the travelers take with them five of his finest scouts to lead the way out of his kingdom, and on this matter they capitulated. The escort would protect them from hazards along their route and would not seriously hamper their speed.

When the travelers went to the stables they found their supplies had been completely replenished, all their clothes cleaned, and their horses had been groomed and given new harnesses of well-tooled leather, thanks to the generosity of King Armandor. The men retrieved Selima from the temple where she'd spent the night, and Jafar filled his daughter in on all that had happened while they were apart. Umar gave his letter for Alhena to Sarojin Fadakir, and the Khmeri high priest promised to dispatch his messenger to Ravan that very afternoon. As the travelers approached the eastern gate of Khmeria they were joined by their escort, five outstanding soldiers in the green and gold livery of King Armandor, and the group set out on the long eastward trek to Punjar.

As they traveled, the prince's party had occasion to talk with King Armandor's soldiers and ask them about the nature of the land they were about to visit, but they received few satisfactory answers. It was not that the soldiers were uncooperative, but rather that so little was known about Punjar. Few people ever visited it, and of those who did, even fewer returned to talk about it. If anything, conditions had grown harsher and more forbidding than they'd been in Ali Maimun's time, and the Punjari were not inclined to travel beyond their boundaries. The rest of the world would have ignored Punjar completely were it not for the riches buried within those mountains.

The kingdom of Punjar was noted as the source for the finest gems in the world; its tunnel-dwelling citizens were constantly unearthing treasures in the course of their excavations, and this was the land's sole source of outside income. Traders came to specified sites, bearing goods; if the Punjari were in the mood to trade, some of them would come forth with raw gems of incalculable beauty. The Punjari, for all their seeming ignorance, were shrewd bargainers and were seldom cheated in any transactions.

Every so often some bold adventurer would sneak into Punjar to steal some gems for himself. If any had ever been successful, his story had not been recounted in Khmeria or any of the lands around Punjar. Most people simply put the thought of those riches out of their minds and ignored the troublesome place altogether.

The party traveled to the north and east toward Khmeria's border with Punjar. As the travelers had discovered on their way into the city, Khmeria was a tropical land with lush growth, verdant and well-irrigated fields, and occasional dense rain forests. King Armandor's scouts were familiar with this territory and guided the prince's party along the fastest routes so they made good time, reaching the ill-defined border in just four days. There, where Khmeri influence ended and the Punjari realm began, the travelers said farewell to the Khmeri scouts who'd escorted them and provided companionship for part of their journey. Umar said a special prayer of blessing over the soldiers as they left, and Prince Ahmad gave the commander of these troops another message of deep gratitude to relay to King Armandor. Then, as the scouts rode off for home, Prince Ahmad's party turned eastward and began the uncertain journey into the heart of Punjar.

It didn't take long for them to notice the difference between the land they'd just left and the one they were entering. A set of sharp, jagged mountains rose ahead of them in the east, and though the temperature remained hot and muggy the ground became less fertile. There were fewer birds and animals about, no forests at all, and the vegetation was harsher, less tamed. Above all there was no sign whatsoever of human habitation.

"I can see Rimahn's hand in this portion of the world, that's for sure," Prince Ahmad commented to Umar.

"Ali Maimun's journal did say the power of Rimahn was great here," Jafar agreed.

"Rimahn's hand is everywhere," Umar said. "It's just that sometimes he disguises it better than others. No corner of the world is free of evil, no matter how beautiful—and sometimes you must look more carefully where the evil is hidden than when it's out in the open for all to see, for then it's more subtle and more dangerous. But by the same token, because Parsina was made by Oromasd, no part of it is totally devoid of good, either. You must look to the balance and have faith in

Oromasd's plan for the eventual redemption of the entire world."

Riding through this eerie countryside the travelers were reminded of all the horror stories they'd heard of Punjar. While they were reluctant to ride boldly through the main gates as they'd done in Khmeria—assuming they could even find them—they also knew it would be futile to sneak into the country and hope no one would notice. The Punjari defended their territory entirely too well; if the intruders looked as though they were trying to be furtive it would make the case against them that much worse. As a result of their indecision they rode at an awkward gait neither bold nor stealthy, placing themselves in the hands of Oromasd to make their destiny come to them.

Cari continued to give Jafar and Selima reading lessons every night and morning when they made and broke camp, and was very pleased with the progress of her two pupils. In addition, as was her custom, she flew invisibly beside the horses and made occasional scouting forays to look for Punjari warriors. If the travelers were attacked by a band of natives, Jafar figured he could play the same trick on them that he had on Nusair ibn Samman. Anything that could give him an advantage in a touchy situation was worth a try.

They traveled for two days through the increasingly barren land of Punjar without seeing a sign of another human being. What water they could find was in small, sluggish streams that only desperation compelled them to drink from. The stillness about them was intimidating. When they made camp for the night they kept a fire going and stood watch in shifts, even with Cari to help them—but the world was quiet all about. In some ways, that worried them more than noise.

By the afternoon of the third day they had almost reached the base of the mountains. The ground was baked and rent with cracks and pitted with large holes, like the burrows of enormous rodents. The travelers slowed as their horses stepped carefully to avoid catching their hooves in the torn ground. The only signs of life by now were hardy bushes at irregular intervals, a few brave birds—perhaps vultures, though they were flying too high to properly identify—and the ever-present insects buzzing about. No one in the group was talking much; it was as though the air was ready to soak up all sound if any were uttered, so the riders just paid attention to the route their horses were picking across the cracked ground.

Appearing from nowhere came an army of tiny men, the tallest of whom would have come no higher than Selima's chin. They came pouring out of the cracks and popping up from the burrows, all armed with spears, bows and arrows, and all with their weapons pointed directly at the travelers. They had dark skin, small black eyes, and coarse black hair that had never seen a comb or brush; they wore the most basic of loincloths and not so much as a simple turban on their heads.

Despite Cari's best scouting, she must have missed seeing these warriors. It was a well-laid ambush; the men had obviously been watching the travelers approach for some time and made the decision to take their stand here. The four horses were completely ringed by the warriors so there was no avenue of escape. The only thing that gave the travelers any hope at all was that the Punjari did not kill them immediately. They stood with spears and arrows poised for battle, dozens of brown-skinned men, but—despite their ragged appearance—they were a disciplined force. They would only attack if ordered—or if the captives tried to escape.

One man toward the front, carrying no weapon, stepped forward and addressed them. "You trespass on Punjari land. Who are you? What is your purpose here?"

Prince Ahmad urged his steed Churash two steps further, taking the calculated risk that the Punjari would not kill him. He thus stood at the front of the formation as he said, "I am Ahmad Khaled from the Holy City of Ravan, and I come on a peaceful mission to speak to King Zargov." He deliberately dropped his title, again a calculated risk; if the Punjari thought he was someone important they might want to hold him hostage—or they might be in league with Shammara and kill him on the spot.

"What is the nature of your mission?" the Punjari captain asked.

"That's for my friends and me to say directly to King Zargov. Only he can hear our message."

The captain looked over their rich attire and trappings and sneered. "You'll talk to me or no one," he said.

"Then we'll talk to no one," Jafar al-Sharif spoke up, "and you can kill us right here. When King Zargov asks you what those strangers with the important message had to say, you can tell him you killed us before you found out."

The captain eyed the strangers angrily, taking particular notice—as others had done before him—of the ghostly girl on the fourth horse. He hated to be outbluffed—but he knew King Zargov would want to know more about these intruders personally.

"You'll meet King Zargov," the captain snarled. "Then you'll wish you'd talked to me first."

The tiny Punjari warriors closed in on their captives and took away their khanjars and saifs, then guided them at spearpoint across the eerie landscape to a large pit at the base of the mountain. Never once did they let down their guard or let their aim waver from their targets. Under these conditions, Jafar felt it would be inappropriate to call on Cari's invisible aid; even as fast as she was, she couldn't stop all the spears and arrows before some found their mark. Better, he decided, to hold her in reserve for some future moment.

He did, however, find an unguarded instant to whisper to her and ask why she didn't warn them of the ambush. Her voice was most contrite as she replied, "In truth, O master, I didn't see them until the same instant you did. If you remember what King Armandor said, King Zargov has some djinni blood in him and may know a few simple spells. I suspect he placed a spell over his men to make them look like rocks and bushes until they were ready to make their attack. I did feel some magic in the area, but wasn't sure what it was. I'm afraid once again I've failed you by being unworthy."

"Cheer up. We're not finished yet," Jafar told her, trying to sound more positive than he felt.

The travelers were guided to the lip of a pit near the base of the mountains, and out of the pit arose clouds of sulfurous steam. The party was ordered to dismount and walk to the edge, where they saw a steep and narrow pathway leading down the side of the rock wall into the darkness at the bottom. At the prodding of their "guides" they started down the treacherous path, taking sure, tiny steps until they reached the floor some twenty cubits below the surface. There, torches lit the way to a tunnel that burrowed into the side of the mountain itself.

The tunnel had been constructed for the diminutive Punjari, and the men from Ravan had to stoop over to avoid scraping their heads on the ceiling as they walked. The tunnel was quite dark, with one torch every thirty or forty cubits apparently sufficient for Punjari eyes. The illuminated areas around the torches seemed to be some kind of hard, black stone, and the walls were chiseled very roughly, with large projections of rock jutting out irregularly from the walls. The floor was littered with pebbles and sand, and it was difficult to walk quietly because feet tended to crunch on the debris. Only Selima made no sound at all, because her feet did not truly touch the gravel on which they walked.

The overwhelming impression of the Punjari tunnels and caves, though—far more than the darkness—was of the stench that permeated the walls. Countless generations of Punjari, never noted for their cleanliness, had lived and died within these narrow tunnels. They'd worked and played, cooked their food and removed their wastes, all within the stuffy confines of rock walls. Some air holes had been drilled to let out the worst of the smoke, but the walls still stank of soot and the accumulated odors of human activity. The travelers coughed frequently at the unaccustomed stench, but they couldn't slow their pace without being prodded along by the spears of their captors.

They walked for what seemed like an hour. The tunnel branched and other tunnels intersected it, but their guides steered them firmly through the maze though the prince's party quickly lost all sense of direction. Buried here in the mountain, away from the honest light of the sun, all directions were equally dark and forbidding.

At last the way before them brightened slightly and the tunnel opened into a chamber that could only have been King Zargov's audience hall. While brighter than the tunnels it was still dimly lit by surface standards, and its size was not much greater than that of an average room in the palace of Ravan. But it was neither the light nor the size of the room that made the travelers gasp in astonishment.

The walls, the arched ceiling, and even parts of the otherwise smooth rock floor were covered entirely in gemstones. Not even in Ravan, a city renowned throughout Parsina for its wealth and beauty, were so many jewels displayed as casually as this. All types of stone were represented: diamonds, emeralds, rubies, sapphires, all mixed together with stones of lesser value but no lesser beauty. The stones appeared to have been set randomly, tourmalines next to emeralds next to spinels next to diamonds next to opals, with no apparent pattern. A good artist could have arranged the gems in breathtaking array—but the raw power symbolized by such haphazard use of untold wealth made its own impression on the visitors' minds. It told them that here was a monarch so wealthy he didn't need to put his wealth in order; he could just scatter it around at his whim. Such a ruler was obviously not to be trifled with.

Aside from the gems and the cresseted torches that gave it light, the room was almost bare of decoration. King Zargov didn't believe in perfume or incense, for the air stank of smoke and generations of Punjari bodies. Seated at the front of the room on a golden throne whose arms, legs, sides, and back were encrusted with gems, sat the wizened creature who could only be King Zargov himself.

The king was a gnome of a man, smaller even than most of his subjects. His bony body was covered by a threadbare cotton kaftan, and he wore simple niaal on his feet. Like his subjects he wore no turban; his head was mostly bald except for a ring of white, unruly hair, and he wore a golden crown set with gems. His fingers, wrists, and ankles were all circled with bands of gold and jewels. His eyes were large, bugging out slightly from their sockets, and his skin looked to be both the color and texture of ancient parchment.

Seated on a pillow beside the throne was a woman whose appearance was equally startling, if for different reasons. She was quite tall—if standing, she'd have been as tall as Jafar al-Sharif—and fair-skinned, in her early thirties. She wore a closed-neck cotton sidaireeya with tight sleeves almost to her elbows, and voluminous sirwaal trousers tightened in at her ankles and slender waist. Both the sidaireeya and the sirwaal were a rich blue, the color of forged steel, with rich gold embroidery around the ankles, sleeve cuffs, neck, waist, and down the front placket of the sidaireeya. There were blue zarabil with leather soles on her feet, and large circular gold earrings dangling on either side of her face. Most of her fingers bore gold rings, and there were half a dozen gold bracelets on each arm.

She wore no veil and had a lovely, slim face with piercing blue eyes and a thin, straight nose. Her most startling feature, though, was her hair—blond and long enough to reach well below her shoulders, had she not arranged it in an upswept fashion. None of the three men had ever seen hair that color, though Umar had heard there were people with yellow hair in the frozen regions of Norgeland. Punjar was as far from Norgeland as it was possible to get, however, and all three men stared at the woman as though she were some fascinating jewel in her own right.

It was the woman, rather than King Zargov, who spoke first. "Do come in," she bade the visitors as they stood gawking on the threshold. "It may be nothing but a jewel-covered quarry, but we call it home."

"Quiet, Leila!" said the king in a harsh whisper. "I will deal with these prisoners."

"With your usual wit and brilliance, no doubt," Leila sighed. She leaned back languidly on her pillow, but continued to watch the visitors with a discerning eye. Her gaze fixed particularly on Jafar al-Sharif, and a couple of times he glanced at her and noticed the hint of a smile at the corners of her mouth.

For the moment, though, King Zargov commanded their attention as he ordered the prisoners to step forward. They did as requested and the king demanded that they identify themselves.

Prince Ahmad bowed and tried to display the proper amount of deference without fear. "Your Majesty, may you live forever, my name is Ahmad Khaled and I travel on a holy mission of great importance to Oromasd. This is Umar—"

"With those white robes he must be some kind of priest," the king interrupted.

"Your powers of deduction never cease to amaze me," Leila drawled from beside the throne.

King Zargov ignored her. Apparently he was quite used to ignoring her. "Go on, wretch, who are the others?"

"The other man is the mighty wizard Jafar al-Sharif, and with him is his daughter Selima, presently under a curse. We travel, in part, to find her cure."

"Yes," continued the king impatiently, "and who is the Jann floating in the air behind this wizard?"

Jafar stiffened, wondering how King Zargov could have known Cari was there when she was invisible. Then he recalled what King Armandor had said, that Zargov was reputed to have some djinni blood in his heritage—and he remembered Cari telling him djinni could not be invisible to one another. King Zargov must have enough djinni blood to spot her. His heart sank as he realized he no longer had as much of a trick up his sleeve as he'd thought he had.

"She is my servant," Jafar spoke up, "a young and innocent member of the tribe of the righteous Jann. She'll cause you no harm if you do none to us."

"I'll not tolerate strange djinni in my kingdom," King Zargov declared. "Bid her depart at once, or you'll both answer for it."

Jafar al-Sharif had no idea how strong the king's powers were, but they were almost certainly stronger than Jafar's. Reluctantly he said, "Return to your home until I summon you again, O Cari."

"But master—"

"Obey my command!" Jafar said harshly. Her spirit was commendable, but she'd get one or both of them killed if she didn't obey instantly.

Cari must have realized that belatedly, too. "Hearkening and obedience," she said with resignation and sadness in her voice. Jafar could not tell whether she'd left, but King Zargov relaxed a bit.

"Why have you trespassed on my domain?" the king asked next. "Have you come to steal my treasures, as so many men before you have tried to do?"

"We do not come to steal," Prince Ahmad insisted. "We seek one item only, the piece of the Crystal of Oromasd left here in the keeping of King Durrego many ages ago by Ali Maimun the mage. If you give us that, we'll leave peacefully and never bother you again."

King Zargov stared at him. "With one breath you claim you're not here to steal, and with the next you deny it," he said. "You would take from me the Crystal of Oromasd, chiefest of my treasures, given to the rulers of Punjar many ages ago."

"It was given to you in trust," Umar spoke up. "The Crystal doesn't belong to you, or to any man. It's the Crystal of Oromasd, and Oromasd alone can say who should hold it. We were directed here by the prophet Muhmad to gather that piece of the Crystal. We must have it if we are to prevent the destruction of the world and the victory of Rimahn."

"It *is* mine," King Zargov insisted. "I've always had it and I always will. Oromasd isn't here to tell me otherwise, and neither is this prophet you mention."

Leila looked at the prisoners before the throne. "My husband's nobility is matched only by his maturity," she explained caustically.

"Quiet," said Zargov, shooting her a warning glance. Then, looking back to the prisoners, he said, "You will find, wizard, that I'm not without powers of my own. Even your magic won't save you from my prisons."

He nodded to the captain of his guards. "Take these thieves away to the lower pits until I decide exactly how to dispose of them."

"Always the same, no imagination," Leila said. "Couldn't we just once talk with them a while, find out what's happening in the world outside these drab little tunnels—?"

King Zargov turned to her, fury in his eyes. "You'll hold your tongue, woman, or I'll have you locked in your room!"

"What, and deprive me of seeing all the other depressing caverns exactly like mine? It matters not to me which blank walls I stare at."

"If you won't keep silent I'll deal you more punishment than that."

"You haven't the imagination," Leila challenged.

While the two prime figures in the room were thus engaged, Selima made a sudden break back into the tunnel from which she'd arrived. An alert soldier tossed his spear at her, but it sailed harmlessly through her phantom body and clanked against the rock wall beyond.

"After her!" cried King Zargov hysterically. "Don't let her escape!"

His soldiers moved to obey. Two of them stepped in front of the tunnel to block the entrance, but Selima simply ran through them into the cavern beyond. Others went chasing after her, but no one could grab her and stop her. She raced through the narrow tunnels, turning and dodging haphazardly until she finally eluded all pursuit and was swallowed up within the underground maze.

Leila laughed as she watched Selima make fools of her husband's soldiers, and the laughter only infuriated King Zargov more. He glared at his wife, then turned to the other prisoners. "The girl will be dealt with in time. No one escapes from Punjar against my wishes. Meanwhile, unless any of you feel lucky enough to challenge a spear through your hearts, you won't try to follow her example."

Thus it was that Jafar al-Sharif, Prince Ahmad, and Umar bin Ibrahim were led down some more tunnels and imprisoned in the black pits of King Zargov's dungeon—a place not unlike the dungeons of Ravan with which Jafar al-Sharif was already entirely too familiar.

15

THE COUNCIL OF THE RIGHTEOUS JANN

FAR back in the early Cycles of history, in the days when Parsina was new and Oromasd's plan was only beginning to unfold, the servants of Rimahn roamed freely upon the earth, their evil unchecked and their lies uncountered. The men and women of that time, unenlightened about the goodness of Oromasd, believed the lies of the daevas, and Rimahn's servants took advantage of their ignorance by seducing them into sexual acts and perversions. The offspring of these unions between daevas and humans became known as the djinni, and their presence upon the earth continued to pester mankind throughout the ages.

As the djinni continued to breed—with daevas, with humans, and with one another—five distinct lineages emerged. Those with the most daeva blood, the most powerful and bloodthirsty of the djinni, became the Shaitans. Though few in number they had the greatest magical abilities and the greatest propensity for evil; they differed from the daevas only because, as descendents of humans, they were mortal while the daevas were not. While their daeva heritage granted them long life spans, they could be killed by men of courage with the proper weapons.

Ranked below the Shaitans were the Marids, then the Afrits, then the Jinn, and finally the Jann. All were long-lived, all were creatures of magic, but the Jann were the weakest and closest to humans. They had the least magical abilities and were the easiest to kill, though they could still seem formidable to the average person not versed in the magical arts.

Most of the Jann were dedicated to evil and to the bedevilment of mankind, as were the rest of their djinni brethren. There was one comparatively small clan, however, that had heard the words of Oromasd and had become enlightened in the ways of his truth. These became known as the righteous Jann, and when their beliefs were made known to their fellow djinni they were cast out and made to dwell apart from the others. Misunderstood by men and shunned by djinni, they lived quietly on their own devices in a cavern measureless to man far below the surface of the earth.

The home of the righteous Jann is indescribable in human terms because it exists in a place beyond human senses. There is no light, no sound, no physical substance, and yet it is as real to its inhabitants as Ravan is to its citizens. The righteous Jann viewed their home as comfortable and secure, while an ordinary man could not have seen anything at all. Magic was a part of this cavern, just as it was a part of every Jann, and here the Jann could live in a plane beyond human reckoning.

It was to this hidden cavern that Cari withdrew when her master Jafar dismissed her from the pits of Punjar. Her heart was filled with forboding and her mind was wracked with worry over her master's fate. It was her duty to be at his side and protect him when she could, but now she'd been ordered away and could only stand helpless until he summoned her again. She felt totally frustrated, and more alone than at any time since the wizard Akar had first ensnared her soul and made her a slave to that simple brass ring.

Cari floated through the cavern, which appeared bright and glittery to her magical eyes. All around her were the insubstantial, yet very real, bodies of the other Jann who inhabited this cave, talking or singing or studying or engaged in other pursuits, oblivious to the concerns of the human world above. Cari could still remember when she'd been as one of them, a spirit free of earthly cares, her sole concern being to live a good and pure life so her spirit would be saved at the Bridge of Shinvar and she'd be allowed to enter the House of Song.

Then had come the horrible shame as she fell into the snare of Akar's magic and the wizard tightened the noose around her soul, enslaving her to his will and his ring. The feeling of constriction was as though he'd bound her chest making it hard for her lungs to breathe—only it was her soul that was bound, and her spirit that couldn't breathe. That had been less than ten years ago, just a tiny portion of her life, yet she was immeasurably and irrevocably changed because of this.

All her former friends avoided her as she passed. It was nothing blatant, no obvious snubs, just a subtle refusal to meet her gaze or acknowledge her existence in their world. Cari was a living reminder of what might happen to them someday if they were careless or some wizard trapped them for his own use. Cari could remember how awkward she felt in the presence of other captured Jann when she was free, and she couldn't blame her fellows for their behavior. After all this time, she was getting used to it.

Cari did not have a home of her own within this vast cavern, but dwelt instead in her family's portion of the cave, a niche her ancestors had occupied for centuries. Even here she was not completely welcomed, though she was tolerated and allowed to stay. When she arrived this day, though, she found the region deserted. Entering the insubstantial abode, she made herself comfortable and waited for her master to summon her.

Time was all but meaningless in the cavern of the righteous Jann, but it seemed interminable to Cari as she hovered in the air and imagined all the horrible things that might be happening to her master and his friends. If anything happened to Jafar, would that horrible King Zargov take her ring and become her new master? What kind of life would she have as servant to that wicked, selfish insect of a man?

A change occured within the house, and she looked to see her uncle, Suleim, approaching. Of all her relatives, Suleim was the most understanding and the wisest. It was he who spoke to her the most, and gave her solace in her servitude. "Men are transient creatures," he'd consoled her more than once. "The ring that enslaves you may pass from hand to hand for many years, but eventually it will become lost and forgotten. Then you will be free once more to live your own life. Until then, trust in the goodness of Oromasd and the Bounteous Immortals to preserve you."

Now Suleim came up to her and greeted her as uncle to niece. "Welcome home, Cari, for however long a time you are permitted. How fare you in the world of men?"

In normal circumstances Cari would have been discreet and kept her master's affairs a secret. But today, as filled with worry as she was, she could not keep the story to herself. Before she even realized what she was doing she told her uncle of the prophet Muhmad's vision, that the world was approaching a change of Cycles and that her master must gather the pieces of the Crystal of Oromasd to withstand the onslaught of Rimahn's forces. Suleim listened patiently as his niece related the story of the adventures with the Badawi, and about the travel on the road to Khmeria and Punjar, and about the audience with King Zargov. Cari was almost crying when she told of her fears for Jafar, that somehow he might not be able to cope with the wiles of this evil king.

Suleim listened thoughtfully to her tale, and was silent for some time thereafter. He looked serious as he said, "I think this is a matter we must bring before our shaykh, that he may decide what should be done."

"I've already spoken to him once," Cari said with resignation in her voice. "He has little sympathy for my master, and cares not for humans in general. I can't ask him to interfere in the affairs of men when he's already told me he disapproves."

Suleim did not argue with his niece for, indeed, the shaykh's aversion to humans was common knowledge among the righteous Jann. Nonetheless, he was resolved to do something to aid his niece's plight. He said nothing to her other than general words of comfort, for he knew he could not promise her anything—but, after excusing himself, he went to pay a visit on the shaykh of the righteous Jann.

The shaykh's palace would have looked no different to human eyes than any other place within these vast caverns, but to the eyes of a Jann it was a place of incredible light and beauty, gleaming and glistening in the glow of a thousand shining jewels. Not the harsh glitter of the brilliants—diamond, ruby, tourmaline, and such—that dominated Zargov's filthy hole. These were like opal, moonstone, and carnelian—more alive, warmer, and softer, as is the love of Oromasd when compared with the life of Rimahn. The palace was formed by the interweaving of strong magical spells, more sturdy than tempered steel, and was a formidable stronghold to anyone who could recognize its power. No Jann could ever approach it casually, but Suleim—as a member of the tribal council—could enter without fear of repudiation.

Suleim was greeted warmly by the shaykh's servant and escorted immediately into the shaykh's presence. Suleim made his salaam and the formal salutation, but was cut short before he could proceed any further. The shaykh of the righteous Jann was old, and had little patience for the formalities he had once reveled in.

"Come straight to the point with me, O Suleim," said the shaykh. "You are known for your wisdom and your forth-rightness, and you're not accustomed to worrying over trivial matters. I can see you're worried now. Tell me the object of your concern, that I might see how to ease it."

"I hesitate to speak of it, O great shaykh, for it concerns my niece Cari and her human master."

"Ah yes, she's told me of him. He's the rogue pretending to be a wizard." He sighed deeply. "I've already given her all the advice I could on the matter of his daughter. I sense she is becoming far more involved in his affairs than she wisely should be, and that disturbs me. She always seemed so level-headed before her capture by the accursed Akar."

"This has become a matter going far beyond this single human, O shaykh. It's a matter that affects all of Parsina and all who profess a love for the beauty and truth of Oromasd."

The shaykh leaned forward and peered intently at Suleim. "Of what matter do you speak, then?" he asked.

"Aeshma has been released from his captivity. The prophet Muhmad says this signifies the changing of Cycles, and will affect the entire world."

The shaykh was thoughtful. "I knew I felt something wrong, but I didn't know what it could be. This is indeed serious, and the righteous Jann will have to be especially care-ful not to cross Aeshma's path, lest we be drawn into his evil schemes."

"We'll need more action than that," Suleim insisted. "The prophet Muhmad—to whom you yourself specifically sent Cari's master—has proclaimed that this Jafar al-Sharif must gather together the pieces of the Crystal of Oromasd that were separated by Ali Maimun, and use the Crystal to defeat the forces of Rimahn."

"That's impossible," the shaykh said flatly. "It took all the wisdom of the greatest mage in history to use the Crystal before; this charlatan Jafar al-Sharif can never hope to repeat that achievement."

"I know," Suleim agreed. "That's why we must help him."

The shaykh's temper flared. "Men are already the protected of Oromasd. I shall not risk the power, prestige, and safety of the righteous Jann to help some human charlatan, no matter how worthy his cause."

Suleim was wise from many arguments with the shaykh, and he knew from the tone and timbre of the other's voice that he would never convince the shaykh of the rightness of his cause. Suleim did have one further avenue of persuasion, however, and he was resolved to do everything he could to fight this matter through.

"In that case," he told the shaykh, "I ask to call a session of the council to hear my petition, that the clan as a body may judge the merits of my arguments."

It was Suleim's right, as a member of the council, to call for a session if some matter warranted consideration. Convening such a session without first obtaining the permission of the shaykh was an insult to the older Jann's leadership, but there was ample precedent for such a move. Suleim considered this situation important enough to risk offending the shaykh.

He could see the shaykh stiffen at his request. "You feel that strongly about the matter?" the shaykh asked. There was no anger in his voice, but he sounded hurt.

"I'm afraid I do, O wise shaykh," Suleim said gently, trying to cushion the blow to his old friend's dignity.

"Then a council will be called," the shaykh sighed. "But I warn you, O my friend, you will not find many friendly ears on the council, either."

And so the summons went out to all the members of the council, representing many of the great families of the clan of the righteous Jann. The call was neither verbal nor written, but a summoning of the spirit that reached to each member who sat on the council. Twenty of them there were, not including the shaykh himself, and they served as an advisory body only. The shaykh was not bound by their decisions—

but a shaykh who too frequently ignored the wishes of his council often ended up being replaced by someone more tractable.

The council members heard the summons, and from all parts of the caverns and from their far-flung journeys they came to sit in session. Even on such short notice, Suleim was gratified to see all the other council members in attendance as well as himself. If he were to have any influence at all, he'd have to convince a significant number of his fellows, probably a majority, that his view of the situation was correct.

When the entire council was assembled in the brightly lit—to a Jann's eyes—council chamber of the shaykh's palace, the shaykh of the righteous Jann faced the assemblage. "We are gathered at the request of Suleim, who wishes to address us on a matter of some concern." With no further prelude, he left the discussion to Suleim.

Cari's uncle began in a matter-of-fact tone, simply stating the facts of the case as explained to him by his niece. He told about Aeshma's release and the threat it posed to all followers of Oromasd, and he explained about Prince Ahmad and Jafar al-Sharif, and the mission they'd been given by Muhmad, the prophet of Sarafiq. He closed his initial speech by saying, "Muhmad told Prince Ahmad to gather together the rulers of the earth and the armies of Parsina to fight against the menace from Aeshma and his daevas. I propose that the righteous Jann should help these men, that they might accomplish their task more easily."

The council was in instant uproar; many of the members held views even more isolationist than the shaykh's. "Why should we help these humans?" one older Jann asked. "Their fight is not our fight."

"Their fight is Oromasd's fight, and Oromasd's fight is ours," Suleim countered. "Can we continue to call ourselves the 'righteous' Jann if we turn our backs on Oromasd's call to battle?"

"We are the righteous Jann because we refrain from evil and live at peace within the laws of Oromasd," an archconservative named Kasman pontificated. "It's the humans who are Oromasd's tool for defeating Rimahn and restoring the world to its perfect order. This battle is for them, not for us."

"We have our own souls to think about," another Jann replied. "All humans will eventually be rehabilitated and share in Oromasd's paradise, but we Jann must be careful how we die or we could vanish forever."

"Are we to hide quaking like cowards in our caves, then," Suleim asked, "while the great battle rages all about us?"

"No one dares question the courage of Kasman!" bellowed that old Jann from the other end of the chamber.

"Then I pose you a question," Suleim responded, trying with all his might to remain calm in the face of chaos. "Who is more righteous—the person who lives apart and ignores the evil he knows exists around him, or the person who fights to exterminate that evil? We can lead innocent lives buried here in our caverns, but will that save us when we reach the Bridge of Shinvar? When Rashti questions us at that fearsome place and weighs the goodness of our lives, he'll see that we knew about this evil and failed to confront it. It's not enough that we refrain from evil ourselves. The absence of evil is not goodness, merely another and subtler form of evil. We must not fall into Rimahn's snare; we must fight this evil if we value our souls."

A short silence followed this eloquent plea as each council member weighed his courage and beliefs against the distasteful idea, and each pondered the gap he found.

"But the project is doomed from the start," another Jann finally protested. "No man except Ali Maimun has ever used the Crystal of Oromasd; you certainly can't expect an untrained rascal like this Jafar al-Sharif to manage it. The mere act of his gathering the pieces will alert Aeshma to his existence, and he'll never be able to stand against the power Aeshma can unleash."

"That's why we must help him," Suleim insisted.

"All the righteous Jann together are barely a match for Aeshma," Kasman said as he tried to shake off the effect of Suleim's earlier challenge. "If Aeshma regains control of his daeva legions, as he is sure to do, our entire clan would be wiped out, to no good end. I refuse to believe that would serve Oromasd's great plan for the reformation of the world."

Around and around the arguments swirled, and every council member had his say, some of them many times over. As the emotions became stronger, the chamber seemed to grow larger to contain them. The walls shifted, not in color, but in the refractions and light thrown by gems of magic. In this way was the energy kept within the home of the righteous Jann and not dissipated into the magical web to benefit all, even Aeshma. The shaykh of the righteous Jann did not participate in the debate himself; the council, after all, was there to advise him, not listen to his opinions.

Even though he was deeply embroiled in this debate, Suleim kept watching the shaykh from the corner of his eye. He saw the shaykh noting every nuance and particle of the argument, and could almost hear him keeping tally of where everyone stood on the matter and why. The shaykh was a veteran of these councils; not a word, not an inflection, escaped his careful notice.

At length the arguments began to wind down, and positions became set and hardened. Suleim had convinced roughly half the council members of his position—but the other half remained firmly opposed. If a vote were called, the tally would be very close one way or other—and in the event of a tie, the shaykh would cast the deciding vote.

The shaykh saw this, too, and abruptly called for an end to the debate. "Since the council is so evenly divided," he said, "there's no point in continuing to bicker or poll our members. I alone, as shaykh of our tribe, must make the decision for all of us—and only Oromasd can judge whether I make the proper one."

He paused and looked around the chamber at the expectant faces staring into his own. "I've made no secret of my feelings for human beings; you all know them. Humans are the favorites of Oromasd and our distant cousins, but their affairs are no concern of ours. The righteous Jann fought on the side of the humans in the last great battle, because Ali Maimun compelled us through the Crystal of Oromasd—but other than that, we have always lived apart and let the humans live their own lives without our interference. I cannot see the need to violate that principle now."

Suleim's spirits sank. He had spent all his energy and placed all his personal prestige on the line, only to see his arguments fail to persuade and his opponents triumph over his ideas.

The shaykh saw Suleim's expression of despair, and smiled. "However," he continued, "since my council, and the worthy Suleim in particular, rightly remind me of our duty to Oromasd, I cannot neglect that. If this impostor Jafar al-Sharif and his friends begin gathering the pieces of the Crystal, they will certainly come to the attention of Aeshma, who is currently in ignorance of them. These people are no match for the might and power that the king of the daevas can wield against them, and they would certainly fall before they complete their ordained mission. It shall be the task of the righteous Jann to shield these travelers from Aeshma and keep them safe—"

"All the righteous Jann together couldn't prevail against Aeshma," Kasman interrupted. "If we try to be their shield, we'll only perish as well as the humans."

"We can't shield them from his power," the shaykh agreed, overlooking Kasman's rudeness out of respect for his old friend, "but we can shield them from his view." A murmur ran through the hall as these, the wisest of the tribe, saw the direction of their shaykh's decision.

"The righteous Jann," continued the shaykh, "will interpose themselves between these adventurers and Aeshma. When a piece of the Crystal is gathered up, it will cause a disturbance on the magical web that Aeshma can't help but notice. When he looks to find its source, though, he will see us in great activity and assume we are the cause of the anomaly. He will be busy with his own evil concerns, and will pay little attention to us because he, too, knows he is greater than we are and we pose little threat to him. If Oromasd favors us, Aeshma will not see past our deception to the truth. This council is dismissed with my thanks for its wisdom and advice."

The council members made their obeisance and departed on their separate ways, leaving Suleim alone with the shaykh once more. "I wish to thank you, O shaykh, for the wisdom of your decision," Suleim said.

"It's only wise so long as it agrees with your own views, of course," the shaykh said wearily.

"Still, you could have denied my wishes totally and the council would not have reproved you."

"Your arguments were not without merit, and a significant proportion of the council agreed. True, they wouldn't have castigated me for ignoring your wishes, but they're not unhappy now, either. Sometimes a delicate balance must be maintained, a compromise struck between principle and necessity. That is what I did here, nothing more.

"And don't be too quick to thank me, for I've given you little of what you asked and it means much work for you. I

command you to set up the details of our operation to camouflage the actions of Jafar al-Sharif from Aeshma's eyes. You
may delegate whatsoever Jann you wish to help you with the
task, except for your niece."

"Why not her?" Suleim asked.

"Two reasons. First, as slave to that ring she is unreliable;
her master could give her commands that interfere with our
efforts and render them useless, or the ring could fall into
other hands and our plans would be revealed. And second, she
would likely tell her master about our work, which I do not
want."

"Why not?"

"If these humans believe they're being guarded by the
righteous Jann, they may grow careless and thus fail in their
mission. As I decreed, the righteous Jann will not interfere in
the affairs of these humans; their success or failure must depend on the will of Oromasd and their own particular skills.
We are merely to hide them from Aeshma's sight so they can
go about their mission unimpeded. Are my wishes clear, O
Suleim?"

"Perfectly, O wise shaykh," Cari's uncle said. "I hear your
commands and shall move to obey them. I will organize our
camouflage so Aeshma will never know of Jafar al-Sharif and
his quest for the Crystal of Oromasd—and I will keep the
knowledge of our actions secret from my niece, so she may
not tell the humans and allow them to grow overconfident."

Although Suleim's loving heart regretted the loss of the
comfort such knowledge would bring Cari, he would obey.
The shaykh watched him retire, wondering afresh at the will
of Oromasd that could make two of the least of his creatures—a half-grown Jann and a would-be wizard—so shake
the mighty . . . perhaps even the mightiest.

Thus it was that plans were made to guard Jafar al-Sharif
and his companions from the sight of Aeshma, thus protecting them from one serious source of evil along their mission.
The humans, however, would find more than enough other
problems to occupy their minds.

16

THE HAIRY
DEMONS

WHEN Aeshma, king of the daevas, broke off his duel of sorcery with the wizard Akar to rescue Hakem Rafi from the flames of the burning palace, he swooped quickly through the thick black smoke, cradled the thief securely in his massive arms, and flew off into the clear sky with him once more. The daeva had abandoned his form as a tower of blue fire and instead was in his more natural shape, manlike and gigantic with pitch black skin and glowing, fiery eyes.

Below them, the magnificent palace of Rashwenath—which had stood for thousands of years as a tribute to the greatness of its creator—burned like dry kindling on a summer's eve. The magical powers of the two combatants were so fierce that nothing, not even such a splendid structure as that fabled palace, could stand before those destructive energies. The servants who'd waited on Hakem Rafi, mostly phantasms created by Aeshma, vanished in the blaze, while the women of the harem ran screaming out of the building to survive as best they could in this forsaken wilderness.

Hakem Rafi cared nothing for the fiery passing of a historical monument or the lives of the women who'd given him pleasure. He was more worried about saving his own skin. He'd thought his life was finally secure with the power of Aeshma behind him, and that at last he'd have nothing in the world to fear. Suddenly this wizard Akar appeared on the scene and presented a direct threat to the life he'd fashioned for himself. Now Hakem Rafi's palatial home lay in ruins, his servant—who'd called himself the most powerful being in all Parsina—was fleeing in ignominious defeat, and Hakem Rafi's own life had hung for a moment by a precarious thread. Hakem Rafi had once lived by his wits, with his circumstance liable to change between one blink and the next, but now he was no longer accustomed to such violent turnarounds—not since Aeshma had introduced him to this leisurely lifestyle. The erstwhile thief was frightened near unto death by this state of affairs.

Aeshma had made his body larger than normal so he might more easily carry his master as he flew through the air. Hakem Rafi was held securely in his servant's powerful black fist, but wriggled uneasily to look behind them as they flew from the burning palace in the middle of the desert. He tried to see whether they were being followed by this powerful wizard Akar, for a great fear was upon him. If Akar could mount so strong a challenge to Aeshma's power, were there other men who could do the same? How long could Hakem Rafi retain control of the daeva he considered his personal slave?

The black smoke from the dying palace formed a column that reached up to heaven itself, and the sky for a hundred parasangs around was polluted by a dark cloud that poisoned all birds and insects that flew through it. That cloud lingered in the air above the northern regions of Fricaz for two weeks, and many were the eyes that looked up at it and pointed and wondered at its origin. In the wake of the scourge that was to sweep through the continent of Fricaz, stories grew that it was an omen of the dark times yet to come.

Hakem Rafi peered through the smoke and the cloud, but could see no sign of pursuit by his wizardly adversary. Eventually the thief relaxed slightly and allowed himself to enjoy the flight. This was his second time in the air, and he was beginning to like the feel of the breeze rushing past his face and the look of the landscape below him, so tiny and unreal. He began to envy the daeva his easy ability to fly through the air, and resolved to ask Aeshma to fly him to other places more often. The peacefulness of the flight soothed his troubled nerves and almost made him forget their abrupt departure from the palace of Rashwenath.

Aeshma flew southward from the palace, into the heart of the continent of Fricaz. As they passed beyond the boundaries of the black cloud the air turned to clear blue and the clouds that floated past them were fluffy balls of white mist. The Afrits of the air who'd so tormented Jafar al-Sharif during the flight of his magical carpet did not disturb them; they knew better than to interfere with the lord of all the daevas, for as djinni they were all mortal while he was not.

The nature of the land below them changed as they flew on. Desert yielded slowly to green, fertile ground cut into parcels for crops or into pastures for grazing. As they flew even further south, the heat grew more oppressive and the character of the land changed again, becoming dense jungle with trees so closely grown together that Hakem Rafi could not see the ground through their leaves. Broad rivers flowed through these jungles, their depths occupied by crocodiles, hippopotamuses, and other creatures new to Hakem Rafi. He was learning, slowly, that all places were not like his native town of Yazed.

Ahead of them, now, a solitary mountain rose out of the jungle, its peak capped with snow even in summer. Aeshma flew for this mountain and landed on its summit, but surrounded the two of them with a bubble of magic so the chill of the air would not affect his master. Here, looking down on the land of Fricaz all around them, master and servant spoke of what should happen next.

Aeshma's form was larger than normal, but otherwise showed the same hideous shape he'd first manifested on the roof of Rashwenath's palace. Hakem Rafi had grown used to his slave's appearance, and no longer found Aeshma as menacing as he'd thought at first. The fear at having to flee his palace had by now left him, tranquilized by the wonder of his flight with Aeshma, but in its place was a cold fury at having been lied to by someone he'd trusted.

"You told me you were the most powerful being on earth," Hakem Rafi yelled at Aeshma, "that no one could challenge your authority to do anything you wanted. Yet today we must run from a mere wizard, a man who shouldn't have even a tenth your power. Are all your promises merely idle boasts, as empty as the desert wind?"

Aeshma was a proud and fiery spirit, and it kindled his own anger to be yelled at by so insignificant a mortal. It took every drop of his self-restraint to avoid venting this anger on the man who'd freed him from his urn and whom he'd vowed to serve faithfully. He held his reply until his temper was under control, then said in a voice all honey and humility, "I spoke the truth as it should be, O master, but you must take the circumstances into account."

"Circumstances?" Hakem Rafi snorted. "Like the circumstances that a mere mortal can best you in a duel of magic?"

"He did not best me, O master, and had I a little more time I could have utterly destroyed him. But that is now, alas, beside the point. The circumstances I refer to are that I was pent up in a tiny urn before the Bahram fire of Oromasd with my strength being sapped for millennia, while the world has changed around me. I sat in that urn impotent to exercise my vast powers, until they have faded with disuse. And still, after all this time without any true experience, still I am able to perform miracles and fight to a standstill the mightiest wizard on the face of Parsina. With each passing day my powers grow stronger, my abilities grow surer, my control grows vaster. And all of my energies, O master, are for your benefit alone."

Hakem Rafi was slightly mollified, but was determined not to show it; Aeshma must be made to pay for the mistakes he'd made in dealing with Akar. "But what good are these powers of yours if I must live in fear that some wizard might come and steal them away from me?"

"If you will but take my humble advice, O my master, I can suggest a course whereby you need live in fear no longer," Aeshma said in soothing syllables.

"What course is this?" growled Hakem Rafi.

"The course suggested by Akar himself: you must become master of the world. As long as you enjoy yourself in a secluded palace and merely sample the pleasures of life, you are a target for everyone with an envious mind. I'll protect you as best I can, as I did against Akar, but unless you give me freer rein my powers are finite."

"Freer rein?" Hakem Rafi was instantly suspicious. He knew Aeshma would try to take advantage of him, as he would have were their roles reversed, and he was on the alert for any tricks his servant might try. "What exactly do you mean?"

"In my earlier days, when I was—as I told you—the most powerful being on earth, I was king of the daevas. All the hosts of Rimahn bowed unto me and called me their lord. Since I've been imprisoned, my former subjects have gone along their own paths, performing such mischief as may occur to them but acting to no organized plan. I have spent all my time serving you, as of course I must, but this has allowed me no time to renew my control over the forces of power that undermine the world. My own powers, which are considerable, are as nothing when compared with the combined powers of all my minions acting at my command. If you but gave me the word, I would subjugate the dark hosts once more under my authority, so that all the powers of Rimahn would be at your disposal."

"To what purpose?" Hakem Rafi asked warily.

Aeshma's true purpose was to unite all his former subjects and control an army vast enough to sweep across the face of the world, annihilating all mankind before him and making Rimahn's victory in Parsina complete. But he could hardly tell this to Hakem Rafi, whose sense of self-preservation would be threatened. Instead he had to find some logical excuse appealing to the thief's greed and selfishness—and he was actually grateful to the wizard Akar for providing the reason.

"To make you the mightiest monarch ever to reign in Parsina," Aeshma answered in seductive tones. "To build you an empire so vast it will dwarf even that of the great Rashwenath. Think of it, O my master: the power of all the djinni, all the demons, all the daevas harnessed to my will, and all at your service to control the fate of the world. You'll have armies so huge they'll cover whole kingdoms when they march. The name of Hakem Rafi will be renowned throughout the world, from the coast of Norgeland to the shores of far Sinjin. People will live or die by the snap of your fingers, and your shadow will be feared by all who value their necks. You need fear no one ever again, for your power over the earth will be absolute and there will be none who dare challenge it. All your fears, all your worries, will then be gone, for no one can touch you or cause you harm. You will be safe and secure for the rest of your life."

Hakem Rafi, raised in alleyways and seedy inns, had heard many pretty lines before, and knew there was always a price at the other end. "It all sounds wonderful," he said, "except that I don't trust you. Akar was probably right that you're looking for some chance to betray me."

"Have I ever failed you in anything you asked of me?" Aeshma asked in wounded tones.

"No, because I've kept my eyes on you all the time," said the conceited thief. "You behave yourself because you know I'm watching you closely. If I gave you the leeway you're asking for, you could do things behind my back, make secret deals with your own servants to counter my orders. I can't give you that much freedom. My life is at stake."

Aeshma struggled hard not to laugh at the thought that this puny human could keep close surveillance on him if he wanted to be away. The daeva king had moved slowly to this point, letting his powers return to him at their natural pace. But while it was true he must obey Hakem Rafi's orders, there were many ways to manipulate this little man into doing what Aeshma wanted him to do.

Never at a loss for a plan of mischief, Aeshma said, "Consider then, O master: you could come with me as I subjugate my former servants. You could watch me as I reestablish my command over them, to make sure I do nothing to harm your interests. The only reason I didn't suggest this before was that I will have to go places where no mortal has ever gone. You will see sights and be privy to things that would terrify a lesser man into an early death—but if you feel capable of accompanying me I will protect you in these terrifying places."

Hakem Rafi strongly considered the daeva's suggestion. He didn't doubt Aeshma wanted to outwit him, but at the same time he knew he could place the king of the daevas under strong constraints. After all, hadn't he made Aeshma serve him well thus far? The plan Aeshma suggested sounded exhilarating. No man in history had ruled the entire world, and the thought of being the first to accomplish this filled Hakem Rafi's black soul with the fire of ambition. He'd learned how boring it was to live simply for pleasure, without any conflict or competition. Being the supreme ruler of all men, being responsible for their lives and their welfare, could provide him the challenge he needed in his life. It would feed the need for revenge he'd felt since his childhood, since he was an outcast from all that was good and decent in society. He would make the whole world pay for treating him so badly. When he gave the commands, the so-called good people of Parsina would regret their superior attitude.

But the plan Aeshma outlined also had its dangers, and Hakem Rafi was not so foolish he could easily discount them. If he let Aeshma go off by himself to subjugate the lesser demons, he had no guarantee Aeshma wouldn't find some way to betray him. On the other hand, if he went with Aeshma he would have to go through some terrifying experiences. It had taken him some time to get over Aeshma's frightening countenance; how much worse would he feel, even knowing Aeshma was there to protect him, if he was surrounded by hordes of evil creatures? The daevas and the lesser demons were created by Rimahn specifically to torment men; how kindly would they take to having a man in their midst, and following his orders?

Mostly, though, it was fear that made him decide. He dared not live unguarded again, when another wizard like Akar could slip in and destroy everything he'd built. If he were master of the world he would have guards around him constantly, and he could have all wizards—and anyone else who posed a threat to him—hunted down and killed. Then there would be no one to challenge his authority; he could live in perfect safety from then on.

"I'll do it," he said aloud to Aeshma. "I'll go with you and together we'll rule the world of spirits and men."

"An ambition worthy of you, O my master," Aeshma smiled, knowing he'd once again seduced his master into following the path Aeshma himself had chosen.

Having made his decision, now, Hakem Rafi was slightly uncertain in his manner. He was more at ease anticipating the ultimate result than in planning the steps to reach it. "What must we do first?" he asked his slave.

"We must start with the simplest," Aeshma said, and it was evident the plan had already been well conceived in his mind. "We shall visit my offspring, the hairy demons. They will easily fall back into line, and once they're on our side we'll use them to build our forces."

Aeshma did not allow his master time for second thoughts or hesitations. Even as he spoke he wrapped his enormous claw with its razor-sharp nails around Hakem Rafi's body and hurled the two of them off the mountaintop. This mighty leap sent them hurtling through the air, with the wind whistling past them as they fell with ever-increasing speed toward the hard ground below. As he watched the earth rushing up at him so rapidly, Hakem Rafi again felt fear, even though he knew Aeshma was supposed to protect him from all harm. They reached ground level and Hakem Rafi closed his eyes and braced his muscles against the shock of the certain impact.

But the crash never came. As they touched the earth they passed right through the surface as though it were nothing but air. Darkness enveloped them, a darkness deeper than Hakem Rafi had ever known before. As a thief, he'd always thought darkness was his friend, but this was such a total absence of light that it smothered all his senses. He became slowly aware of the stale, dead smell of late autumn and damp, moldy earth. Gone was the light of the sun; gone, too, was the honest darkness of nightfall. Instead they plunged through an oppressive blackness that pressed in from all sides like a vise, a blackness from the worst tunnel nightmare a man's mind could devise. Even though Aeshma made sure the air was sufficient for him, Hakem Rafi began gasping for breath. He suddenly wondered whether world domination was indeed worth the effort.

Time lost all meaning for him in this abyss, and minutes passed with agonizing slowness as their plunge through the earth continued. Hakem Rafi looked out and could see nothing; he wondered how Aeshma knew where he was going. All the blackness looked the same, left, right, ahead, and behind. Would they be lost forever in this hellish pit, to wander madly through the earth like dispossessed souls unable to find the Bridge of Shinvar?

Then suddenly the blackness was over and they were in a place of blazing radiance and deafening noise. Hakem Rafi quickly sealed his eyes tightly shut to avoid blindness after straining so long at the dark, and lifted his hands quickly to his ears to shut out the maddening shrieks that surrounded him on all sides. His face, unprotected by the clenched fist of Aeshma that held most of his body, felt a blast of heat as though from a blacksmith's furnace. The hot wind blew a sour odor into his nostrils and he wrinkled his nose to keep out, as much as possible, the noxious smell.

After a few moments he could open his eyes a tiny crack and squint out at the sights around him, though he still dared not take his hands from his ears lest the horrible high-pitched shrieking drive him insane. The light everywhere was still brilliant, as though he were looking directly into the sun at midday, and his eyes watered from the pain. The glare made the colors around him seem pale and washed out, and the scene appeared two-dimensional and unreal. Nothing had a sharp edge to it; everything blurred into everything else, making the details hard to establish in his mind.

There was movement all around him, indistinct shapes flitting from place to place in constant turmoil, as though nothing in this hellhole remained put. The beings who darted about looked vaguely human, but their bodies and limbs were grotesquely distorted and elongated to give them a skeletal appearance. Their faces were shadowy and indistinct, but their mouths seemed full of fangs and their noses were flat against their faces. Their skin appeared sometimes red, sometimes yellow, sometimes orange in the strange glare, and their eyes were tiny black pinpoints in their skulls. They were unclothed, yet they did not appear naked; it was as though some indescribable film covered their bodies without concealing anything. Some of the creatures had long tapering tails, while others apparently did not. As they darted back and forth they screeched at unearthly volumes, filling the air with their hideous cacophony.

Their most unusual feature, though, was their hair. They all had long masses of it flowing from their heads, yellowish white in stark contrast to the deep colors of their skin. The hair was fine and brittle, often tangled and totally unmanageable. It snarled and matted and flew about as the demons darted through the air and shrieked their hideous cries, giving them a disheveled appearance.

Aeshma and Hakem Rafi appeared in this vast cavernous area beneath the earth, and the king of the daevas stood with legs apart in a stance of command. He held Hakem Rafi securely in his left hand, while his right hand was held up in a powerfully clenched fist.

"Your sire has returned," Aeshma proclaimed in a voice that boomed throughout the cavern. "Bow down to me, you hairy demons, and pay your proper homage."

This announcement produced varied reactions among the demons. Some flitted about more wildly than before, shrieking ever more loudly and being panicked beyond human understanding. Others stopped dead still as though afraid to move, their beady eyes peering through the glare of this unearthly light to distinguish the forms standing there. After a pause for the facts to sink into their minds, many made a deep salaam to acknowledge the return of their master—but some few stood defiantly by and made no gesture of obeisance.

Aeshma paid particular attention to these rebels. "Why do you not bow to me?" he roared at them in a voice calculated to make even the sturdiest souls quiver.

One of the defiant demons, bolder than the rest, spoke up immediately. "You've been away for many centuries, O Aeshma," he said, his sharply pointed tail waving forcefully. "Do you expect just to come in here and have us surrender ourselves to you?"

"I am your father and your master," Aeshma said sternly.

"And you led us into a useless war and you paid the price," the rebel replied. "We've developed other plans, other methods of tormenting mankind without your help while you were gone. We don't need you any more."

Aeshma puffed out his chest and grew even larger in stature, until his head reached to the very top of this enormous cavern. "You'll pay for this insolence!" he bellowed at the throng of demons. "From nothing did I create you, and to nothing shall you return!"

Even as he spoke, Aeshma extended his right hand toward the demon who'd spoken so harshly to him. The heat of the earth's internal fires—which had been as a mother to these demons—was sucked from the rebel's body and flowed like a piped stream into Aeshma's hand. The daeva laughed cruelly as the energy he drew strengthened him.

The rebellious demon let out a scream that was the embodiment of nightmares, and twisted about in agony. Then slowly did he curl up at the edges, like a piece of dried parchment tossed into a fire, until he folded in upon himself and became no more.

Some of his comrades in the revolt leaped at Aeshma in their anger, and the air was filled with their bodies flying in attack. Hakem Rafi shrank back, trying to hide within the safety of Aeshma's huge fist and certain he had reached the appointed hour of his death—but, as Aeshma had sworn, no harm befell him. Though the angered demons swarmed all around like bees in a frenzy, shrieking as loud as they could and spitting poison at Aeshma, none of their anger or their venom could touch the thief. Aeshma shielded him as carefully as he'd promised, meanwhile launching a counterattack of his own.

The air became supercharged and everything was a blur, but Hakem Rafi could see that one by one the attacking demons were shriveling as their leader had done under Aeshma's assault. Most of the other demons stood about silently awaiting the outcome of this battle, not wanting to defend Aeshma but unwilling also to join the rebellion against his authority.

When it became clear that Aeshma would win, some of the rebellious demons fled—but they were no more successful in that than they'd been in their attack. Aeshma strode through the cavern in mighty steps, pursuing all who tried to escape and blasting them to nothingness with the power of his magic. Some of the rebels turned to plead for mercy, but Aeshma had none to give. Before too long, all those who dared challenge his authority were vanished from the world and the rest of the hairy demons stood quietly humble before their master.

"I say again, pay your homage!" Aeshma roared. "All who hesitate will share the fate of those now departed." And this time the demons, as though with one mind, made the deep salaam of reverence to their acknowledged leader.

Hakem Rafi, peeking out from his place of hiding and seeing that all threat was gone, was now emboldened to make his presence known. "Make the air cooler and the light dimmer, O Aeshma, that I might be more comfortable," he commanded.

"I hear and I obey, O master," said Aeshma, and immediately the light and temperature were reduced to a level more bearable to humans. The hairy demons, however—startled by this abrupt change in their living conditions—began flitting about the cavern once more and shrieking in their high voices, trying to keep from freezing. Many collided with one another as, in the dimmer light, they were nearly blind.

"Make them stop shricking," Hakem Rafi said with his hands once again to his ears. "I can't stand that noise."

"Silence!" Aeshma obediently commanded his progeny. "You must cease your screaming and yelling this instant, or face my wrath."

The shrieking stopped, though the demons continued flitting about to keep warm and kept bumping into one another. One of the hairy demons, trying hard not to appear disobedient but still wanting an explanation, said, "What is happening, O wise and revered master? Have you not yourself taught us that mankind is our hated enemy and that we exist for the purpose of plaguing and killing them? Do you now follow the commands of a mere mortal, even as we must obey yours?"

Aeshma scowled, and the demons withered visibly before his displeasure. But he took no punitive action as he explained. "Hakem Rafi, who stands here before you, is no ordinary man. It was his bravery and daring that freed me from my imprisonment, and I have sworn to serve him as faithfully as you must serve me. Therefore, as you acknowledge me as your master, so must you acknowledge Hakem Rafi as my master, and do his bidding as though it came directly from me.

"And too, while he is a mortal and created of Oromasd, still his soul follows the path of Rimahn. He has been a liar, a thief, and a murderer, and for these acts alone we should do him homage. We shall become his army, and with our help he shall rule the entire world. All men and all spirits will bow before him, and he shall help us deliver the world unto Rimahn.

"So bow, now, before Hakem Rafi, the man who is more than a man, and who will lead us to victory over the forces of Oromasd."

Aeshma held out his giant hand with Hakem Rafi standing on his palm, and in the subterranean cavern did the legion of the hairy demons bow before Hakem Rafi and call him master, and swear to help him conquer the human world. And from this beginning would Hakem Rafi the blackhearted, the thief, set out on his conquest with an army that would grow to a size no man on Parsina had ever witnessed before.

17

THE CLOAK OF INVISIBILITY

 AFAR al-Sharif, Prince Ahmad, and Umar bin Ibrahim were led away from King Zargov's audience chamber still protesting their innocence. A squad of alert guards, walking before and behind them, escorted the prisoners through the downward sloping corridors of Punjar into the heart of the mountain that was their home. The men from Ravan again had to duck to avoid bumping their heads on the low ceilings; the gravel that littered the floor crunched beneath their boots, and the smells within the walls—which they'd thought were bad before—grew steadily worse. Eventually the trio was breathing exclusively through their mouths to avoid smelling the awful stench.

Their hearts were heavy at the thought that their mission would be curtailed this quickly. This was only the first piece of the Crystal, and already they seemed doomed to failure; how could they have ever hoped to gather all four pieces? What rash conceit led them to think that three men could accomplish this monumental task? Now they wondered whether they'd even see the light of the sun again. Too many were the treasure hunters who'd disappeared in Punjar to let them believe they stood a good chance of escape.

Even Umar suffered doubts—not that Oromasd couldn't release him if that was his will, but whether he was actually following the path of the lord of light or merely being a vain old man who pretended he knew a fraction of Oromasd's great plan.

The captain of the guard, sneering triumphantly at having called the prisoners' bluff and been vindicated by his king, led them into the dimly lit dungeon area, where the key master found an empty cell to house the new visitors. This cell, only slightly bigger than the narrow one Jafar had occupied in Ravan during his brief but painful incarceration, had no window in the door to let in light, and no furnishings or amenities—not even a pallet of straw to use as a bed or a bucket for a lavatory. Bare stone walls were all they'd have as comfort. The three men were shoved into the narrow confinement and the heavy iron door slammed shut behind them. They could hear the key turn in the latch with a rasping sound as they stood, cold and afraid, in total darkness.

"What kind of a hellhole is this?" Prince Ahmad asked angrily. "What king would treat his subjects or his visitors this way?"

"This is only slightly worse than the accommodations Your Highness himself keeps in Ravan," said Jafar al-Sharif, so overcome with his despair that he was unable to keep the bitterness out of his voice.

"What do you know about Ravan's dungeons?" Umar asked, suddenly worried about the background of the man they'd been traveling with, but about whom they really knew so little.

"I've visited them and seen what goes on, which is probably more than you have," Jafar said carefully, realizing he'd almost made a major slip and trying not to let on how firsthand his knowledge was. He described the cells and the accommodations, and the tortures the prisoners were routinely subjected to.

"What would you have us do with thieves and murderers?" Umar said indignantly. "Should we rest them on pillows and feed them sweetmeats?"

"There were many in there who deserved no punishment at all, who were tortured merely at the whim of your wali of police," Jafar countered. "Guilt should be established *before* sentence is carried out."

Prince Ahmad had listened quietly to Jafar's descriptions, and even in total darkness the somber tone of his voice indicated he was paying serious thought to the matter. "There must be a system of justice," he said. "When I am king, criminals will be punished according to their due, but I'll see that the innocent have naught to fear." He paused, and added in an almost inaudible whisper, "*If* I am ever king."

Umar, hearing the tone of hopelessness in the young man's voice, changed the subject to prevent him from falling into a mood of resignation. "A discussion on criminal justice can wait for some more relaxed moment around a camp fire one night as we travel. For the moment we must bend our minds to getting out of here and finding the piece of the Crystal we need.

"In our current straits, the prince's strength and skill are of no help to us. You're along to solve situations like this, O wizard. How can we get out of here?"

This was what Jafar al-Sharif had feared, that the others would turn to him in times of crisis and he'd be unable to use his supposed magical powers to help. Still, he might be able to do something in this particular instance. Cari had gotten him out of a dungeon before; perhaps she could again.

"I'll summon my Jann," he said aloud. "She's particularly helpful in situations like this." Rubbing the ring on the middle finger of his left hand he intoned, "By the ring that bears thy name, O Cari, I command thee to appear before me."

He stood and waited for the pinkish haze that would form into the lovely and familiar shape of Cari the Jann. Even though he couldn't see it in the blackness of this cell, he'd still smell the faint aroma of ylang-ylang and hear her voice as she materialized and acknowledged his command.

But nothing happened. Cari did not come. When a minute passed with no response, Jafar tried the invocation again, fearing he'd done something wrong. Still nothing. Jafar felt a cold knot of fear clutching at his innards. He'd grown very used to having Cari to depend on. Had the ring now ceased to work? Was the power of Cari lost to him forever?

"What's the matter?" Umar asked. "Why isn't she here?"

Jafar didn't know either, but he couldn't admit that to his companions. "King Zargov has some magical abilities of his own, as we've seen. He was able to camouflage his soldiers so we didn't see them until the ambush, and he could spot Cari when she was invisible. He must have made the walls of this dungeon impervious to magic, so the spell of my ring cannot reach Cari and she cannot be summoned."

"Is that possible?" asked Prince Ahmad.

"All things are possible, Your Highness," Jafar said. "I see more and more impossible things happening every day."

"In that case, O Jafar," the priest said testily, "it should be possible for you to get us out of here."

"Had I the proper equipment, it would be child's play," Jafar replied. "As it is, I'm rather bereft."

He paused as an idea occured to him. "Hmm. We found a key in the sand Jinn's cave, a key that Oromasd must have given us for a purpose. Could it possibly be a key to this cell?"

He reached into his robes and pulled out the thong on which he'd hung the mysterious key. Taking it from his neck, he stepped forward to the door and felt for the keyhole with his fingers. When he found it he inserted the long brass key into the hole and began turning it slowly. The key fit within the slot, but nothing happened when it was twisted, the door remained locked as securely as ever.

"Oh well, it was worth a try," Jafar said, putting the thong back around his neck and tucking the key inside his kaftan once more.

"What will you try now?" Umar asked him.

"Now it's your turn."

"Mine?"

"Yes," said Jafar al-Sharif. "You're the expert on prayers, O priest. I'd suggest you find a good one for us. Maybe Oromasd, in his infinite mercy, will find a way to free us from this cell where my humble abilities have failed."

Selima ran as fast as she could when she broke away from the others in the audience chamber. It was her first intention to run back to the entrance where they'd left the horses, though she had no idea what she could do when she got there. They'd taken so many branching corridors in coming down here, however, that she quickly became lost in the maze of tunnels. She ran away from the sound of pursuit, but she had no idea what she was running toward. In her insubstantial condition she could not become tired or short of breath, so she easily outraced those chasing her, only to find herself lost and alone in an endless series of dark tunnels.

A lesser girl might have broken down and cried, but Selima was too strong willed and had been through too many crises already in the past few weeks to become discouraged in this situation. She knew there would be a solution if only she kept her head and worked things out sensibly.

The darkness and the stench of these foul tunnels closed in about her, but now that she was no longer being chased she could move through them in a systematic way to see where they led. Her feet made no sound as they trod upon the gravel on the tunnel floors, while anyone approaching her made a characteristic crunching noise to warn her they were coming.

Some of these tunnels, she discovered, had been formed naturally within the earth, while others had been carved from the hard, black rock; during the millennia the Punjari had lived within this mountain, they had honeycombed it with passages. Torches in the walls provided illumination at intervals no closer than every thirty or forty cubits and sometimes as much as a hundred, but this dim illumination worked to Selima's advantage. Being as insubstantial as she was made her almost invisible in the darkness; whenever she heard anyone coming she could easily disappear into the shadows at the side and the people would pass without even noticing her presence.

At times, though, she came to larger caverns where the smell became correspondingly greater. Many of these had a large wall with smaller holes drilled in it, some of them as high as five stories above the ground level, with ladders cut into the rock to reach their entrances; Selima guessed these served as homes for Punjari families, though she didn't investigate any of them. She also passed through one large cave that served as a communal kitchen area; fires burned there constantly in primitive-looking ovens, and the air smelled of unidentifiably mixed cooking odors. Nearby were doors to recesses in the rock walls that served as storerooms for many of the Punjari cooking supplies.

Selima had a little more trouble traversing these larger caverns because they were much better lit than the tunnels. Here she had to wait at the mouth of the tunnel she was leaving until the chamber was empty—or at least sparsely populated—and then sneak across to the next corridor hugging tightly against one wall, keeping as much in shadow as she could. Since she made no noise her tactics worked, for she passed through these living quarters without once being spotted by their inhabitants.

All the things she saw were interesting in an abstract way, but it did nothing to solve the problem of how to rescue her companions, get the piece of the Crystal, and escape from this wretched kingdom. Selima wandered aimlessly through the tunnels of Punjar, not knowing what she was looking for and hoping she'd be smart enough to recognize something worthwhile if fate presented it to her. The more she wandered, though, the more hopeless her task seemed and the lower her spirits sank.

Eventually her wanderings brought her to a section of the tunnels that looked different than the rest. The ceilings were higher and the floor was swept clean of rubble; the tunnels were broader and their walls were smooth in contrast to the rough-hewn nature of most of the tunnels she'd seen. There was much more light, with torches burning every few cubits, and there were more private rooms sealed off with their own doors, rather than being open holes in the cave walls.

Selima peered through some of the doors that were hanging ajar and saw furnishings fancier than she'd seen elsewhere in the tunnels. This led her to conclude that she'd circled around and returned to the "royal" portion of the mountain where King Zargov and his retainers lived. Selima didn't know whether to be cheered or depressed at this development, but she did have to be more careful because the brighter lighting meant it would be easier for passersby to spot her and send up an alarm.

As she was traversing one corridor whose walls were not only smooth, but polished as well, she heard a group of people approaching in front of her. She turned and started to retrace her steps when she realized more people were coming from that direction. Selima looked frantically for a hiding place and saw across the corridor a wooden door that was open enough to let her slip through. Hoping there'd be no one inside the room to spot her as she entered, she squeezed through the opening and looked around at this new environment.

Her first and strongest impression was that this was a place that didn't stink; the air held the refreshing fragrance of a rose incense that drove all the unpleasant odors of Punjar before it. The room was as lavishly appointed as any she'd seen in Punjar. The bare rock walls were draped with airy fabrics of pastel blue, yellow, and white; there was a large mirror on the right-hand wall with a table in front of it, on which were a set of combs and several jars. Stools and chairs were spaced about the floor; another door in the opposite wall led to a second chamber beyond. This was quite obviously a woman's room; there was still danger for a fugitive like Selima, but the soft tones of the room mitigated it a little.

The voices from the corridor outside grew louder, and it soon became clear their destination was this very room. Cursing under her breath at her bad luck, Selima retreated into the second room and found this was a bedroom with a single canopied bed draped in blue and yellow gauze; a closet dug into the wall; and a bureau with more furnishings that made it clear a woman lived here. There was no other way out of this room.

A group of people entered the outer chamber. From the sound of their voices they were all women—and Selima recognized one deeper, cynical voice as that of Leila, the woman who'd sat beside King Zargov in the throne room and taunted him so relentlessly. Selima couldn't make out individual words as these women spoke, but it seemed clear that the other women were serving in attendance to Leila.

Then the voices came toward the bedroom, and Selima had no choice but to dash into the open closet and try to hide behind some of the clothes that were hanging there. It was not the best of hiding places; Selima would have to hold perfectly still and trust to her transparent nature to keep her from being conspicuous.

Leila entered the bedroom, following closely by four serving women. The tall blond woman had removed her jewelry and had let down her long yellow hair so that it flowed to the middle of her blue sidaireeya. It was quite a contrast to see the fair Leila towering above the dark-skinned Punjari servants who fussed about her. The servants jabbered constantly in a thick accent about things that made no sense to Selima, and their incessant chatter even wore on Leila's nerves. Their mistress finally shooed them all out of her suite so she could be alone.

When the servants had finally departed, Leila closed the door to the outer corridor and breathed a sigh of relief. "It's all right now, O fleet-footed phantom," she said. "You can come out of hiding."

Selima was startled, for she hadn't made any noise to let the woman know she was there. She wondered whether to acknowledge Leila's words or ignore them—but Leila was looking straight at her hiding place, and spoke with a certainty that Selima was there. If Selima didn't come out as requested, the older woman would simply come to the closet and see her there.

Sheepishly, then, Selima stepped out of the closet into the light of the bedroom. "How did you know I was in there?" she asked.

"Your feet showed beneath the clothes. I don't own niaal like those."

"Your servants didn't spot them."

"I see a great many things other people miss. It's a curse or a blessing, depending on how you view it."

Selima took a deep breath, afraid to ask the next question. "Are you going to turn me in?"

"That all depends," Leila said, "on the story you tell me. I certainly won't do anything rash; life in Punjar is entirely too boring to pass up an opportunity when it presents itself, no matter what that lump of a king says."

The tall blond woman crossed the room and sat down cross-legged on the bed. She leaned forward with her elbow against her knee, her head resting on top of the arm, and looked straight at Selima. "If you entertain me," she continued, "I won't call for the guards and set you running again. But be careful not to lie, for I'll spot that in an instant."

Selima took another deep breath, wondering where to start. She wished she had her father's talent for storytelling, for he could certainly have bound this woman in the spell of his words. Selima was not nearly as sure of her own abilities to tell their tale correctly—she was certain she'd tell things in the wrong order or omit some vital detail, or say things in a way that the story did not seem clear. Nevertheless, she was here and her father wasn't, so she'd have to do his job for him as best she could.

She explained how her father, the wizard, had dueled with the blind wizard Akar, stolen the magical carpet, and escaped from the mountain castle at the top of the world, only to have her fall under Akar's death curse. She told of the battle with the Afrits and losing the carpet, and of meeting Prince Ahmad in the desert. She told of the journey to Sarafiq, where her father and the prince consulted the prophet Muhmad and learned they must travel across Parsina and find the pieces of the Crystal of Oromasd for the upcoming battle between the forces of good and evil. She told of their adventures with the Badawi, of fighting the Jinn Estanash, and of King Armandor's hospitality in the city of Khmeria. Throughout it all, Leila subjected her to a cold, silent stare as though weighing the truth of every word.

"I must beg you for your help, O gracious lady," Selima concluded. "My father and my friends are locked in your husband's dungeon and I know not where to turn. Unless you can intercede with the king, our mission is a failure and the whole world might be doomed to destruction."

"Intercession is hopeless," Leila said with a shake of her head. "The king's mind is harder than the rocks of these walls—and you saw how much influence I have over his opinions."

She paused. "I knew your fellow Ahmad was much more than he presented himself—there was too much poise in his manner and demeanor. A prince of Ravan, you say? Very interesting."

"A prince in exile," Selima corrected hastily.

Leila appeared not to hear, so lost was she within her own thoughts. She stared vacantly at a point in space somewhere beyond Selima, and her face was a mask that revealed none of the thoughts behind it. Selima fidgeted, not knowing quite what to do—whether to say more on her companions' behalf or to remain silent and let Leila convince herself of what action she must take.

After several silent minutes Leila broke out of her reverie. "Your father is a most handsome and interesting man," she said. "You say he's a wizard?"

"Yes," Selima said nervously, wondering whether Leila could indeed tell if she were lying.

"I'll bet he works a spell on all the ladies," Leila said with a smile.

"He's been celibate since my mother died two years ago," Selima said, not sure whether she resented the other woman's implications or not.

"Oh. I'm sorry for your loss, little one. He must have loved her very much."

"He did," Selima nodded.

Leila was thoughtful for yet another minute. Finally she spoke again. "What are you prepared to offer me in exchange for my help?"

Selima was at a total loss. "I don't know what you need, O my lady. You already seem to have more riches than we could offer—"

"I need my freedom," Leila sighed. "I need to be away from these stinking pits, out in the open air where the breeze can blow through my hair. I need to see the sun, the moon, the stars, the clouds, the whole panorama of sky that's more than a cavern ceiling. I need freedom from a husband whose brain's no larger than a rooster's testicle. I need to eat real food and breathe fresh air. I need a chance to roam the world and see what I've missed while I've been cooped up here like a cut flower in a vase."

She stopped abruptly and looked straight into Selima's eyes. "If I help your father and his companions escape, will you give me your word that I can come with you on your mission, wherever it leads you?"

"It could be very dangerous," Selima began.

"There's no death worse than death by boredom," Leila said. "I've been dying for ten years. This will give me a chance to live again."

"But I'm not in charge of the group, I don't have the authority to invite you along," the girl protested.

"If you have the authority to ask for my help, you have the authority to include me in your adventure," Leila insisted. "I take you to be an honorable woman. If you'll give me your word, I'll help your father and the others. If not. . . ."

She shrugged. "If kismet decrees I should die of boredom in this accursed mountain, I'll at least have interesting company for a short while."

Selima didn't know what to make of this very forward woman who spoke her mind so bluntly. She remembered all too vividly how she'd been betrayed by a supposedly friendly woman in Ravan's hammam when she'd been fleeing the police. Even if Leila was being honest with her, would she be an asset to the group? At the very least, though, she could get them out of the dungeon; anything beyond that would have to be in Oromasd's hands.

"All right," Selima said aloud, "you have my word that you can come with us when we leave Punjar if you'll help us get out."

"Good," Leila smiled. "I was hoping you'd see reason."

She stood up and paused, looking around the room with a curiously wistful expression on her face. "You know, ever since I came here I've dreamed of nothing but leaving again—and now that I'm set to go, I'm not sure what to take. Whether I liked it or not, this dreary little cave has been part of my life for ten years; leaving it is going to feel strange."

She stared into the closet for a moment before making a decision. "I suppose it's rough out on the trail; I'd better take the most durable of my clothes. And maybe just a few of my better jewels in case of emergency."

She took out a simple cloth bag that contained her sewing supplies, dumped the contents out, and began filling it with the items she wished to take. She took off her blue zarabil and placed them in the bag, putting on her feet in their place the sturdy but soft leather boots she wore when hiking through the more remote, unfinished tunnels of her husband's realm. The boots looked a bit strange with the sirwaal she was wearing, but she was dressing for convenience, now, rather than style.

Though the climate in the tunnels of Punjar was temperate, it often seemed cold and, as a result, Leila had a good selection of heavy cotton and linen clothes and quilted robes. There were brightly colored sidaireeya with short and long sleeves, several pairs of sirwaal trousers, a thin but sturdy cloak, and a pair of handsomely striped and embroidered milaaya to cover her head. As a final thought, Leila grabbed a long, warm sleeping gown; she normally didn't wear one, but it might be handy on the trail.

Selima was impressed by the number of clothes Leila was leaving behind and the quality of things she stuffed into her bag. Having watched the Badawi women's supply, she knew Leila showed a good deal of trail sense in her selections; the clothes she'd chosen would stand her in good stead during their travels. Selima did notice one significant omission: Leila had packed no milfas. It must be the custom in Leila's country to go barefaced. So much had Selima's travels and conditions changed her that she wasn't really shocked by this, merely observant.

Leila took a small box and placed within it some of her rings, necklaces, bracelets, and earrings. She paused for a few moments and looked around the room. Grabbing a set of jeweled hairbrushes off the bureau, she tucked them in her well-stuffed bag and gave a deep sigh. "I'm ready," she said.

She opened the door to the outer hallway and looked down the corridor, but could see no one about. "The way is clear," she told Selima. "Follow me. Stay in shadow as much as possible so no one will see you. I can go almost anywhere I wish within these tunnels, but your presence would be a little harder to explain."

The tall Leila had to stoop slightly in these low-ceilinged tunnels as she guided Selima downward into the mountain through a series of back corridors where they encountered no one. Finally they reached a particularly dark and gloomy section that Leila said was the perimeter of the dungeon.

"We'd better be careful that the guards don't hear us," Selima whispered.

"There's only the one key master," Leila explained. "No one's ever dared challenge the king's authority to lock people away, so they don't have more than one guard down here at a time. You wait here and be quiet; I'll take care of him."

As Selima obediently waited in the dark and empty corridor, Leila walked boldly out into the dungeon's antechamber and spoke to the key master, a dim-witted man slow to comprehend any change in his daily routine. Leila patiently explained to him several times that King Zargov demanded his presence in one particular chamber clear on the other side of the mountain, and that she would stand guard over the dungeon until he returned. Finally the key master departed on his supposed errand, leaving the keys in Leila's possession. When she was certain the man would not return to ask yet another question, Leila called Selima out of the shadows and together they walked down the length of the dungeon, noting the many heavy steel doors, all closed and locked.

Able to contain her impatience no longer, Selima ran ahead of her guide through the narrow, dimly lit hallway. "Father?" she called. "Father, where are you?"

After a few moments, an answering voice came from behind one of the doors. "Selima? Take care, don't let the guards hear you."

"We've sent the only guard away, Father. We came to rescue you."

" 'We'?" Jafar asked. "Who's with you?"

Leila now spoke up. "I am Leila, wife of King Zargov. Am I addressing Jafar the wizard?"

"You are indeed, O beautiful queen of these dismal tunnels, who shines far brighter than any jewel in your husband's throne room, who lights the dim caverns with—"

"Yes, I can tell you're Jafar," Leila interrupted. "Please spare me the soliloquy; I'll be happy to hear it later when we've got more time. Your daughter came to me and told me your story. She's given me her word that if I rescue you now I can come along with you on your journey."

"We can't have too large a group," Jafar spoke hesitantly. "We'd already resolved to travel light and fast."

"How light and fast can you travel in that cell?" Leila asked tartly.

"A valid point, O lovely lady of Punjar," Jafar replied. There were a few moments of whispered consultation with the others, then he went on, "Very well, it's agreed. We'll take you with us if you rescue us now."

"Let me have the oath of the priest on this matter," Leila insisted.

The voice of Umar bin Ibrahim came through the door, swearing in the name of Oromasd and the Bounteous Immortals that Leila would be allowed to accompany them on their journey around Parsina—although he added he was mystified why she'd want to undertake a venture so hazardous and unladylike.

Assured now that there would be no double crosses, Leila turned the key in the lock and pulled the heavy door open. The three men staggered out into the hallway, blinking at even this dim light, after the total darkness of their cell. Prince Ahmad bowed his head to Leila and said, "We thank you for your kindness to strangers, O noble lady."

"The gratitude can wait. I'll lead you to your horses and we can get away."

But Prince Ahmad shook his head. "We can't leave without the piece of the Crystal in your husband's possession."

"I don't know where it is," Leila admitted, "and he'd never tell us of his own accord."

"He could be made to talk," Umar said with a most unpriestly tone of vengeance in his voice.

"You couldn't even reach him," Leila said. "He so fears assassination that he surrounds himself with guards night and day. These dungeons are filled with people who've tried to kill him—or who he's imagined have tried. It's all one and the same in his mind."

A smile crossed Jafar's face. "In situations like this," he said, "I've found it helpful to empty all the prison cells—it adds to the general confusion. Please hand me the key."

Leila's smile mimicked his own as she obeyed his request. Jafar al-Sharif went up and down the corridor opening the dungeon doors and telling the inhabitants King Zargov had pardoned them. Many were unbelieving, at first, but when no evil befell them they left their cells and made a speedy exit from the dungoen before the king could change his mind again. The travelers were soon standing alone in the corridor.

"A very humanitarian gesture," Leila nodded, "but it does nothing to solve our problem."

"Still, we must try," Jafar said. "We can't leave without the Crystal, or our whole mission will become pointless. Surely there must be some way to get through to the king."

"Not even a mouse could slip by unseen," Leila insisted.

The word "unseen" suggested a plan to Jafar's shrewd mind. "I have the glimmerings of an idea," he said, "if I can get something out of my saddlebag."

"Your gear was all unpacked from the horses and brought down to the treasury for inspection," Leila said. "I heard the king tell his ministers he'd examine the stuff in the morning."

"How does he know when it's morning in these tunnels?" Selima asked.

"Morning is whenever the king wakes up," Leila explained.

"As long as our things are intact, that's all that matters," Jafar said. "Lead us to the treasury, quickly. The sooner we retrieve our gear, the sooner we can be away."

It was more difficult for the group to reach the treasury than it had been for the two women to reach the dungeon— first because the party was larger and easier to spot, and second because they were going into a far more populated section of the tunnels. Leila took them as far as she could via the unused back corridors, but there came a point at which they would have to go through major routes that were both well lit and well traveled. For the whole party to go any further would invite discovery.

Jafar gave the matter some thought. "Are there any here beside your king who can see an invisible Jann?" he asked Leila.

"The Punjari have weak eyesight from spending so much time in these caves," Leila said. "I doubt they can see their toes clearly enough to count them—assuming they could count, that is."

Jafar al-Sharif looked at the ring of Cari on the middle finger of his left hand. His failure to summon the Jann in the darkened cell had shaken his faith more than he cared to admit. What if the ring no longer worked? Could he continue his brazen masquerade without Cari's faithful assistance? He felt the same chill in the pit of his stomach that he'd felt in Sarafiq when the acolyte asked him to give up the ring before visiting the prophet. Cari had become a very important part of his life, and the thought of her vanishing from it so abruptly left a hollow place in his heart.

Still, there was only one way to find out. Cursing himself mentally for his hesitation, Jafar al-Sharif rubbed the ring and said, "By the ring that bears thy name, O Cari, I command thee to appear before me."

There was a heart-stopping second in which nothing happened, and then the familiar pink haze, scented of ylang-ylang, began to coalesce in front of him, solidifying into the reassuring form of the Jann. "I come at your command, O my master," Cari said, making the formal salaam and averting her eyes as she always did, though in her heart she was delighted to find her master safe from harm.

The relief that washed over Jafar had the strange effect of making him appear more callous. "Why didn't you come when I summoned you in the cell?" he demanded.

Cari looked up at him with eyes wide. "I felt no such summons, O master. I must always come when I'm called."

Her innocent look made him instantly regret upbraiding her. "I'm sorry," he said. "My assumption must have been correct, that there was a spell on the dungeon to prevent magic from working there."

"My husband has some slight powers," Leila confirmed. "That may have been within his abilities."

Time was short, and they couldn't stand here indefinitely without being discovered. Jafar explained briefly to Cari that Leila was helping them, then outlined some of his plan. "You," he said to Leila, "must go to the treasury room where our saddlebags are; no one will question you, I'm sure. Cari, you go with her invisibly. Bring our gear back here to me."

"Hearkening and obedience, O my master," Cari said, and set off following Leila.

Nearly half an hour passed, and the fugitives waited in their dim corridor with growing panic that their plans might somehow have been thwarted. Then Leila returned, and behind her came floating the heavy saddlebags; Cari could make herself invisible, but not the things she was carrying. Leila apologized for the delay, explaining that the treasury guards weren't as simpleminded as the key master; Cari'd had to use more physical persuasion—actually, a rock to their skulls—to get past them.

The invisible Jann laid the gear down in a corner of the hallway and, after thanking her, Jafar knelt and searched quickly through their possessions until he found what he wanted.

"King Armandor told me this would make me invisible to human and djinn alike," he said, holding up the cloak of invisibility. "Cari tells me she can't see me when I use it; let's hope the king won't see me, either."

The khanjars and saifs that the guards had taken from them before they entered the tunnels had been stored with the saddle pouches, and Cari had thoughtfully brought those along as well. "What I do now I must do alone," Jafar said as he slipped his dagger into his sash where it belonged. "I will become invisible and you, O Leila, must lead me past the king's chambers and point them out to me. I'll slip inside and you come back here. Lead the others to where our horses are being kept and wait there with them for my return. Cari, the king would see you if you came with me, so go with the others and help them fight off any trouble. I'll join you all as soon as I persuade King Zargov to give me the Crystal."

Jafar donned the magical cloak and muttered the secret word taught to him by King Armandor: "Decibah." To the astonishment of all but Cari, who'd seen him do it before, he immediately vanished from their view. Still, his voice was known to them as he said, "Lead on, O Leila."

Recovering quickly from her surprise at his disappearance, Leila set off down the maze of corridors with Jafar al-Sharif following closely behind her. They did not speak, lest anyone see her talking to empty air and wonder about her sanity. Their path wound up, down, and around through the dim, low-ceilinged tunnels, until finally they reached a brighter portion of the caverns where there were many guards standing watch. Leila nodded her head in the direction of a well-guarded door as she walked a little way past it.

"Good luck, O thou marvelous impostor," she whispered, then turned and walked back the way she'd come.

Jafar al-Sharif stood before the door, slightly stunned, watching her go. She knew, then, that he wasn't really a wizard. But how did she know? Had Selima told her? He made a mental note to speak with his daughter privately as soon as they had a moment together. From Leila's tone and behavior she seemed willing to keep his secret—but the why and how of it puzzled him. There were many questions about this woman Leila that would need answering.

But right now he had other business to attend to. He was standing invisibly in the hallway while members of the king's guard stood on either side of the door to the royal chamber. Jafar couldn't walk *through* the wooden door, nor could he open it without being noticed. This was a problem that hadn't occured to him, and he took his time to consider it.

As he stood there watching the scene, servants scurried in and out of the room, opening and closing the door every few minutes. Jafar finally decided to take a chance, and slipped in behind one of the servants entering the king's chamber while the door was still open.

The royal chambers were not nearly as ostentatious as the audience hall. The rock walls were not studded with gems, but torches did burn more brightly here than elsewhere in these honeycombed passages. Heavy tapestries hung on the walls, and uncomfortable-looking wooden furniture was spaced about the floor. The royal crest was carved or emblazoned on everything in the room, and there were half a dozen servants scurrying about tending to details. Invisible as he was, Jafar al-Sharif had to step lively to keep out of their way.

King Zargov stood in the middle of this chaos, bellowing orders and sending his attendants chasing to and fro, in and out of the room. Jafar watched these antics for a second, pitying the servants, then drew his khanjar from its sheath and stepped up right beside the king. As the monarch paused in his bellowing to draw a breath, Jafar nudged the point of his dagger against the royal ribs. "Make one sound and your heir will inherit your kingdom prematurely," he whispered in the king's ear.

King Zargov jumped and looked around, but could see no one. The feel of the knife point against his ribs, however, was unmistakable. "Who are you?" he asked hoarsely.

"I am Jafar the mage, whom you thought to imprison in your puny little dungeon. Your skills are no match for mine, O king of pismires. You should not interfere in the business of true wizards; you're liable to regret it."

The king's bony frame was shaking with fear now. "Wh-what do you want from me?"

"Only what I asked before: the piece of the Crystal of Oromasd that was entrusted to King Durrego these many ages ago. When I have that, my friends and I will depart in peace."

King Zargov gulped loudly. "Very—very well. I'll go get it for you."

"No," Jafar insisted. "You'll stay here with me and send one of your servants for it. What's the point of having lackeys if you don't use them now and then?"

Accordingly, King Zargov called one of his attendants to him and directed him to the throne room. There he would find a jeweled box beneath the throne. The servant was to bring the box back here immediately.

After the man departed, Jafar al-Sharif ordered the king to send the rest of his servants from the room, digging the knife point into Zargov's ribs to emphasize what would happen if the king were less than cooperative. Within a minute the two men were alone in the chamber, and King Zargov stood in sweat at the thought of what this unexpectedly powerful wizard might do to him.

Finally, after about ten minutes, the servant returned carrying the indicated box and handed it to the king, who took it with trembling hands. The servant could see his lord was not behaving in his normal manner, but didn't dare question this; servants who asked too many questions often ended up in the dungeons.

The king dismissed this servant as well, leaving him alone with Jafar and holding the box, unsure what to do next. Jafar had King Zargov open the jeweled box, and there inside was a piece of unpolished crystal with rough edges, somewhat larger than a man's fist. Jafar realized he faced a problem: he had no way of knowing whether this was the piece of the Crystal of Oromasd he'd been sent here to get. It was about the right size as the piece described in the journal of Ali Maimun, but there was nothing about it that looked special; it emitted no strange glow or aura to show it was divine in nature. How could he tell whether King Zargov was trying to fool him?

He recalled the story of Harban and the treacherous ferryman, and smiled. Digging his blade deeper into the king's ribs, he said, "What trick are you trying to play on me? That's not the Crystal of Oromasd."

"Yes it is, O wizard," King Zargov squeaked in panic. "The very same one, I swear it."

"It looks not right to me. I think you're lying, and for that you'll die."

King Zargov dropped instantly to his bony knees and began weeping like an infant. "Please don't kill me, O powerful wizard. This is the only crystal I know of. If what you seek is different, I know not where it is."

Finally convinced the king was not lying to him, Jafar said sternly, "Very well, I'll accept this one—for now. I give you warning, though: if it turns out to be false, I'll return to you in dead of night and turn your hands into deadly snakes and your hair into a carpet of scorpions."

Jafar al-Sharif took the Crystal out of its jeweled box and tucked it inside the pocket of his kaftan, where it promptly became as invisible as the rest of him. And at this moment, as possession of the Crystal switched to Jafar, a tremor of some magnitude shook the magical web that underlay the world. Far away, in Fricaz, Aeshma noticed the disturbance and looked to find its source—but by that time Cari's uncle Suleim had organized the righteous Jann, and they created so great a commotion of their own that Aeshma, seeing them, decided this was all the work of insignificant djinni and paid it no further heed. Only the prophet Muhmad, in his shrine at

Sarafiq, realized the true importance of the moment and smiled.

Unaware of these happenings about him, Jafar al-Sharif continued to badger Zargov. "Now," he told the blubbering king, "get back on your feet and lead me to where you're keeping my horses. My friends will meet us there, and we'll leave your accursed kingdom in peace."

King Zargov rose shakily from the floor, and Jafar jabbed him with the knife just to remind him of the danger that still threatened. Slowly and carefully, with Jafar behind him every step of the way, the king walked out of his inner chamber and past his guards. Some of them wanted to accompany him as a matter of course, but he hurriedly told them not to, saying he preferred to be alone for a few moments—a sentiment that was truer than they realized.

The royal prisoner led Jafar along a series of tunnels slanting upward toward the surface of the earth once more. It was nighttime outside as they came to the main entrance of the cave, and they found that a short battle had taken place here. A few of the guards standing watch over the horses had been killed by Prince Ahmad and Cari, but no warning had been given to any other Punjari troops. As they'd been instructed, the party was waiting for Jafar, and they were quite surprised to see King Zargov appear, seemingly alone. Prince Ahmad started to reach for his sword, but Jafar called out to reassure him that all was well.

King Zargov was also startled to see his wife in this company, seated on the horse that was usually reserved for supplies with Selima seated in front of her. "Leila!" King Zargov cried, then turned and tried to confront the invisible Jafar. "What are you doing with my wife, O wizard?"

"We're taking her with us as a hostage," Jafar replied casually. "We want to make sure you don't sent any of your troops to hunt us down after we leave this cave. Don't worry—as soon as we reach your borders we'll free her safe and sound. You have my oath as a wizard on that."

"If you harm her, wizard or no wizard, I'll see you pay dearly," King Zargov said, rising above his normal level of cowardice.

Now that they were out of the tunnels Jafar al-Sharif removed the magical cloak and became visible once more. "If anyone harms her, it won't be us," he promised, walking to his own horse and mounting quickly. The rest of the party had acted efficiently—the saddlebags were back in place and prepared for instant escape.

Now that they were all ready, Prince Ahmad spurred his steed Churash forward, disdaining even a backward glance at the Punjari king. The others followed his example, and the string of horses climbed up the steep path from the floor of the pit to the surface of the earth, leaving King Zargov standing in the dim torchlight watching his one-time prisoners disappear into the dark of night.

Leila rode her horse up beside Jafar. "Does your word mean so little to you, O Jafar, that you would betray it to send me back once you've crossed the border of Punjar?"

"I merely told your husband you'd be our hostage that far, and we'd set you free thereafter," the storyteller said. "If you freely choose not to return to him, can I be blamed for that?"

Leila laughed, a fine sound like the clear tone of a bell. "So I was right about you," she said mysteriously. "This promises to be interesting. We'll talk more later." Then she guided her horse away from his and did not speak to him again for the rest of the night.

18

THE ASSASSIN
AND THE
PROPHET

 BDEL ibn Zaid, high priest of the rimahniya temple, remained closeted in his private quarters long after Shammara had left the caves to return to the city of Ravan. He knelt on the hard stone floor of his cell, facing the niche that held his personal shrine. In the niche was a piece of solidified tar half the size of a man's fist; it was said to be a small piece of pitch taken from the Pits of Torment, domain of Rimahn and his daevas. This was a symbol of ibn Zaid's master, a token bequeathed to each high priest of the rimahniya in his turn. It was to this black rock that Abdel ibn Zaid now fervently prayed.

The rimahniya had tried before at Shammara's request to kill Prince Ahmad, and each previous attempt had failed. Ibn Zaid was convinced the failures were not the fault of the rimahniya; in each case, Prince Ahmad had been protected securely within the Temple of the Faith in Ravan itself, and it was hard for even the best assassins to slip past the watchful eyes of those priests. The servants of Oromasd had sometimes given their lives to protect the prince, and always the rimahniya assassins had been stopped short of their goal. Abdel ibn Zaid considered these failures a blot on the record of the rimahniya; now, facing his shrine, he vowed to his master Rimahn that blot would be erased for all time.

He removed his robes and picked up the small scourge he kept beside the shrine. His fingers ran caressingly over the black leather handle and the long, delicate lashes that ended in hard knots. He corrected his posture slightly so his back was absolutely straight. Then, staring straight ahead, he began to beat himself with the scourge.

Not a sound escaped his lips, not a muscle twitched on his face as he repeatedly flailed at his chest and back with the whip. Each stroke brought fresh pain, each stroke drew new blood, but Abdel ibn Zaid kept at his flagellation with single-minded fervor. His mind was filled with hatred for Oromasd and all who followed the path of truth, and he repeated to himself his oath to follow the way of darkenss and of lies, and to revere Rimahn above all else in life. The stings from the lashes faded to insignificance at the high priest withdrew into his trance of hatred.

Much later, with the skin on his upper body raw and soaked in blood and with his arm so tired he could barely lift it, Abdel ibn Zaid placed the scourge gently down in its familiar nook beside the shrine. Standing, he moved proudly and erect to the door and called for his servant, who came and rubbed ointment into the wounds to prevent infection. The ointment stung as badly as the lashes, but still the high priest did not flinch. Prince Ahmad was going to die, and Abdel ibn Zaid was showing his dedication and determination before his master Rimahn, to prove his worthiness to undertake such a mission.

With his wounds dressed and the pain from them being ignored, Abdel ibn Zaid again donned his cloak and summoned his most capable followers, ordering them to assemble in the main temple. One hour later he went down to inspect them and assemble the group he would take with him on this arduous journey.

They lined up in a single row, fifty of the most skilled assassins on the face of Parsina. All were tough, all were dedicated to the cause of Rimahn. And Abdel ibn Zaid walked down that line, a general inspecting his troops, examining each assassin for some tiny flaw, some iota of weakness in either flesh or spirit. He would stare into the eyes of each, looking for the flame of fanaticism that would mirror his own. Many of the followers, even as dedicated as they were, could not meet the cold, even stare of their leader and would look away nervously. These Abdel ibn Zaid discarded as unworthy of participating in so supreme a task. Only those followers who could meet his gaze without flinching, without fear or pomposity, were worthy of accompanying him on the journey to kill Prince Ahmad and help the rimahniya gain their long-desired foothold in Ravan.

Of all the group, he selected twelve to accompany him on his mission. The nine men and three women were the toughest, most callous, and most fearless servants of Rimahn stationed within this main temple. All were hardened assassins, fast and experienced. Individually, each could fight and defeat a squadron in open combat; together they were a match for a small army.

Prince Ahmad was no longer protected by the high walls of the Royal Temple, nor by the devoted flocks of Oromasd's priests. Even if he still had a cadre of men around him, he was out in the open without a protective base. He would present a ready target for the rimahniya assassins.

The next day, Abdel ibn Zaid and his party set out from their mountain hideout well provisioned and prepared to move quickly. Their saddle pouches were filled with maps, food, and weapons, and with money to buy more if the need arose. They carried no luxury items such as tents; the followers of Rimahn were accustomed to the rigors their discipline demanded.

Riding down from their mountain retreat, they quickly reached the forest trail that Prince Ahmad's wedding party had taken, paralleling the foothills. The assassins rode eastward through the forest with the Tirghiz Mountains towering to their left. They passed other travelers who instinctively avoided contact with them. Even though the rimahniya had no special clothing to identify themselves as such, their demeanor was so intimidating that no one else wanted to come near them or attempt communication.

After a day's hard travel, the rimahniya reached the spot where King Basir's soldiers had ambushed Prince Ahmad's party. Abdel ibn Zaid and his followers examined the site closely, their sharp, experienced eyes overlooking no detail of the scene. Signs of a struggle were evident, and the stone cairn beside the road gave silent testimony that many men had died here recently.

Abdel ibn Zaid was not concerned with the outcome of that battle; Shammara had already related those details. The high priest of Rimahn was much more interested in what had happened when the fighting was over. The prince, a few dozen men, and a trainload of supplies did not simply vanish into thin air, since they did not go either to Marakh or to Raven, they must have gone somewhere else. Abdel ibn Zaid had to find out where that was.

With the ambush site as the center of a circle, ibn Zaid sent his followers fanning out in ever widening radii to look for signs of the prince's entourage. Over a hundred horses and asses had left Ravan; that many beasts could not travel through the forest without leaving some sign of their passage. Many people had passed this point since the battle, and some had stopped to scavenge the horses, saddles, arms, and supplies the prince hadn't taken with him. Some of these hadn't left the scene by the main road, leaving false trails that confused the story even further. The rimahniya added up such tiny clues as torn turf, snapped twigs, and horse droppings before reaching the conclusion that the largest party leaving this site recently—most likely the prince's entourage—had moved southward, heading off the main road and toward the Kholaj Desert. Abdel ibn Zaid accordingly turned his own group in that direction and started off in belated pursuit.

As long as they traveled through forest and farmland the trail, even after two and a half weeks, remained plain enough to follow—but when they reached the edge of the Kholaj Desert, the tracks of the prince's entourage were swallowed up by the shifting sands. There was no way to know which direction the travelers had gone through the desert.

Abdel ibn Zaid checked his maps and plotted the course the prince's group had taken so far. Assuming they had a definite destination in mind when they left the forest road, they would probably have moved toward it in the shortest possible route. Following a straight line path from the spot of battle and extending it forward, ibn Zaid saw that the line passed right by the oasis of Sarafiq, home of a famous shrine and a noted prophet. That was indeed a likely goal for a prince who suddenly found himself without a realm; he'd want to consult a seer to learn what his destiny was to be.

Abdel ibn Zaid frowned when he reached this conclusion, and his eyes burned with the glow of hatred. Everything connected with Oromasd was loathsome to such a devoted follower of Rimahn, and the thought of venturing into a consecrated area filled him with disgust. He would be entering enemy territory, and if Prince Ahmad was still there it would make the assignment cumbersome.

The code of the oasis was strict, for life in the desert was harsh on followers of Rimahn and Oromasd alike. All who came to an oasis must be granted sanctuary. Within the oasis there could be no fighting, even between the most vehement of enemies. There were no exceptions to this arrangement. Even the rimahniya, as cold-blooded and treacherous as they were, realized the need to keep oases as free havens. Once they were inside the oasis of Sarafiq, they could perform no violence until they'd left again.

Of course, the code worked in the other direction as well. Even if the priests of Oromasd guessed that ibn Zaid and his party were of the rimahniya, they could neither deny them the sanctuary of the oasis nor set upon them and kill them. An uneasy truce would remain while the opposing groups shared a roof in the middle of the wastes.

Realizing he had no choice but to visit the oasis, Abdel ibn Zaid led his band of assassins across the shifting sands to the shrine of Sarafiq. The rimahniya paid little attention to the burning desert heat; they gave no heed to their own comfort. They took what care was needed to keep their horses well, the same as they would treat any necessary tools. Other than that, their pace was relentless, their determination fanatical. Nothing would stand between them and their objective— nothing but death and destruction.

After four days of hard riding, the shrine of Sarafiq stood out of the sands ahead of them. Abdel ibn Zaid looked scornfully at the simplicity of the place. A white plaster wall, barely taller than a man's head, enclosed the rectangular oasis. The wall was broached by four arched gateways, one on each side of the rectangle. Within the wall was the small caravanserai where visitors stayed, and a clump of little houses where the few permanent residents dwelled. A tiny bazaar and fountain were shaded by a cluster of palm trees, and the all-important well was located almost directly in the center of the enclosure.

Dominating the oasis, though, was the shrine itself, a large building made of alabaster and trimmed with gold that gleamed beneath the desert sun. The temple, like most temples, had a large sahn and arched colonnades. The roofs at either side of the front end were large onion-dome spires. A minaret stood at the northeast corner, its eternal flame burning as a symbol of Oromasd and a welcoming beacon for desert travelers.

A small force of rimahniya could capture the oasis easily, ibn Zaid thought with disdain. *Leave it to the priests of Oromasd to worship something so simple and weak. We have little to fear here.*

At his signal the rimahniya rode down the slope of the dune toward the nearest of the arched gateways. As the thirteen riders approached, a group of acolytes in white robes came out of the gateway to welcome them.

"May the peace of Oromasd be upon you as you enter this oasis of tranquility," the chief acolyte greeted the riders. "Allow us to offer you the hospitality of Sarafiq. The prophet Muhmad has been expecting you. Come share our food and water, and then he will impart his vision to you."

"I ask no vision of your so-called prophet," ibn Zaid growled testily, wondering whether Muhmad had really known of his coming. "I seek only the whereabouts of a certain traveler who passed through here recently. When I have that I'll bother you no further."

The chief acolyte shrugged. "The prophet will discuss all such matters with you. In the meantime, enter our gates and be at peace."

The rimahniya rode warily into the oasis, suspecting a trap even though they knew the strict desert code expressly forbade such duplicity. The priests were being entirely too accommodating—particularly if, as the acolyte had said, the prophet Muhmad knew who they were and had been expecting them.

They were guided to the small caravanserai, which was staffed by priests and the students of the madrasa. Their horses were taken and attended to, and the riders themselves were given rooms in the caravanserai. They were assigned three to a room except for Abdel ibn Zaid, who received a room all to himself. Though the quarters were simple by most standards, they were far more comfortable than the rigorous rimahniya were used to—and that fact made them distinctly uneasy.

The visitors were fed well on the plain fare served in the caravanserai, but whenever they questioned the priests about Prince Ahmad's group they received either evasions or total silence. The prophet Muhmad, they were told repeatedly, would deal with the questions personally. When ibn Zaid pressed about *when* the prophet would communicate with them, he was told that all would be made clear to him in the morning.

There was a prayer session in the sahn after dinner, which Abdel ibn Zaid and his followers pointedly avoided. They settled, instead, for a short service of their own in the room of ibn Zaid, and the high priest of Rimahn exhorted them in their hatred of all things good and truthful. Afterwards he dismissed them to their own rooms, while he lay awake in the darkness for several hours before finally falling asleep.

He awoke suddenly in the night with the certain knowledge that something was wrong. He lay on his mat unmoving, relaxed, so as to appear still asleep and thus not lose the element of surprise; his dagger was already in his hand, prepared to kill any attacker who would violate the truce of the oasis in the dark of night. His ears and barely opened eyes were straining to detect any signs of something amiss within the room.

As he slowly rotated his head he could see a dim shape outlined in the moonlight that filtered through the window. The figure was seated cross-legged on the floor a few cubits from the foot of the mat on which the assassin lay. Abdel ibn Zaid was furious at himself, since he took pride in his ability to wake at the slightest hint of danger; it was unthinkable that someone could have entered his room and sat down calmly without his waking until now.

"Who are you?" he asked. There was no fear in his voice, just the measured threat that the answer had better not displease him.

"I am Muhmad," came the gentle reply. "I am unarmed. You need fear nothing from me except that I might speak the truth you so abominate."

."What do you want?" ibn Zaid continued as he finally sat up.

"You're the one who wanted me," the prophet said. "I understand you seek the whereabouts of Prince Ahmad of Ravan."

As his eyes became more accustomed to the dim moonlight, Abdel ibn Zaid saw that his visitor was a slight man, very old and frail, dressed in white robes and wearing a white turban. "Very well," the assassin said. "Talk, then."

"I normally conduct my audiences in the shrine, before the altar and the Adaran fire," Muhmad began casually, "but in your case I was forced to make an exception. I doubt you could have gotten all the way through the shrine to see me, and in any case the presence of a rimahni would have polluted the sacred flame. So tonight I come to you."

"How do you know I'm of the rimahniya?" asked Abdel ibn Zaid. "How did you know I was coming here?"

"It was inevitable that the forces of darkness would pursue the prince on his quest. If it were not you it would be someone very much like you. The world moves on and kismet charts its course through the reefs of our lives."

"Your stalling will do no good, O priest. I'll find your precious prince whether you help me or not."

"I'm not stalling. You'd depart this oasis no earlier if I give you the answers you seek now or ten minutes from now. I'm merely humoring my own curiosity, nothing more."

"Sizing up your enemy?"

"You're not my enemy, O assassin. The fact that you believe you are stems from some of the many lies Rimahn, the inventor of lies, has told you. So caught up are you in the web of these lies that the truth strikes you as unbelievable."

"And what is this 'truth' that I don't believe?"

"That all men and women, yourself included, are servants of Oromasd; that we were all placed here on Parsina to serve as soldiers in the battle against Rimahn; and that each of us plays his own crucial role in that battle. No matter what lies Rimahn makes you believe, you cannot alter that—and Rimahn himself cannot tell you the truth, because he is so much a part of his lies that he can't see past them. Your destiny, as with all men, is to fulfill the great plan of Oromasd. Since that is so, you cannot be my enemy."

In one quick motion, Abdel ibn Zaid leaped from his mat to stand beside the prophet. He held his blade against the older man's throat while with his other hand he pushed the man's head back, exposing the throat even more. "And what if it's my destiny to kill you on the spot?" he asked coldly.

Abdel ibn Zaid was used to terrifying people. He knew the feel of muscle tensions when a potential victim was paralyzed with dread, the fear of moving lest ibn Zaid follow through on his threat. Even the mighty Shammara, as coldly aloof as ever a lady was, had feared the strength of his hands on her throat.

But the prophet Muhmad showed no fear. He did not move in any way. His muscles did not tense and his breathing remained calm as he said, "You won't kill me."

"Why not?" asked ibn Zaid with all the power of his rank resonating in his voice. "I'm sworn to destroy all who venerate Oromasd."

"Because then you wouldn't hear my vision of your future."

Abdel ibn Zaid stood silently for minutes with his blade at the old man's throat, until at last his hand began to tremble. Disgusted at this unaccustomed sign of weakness, he pulled the hand away. "The code of the oasis forbids me from killing even my enemy here," he said. "It's that, not your supposed vision, that saves you from the folly of your impudence."

"My impudence, as you call it, will kill me yet," the prophet said calmly. "But that is no concern of yours. You were asking the whereabouts of Prince Ahmad. You no doubt think I withhold the information because I know you intend to kill him."

"It's what the sensible man would do," ibn Zaid growled.

"The ways of Oromasd are beyond human sensibility," Muhmad proclaimed. "Prince Ahmad is on a quest that will take him to Punjar in the east, to Varyu's castle in the north, to Atluri in the west, and to Mount Denavan in the south. His goal, in part, is to unify the forces of mankind to oppose the growing legions of your master, Rimahn, and restore the balance between good and evil."

Abdel ibn Zaid's eyes flamed with anger. "Then it's even more important that I kill him before he achieves his end," he said. "You must know that. Why did you tell me?"

"It makes no difference. You'd find out in other ways, and possibly hurt innocent people in the process. This will save those people a great deal of pain." The voice of the prophet was so calm it could have been mistaken for indifference toward those innocent people. Somehow, though—quiet as it was—it was the embodiment of strength and purpose.

Abdel ibn Zaid stared at the cagey old man, and his first thought was that the prophet must be lying to him to save the prince. It was exactly what ibn Zaid would have done in his place, sending the hunters off in the wrong direction and leaving the prince free to pursue whatever course he chose.

But that wouldn't be in character with the nature of the priesthood. The followers of Oromasd believed firmly in the truth—and this prophet, as a particularly holy man, would revere it even more. For him to lie that blatantly would be a betrayal of his entire life's work and could, by his own beliefs, damn him to the Pits of Torment until the rehabilitation at the end of the world. No, he would not lie merely to save some temporal prince. Whatever his reasons for doing so, he had told the truth.

"Did you tell me this because you think I'll fail in my mission to kill him?" ibn Zaid asked.

Muhmad waited a couple of heartbeats before replying. "Prince Ahmad will be betrayed by a member of his own party, but that will have nothing to do with you."

"So you are claiming my mission will fail."

"That depends on what you consider your mission to be. You profess to serve Rimahn and work for his greater glory, is that correct?"

"Rimahn is the ultimate power in the universe. Oromasd has never won a lasting battle against him. Only by serving the forces of evil does one find his true niche in life."

"And your allegiance extends to his personification, Aeshma?"

"Unquestioningly."

The prophet smiled. "Then your mission will succeed admirably. You will serve Aeshma faithfully and be justly rewarded. Your blade, used in his service, will topple an empire and help shape the future course of Parsina. To that extent, you will succeed beyond your wildest imaginings."

The prophet of Sarafiq finally stirred himself from the floor, rising gracefully to his feet. "And now I must end our conversation. While I find I need less sleep as I grow older, I still require *some*. I assume you'll want some more yourself, since you have a long journey ahead of you."

The prophet Muhmad walked past the assassin to the doorway, then stopped and turned for a final comment. "Many men have come to me pleading for a vision of their future, and if they are worthy I grant it. You have not really asked and you are not at all worthy, but I granted it anyway. May you make of it as your heart requires."

And then he was gone, so silently that even with all ibn Zaid's training the assassin couldn't say just when he crossed the threshold. Abdel ibn Zaid was left alone in the darkness of his room to contemplate the mysteries and the methods of the man who, by all rights, should have been his archenemy and deadliest rival.

And for the prophet Muhmad as he walked back to his simple quarters, his heart was heavy with sadness. Tonight had begun the final cycle of his own life, and his energies from this point must be directed toward the dissolution of all he'd worked to maintain. The oasis of Sarafiq was drying up. A replacement had been found, and the citizens, priests, and students must go and build a new town upon that site. Word must be spread among the Badawi and all the caravans that traveled through the Kholaj Desert that Sarafiq would soon be no more. The shrine must be deconsecrated so that the final act could be played out here—Muhmad's own death.

The prophet sighed. The inevitability of this plan and of Oromasd's triumph, which it would bring about, did not lessen the grief he felt for this beautiful spot among the desert dunes where he'd made his home most of his life. But a servant may not question his master and Muhmad was, above all, a faithful slave to the will of Oromasd.

19

THE WARRIOR

AFTER leaving the dismal caves of Punjar, Prince Ahmad and his companions took their bearings from the stars and rode northward through the clear night, ever mindful of the cracked and broken landscape around them. So eager were they to be away from this hateful place that they rode continuously on into the morning. The horses wearied and had to be walked occasionally, but they didn't cease their progress until the character of the land about them changed. The ground here was fertile; trees, bushes, and grass grew in abundance. While the terrain was still hilly and they saw no farms, the softer nature of the land assured them they were beyond the immediate influence of King Zargov of Punjar.

Finally feeling safe from their enemy's reprisals and totally exhausted after their long ordeal in Punjar, the travelers picked an open spot to make camp and rest. The Jann Cari, working at magical speed, set up the tents in short time, while the men prepared a simple meal to satisfy their ravening hunger. Selima, as always, stood by and watched—and Leila stood beside her, claiming she'd never been taught how to perform such practical tasks.

They were so hungry there was little talking while they ate; it was all they could do to stuff the food into their mouths and satisfy the gnawing in their bellies. Cari and Selima sat apart as they normally did during meals and respectfully watched their companions eat.

When the meal was done and there was no other pressing business, it was time for some questions to be answered. It was Umar bin Ibrahim who turned to their newest companion and said, "We're most grateful for your help, O Leila, but you remain a mystery to us. We have no idea who you are or why you helped us at your husband's expense. If you expect to be a full member of our party and travel amicably with us, you'll have to explain yourself more completely."

Leila sat upright facing the others and folded her hands neatly in her lap. Her blue eyes looked from face to face to emphasize her words as she spoke. "I realize I intruded most impolitely into your party, O venerable priest," she began formally, "and were my circumstances not so desperate I would not have done so. But once you hear my story I hope you'll forgive my boldness and learn to accept me as one of your number."

Jafar al-Sharif recognized a preface when he heard one, and settled back comfortably to hear what might possibly be a good story—which to him meant one worth stealing. He had to admit that Leila, for all the sharp tongue and sarcasm she'd shown in Punjar, knew how to assume a demure demeanor when it suited her tale.

"Far to the north and west of here," Leila began, "lies the part of Parsina known as Norgeland. My dear mother, may she be dwelling now in the House of Song, was a princess of that land. It was from her that I inherited my height, my fair skin, my blue eyes, and my hair color at which I know you've all been marveling. As she was a younger princess and not particularly important in the line of royal succession, she was married to my father, a younger prince of Tatarry, a land west of the Altai Mountains. Thus did she leave the land of her ancestry and move southeast, where she was given a new home and made to feel most welcome and happy.

"There in Tatarry was I born and raised, a princess of royal lineage on both sides of my ancestry. I lived a comfortable life as a member of the royal household, and had a staff of servants to do whatever chores I required—though since my father was a younger prince and his brother, my uncle, the king had plenty of his own children to assure succession, I was definitely of lesser rank.

"When I was sixteen my family arranged a marriage for me with an older man, a merchant from a highly placed and noble family. He was a good man, and quite wealthy. He treated me, his pretty young wife, with great indulgence—and his senior wives were careful to treat me with respect because my uncle was the king. As a young girl, not knowing any better, I took shameless advantage of their kind and patient treatment; I spent much of my husband's money on jewels and frivolous fancies for myself, and I often insulted the other wives and concubines. It was probably for this selfish and wrong-headed behavior that Oromasd saw fit to punish me as he did.

"The kingdom of Tatarry maintained trade with most regions of the world, but to the lands of Sinjin we relied only on the occasional traders to bring our commerce. These traders were proving more and more undependable, and so my uncle the king sought to open more direct avenues of trade. About five years after my marriage a formal arrangement was made with the emperor of Sinjin. Letters of agreement were signed and rates of exchange were decided, and it was agreed that permanent ambassadors would be assigned by each kingdom to the court of the other. As a reward for his loyalty and fine service to the king, my husband was chosen to be ambassador from Tatarry to Sinjin. Our entire household was uprooted and we set out for our new home.

"Many are the sights I could describe that we saw along our travels, and many are the strange people and customs we encountered along the way. It was on this journey that I began to grow up and appreciate the true wonder of the world. We traveled through a pass in the Altai Mountains down to the southwestern edge of the Bitter Sea, then east along that sea's southern edge through Marakh and into Formistan.

"It was in a forest in Formistan that we ran into bandits. We had some men-at-arms with us as a precaution and we were able to drive the outlaws away, but our guides were killed in the fighting. Rather than turn back, we decided to press on. We knew that Sinjin was a vast land to the southeast, so we kept moving in that general direction, hoping to find someone who could give us accurate instructions. No one we found knew the way any better than we did, though, and we ended up going far out of our way.

"Eventually we stumbled into the desolate country of Punjar. We were captured by that ridiculous little king, just as you were. As usual, he thought we were thieves come to steal his precious jewels, and no amount of protesting could convince him otherwise. He put my husband and the rest of our party to death, but because I was tall and fair—unlike everyone else in his wretched kingdom—he took a fancy to me and spared my life.

"Since as king he could do as he pleased, he declared me to be his wife. There was no religious ceremony, for Zargov has no religion but greed, and I never swore unto Oromasd to take him as my husband. I was in no position to deny him if I wanted to live, but I scarcely consider him my husband and I don't view what I've done as betrayal or abandonment.

"He seldom bothered me or made demands; merely owning me was enough of a thrill for him. I was just a possession, nothing more than one of the jewels in his throne room wall. I tried to escape a number of times, but he always sent his soldiers to bring me back. Through time I learned that I could say anything and do anything except try to escape, and it didn't matter; I was still a jewel no matter how sharp my tongue was. And there I remained for ten years, with little to do but contemplate the follies that brought me to my fate. The only thing that relieved the oppressive monotony of my days was the occasional intruder like yourselves—but no matter how hard I tried to argue on their behalf, Zargov always killed them eventually."

She paused to take a sip from the water pouch, and looked at each member of her audience in turn before continuing. "Do you see now why I longed so for my freedom, why I leaped at the chance to escape with you? I had to be away from there before my mind turned to dust and my soul grew too old for me to bear. That's why I helped you outwit my 'husband,' and that's why I'm with you now."

She bowed her head slightly to signal she was finished with her tale, and sat awaiting the verdict of her companions. The others shifted restlessly in their places, looking from one to another for silent opinions about this woman who'd come into their midst. Finally Umar replied to her.

"Your story is certainly a sad one, and we will gladly repay your kindness to us by helping you in return. Our path now takes us northward, and we must pass near Tatarry along the way. When we reach some friendly town, we'll be all too happy to pay a guide to transport you across the Altai Mountains, or perhaps buy you passage in some caravan traveling to your home. That way—"

But Leila was shaking her head defiantly. "You don't understand," she said. "Tatarry isn't my home any more. I have no reason to go back there."

"You have family there," Umar said.

"They were just as glad to get rid of me ten years ago," Leila said. "If I returned now I'd be an embarrassment to them, nothing more—someone to live in their house and eat their food until they could find another way to get rid of me. You gave me your word you'd let me accompany you on your entire journey. I'll settle for nothing less, or revile you as a liar before Oromasd."

"But the road we'll take will be hard," Prince Ahmad argued. "We'll face great danger, hardship, deprivation, possibly even death. That's no journey for a woman of your breeding to undertake."

Leila railed even louder against the prince. "I've been a protected little flower all my life," she said. "First I was a superfluous princess, then a pampered young wife, then a prized and neglected treasure. If I go back to Tatarry, I'll have to be a grieving widow until I'm lucky enough to remarry, and then the cycle starts all over again. I've had plenty of time to think about my position in life during these last ten years of boredom, and no more can I accept such a degrading situation.

"You say you may face suffering and hardship. Well, I suffered ten thousand deaths a day sitting bored beneath King Zargov's mountain; nothing you'll find along your path will frighten me more than the prospect of spending the rest of my life in those stinking tunnels. Let the world do to me what it will, it can't be worse than the ten years of torture I've already endured. I'm more than ready to see the world—and what's more, if young Selima is correct and you're traveling in a holy cause, that's even more reason for my being along. I have much atoning to do in the eyes of Oromasd for the errant behavior of my youth. I must build a store of good deeds to counter my bad ones at the Bridge of Shinvar.

"I'll work as hard as any of you to make your mission a success, and I'll contribute all my knowledge and abilities to

236 / STEPHEN GOLDIN

your cause. In particular, I have one skill you might find useful along the way."

"And what skill is that?" Umar asked.

"My mother dabbled a little in the magical arts," Leila replied. "Never in a major way, just little tricks about the household—love spells for some of her serving maids, or amulets to ward off evil djinni. She never even bothered to teach any of them to me. But because of her talent, I was born with a unique gift: the ability to see things differently from the way they appear to others. Though I can't always see them as they really are, I can easily tell when something is not as it pretends to be. You for instance, Your Highness—I knew you were more than some simple traveler the minute you entered my sight, though I might not have guessed how highly ranked you truly were."

As she looked around the circle of faces in front of her, her gaze locked onto Jafar's for a brief moment. There was a flickering there of something unsaid, a secret shared. Then Leila looked casually away as she continued, "You might sometime have need of someone who can tell the real from the illusory. Let me serve as your guide through the path of lies Rimahn may throw in your way."

Despite her arguments the men were reluctant to bring her along. Still, they had given their word and did not feel they could honorably break it, even to a woman. Leila refused to be dissuaded from her position, and after further discussion the men agreed she could accompany them on their travels, though they warned her they couldn't guarantee her safety in case of trouble. Leila accepted that provision willingly, so delighted was she to be away from her confinement in the pits of Punjar.

By the time this discussion was finished it was nightfall again, and sleeping arrangements had to be decided. Until now Umar and Prince Ahmad had shared one tent while Jafar and his ghostly daughter took the other. For propriety's sake Jafar agreed to share the other men's tent while Leila and Selima took the second.

Later that night, while the others were sleeping and Cari the Jann kept watch against wild animals and human intruders, Jafar al-Sharif awoke, feeling very uneasy. He slipped quietly from the tent without disturbing the other two men and went outside to his horse. Taking from his saddle pouch the journal of Ali Maimun and the piece of the Crystal of Oromasd he'd acquired in Punjar, he sat cross-legged on the ground near the embers of the dying fire and began to look at them.

Cari's reading lessons had been coming along very well, and he'd learned all of the alphabet. Soon he would have mastered the written language completely—digraphs, alternate forms, and accenting rules included—and then there'd be no word he couldn't piece out quickly. Already he could recognize many words in the book and manage to figure out others from context. That gave him a feeling of power matched only by the ring of Cari on the middle finger of his left hand.

But all this newfound skill would go for naught if the book he must read would not be more cooperative. Now that he had the first piece of the Crystal he tried to open the pages of the journal to the next section, but they stubbornly refused to open for him. He was no wiser than Umar or the prince on the matter of finding the other pieces of the Crystal, but they would look to him as the expert.

He put the obstinate book down and picked up the piece of the Crystal King Zargov had given him. In the starlit darkness it might have been simply a lump of coal for all the energy or special glow it had. Other magical objects Jafar had handled, such as the ring of Cari and the flying carpet, had a special feel to them, a vibration of magical energy. This Crystal had nothing at all to distinguish it from the rocks all around the camp.

He looked from the Crystal to the book, and back again. Would the book deign to tell him how to use the pieces of the Crystal when the time came—and even if it did, would there be enough wisdom in the writings of Ali Maimun to teach a total novice how to master the Crystal of Oromasd?

He thought back on the words of the prophet Muhmad: "No man can control the Crystal of Oromasd." If that was true, what was the point in even trying? What double-talk nonsense had that old hermit been feeding him—and how much of a fool had he been to believe it?

"It's time for our talk now, O crafty Jafar," came a soft voice behind him.

Jafar jumped, not realizing how absorbed he'd been in his contemplations or how quietly Leila had crept up to him in the darkness. Cari, too, must have been alarmed, for suddenly she was at Jafar's side with a look of protectiveness upon her face. "Do you need my help, O master?" she asked, glaring pointedly at Leila.

Jafar al-Sharif looked from Cari to Leila and back again. "I'll be all right," he told the Jann. "Return to your duties of guarding the camp."

Cari glared at the blond woman, but could not contradict her master. "Hearkening and obedience," she said, and was gone once more.

"She's very protective of you," Leila commented.

"I'm her master, and she'd bound to me by magical commands," Jafar said with a shrug. "She must protect me if she possibly can. She has no choice."

Leila gave him a mischievous half smile and sat down beside him, but said nothing further on that subject. Instead she looked straight into his eyes and said, "You intrigue me, O Jafar. I told you earlier about my ability to see past illusion. You're no more a mighty wizard than I am."

"If you're so certain of that, why didn't you tell the others about me?" Jafar asked.

"Only a fool tells all he sees. I hesitate to speak where I'm not sure what it will profit me," she told him bluntly. "I knew your daughter wasn't telling me the full truth when she related your story, but it wasn't to my advantage to challenge her then. Perhaps it's to my benefit even now to go along with your tale. I must consider all the possibilities."

Jafar al-Sharif looked at her carefully in the dim moonlight, studying her face to evaluate her trustworthiness. He scarcely knew her except as the sharp-tongued wife of a hostile king—and then as a woman who betrayed her nominal husband to win her freedom. She had a selfish shrewdness about her that made her seem a risky gamble—yet there was a basic honesty and openness that made him want to take the risk.

Her candor in admitting her motivations was refreshing, and she *had* been willing to help the party escape from Punjar. She must have sincerely wanted to share their adventure to turn down the chance of returning to Tatarry, where she'd be a wealthy widow of the royal house—providing she'd told the truth about her background. Jafar had told enough lies himself on this journey to doubt the honesty of strangers.

A sudden thought occurred to him. He stood up and walked over to his saddle pouch, where he removed the magical cap they'd taken from the cave of Estanash, the sand Jinn. According to its embroidered inscription, it had the ability to make its wearer answer up to three questions truthfully. If he could use it on Leila, it would give him a better idea of the sort of person he was dealing with.

Bringing the cap back to where Leila sat, puzzled, he handed it to her and said, "Put this on your head."

She looked at the silvery material of the cap with a silent, perplexed expression, but donned it as he suggested. Jafar al-Sharif sat down beside her on the ground once more and asked, "Were you telling us the truth tonight about your history?"

"Yes I was," Leila answered without hesitation.

"Do you really want to come with us out of a sense of adventure, without thought of betraying us or of profiting from any misfortune that may befall us?"

"Yes I do."

Jafar paused, considering the wording of his third and final question. "If I tell you my own true story, will you give me your honest oath by lord Oromasd and the Bounteous Immortals that you'll keep it to yourself and not betray me?"

Leila was slower to answer this time; she was considering her reply just as carefully as he'd considered the question. "In all honesty, I can't give you such a blanket oath. I will vow to keep any secrets as long as I know no one is being hurt by my silence. If there turns out to be harm done, and the harm outweighs the benefit, I'd feel compelled to speak the truth."

The integrity of her answer astonished him. Even wearing a cap of truthfulness, she'd given a more complete and thorough reply than was necessary—and in the process had shown herself to be a woman of high ethical values.

He made the decision that he could indeed trust her—and, in fact, that he needed to. The burden of his masquerade was a heavy one. Umar and Prince Ahmad and all the strangers they met expected so much out of him; it was good to have people for whom he didn't have to pretend. Selima and Cari were restful to be around for that reason; Leila could be the same way. Besides, a good liar needs a lot of accomplices to support his stories and cover his back in a moment of crisis. Leila, with her sarcastic sense of humor and quick wit, would be a welcome ally.

Taking the magical cap from her head and putting it away, he said, "Very well, O Leila, I'll tell you my own history—and it'll be for you to decide whether anyone's hurt by my deception."

He then began, in his most entertaining manner, to tell his own story—from the day when he found the accursed altar cloth lying in the street in Ravan to his imprisonment, his rescue by Cari, the fantastic flight to Akar's castle, the escape and the curse placed on Selima, the prophet's vision, and the subsequent travels up until they reached Punjar. He was careful to explain that he never *wanted* to pass himself off as a wizard, but that the situation and his continued survival had required such an imposture. Now that he was caught up in the lie—and with the prophet Muhmad's seal of approval, no less—he was forced to behave as though he were such a wizard, even though he didn't feel up to the responsibility.

"Indeed," he concluded with a flourish of his hands, "if the truth were to be told now, I think *that* would cause harm to our noble mission; it would lead Umar and Prince Ahmad to doubt my ability to help them. If they have confidence in me, however misplaced, perhaps it will help them find the strength to deal with their own problems. And I must admit, kismet has aided me when I needed it. First Cari came to help me, and now, apparently, you. As in the story of the farmer with the three-legged ox, even unusual blessings are worth counting."

"I'll take that as a compliment—I think," Leila said. She reclined on her right side, leaning on her elbow and studying his face in the dim moonlight as carefully as he'd studied her earlier.

"You're a remarkable man, O Jafar al-Sharif," she said, "but I do agree your deceptions aren't intended to harm. I think you may even surprise yourself before our journey is over—for I can see past illusion, even the illusions you tell yourself."

Leila reached up with her left hand and stroked the side of his face. "I had my eyes on you the instant your group walked into the throne room," she admitted. "You fascinated me from that first moment. Umar's a good man, but he's old and very married; your princeling is handsome, but just a boy with much growing yet to do. You, by contrast, are a man full and strong, handsome and daring. You don't foolishly embrace danger, but when it comes you face it with the wits Oromasd gave you.

"My first husband, my real husband, was kind and gentle, but also old and tired. King Zargov was a cretin, and the best thing I can say for him is he left me alone most of the time. I've needed a lover of mature years and strength. I've waited all my life for a man like you."

The feel of her fingers stroking his beard and the subtle scent of her jasmine perfume were slowly arousing Jafar as nothing had aroused him in the two years since the death of his beloved Amineh. At first he sat paralyzed with fear at the notion of being unfaithful to his late wife's memory—but as Leila reached behind his neck and pulled his face down close to hers, he relaxed again and allowed himself to be swept along in the sensuality of the moment.

Their lips met and she pulled his body down upon her own, and for a while there were no thoughts except of the two of them, lying passionately together on the ground beneath the early morning stars.

The kingdom of Punjar, for all its unknown and forbidden aspects, was still a well-defined territory on civilized maps. There were no known maps, however, giving the location of the citadel of Varyu, king of the winds. The prophet Muhmad had merely said it was in the north, and the maps from the shrine of Sarafiq were equally vague. The few legends that Jafar al-Sharif knew simply described it as being at the north edge of the world, beyond the rim of the Altai Mountains.

Umar had been keeping the maps all through their travels, but it was clear they would only be of general help in this case. He repeatedly consulted Jafar on the matter, and all the storyteller could do was explain patiently that the journal of Ali Maimun was not cooperating. They had no recourse but to travel northwest toward the Altai Mountains until such time as the book decided they needed the information it contained.

They stopped at the first large town they found beyond the northern border of Punjar and purchased a fifth horse so Leila could have her own. They also bought a third tent and restructured the formal sleeping arrangements: Umar and Prince Ahmad shared their tent, as before, Leila and Selima

shared the second; and Jafar had the third to himself, along
with the packs and supplies.

Since Leila had insisted on being an equal member of the
group, she was taught how to set up her own tent and was
expected to do her share of the chores. Though she'd scarcely
done a day's work in her life, she was so happy to be freed of
her boredom that she pitched in with enthusiasm and even
learned the basics of cooking from Selima, who took charge
of her practical education. Selima found it amusing to instruct
a woman almost old enough to be her mother on the funda-
mental necessities of everyday life.

The travelers rode for two weeks across fields and plains
up through Formistan toward the eastern edge of the Bitter
Sea. They had to proceed very carefully through this territory,
since Formistan had been conquered years ago by neighboring
Marakh, and as such was under the rule of King Basir. For all
they knew, the prince's description had been spread to all the
towns and villages, with a reward offered for his capture or
death. King Basir had already made one attempt on the life of
Prince Ahmad; the travelers didn't want to offer him a second
opportunity.

One advantage they had was that so much time had
elapsed since the ambush that King Basir's forces might be less
alert for someone resembling the prince. Another advantage
was that King Basir would not be expecting Prince Ahmad to
be traveling up from Indi in a northerly direction or with so
small a group. Still, the travelers didn't want to press their
luck too tightly in what had to be considered enemy territory.

They avoided the towns and stayed off the main roads
wherever they could. They preferred to travel through open
farmland, waving politely to the peasants as they passed and
occasionally stopping to ask directions. Since they were not
along a well-traveled route they could not stay in established
caravanserais, forcing them to camp out under the stars every
night. When they had to stop occasionally for supplies, they
picked the smaller towns where they were less likely to encounter significant opposition. Umar and Prince Ahmad,
whose descriptions might have been spread throughout the
land, remained behind, as did Selima, whose ghostly form
would attract too much attention. Jafar al-Sharif and Leila
would take a few coins and go into town—with Cari flying
invisibly beside them for protection—and stock up on what-

ever supplies they needed. This system worked quite well, and there was no hint that anyone suspected them of being people King Basir would want to kill.

They grew more concerned about the deadline facing them. They'd begun their journey in early summer, and already summer was past its height. Muhmad had told them they must be ready to do battle on the Leewahr Plains by the first floods of next spring, and they yet had only a single piece of the Crystal. The path outlined for them would take them all around the world, yet there seemed impossibly little time to complete it. No one spoke of the problem aloud, but each member of the group prayed often that Oromasd would find a way to accelerate their progress.

Prince Ahmad took more and more to leading Selima's horse as they rode along. He found himself having long conversations with her, and he thoroughly enjoyed her charm and wit. He rationalized this to himself by arguing that they were both roughly the same age, even if they did come from separate worlds.

It was their differences, in fact, that gave them the greatest source of their conversation. Selima was fascinated by the concept of royalty, and kept up a constant barrage of questions about what it was like to be a prince and live in luxury. The thought of being pampered in such a way, of having servants to do all the simple chores of daily living, was almost beyond her comprehension. Prince Ahmad admitted that it was only recently, on the trail, that he'd learned to prepare his own food; had he not been given such a rigorous upbringing in the madrasa within the Temple of the Faith, he might not even have learned to dress himself.

At one point as they rode, Selima shook her head and exclaimed, "It's all so different from how real people live."

"Oh?" asked Ahmad with a smile. "And how do 'real' people live, then?"

Selima looked away shyly and begged his forgiveness for her insolence, but Prince Ahmad said he wasn't angry and insisted on an explanation. Thus were their roles reversed for a while, the prince asked questions about how the common people lived and Selima gave long lectures about what it was like to be poor and live crowded into small rooms among the trash of the city, not knowing where the next day's food was coming from.

"How do you know so much about this?" Prince Ahmad asked at one point. "Surely a wizard's daughter must have lived better than a pauper."

Selima cursed herself silently for making such a stupid mistake. "A wizard's apprentice travels widely," she said to cover her blunder. "Though we lived mostly in my father's citadel, we made many journeys and saw many things. My father is a good man, and takes his clientele from all classes of people—even the poor who can't afford to pay him for his efforts. Oromasd teaches us the goodness of charity, and I've seen far more of poverty than I'd ever care to repeat."

The prince accepted her explanation, and after that questioned her both about life in the lower classes and her own life as a wizard's apprentice. Questions in the former category were easy to answer, but the latter tested Selima's resourcefulness to the limit. Time and again she thanked Oromasd that life with her father had provided her with a good imagination and a ready wit. She made up answers and stories of her own, knowing they were not as good as her father could have done. Fortunately for her Prince Ahmad was not inclined to be critical; he seemed more interested in the speaker than in the words being spoken.

Prince Ahmad absorbed what Selima said about daily life in the lower classes and tried to learn from this new information. Even Umar's many past lectures about the lot of the common people had never been as vivid as Selima's descriptions, and Prince Ahmad gained a new understanding of the vast differences between the classes. He made careful mental notes of everything Selima told him, for he knew that a good ruler—which he still hoped one day to be—must understand the people he governed.

For her part, Selima was learning as well. She mastered Cari's reading lessons as avidly as her father, though she rapidly grew bored with the dry text of Ali Maimun's journal. One evening by the camp fire she saw Prince Ahmad reading a small book and asked him about it. He'd packed a few of his schoolbooks in his saddle pouch to bring along on the journey—books of history and poetry. Selima would have loved to borrow the books to improve her own reading skills, but she could neither hold the volumes nor turn the pages.

She hit instead upon the solution of asking Prince Ahmad to read aloud to her, while she looked over his shoulder and tried to recognize what words she could. They spent many nights sitting late into the evening beside the camp fire after their companions had retired, with the prince reading passages of history and poetry to her, and with them discussing the works afterward.

Jafar and Leila were also growing closer as their journey progressed. Though they ostensibly had separate tents, Leila would visit Jafar's tent every night for longer and longer intervals. At first she tried to be discreet about it, but when it was clear that everyone else knew what was happening she abandoned all pretense and spent her nights with Jafar.

This development evoked varied reactions from the others in the group. Prince Ahmad didn't care what Jafar and Leila did together, and Selima was content that her father was looking happier than he had in years. She liked Leila well enough to consider her an acceptable replacement for her poor departed mother.

Umar the priest got a bit ruffled at these goings-on. He started to make stronger and stronger references to Oromasd's instructions that men and women should *marry* before engaging in such activity, and offered his services as a priest in formalizing the relationship. Jafar al-Sharif would not have objected strongly, but it was Leila who absolutely refused.

"All my adult life," she said. "I've been some man's wife, and I nearly smothered because of it, Now that I've tasted some freedom I'm not going to give it up. It's probably my Norgic heritage—we've always been an independent people, stubborn and proud. I'm not going to trade my freedom for the sanctity of a few holy words. I'm sorry if that offends you, O Umar, but that's the way it must be."

And Umar grumbled, but accepted her wishes.

The one who reacted most strongly, though, was Cari. As Jafar's slave she could not openly challenge her master's lover, but she kept carefully balanced along the fine line between insolence and grudging courtesy. She avoided Leila whenever possible, and couldn't look at her without a smoldering glare. She often pretended not to hear what Leila said to her, and made exaggerated efforts not to intrude on Jafar's private moments with the woman. Jafar was puzzled by the Jann's uncharacteristic behavior, but Leila merely accepted it with one of her small, enigmatic smiles and said nothing on the matter.

With Jafar and Leila sleeping together in Jafar's tent and with Prince Ahmad staying up later and later by the camp fire to read to Selima, Umar bin Ibrahim had much time at night alone in his tent, staring up at the darkened top before sleep claimed him. Often his lonely thoughts turned to his wife Alhena. At times those thoughts would be warm and comforting as he remembered the love she'd given him throughout their many years of marriage—but at other times his thoughts were dark and brooding as he wondered whether the priest from Khmeria had arrived safely in Ravan to deliver Umar's important message to her. So many things could have happened along the way. What if Alhena never received word that Umar was still alive? Would she grieve needlessly for him? Would Yusef bin Nard treat her fairly when he became the new high priest, or would he throw her out on the street? Would Shammara let Alhena live, or would such a virtuous woman be eliminated in the vicious purge Shammara was certain to launch as she tightened her grip on Ravan?

Such were the worries of Umar bin Ibrahim late at night while, around him, his companions indulged in lighter thoughts. It's to the priest's credit that he could banish his gloomy thoughts during the daylight riding; only at night did these apparitions appear to him.

Summer was fast fading into fall as they reached the eastern shore of the Bitter Sea, marking the northern boundary of Formistan. They could scarcely afford to relax their precautions, because they couldn't know for certain whether neighboring kingdoms had been alerted to kill Prince Ahmad—but the mere knowledge that they were past the borders of a known enemy was a great comfort to them.

Jafar and Selima had finally mastered all the basic reading skills, and were now recognizing many words without sounding them out. The few they needed help with now were words adapted from foreign or ancient languages, or specialized words related to Ali Maimun's arcane craft. These words didn't always follow the standard rules, and a page of writing could still take more than an hour to read. Leila would have liked to help them, but she couldn't read either; reading was a skill that young princesses were seldom taught because it was assumed they'd never need it. Nevertheless she provided moral support to father and daughter in their efforts to achieve literacy.

Jafar al-Sharif would sit cross-legged with the journal of Ali Maimun open on his lap piecing out unusual words. He'd make the sound of each letter in turn, then try to integrate them into one continuous sound. By the second or third try he could usually guess what the word was, and Cari would tell him whether he was right or wrong. After a while he caught onto the fact that certain letters frequently appeared in given combinations, and that those combinations often formed words embedded in other words. If the need and the conditions had not been so desperate, Jafar would have been utterly elated at the thrill of these new discoveries in his life.

The travelers skirted the eastern shore of the Bitter Sea, through that narrow tract of fertile land between the inland ocean and the Gobrani Desert. The land became rougher and the farms appeared less prosperous here, but the people seemed sturdy and used to their harsh existence. Umar told Prince Ahmad this was further proof that men were the chosen implements of Oromasd in the eternal war with the powers of Rimahn—for only man, of all the animals and plants in all Parsina, could adapt to the many different climates and conditions Rimahn could devise. Men could live in mountains and deserts, on tundra and fertile plains, wherever it was necessary to carry the plan of Oromasd to fruition.

The shoreline turned to the northwest now, and they continued to follow its curve. This was a land that was little known to the people of Ravan and the central portion of Parsina, and the boundaries and names of kingdoms were vague or nonexistent on the maps. The terrain became more heavily forested and human habitation became sparser, but still the travelers pressed onward in their quest.

They were camped near a ravine in a wooded area for the night. The eastern sky behind them was just starting to lighten with the dawn when Cari shook Jafar awake. "We have trouble, O my master," she said. "A band of armed horsemen is descending on us quickly. They should be here within fifteen minutes."

"How many of them?"

"About fifty."

"Do they know we're here?"

"I believe so."

Jafar cursed under his breath. He'd carried off his wizardly bluff against the Badawi, but they were only a party of about a dozen. It might be foolhardy to try such a trick against a force four times that strength.

Rising to his feet and starting to dress, he said, "Wake the others, quickly, starting with the prince. Let them know the danger we face."

He shook Leila awake and quickly explained the situation as he reached into his saddle pouch and pulled out some of his more courtly robes, rather than the ones he'd been using for travel. Whether this force was hostile or friendly, it was always wise to make a good impression.

The prince and Umar woke and quickly evaluated their situation. Their camping gear was all spread out, and they couldn't pack it away very quickly. Flight was therefore an unattractive option; they'd have to leave too many things behind, with little guarantee they could outrun the band that was sweeping down on them. "Once again we must place ourselves in the hands of Oromasd," Umar decided. "If we're performing his mission, he will protect us."

"Faith is all very well," Leila said, "but I'd feel more comfortable with an army backing me up."

Jafar was inclined to agree with her. He took the cloak of invisibility from his pouch and put it around his shoulders, though he did not say the magic word that would enable him to vanish. He would save that feat for some more opportune moment, if needed, though he wasn't sure how much it would accomplish other than saving his own life. He also grabbed the heavy wooden staff of Achmet the terrifying they'd taken from Estanash's cave, the staff that supposedly could draw lightning down from the clouds. Jafar didn't know how to use it, but it looked impressive nonetheless.

They dressed in the dim dawn light as best they could and mounted their horses, the better to face the unknown force. Prince Ahmad sat astride his steed Churash several steps ahead of the others, making it clear he was the nominal leader of their tiny group. He sat with back erect and face composed, prepared to confront any situation with the dignity that befit his rank.

The sound of hoofbeats rumbling across the bare ground signaled the arrival of the newcomers, and soon the riders themselves came into view over a small hill. They were all well armed, as Cari had said; they were also liveried in gold and green, a point she'd failed to mention. That in itself was a great relief, for it meant they were not a group of bandits who'd descend on the travelers for mere plunder. As soldiers of the local king they might be friendly or hostile, but at least they could be dealt with on some official level.

The riders pulled to within a dozen cubits of the camp and reined to a halt. One armor clad figure pulled out of the group a couple of paces, as had the prince, and stopped. His shiny brass helmet curved to a point over his head and down the sides of his face, covering hair and ears and exposing just the beardless features. He carried a lance currently tucked in against the stirrup, and the sword at his belt was ready for easy drawing.

For a long moment both sides stood silently staring at one another, evaluating the possibilities. The soldiers looked particularly at the ghostly Selima, as everyone did, wondering what strange, unearthly being she might be.

The leader, looking slender even in the armor that covered his form, spoke in a surprisingly high voice, as might a teenage boy. "What business have you trespassing on the lands of Buryan? You're obviously not traders, and you have no permission from the king. Perhaps you're spies sent to scout our weaknesses."

"I am no spy," Prince Ahmad insisted strongly. "I'm a warrior like yourself, on a mission of great importance on behalf of our lord Oromasd."

"A holy pilgrimage?" the leader asked. "Ravan is in that direction. You're all turned around."

"Not a pilgrimage, but a mission of utmost importance to all who follow the way of Oromasd," Prince Ahmad explained. "I am Ahmad Khaled, and these with me are the priest Umar bin Ibrahim and the wizard Jafar al-Sharif—"

Prince Ahmad got no further in his introductions, however, as the leader's hand went instantly to the hilt of his sword. "A wizard?" he growled, glaring directly at Jafar.

Jafar al-Sharif kept the word that would make him invisible near the tip of his tongue. Wizardry was obviously an unpopular profession in this land. "A very gentle wizard," he said softly. "A wizard who follows the way of Oromasd, who loves the beasts of the fields and the flowers of the earth, a wizard who has never harmed an innocent man nor caused hurt to an honest soul."

"It's the wizard Kharouf with whom we're at war," the leader said sternly.

"Well, there you have it," said Jafar. "I'm not this Kharouf, and I've never even met him. I'm sure he must be a vile villain and a horrid despoiler of purity to make war upon such fine and decent people as yourselves. I'll happily spit upon his shadow if ever I see him, and curse him roundly on your behalf."

Prince Ahmad decided to bring the conversation back to its original subject. "We are innocent travelers in your land, not spies for the wizard Kharouf. We travel to the Altai Mountains; we wish only to traverse your land and will leave without harming anything or anyone. Although, if it were possible, I'd wish an audience with your king, to discuss with him matters vital to the future of all mankind."

"The future of all mankind?" laughed the leader in a mirthless tone. "We fight now for the future of Buryan, and that future is shaky enough. We cannot let you cross our lands, nor can we take the chance of giving you an audience with our king—not with a wizard in your midst, even a very gentle one."

That was dismaying news indeed. If they couldn't pass through this land, they'd have to go back around the southern edge of the Bitter Sea—which meant going through the heart of King Basir's territory, not to mention an unconscionable delay to their mission.

"Is there no way we can prove our righteous intentions?" Prince Ahmad asked.

The leader sat thoughtfully for a second. "You claimed to be a warrior?"

"Of noble blood and honorable teaching," Prince Ahmad said.

"I'm known as the finest warrior within the northern kingdoms," the leader said. "Would you care to put your claim of honor to the test of metal?"

"If I may be given the time to put on my own armor," Prince Ahmad replied. "I fear no mortal man on the field of combat, for no man has ever bested me."

"Then we shall test your worth, and if you prove brave and strong perhaps you may win the right to meet our king."

Beside Jafar, Leila was grinning broadly. "Our young prince is in for a bit of a surprise," she whispered to Jafar, and then would say no more on the matter.

Prince Ahmad dismounted and Umar helped him take his armor from the saddle pouch where it was packed. Because they'd chosen to travel light and in as practical a manner as possible, the travelers had abandoned the prince's finest armor back at Sarafiq; the prince had with him now only such plain armor as an ordinary soldier might wear. Umar helped him slip the shirt of lamilar armor over his head; the thick linen cloth with overlapping bronze scales covered Ahmad's chest and back down almost to his knees. The shiny brass helmet fit snugly over his head, and Ahmad slipped his left forearm through the two handles on the back of his adarga. That oval shield was more than one and a half cubits long and covered in black leather, with metal around the rim to protect the edge. Prince Ahmad proceeded with his armament in such a matter-of-fact manner that even the Buryani leader realized this young man had some practice in the martial arts.

Prince Ahmad remounted Churash, drew his saif from its sheath, and sat with proud, erect bearing in his saddle. His opponent on the other side drew his own sword and watched the prince's every move, carefully appraising this unknown adversary.

The Buryani soldiers backed off to a respectful distance, giving the combatants plenty of room to fight and loudly placing their bets on how many minutes the stranger would last. The travelers were warned that at the first hint of sorcery used to aid Prince Ahmad, the soldiers would attack and kill them without mercy; Jafar promised solemnly he would not interfere.

The two warriors sat atop their mounts at opposite ends of the makeshift field. At a prearranged signal from one soldier they charged at one another, swinging their swords and yelling their respective battle cries. There was a clanking of sword on sword, metal on metal, as the combatants met in the center of the field. Their horses, both trained expressly for combat, held their ground firmly as the riders swung their weapons with the full strength and power at their disposal.

Hours went by as the two armored figures fought in that empty ground, swinging and pounding in furious assault, wheeling their horses around and charging at one another time and time again. Dust was stirred up by their horses' hooves, sometimes so thickly it was impossible for the spectators to see what was happening. Yet for all the speed and all the strength of the blows, neither fighter could unseat the other nor deliver a blow that couldn't be parried. At first the soldiers cheered their companion while the travelers yelled encouragement to Prince Ahmad—but as the battle wore on, the spectators' voices became more subdued until at last they all watched in silent frustration, and with growing respect, as the two well-matched rivals battled on horseback.

Both warriors were young and strong, but even so fatigue began to take its toll. As the sun reached the zenith it was clear that the shields were growing heavier and harder to lift; the only reason any blows could be parried was because the opponent's sword arm was also growing tired and slow. Neither fighter swung very often and the blows barely reached to the other contestant. Both fighters looked unsteady in the saddle, and it was only a matter of time before one or both simply fell from exhaustion.

Umar decided to call a halt to this madness. "Enough!" he bellowed in his strongest voice. "The point must be conceded that never in this age have two stouter fighters contended one with the other on the field of honorable combat. The only outcome yet to be determined is which of you is the luckier in outlasting the other. There's nothing to be gained by that."

The two fighters stopped their swinging and eyed each other across the short gulf that divided them. Then the Buryani knight put up his sword in a gesture of salute. "I hail thee, O Ahmad Khaled, as a skilled warrior and an honorable fighter. Your request shall be granted: you will be brought before King Brundiyam and permitted to explain your holy mission. If your words prove as strong as your sword, perhaps you'll convince him as ably as you've convinced me."

20

THE ARMY OF
THE DEAD

FTER the leader of the soldiers agreed to let Prince Ahmad's party have an audience with the king of Buryan, the travelers hastily packed up their camp, mounted their horses, and followed their military escort northward through the dismal countryside. The soldiers rode hard, hoping to reach their destination before nightfall, which gave the travelers little chance to admire the Buryani scenery. They passed some scattered farms, where hardy peasants toiled to make what living they could from the stingy land that lay between the Bitter Sea and the Gobrani Desert.

There was little talking between the two groups. Prince Ahmad may have won the soldiers' respect with his show of prowess on the field of combat, but he still had not proved how friendly he was or how worthwhile was his cause. He was dead tired from the morning's fight; it was all he could do to ride Churash without falling off, and his companions clustered tightly around him to lend their support. Another ordeal would await them in the royal court, and they wanted to be as ready for it as they could.

The sun was touching the western horizon when they finally reached Astaburya, the capital city of Buryan. Compared to the splendid cities of Ravan and Khmeria, Astaburya was very much a disappointment. It was set on a small hill and surrounded by a stone wall no higher than five or six cubits.

The houses were simple stone structures, few more than a single story tall; even the minaret of the local temple, shining its eternal flame as the symbol of Oromasd's welcome, was a bare three stories high. The entire city could not have had a population greater than a thousand people—and most of them were in their homes for the evening by the time the mounted party entered the main gate and made its way through the narrow, winding streets to the palace in the center of the city.

King Brundiyam's palace wouldn't even have ranked as a great mansion in Ravan. It was two stories tall and also built of stone and marble, though of finer quality than the houses surrounding it. Some of the stones were carved into friezes and ornate designs, but they seemed to be the only embellishment on an otherwise drab edifice.

Inside, the palace was no more impressive. There was no glittering of gold or polished gems to catch the eye and capture the imagination. The floor was of black, copper, and white tiles, and the arched stone ceiling was supported by pillars of age-worn alabaster. The tapestries on the walls were of good construction, but their designs were faded and their edges showed signs of mending. Buryan was obviously a poor country, and its king fared little better than its peasants.

The travelers were ordered to wait in an antechamber for a few moments while the leader of the soldiers went directly into the king's presence with their request for an audience. Their rumbling stomachs reminded them it had been a full day since they'd last eaten, but they were resolved not to show any weakness in the face of this monarch. They had to gain his help in their mission; if they were sent the other way around the Bitter Sea, they would fall even further behind in their rigorous schedule.

Finally, after fifteen minutes of waiting, Prince Ahmad, Umar bin Ibrahim, and Jafar al-Sharif were summoned into the king's throne room. Selima and Leila waited patiently behind, but Cari attended invisibly with her master, prepared to protect him in case of trouble.

The audience chamber was brightly lit with torches, and the air was filled with incense of cloves to dispel some of its gloomier aspects, but nothing could disguise its poverty. The throne was an impressive seat carved of oak with majestic beasts in bas-relief, but it was clearly the product of a much earlier and richer age, and the wood was well-worn and polished.

Seated upon the throne was King Brundiyam, a thin old man with a white beard reaching halfway down his chest. His face was well creased, but his eyes still showed the spark of life and intelligence. He wore a simple gray kaftan, and the gold embroidery around the sleeves and placket was well done but obviously mended; the new threads were bright against the old. His white turban, however, was meticulously wrapped, showing he still cared about some items of his apparel.

King Brundiyam eyed the travelers carefully even as the young warrior who'd fought Prince Ahmad stood at his side, still covered in battle armor. "O my father, I bring before you the travelers I've described. They claim they have a matter of great urgency to put before you."

The three men were startled enough to learn that their adversary was King Brundiyam's offspring, but their eyes opened even wider when the armored figure removed the polished brass headpiece to reveal a mass of long, flowing black hair. Prince Ahmad's mouth hung slightly open at the idea that a woman, a princess, could have fought him to a draw in prolonged battle.

King Brundiyam noted the strangers' reaction, but made no comment. He merely said, "Does my daughter speak the truth, O strangers? What is this mission of Oromasd she's told me about?"

Normally it was Prince Ahmad's duty to deal with royalty, explaining to them in his finest courtly manner the task Muhmad had assigned them—but after the hard fighting of this morning and now this added surprise, he fell speechless. Seeing this, Jafar al-Sharif stepped up and began a dramatic rendition of their tale. Not knowing whether or not King Brundiyam was in league with his neighbor King Basir—and therefore part of Shammara's alliance against the prince—he did not reveal Ahmad's true identity; instead he referred to him as "a noble warrior from a distant land," still making it clear the young man was of high birth and impeccable ancestry.

King Brundiyam listened to the story with his eyes sad and teary, and when Jafar had finished speaking he said slowly, "Your quest is certainly a noble one, and as a devoted follower of Oromasd I won't hinder you on your mission. But as for helping you in the war against Rimahn—I'm afraid we might not even be able to help ourselves."

He spread his arms in a gesture of resignation. "Buryan itself is under attack and fighting for its very survival. Just five days ago an enormous raven flew into the palace, carrying in its beak a scroll signed by someone calling himself the yatu Kharouf. He demanded I instantly surrender to his authority, or my land and all who follow me would be put to death. He claims his army is unkillable and unstoppable, and the deadline for his ultimatum is tomorrow.

"My army, under the leadership of my daughter, Princess Rida, has been preparing for the struggle as best it can—but we have barely three hundred men to counter Kharouf's unknown horde. I fear many of us may not live to see the sun set another time."

Prince Ahmad, finally recovering his tongue, stepped forward and addressed the king. "Your Majesty, in our battle today a bond of chivalry was formed betweeen your daughter and me, as between any two honorable warriors. I'd be honored to fight at her side tomorrow against the wizard's army."

"We have a mission of our own, Your Highness," Umar whispered to caution the young man against his excessive enthusiasm.

But King Brundiyam's words drowned out the whisper. "That's a noble gesture," he said, "but I doubt one more sword—even one as good as my daughter tells me yours is—will prevail against a yatu's army."

"You forget we have a wizard of our own," Prince Ahmad said. "Jafar al-Sharif is noted as the greatest wizard of the southern provinces. His powers should be more than a match for this upstart Kharouf."

Wishing that other people wouldn't be so quick to volunteer his services, Jafar spoke up hastily. "My young friend is too kind in his praise. While I have many talents—"

Again King Brundiyam spoke. "It wouldn't matter how skilled you are. Kharouf wears a medallion about his neck making him immune to all harm from magical sources. You cannot stop him, and my army can't stop his army. Buryan is doomed."

"But still we must fight," insisted Princess Rida, "for every person in Parsina is a soldier of Oromasd. To give in to this wizardry is to betray our creator and surrender to the power of the lie. We'll lose if we don't fight, that's for certain—and if we do fight, perhaps Oromasd will find a way to aid us in battle."

"Fight we will," sighed the king with a nod. "And die we probably will, too. But if you wish to fight at our side, O strangers, your blades will be accepted with the thanks of a grateful kingdom."

As the three men left the throne room they were joined by the armor-clad Princess Rida, who offered to lead them to the kitchens for dinner. She was a tall woman, about the same height as Leila, with strong features and thick eyebrows that met in the center of her forehead. She was not beautiful in the conventional sense except for the large, deep-set black eyes gleaming from between long lashes; her face had the seasoned toughness of a warrior rather than the delicate softness of a royal princess. But there was attractiveness in that face, surrounded as it was by her mound of black hair.

"I must thank you for volunteering to help in the battle tomorrow," she said, primarily to Prince Ahmad. "While one more fighter, however skilled, may make no difference to the outcome, we'll certainly need every sword we can get in the field. And while I've no great love of sorcery, I hope your wizard can pull a few tricks to surprise Kharouf."

"I'll do all in my power, Your Highness," Jafar pledged sincerely, even as he wondered what that could mean.

"If I may be so bold, Your Highness," said Prince Ahmad, "I'd like to ask—that is, I'm curious about—"

"About how a maid became a warrior?" she finished for him. Her voice was perfectly regulated, and it seemed clear she never smiled.

"It's not unprecedented," Jafar said. "There's the classic story of King Khaled and the warrior maid of the Altai, one of my favorites—"

"I am my father's only child, born late in his years," Princess Rida said, ignoring Jafar's comment. "There's no one else to inherit the throne, so I must be his heir. You may have noticed that Buryan is a poor country, and its ruler must be as tough and hardened as its people. My father schooled me in the arts of warfare and statecraft so I could survive after his death; otherwise the neighboring kingdoms would swallow us up as though we'd never existed. I've been trained since childhood to think and fight like a man, and as you saw this afternoon there are few who can best me."

She turned to Jafar. "I'd advise you never to mention that story again in my presence. It was told to me so often as I was growing up that I swore to have the head of the next person to tell it."

"Familiarity does indeed breed contempt," said Jafar al-Sharif. "Your advice is noted, O mighty princess."

They arrived at the kitchens, where Princess Rida left them in the hands of the palace staff. "Your woman Leila has already been fed," she told them. "When you finish your meal, the chamberlain will show you to your rooms. Sleep well until the morrow, and may the light of Oromasd guide your steps."

She left them in the hands of her servants, who gave the men a simple, filling meal and led them to individual rooms. Jafar asked to be guided to Leila's room, and conferred with her and Selima on how he could help the war effort tomorrow with his scant knowledge of magic. Cari materialized so she, too, could take part in this conference.

The Jann admitted having heard vaguely of Kharouf, and that he was indeed rumored to have an amulet protecting him from any magic used against him. "That hardly matters," Jafar pointed out. "I don't know any magical spells anyway."

They took an inventory of what they had available. There was Cari herself, though it was doubtful a minor Jann could affect a wizard of Kharouf's strength. There was the key that hung about Jafar's neck—and they still didn't know what it was good for. There was the magical cap, which didn't seem appropriate to the occasion, and the cloak of invisibility, which didn't sound very promising against a wizard's army.

Finally there was the carved wooden staff of Achmet the terrifying that claimed the power to draw lightning down from the clouds. "But there are no instructions for its use," Jafar complained. "I don't know how to focus it or what magical words to use."

"As with the carpet when we escaped from Akar's castle," Cari said, "the object was imbued with its magic by the person who created it. Magical words are useful tools to help you focus your will onto the magic in the staff, but magical words aren't essential. The prime ingredient is your will, and anything that helps you concentrate that should work. If you can recreate the feeling you felt when you made the carpet fly, you can force the staff to pull down the lightning and direct it against the wizard's army."

Jafar al-Sharif took the journal of Ali Maimun from his saddle pouch and shook it, as though trying to open some of the pages that were yet closed to him. The book, however, refused to cooperate, showing him only those pages he'd seen before, and whose contents he'd already memorized.

"If only this book were more helpful," he sighed. "As great as Ali Maimun was, I'm sure he's got some secrets in here for dealing with an upstart like Kharouf. But all he gives us is travelogues."

He closed the book once more and returned it to its place. "We'll just have to try the staff and hope I can make it work. And may Oromasd have mercy on us all."

Like the wizard Akar, Kharouf had also detected the tremors in the magical web indicating the freeing of Aeshma from his centuries-long imprisonment. He had not Akar's ability to trace the disturbance back to its roots and determine the true nature of the event, but he was shrewd enough to realize that something big was happening and greedy enough to grab his own share of the rewards while the universe was in such a state of flux.

Kharouf was a man of large ambitions and tiny scruples. He lived in a cave within a set of hills along the northern rim of the Bitter Sea, and he spent years in these dismal surroundings mastering and perfecting his craft. While he lacked the intellectual background that characterized Akar and many other wizards, he had in common with them the acquisitive drive, the discipline, and the furtiveness that kept him apart from normal people. He molded himself into a master of the magical arts and waited with growing impatience for the day his studies would pay off.

His greatest accomplishment to date had not been entirely of his own doing. Having learned that a colleague was working on a talisman to protect himself from magical attack, Kharouf visited the other man on the pretext of friendship, then poisoned him and took the amulet—and all the other man's secrets as well—for himself. Kharouf let it be known far and wide that he had developed this power on his own, and then discouraged visits from other practitioners, lest they try to duplicate his true methods.

The yatu did have powers of his own, however, and on the day when Aeshma was released and Kharouf realized the world would be undergoing a great change, he became determined that the change would be for his benefit. Now was the time to achieve the rightful rewards of all his study.

Like most wizards, Kharouf acted with caution. He studied the local situation and realized that a man with a strong army behind him could conquer vast areas in a short period of time. The nearby kingdom of Buryan was ideally suited to his purposes. In itself it was not a great prize, being poor and largely barren, but it would be an easy stepping-stone on his path to greater glories. The Buryani king was old and weak, the army virtually nonexistent—yet the conquest of a kingdom, any kingdom, would gain him a reputation that would strike fear into all the lands around Buryan. With each successive conquest, his reputation would grow that much larger, making the next one that much easier. Fear would travel ahead of him, working as much destruction on his enemies as any army.

He laid his plans and checked his spells, and when he was finally ready he sent a raven as his emissary to King Brundiyam, demanding the immediate surrender of Buryan. He hoped privately that the king would put up a fight so he could demolish the Buryani army with his own and thereby begin his reign of terror through the northeastern portions of Parsina.

When King Brundiyam obliged him by refusing to surrender, Kharouf smiled and set about working the most powerful spell he'd ever attempted. Deep in the bowels of his cave he charted out the runes, burned the proper powders, and spoke the secret spells to invoke Nasu, the daeva of death, decay, and decomposition. Never before had he attempted to conjure a druj, but the power of his ambitions made him bold and he succeeded beyond his greatest expectations.

The candles in his cave wavered and dimmed, and the air filled with a choking green smoke that carried the gagging stench of rotting flesh. Through the dismal gloom he could make out the silhouette of his quarry, this powerful being he'd invoked into his presence. Nasu was of such a size that she filled the entire cavern, and her skin was pocked with ugly pustules and open, bleeding sores. She was skinny and bent, more bone than meat, and her sparse gray hair was long and scraggly, flying in all directions at once. As she opened her mouth to scream at him, he saw the worms of decay wriggling in place of her tongue.

The druj shrieked and cursed at this mortal who dared summon her from her home in Mount Denavan, but Kharouf had confidence in the spells he'd used to bind her within his cave and felt no fear. He let the daeva rant and rave against him for an hour, and the more she shrieked the safer he felt. If she'd been able to work him any harm, she'd have done it immediately rather than wasting her energy on harmless invective.

When he finally tired of this amusement, Kharouf gave his commands. "I will trade you your freedom, O druj of the dead, if you will give me an army to fight at my command."

"Do I look like a general, O thou hated son of Gayomar?" she replied angrily.

"What you look like, I could not begin to catalog," Kharouf responded, "but you do command the largest army in the world, the army of the dead. At your command corpses will rise from dakhmas and walk with a power of their own. If you will bring these corpses to me when I ask for them and subordinate them to my will, I'll let you return to your home and bother you no more."

And though she protested further, in the end Nasu capitulated and gave the yatu what he wanted. From every tower of silence in every town across the face of Parsina, every corpse that was not so decomposed it would fall apart rose up and flew through the air to assemble on a plain several parasangs northwest of Astaburya. The souls of these men and women had long since departed for the Bridge of Shinvar to earn the reward of their lives in mortal form—but these decrepit remains would stay to serve the cause of their evil master, Kharouf.

There was little sleep for anyone in the royal palace of Astaburya, as everyone lay in bed anticipating the battle tomorrow against the yatu's forces. A feeling of doom hung over the Buryani capital like a leaden cloud, weighing down everyone's spirits and roiling everyone's fitful dreams.

Dawn came with clear and sunny skies—and with the dawn came reports that a large army was assembled in the northwest. Princess Rida roused and rallied her men. The soldiers donned their armor and mounted their horses, while their loved ones stood to the side and cried their tearful farewells, positive they'd never be reunited. The populace of the city spent much of the day packing their most valued possessions, prepared to flee their homes if, as was feared, the wizard's forces proved too strong for the defenders. No one wanted to live in a land ruled by Kharouf the dark wizard.

Prince Ahmad, looking resplendent even in his plain armor, rode in formation next to Princess Rida, with Umar bin Ibrahim riding a few paces to the rear. Though the priest had not wanted his young pupil to get involved in this struggle, now that they were part of it he was determined to do his share in a battle that clearly was against forces instigated by Rimahn. Though this was not the battle Muhmad had foretold, this was certainly a war in defense of Oromasd.

The sun was barely over the horizon as Prince Ahmad and Princess Rida led the procession of defenders through the gates of Astaburya. It was a far less impressive sight than the prince's departure from Ravan, or even from Khmeria; no crowds stood and cheered, no banners waved, no speeches were declaimed. The mood was somber and subdued; people were convinced that by nightfall the peaceful pattern of their lives would be shattered for all time. King Brundiyam, too feeble to fight any more, stayed behind to oversee the dissolution of his kingdom in the probable event of a loss to the yatu's army.

The army's horses paraded slowly out the city's gates as though to a funeral—a funeral for an entire nation. Well in the back, bringing up the rear, were Jafar al-Sharif, Selima, and Leila, with Cari flying invisibly beside them as usual. The women refused to stay behind and wait in suspense for news from the battlefield, and Jafar could see no reason not to bring them along—provided they stayed well clear of the fighting.

The Buryani army rode for three hours until, at midmorning on a dreary plain several parasangs northwest of Astaburya, they confronted the army of Kharouf the yatu. Princess Rida ordered her column to halt and spread out in a line facing the opposing army across the open field.

Although the yatu's legions were still too far away to make out any details, their numbers looked impressive indeed. They were all on foot, hundreds and hundreds of them, each carrying a sword and dressed in meager rags, standing silently in rows covering the plain to the rim of a distant hill where the yatu Kharouf himself stood and looked over his troops. The enemy outnumbered the Buryani army many times to one as they stood with eerie stillness, awaiting the order to attack.

In true chivalric tradition, Princess Rida rode out into the field between the two armies carrying a flag of truce. She called aloud for any champion of Kharouf's army to battle her in single combat, to spare the lives of innocent men who might otherwise fall this day. Her horse pranced up and down the line as she spoke, but her words had no effect on the opposing soldiers. They stood rigid as statues in utter silence, unaffected by her words or her gallantry.

Then the yatu Kharouf spoke, and though he was on a hill so far away he could barely be seen his voice carried plainly to all the soldiers of Buryan. "You've had time to consider my offer. I will accept nothing less than unconditional surrender. If the throne of Buryan is not mine, prepare to be slaughtered to the last man, without mercy."

Princess Rida drew herself even taller in her saddle. "The people of Buryan are poor in material possessions and humble before Oromasd, but we nevertheless have our pride and our principles. We can never submit to the power of evil you command."

"Then you will die," Kharouf said simply, and the matter was closed. The princess rode back to her front ranks and readied her troops for battle.

Jafar al-Sharif, with Cari and the two women, had stopped at the crest of a hillock a short distance behind the Buryani army, and from there they could look out over the panorama of battle that was soon to be. Jafar viewed the opposing army with awe, and with the growing fear that his ignorance would prevent his helping the Buryani to victory.

Beside him, Leila was peering intently at the enemy soldiers, fascinated by something only she could see. As the truth suddenly dawned in her mind, her face went pale with fear. "Blessed Ashath!" she exclaimed. "Those aren't living men out there!"

And indeed this truth was beginning to dawn on the rest of the Buryani as well. A chance breeze blew across the field, carrying the scent of the decomposing bodies that made up Kharouf's army. The Buryani soldiers began gagging at the nauseating stench, while across the field Kharouf's troops stood rigidly at attention, staring straight ahead, attuned solely to the will of the yatu. They would stand, they would march, and they would fight with passionless determination.

The seconds dragged on interminably as the two sides stared at one another across the empty field. An unearthly silence fell upon the plain, the calm that preceded the battle between the forces of life and those of death. Jafar gripped his wooden staff tightly. If he was going to do anything to affect the outcome of this battle, he'd better do it now.

Closing his eyes, he cleared his mind of extraneous thoughts and concentrated on the feeling he needed to make the magic work. He remembered the feeling he'd captured when he flew Akar's magical carpet through the air from the wizard's castle high in the Himali Mountains all the way to the Kholaj Desert, before the Afrits of the air dislodged him from his perch.

It was a feeling he'd felt many times before, without ever realizing it—the feeling when the story he was telling came out perfectly, when he had his listeners enrapt in the spell of his words and his craft transported them to other worlds and times. In those instants he knew he had the power to make them believe anything he said, to make his thoughts and ideas come alive out of nothingness. This feeling, then, was the essence of all human magic, and all those special people with the talent for creating felt it at some time in their lives: the weavers who made beautiful tapestries, the potters who formed exquisite vases, the musicians who poured forth music to soothe their listeners' souls. The magic itself was common to all men; wizards merely molded it into strange and exotic forms.

Jafar al-Sharif now let this feeling well up from the bottom of his soul until it captured him completely and the rest of the world virtually disappeared. There was just himself and the magical staff of Achmet in a darkened universe. Nothing else mattered; nothing else existed.

"O powers of Achmet's staff, I conjure thee," he intoned in his most commanding voice. "Draw the heavenly fire of the lightning down from the skies. Use this fire to destroy our enemies. Strike them down and burn their bodies to cinders. Decimate the legions of Kharouf the yatu."

Jafar knew his spell was working. In his hand he could feel the wood of the staff begin to glow, gradually growing to a white heat that burned and yet somehow did not hurt his hand. The staff became an extension of his arm, a part of himself that he could wield and direct at his slightest whim. He could feel the surge of the power that had been invested in it, and his breathing increased to feed his need for air.

After several minutes he could hear Leila, as though from very far away, saying, "A very impressive show, but no results."

Jarred from his trance, Jafar al-Sharif opened his eyes and looked about him. Despite the feeling of power he'd gotten, there had been no lightning. The army of corpses still stood silently across the plain with not a flicker from the heavens to mar their composure.

Jafar looked at the wooden staff as though at an old friend who'd betrayed him. His breath was ragged as he muttered, "It was working, I know it was."

"From what you told me," Leila said, "the inscription says the staff will bring lighting down from the clouds. May I point out there's not a cloud in the sky today? There's no place to bring the lightning from."

With a sinking feeling in his heart, Jafar realized Leila was right. He was doing his part correctly, but the conditions weren't right for the magic to work. Trying to operate the staff under a clear sky was like putting the ingredients for a stew into a pot and then not having a fire to cook them on; the ingredients were all fine, but they lacked the crucial element to make them a cohesive whole.

On the hillock far across the plain, the yatu Kharouf must have felt he'd waited long enough to unman the Buryani, for he finally gave the order to attack. His legion of the dead did not charge across the open ground the way a normal army would have; instead the corpses plodded slowly forward, row upon row in uniform precision. A tide of decaying human flesh surged over the field as though with one mind, as relentless and unstoppable as clouds moving across the face of the full moon, obscuring its light and bringing darkness to the earth below. The only sound they made was the tromping of thousands of feet marching in unison across the open plain.

Princess Rida held her army in check, awaiting the approach of the enemy. As the dead soldiers drew near, the Buryani could see them even more clearly, and became further horrified by what they saw. The army that faced them comprised both men and women, carrying swords and wearing only the shabbiest of rags to cover their decaying forms. The vultures had begun their work on many of these bodies; flesh had been pulled from their bones, leaving raw patches that festered like open sores. Hair was torn away from their heads, and in many cases one or both eyes had been eaten out of the sockets, leaving the bodies to walk forward in blind obedience to their magical master. Skin had grown shriveled and taut across the faces; teeth and skulls showed at odd places on their countenances. The stench grew even stronger as the corpses neared, and several of Princess Rida's weaker men fainted from the smell and the thought of contact with these unholy beings.

Realizing that waiting would only unnerve her troops further, Princess Rida finally gave the order to attack. Summoning up vast courage to match their leader, the Buryani army charged down upon the vastly superior forces of Kharouf, yelling their battle cries at the top of their lungs. Clouds of dust were churned up by the horses' hooves, and the soldiers swung their swords with enough enthusiasm to terrify any mortal enemy.

But the legion of corpses was beyond caring. They marched patiently forward to meet the oncoming cavalry, their own swords at the ready. Their gaze remained fixed as they walked silently into the teeth of the Buryani charge. They had no fear of death because they were simply automata of rotting flesh serving the commands of their evil master.

Now the Buryani horses had met the enemy front lines, and the mounted fighters slashed vigorously at their opponents. The corpses wore no armor, just rags to cover their horrible nakedness, and made no attempts to parry the blows. Ordinary foes would have been howling in pain from the cuts they'd received; the corpses felt no pain. Serious wounds that would have disabled mortal men meant nothing to them; the only tactic that worked was dismemberment, rendering the bodies incapable of inflicting further harm. Even then they continued to twitch in an effort to obey their master's commands.

Meanwhile, Kharouf's soldiers were wielding their own swords against the Buryani army. Their reflexes were not fast and their physical strength was not great, but they could stand and suffer great punishment while chopping away at the living men and horses.

Princess Rida and Prince Ahmad rode into battle with great zeal, their blades flashing with speed and courage, every blow they struck solid. The rest of the Buryani army fought with equal ardor, but it was like fighting against the raindrops. The army of the yatu Kharouf could not be stopped by steel alone.

Prince Ahmad waded into battle astride Churash, swinging at the foe lke a reaper mowing grain. This was only his second experience with real combat, and the blood was pounding so fiercely in his temples that the whole scene took on a red haze. Hack and slash, and another enemy was laid to the earth again, but always there were more and they kept coming with relentless determination. As with the brigands in the forest, there seemed no end to their number.

While he was cutting down two of the enemy on his right, one of the corpses came up on his left side before he could swivel around to parry the blow. The dead man's sword cut into Ahmad's left leg, bringing with it a searing pain the likes of which the young man had never felt before. Ahmad screamed, even as his well-honed instincts brought his sword around to decapitate the corpse who'd struck him.

Blood flowed from the wound even as a fire burned through Ahmad's soul. He wavered in his saddle, and only long hours of training kept him from falling to the ground where he would certainly have been killed by the enemy. He clung to the saddle horn as a drunkard clings to a post, while the battle around him grew faint and indistinct.

From a short distance away, Umar bin Ibrahim saw the prince take the cutting blow. Realizing he had to save the young man at all costs, the priest spurred his own horse forward, heedless of the danger to himself, until he reached Ahmad's side. Grabbing Churash's reins, Umar led the two horses toward the rear, away from the fiercest part of the battle. From his own slight knowledge of medicine he guessed the prince's wound was serious, but probably not fatal—if he could be saved from further damage by the enemy.

Standing safely on his hilltop, Jafar al-Sharif also saw Prince Ahmad get wounded. Selima gave a cry of anguish, and Jafar realized with dismay that his allies were destined for a tragic defeat unless he could think of something to save them. Only magic would defeat Kharouf's army of the dead, and the one relevant piece of magic Jafar had was useless under these conditions.

Jafar could see Kharouf standing atop his hillock at the far end of the field, overlooking the scene of his inevitable victory. The evil wizard was the key to the battle; if he were captured or killed, he could no longer put his will into animating the corpses, and the invading force would fail. But Kharouf was protected by his amulet that warded off all magic spells against him. How could anyone get through that defense?

Then a story occured to Jafar, the old tale of the hero Argun and the citadel of Desmarekh. The ancient castle had never been breached and was in the hands of an evil warlord whom Argun opposed. Argun and all his army could not breach the castle's defenses. The lion king, who owed Argun a favor, could not break through the walls even with all his strength and ferocity. Then a little mouse volunteered to help. The lion king laughed and Argun's army ridiculed the mouse, but Argun was humble enough to let the tiny creature try where all the combined strength of more powerful beings had failed.

The tiny mouse burrowed his way under the walls until he was inside the castle, then gnawed through the wooden bars that held the gates secure. When he was finished, Argun's army was able to storm through the gates and defeat the forces of the evil warlord.

As he recalled this story, Jafar al-Sharif was struck with an idea for defeating the yatu Kharouf. He knelt on the ground and uttered a quick prayer. "O blessed Oromasd, more than ever do I thank thee for making me a storyteller, for surely no other profession would so prepare me to cope with the disasters that have befallen me."

Selima and Leila looked at him as though he'd lost his wits, but he had no time to explain his plan to them. Fetching the cloak of invisibility from his saddlebag, he threw it around his shoulders and said, "We must improvise a plan, O Cari, or our friends on the field are lost; we must become as a mouse where the strength of lions has failed. Carry me invisibly to the hillock where Kharouf stands. He may be invulnerable to magic, but I've yet to see a man live with a sword through his heart."

"Hearkening and obedience," Cari said. Jafar felt himself being lifted gently into the air and he hastily uttered the magical word, "Decibah," that made him invisible. They flew above the open field with the battle raging below them, until they neared the hill where the yatu Kharouf stood and commanded his forces.

As they came within a hundred cubits of the hilltop, Cari suddenly said, "I can go no further, O my master. Kharouf has surrounded himself with a spell that bars all djinni from approaching him closer. To do so would mean my death."

"Could I get through on my own?" Jafar asked, suddenly worried.

"Magical spells work best against magical beings. It's possible to bar normal humans as well, but that would take so much power I doubt he could manage his army at the same time."

"Then set me down and I'll walk the rest of the way."

Cari's voice was concerned as she said, "I won't be able to protect you in there."

"My cloak will protect me well enough. He can't defend himself from what he can't see."

Cari reluctantly set him down on the ground. "May the blessings of Oromasd go with you, O my master," she muttered under her breath, so softly Jafar could not hear her above the din of battle.

Jafar's hand went to the hilt of the saif tucked into the hizam at his waist. To date it had been purely a ceremonial weapon, used for proper elegance in dress and nothing else. Now he might be called upon to use it, and he hoped he'd find the courage to do so.

He walked briskly up the hill until he reached the top, where he paused to consider the situation. Kharouf the yatu, dressed in a kaftan of deep purple with a yellow turban, stood looking over the battlefield. His jowly face was a picture of intense concentration, and Jafar realized how much willpower he must be projecting to control the army of corpses on the plain below. Surrounding the evil wizard were three more of the animated corpses, guarding their master against any physical danger that might threaten him.

Unseen by Kharouf or his ghastly guards, Jafar al-Sharif walked quietly up behind the wizard and stood with his hand on the hilt of his saif. One quick stroke would do the deed; the wizard would never know what had hit him, and without his willpower to animate the corpses, his army in the field would simply collapse, giving the victory to the Buryani.

But Jafar al-Sharif hesitated. He'd never killed a man before and it was a frightening thought. An inborn sense of honor also told him he could not strike a man down unaware, even with so many lives at stake on the field below. He at least must try to convince Kharouf to surrender peacefully before relying on the ultimate solution.

Taking a deep breath to hide the nervousness in his voice, he said in his deepest tones, "Your hour of defeat is at hand, O Kharouf. Lay down your weapons and surrender your forces to the throne of Buryan."

The wizard wheeled and looked wildly about for the source of the words, but he could see no one. His hand went to the hilt of his own sword as he said, "Who speaks? Who dares defy the power of Kharouf the Mighty?"

Jafar moved two steps to his left so the words would seem to come from another spot. "It is I, Jafar al-Sharif, wizard of the southern provinces. If you would not have this be your death day, cease your fighting at once."

Kharouf drew his sword and swung it at the empty air. Jafar easily dodged the blow and stayed but a single step away from his opponent.

"I've never heard the name Jafar al-Sharif," Kharouf sneered.

Moving around behind the yatu once more, Jafar said, "Neither had the wizard Akar, but he now regrets the day he became my enemy. Surrender at once or face the consequences."

Akar's name meant something to Kharouf, for his face suddenly showed a moment of doubt. In the field, his army faltered in their fight as his willpower temporarily slackened. The hesitation gave new heart to the army of Buryan, and with the battle cry of their princess ringing about them they plunged forward with new vigor.

Then Kharouf regained his confidence. "I fear no wizard," he said. "My amulet protects me from magical harm."

Even as he spoke, his trio of guards was converging around him. They might not see where the danger was coming from, but they could stand physically between their master and the rest of the world to protect him with their bodies as best they could.

Jafar al-Sharif had no qualms about striking one of these corpses, since they were already dead; "killing" them would be no sin against his name at the Bridge of Shinvar. Drawing his sword he swung it with all his strength at the neck of one advancing guard.. His sword went halfway through, and Jafar had to wrench it free and swing a second time before he completely severed the head from its body. The corpse tumbled to the ground, its arms and legs flailing feebly about, but it was no longer a threat to anyone.

While he was dealing with the first guard, the other two converged on his position. Though they still couldn't see him, they could guess where he had to be if his sword was attacking their comrade. They moved forward with their arms waving about in an effort to locate him.

Jafar ducked and dodged, trying to get closer to Kharouf, and as he did so one of the guards' hands managed to hit his shoulder. Jafar backed away, but the corpse grabbed the fabric of his cloak and pulled it from his shoulders. Sudden Jafar al-Sharif was perfectly visible to all the world.

The storyteller froze, unprepared for his unveiling. Kharouf smiled at his quick triumph and directed the two remaining slaves to capture his sidestepping opponent. The grisly guards lumbered around ther master toward Jafar, their swords ready to slice him into pieces.

Without thinking Jafar al-Sharif lunged forward, thrusting his sword at Kharouf with all his might. The blade pierced the yatu's chest and slid right through the body, emerging on the other side. The wizard's eyes widened and he tried to say something, but all that came out was a soft wheeze and a bubbling of blood at the corner of his mouth. As Jafar had guessed, Kharouf had placed so much faith in the powerful amulet that protected him against magic that he hadn't bothered to protect himself against such a simple thing as a sword blade.

For a long moment the yatu stood at the end of Jafar's sword as though suspended in the air. Then he fell forward onto the ground and the sword was wrenched from Jafar's grip. Jafar just watched, stunned by the results of his own actions. Kharouf's eyes remained open but unseeing as his hands twisted a few times and then were still. Blood oozed from the sword wound and dripped onto the grassy ground of the hilltop overlooking the battlefield.

Jafar al-Sharif stared at the body of his opponent, a stranger who'd sought the deaths of so many people. But the storyteller could claim no sense of victory, just the horrible feeling that he'd murdered another man. His mind replayed over and over the sensation of resistance as the sword started through Kharouf's living flesh, and the sight of the other man's body as it crumpled to the ground. The dead man's eyes, those ever-accusing eyes, were still staring at him, and Jafar knew they would haunt his nightmares for months, if not years, to come.

Jafar al-Sharif fell to his knees beside the man he'd killed and, leaning forward, began to vomit. He'd told many tales of killing and fighting, but none of them had prepared him for the reality of the experience.

As Jafar al-Sharif knelt, weak and nauseated, on the hill-top, the battle below him came to an abrupt end. The dead soldiers animated by Nasu's spells suddenly collapsed when Kharouf's will could no longer control them. As the bodies fell, the magic that held them together dissipated; they turned to a fine powder that sprinkled the ground with a thick layer of ash, leaving nothing behind but their swords and the rags they'd been wearing.

In later years this field became the most fertile ground in Buryan, thick with grass and flowers of all hues and scents. The local peasants would bring their children here to tell them the story of the battle that raged on this fateful day, and Jafar al-Sharif—who had told so many stories about others—would find himself the center of a new heroic legend. But that was still years in the future, and right now Jafar al-Sharif knelt retching on the hilltop while in the field below Prince Ahmad was bleeding from the wound he'd received in battle—and halfway around the world, Aeshma and Hakem Rafi assembled their forces on their quest for total conquest of Parsina.

GLOSSARY

abaaya: a cloak or mantle worn by women
abdug: a cold yogurt drink
Adaran: the second-highest class of sacred fires; must be tended by priests.
adarga: plain round or oval shield, covered with leather or metal
Afrit: a member of the third rank of the djinni
alif: the first letter of the Parsine alphabet
Ashath: the Bounteous Immortal who represents truth; the most beautiful of the Immortals, she preserves order on earth, protects the fire, and smites disease and evil creatures
ba: the second letter of the Parsine alphabet
Badawi: (pl.) tribes of the desert nomads
Bahram: the holiest class of sacred fires; must be tended only by highly purified priests; the king of fires, overhung by a crown
baklava: pastry rolls filled with chopped almonds, flavored with cardamom, and drenched in honey after baking
bazaar: an open-air market of many individual stalls
Bounteous Immortals: seven personifications of ideal qualities, aides to Oromasd
burga: a stiff mask worn by women, often embroidered or embellished with coins and other decorations
cadi: a judge or civil magistrate

camekan: the outer room of the hammam, where clothes are taken off and piled neatly

caravanserai: an inn providing merchants and wayfarers with shelter, food, and storage facilities for their beasts and goods; fee is generally based on one's ability to pay

chelo: a steamed rice preparation

cubit: a unit of length, approximately twenty inches or fifty centimeters

Dadgah: the third-highest class of sacred fire; may be tended by laymen

daeva: a demon, spawn of Rimahn, created to torment mankind and promote chaos

dahkma: a tower of silence, on which corpses are placed for vultures to eat the dead flesh

dhoti: a loincloth fashioned from a long narrow strip of cloth wound around the body, passed between the legs and tucked in at the waist behind

dinar: a gold coin of high value, equal to 1,000 dirhams; one dinar could buy a small village brewery

dirham: a silver coin of moderate value, equal to 100 fals; 1,000 dirhams equal one dinar; one dirham could buy a pony keg (150 glasses) of beer

diwan: a couch for reclining; also, an official audience or court held by a king or other ruler

djinn: a descendent of the illicit union of humans and daevas in the early ages of the world; mortal, but magically powerful and longlived; pl.: *djinni*

druj: (s. & pl.) an evil creature who worships Rimahn and the lie; may have some magical abilities

durqa: a square, depressed area in the center of a qa'a, usually paved with marble and tile and containing a small fountain

emir: a nobleman ranked below a wazir

fal: a copper coin of low denomination; 100 fals equal one dirham; one fal could buy one glass of beer

fauwara: an ablutions fountain in the center of a sahn

fravashi: a person's heavenly self, to be reunited with the soul after the great Rehabilitation at the end of time

ghee: clarified, browned butter

gnaa: a rectangular headcloth for women, usually worn over the top of the shayla

hammam: a public steam-bath house

haoma: the ephedra plant; grows on mountains; is ritually pounded and pressed to yield a fluid that is tasted during rituals, symbolizing man's eventual gaining of immortality

hizam: a waistbelt to secure weapons to the body, hold money and other items

hookah: a water pipe

hosh: the central courtyard of a house, off of which other rooms open

Jann: (s. & pl.) a member of the fifth and lowest rank of the djinni

Jinn: (s. & pl.) a member of the fourth rank of the djinni

kaftan: a long, floor-length overrobe with full-length sleeves

khandaq: a sewage sump, a pit for gathering the city population's bodily wastes

khanjar: a curved bladed dagger, worn in a sheath in the hizam

kismet: unavoidable Fate

Kushti: (s. & pl.) a ritual rope or thread given to a child at investiture; its interwoven threads and tassels are highly symbolic; used during prayers

leewan: a paved platform about one quarter of a cubit above central floor level, usually covered with mats or carpets

madrasa: a school, usually attached to a temple; teaches both secular and religious topics

maidan: a central square or plaza within a city

Marid: a member of the second rank of the djinni

milaaya: (s. & pl.) a colorful sheet worn by women as a mantle

milfa: a semitransparent black scarf drawn over the lower part of the face; worn in public by women

minaret: a tall, slender tower attached to a temple, where an everlasting flame burns in tribute to and as a symbol of Oromasd

minbar: a high raised pulpit with a flight of steps, from which sermons are preached in a temple

musharabiya: a carved wooden grill of close latticework covering the street-facing windows of a house

nan-e lavash: a thin, dinnertime bread similar to flour tortillas, but crispier

niaal: (pl.) thonged sandals

Oromasd: the world's creator, ultimate power of light, truth, and goodness

parasang: a unit of length, approximately three miles or five kilometers

peri: a descendant of the union of humans and yazatas in the early ages of the world; mortal, but magically powerful and longlived

pilau: a boiled rice dish, often with other spices and ingredients such as almonds, raisins, etc.

qa'a: principal room of a house, where guests are entertained

rahat lakhoum: an expensive confection of lichi nuts, kumquat rind, and hashish

Rimahn: the lord of darkness and the lie, opponent of Oromasd

rimahniya: (pl.) fanatical cult of assassins who worship Rimahn and welcome chaos

riwaq: a covered arcade with pillars dividing it into open sections surrounding on three sides an open area (sahn) in the center of a temple

rukh: a gigantic magical flesh-eating bird

saaya: a jacket with gold embroidery, worn by men

Sadre: a white shirt given to children at their investiture, which they are supposed to wear always next to their skin; putting it on symbolizes donning the Good Religion

sahn: an open courtyard in the center of a temple where the faithful gather to pray and hear sermons

saif: a sheathed short sword worn in the hizam at the waist

salaam: a word of greeting, meaning both "hello" and "peace"; also, a deferential bow of greeting or respect

sari: a full-length dress wrapped around the body

satrap: a provincial governor

Shaitan: a member of the first, and most powerful, rank of the djinni

sharbat-e porteghal: an iced drink of orange and mint

sharshaf: an oversize shawl worn when a woman leaves her mother's home for her future husband's; also worn at prayer

shaykh: the leader of a tribe, profession, or other group; usually elected for his age and wisdom

shayla: a rectangular tasseled headcloth worn by women as part of a two-piece headgear; the tassels at the top dangle on either side of the face

sicakluk: the inner room of the hammam; the steam room

sidaireeya: a high-collared, open front, waist-length jacket with elbow-length sleeves, worn by women over the Sadre; often highly decorated

simurgh: the magical bird who perches in the Tree of Knowledge

sirwaal: (pl.) long baggy trousers, gathered at the ankles, with a sash to draw in the waist; worn by men and women

sofreh: a cover placed over a carpet or over the ground while eating to give stability to the plates and protect the carpet; usually one of stiffer, waterproof leather is covered by another of cloth

soguluk: the middle room of the hammam where bodies are washed and massaged

taraha: a rectangular black gauze scarf with beaded, embroidered, braided, or tasseled ends; worn over the head by women

thawb: a full-length, long-sleeved garment similar to the kaftan but cut fuller; also a capacious overdress worn by women

turban: a fine cloth worn wound around a man's head

wadi: a ravine formed by runoff rainwater

wali: a superintendent

wazir: a royal minister and political adviser

yatu: an evil magician

yazata: a heavenly being such as a saint or angel

zarabil: (pl.) cloth slippers, often embroidered

zibun: an ankle-length outer garment opening down the front; closes right over left at the waist, forming a waist-deep open vee in front; slits upward along each side from the hemline and slits at underarm seams from the edge of the short sleeve to the shoulder seam, to allow the decorated robes underneath to show through

ziyada: an outer courtyard surrounding a temple on three sides

Hakem Rafi steals the Sacred Jewel of Oromasd
for the riches it promises.
What he is promised and what he gets are two
different things . . .

The Parsina Saga
by
Stephen Goldin

Kismet draws together Hakem Rafi, a small time thief;
Jafar al-Sharif, a simple storyteller; his daughter Selima
and Prince Ahmad of Ravan when Rafi steals the most
sacred relic of their country. Its disappearance puts into
motion the wheels of a war which will forever change
the earth, the gods and each one of the people involved.

☐ Volume One: **Shrine of the Desert Mage**
   (27212-8 • $3.95/$4.95 in Canada)
☐ Volume Two: **The Storyteller and the Jann**
   (27532-1 • $3.95/$4.95 in Canada)

And don't miss volume three of *The Parsina Saga:*
Crystals of Air and Water, to be published in
January, 1989.

Buy **Shrine of the Desert Mage** and **The Storyteller
and the Jann** on sale now wherever Bantam Spectra
books are sold, or use this page to order:

Special Offer
Buy a Bantam Book
for only 50¢.

Now you can have Bantam's catalog filled with hundreds of titles plus take advantage of our unique and exciting bonus book offer. A special offer which gives you the opportunity to purchase a Bantam book for only 50¢. Here's how!

By ordering any five books at the regular price per order, you can also choose any other single book listed (up to a $5.95 value) for just 50¢. Some restrictions do apply, but for further details why not send for Bantam's catalog of titles today!

Just send us your name and address and we will send you a catalog!